CW01338140

Praise for the *Fractal* Series

'*Fearless* is a brilliant achievement, and one of the best science-fiction novels I have read in a very long time.'
The Sci-Fi and Fantasy Reviewer on *Fearless*

'A sequel that actually improves on its predecessor. Stroud presents us with a complex, multifaceted science-fiction experience that offers a deeply compelling narrative, interlaced with rich and complex worldbuilding and three-dimensional characters.'
The Sci-Fi and Fantasy Reviewer on *Resilient*

'Fast-paced, gripping hard SF with death in hard vacuum waiting at every turn.'
Adrian Tchaikovsky,
Arthur C. Clarke Award-winner on *Fearless*

'Space battles, sabotage, and treachery envelop a gripping whodunit. *Fearless* is a fabulous read from a writer who knows how to deliver.'
Ian Whates, Winner of the Karl Edward Wagner Award on *Fearless*

'A wonderful, modern, inclusive and clever science fiction that deserves to be a part of anyone's collection.'
SFBook Reviews on the *Fractal* series

'Gripping, intense, military SF. Stunning and urgent.'
Anna Smith Spark on *Fearless*

'The depths of outer space test the strength of a dynamic heroine's inner resolve in Stroud's smart, introspective space opera set in the year 2118. [...] With an attention to detail that will please hard science fiction fans, Stroud raises fascinating questions about the politics of space exploration. This is one to be savored.'
Publishers Weekly Starred Review of *Fearless*

'Rigorous hard SF with a powerful but flawed protagonist and a fascinating historical background, *Fearless* is a treat for just about any *Analog* reader.'
Analog Science Fiction & Fact on *Fearless*

'Allen Stroud brings a Clarkian feel that grounds the story in the best tradition of science fiction. He keeps the action going, and does a fine job of showing the difficulties of conflict in space. Highly Recommended.'
Amazing Stories on *Fearless*

ALLEN STROUD

VIGILANCE

Book Three of the *Fractal* Series,
Following *Fearless* and *Resilient*

This is a **FLAME TREE PRESS** book

Text copyright © 2024 Allen Stroud

All rights reserved. No part of this publication may be reproduced, stored in a retrieval system, or transmitted in any form or by any means, electronic, mechanical, photocopying, recording or otherwise, without the prior written permission of the publisher.

FLAME TREE PRESS
6 Melbray Mews, London, SW6 3NS, UK
flametreepress.com

US sales, distribution and warehouse:
Simon & Schuster
simonandschuster.biz

UK distribution and warehouse:
Hachette UK Distribution
hukdcustomerservice@hachette.co.uk

Publisher's Note: This is a work of fiction. Names, characters, places, and incidents are a product of the author's imagination. Locales and public names are sometimes used for atmospheric purposes. Any resemblance to actual people, living or dead, or to businesses, companies, events, institutions, or locales is completely coincidental.

Thanks to the Flame Tree Press team.

The cover is created by Flame Tree Studio with elements courtesy of Shutterstock.com and: Dotted Yeti, joshimerbin, non c, Vezdehod and ZamajK. The font families used are Avenir and Bembo.

Flame Tree Press is an imprint of Flame Tree Publishing Ltd
flametreepublishing.com

A copy of the CIP data for this book is available from the British Library and the Library of Congress.

HB ISBN: 978-1-78758-937-7
US PB ISBN: 978-1-78758-936-0
UK PB ISBN: 978-1-78758-939-1
ebook ISBN: 978-1-78758-938-4

Printed and bound in Great Britain by Clays Ltd, Elcograf S.p.A.

ALLEN STROUD

VIGILANCE

Book Three of the *Fractal* Series,
Following *Fearless* and *Resilient*

FLAME TREE PRESS
London & New York

FOREWORD

The first idea for the *Fractal* series came to me when I was ten years old.

I was always an imaginative child. In my bedroom, I invented worlds. These were inspired by the games, books, television, and films that I experienced. My generation feasted on a diet of *Star Wars*, *Battlestar Galactica*, Dan Dare, Asimov and Elite.

My late father was a good artist. His preferred weapon, a blunt pencil. I never had the same talent, but always wanted to be able to put something on paper that captured the images in my mind. I would try to draw them, again and again.

Eventually, some of the comics and picture books inspired me to draw ship plans. These blueprints were for 'The United Nations Space Force', an organisation born out of existing bureaucracy. Their mission, a mixture of exploration and enforcement. The regulators of humanity's gradual expansion into the solar system.

An array of crudely drawn ships in a sketchbook, made during car rides, or visits to godparents, aunts and uncles. The papers long lost, faded away into memory. The ten-year-old boy who made them tried to imagine the lives of people living in that far-flung future. How their world worked and functioned.

I remember being given big folders at school and being told we could decorate them as we wanted. Other children made interesting art, used cut-out pictures to make a collage, or created an homage to their favourite football team.

I drew spaceships. Badly.

But these imaginings were broad strokes. The stories behind them were clear and vivid to me. Those shaky pencil shapes were poor renditions of what I saw when I went to bed. In my mind, the spaceships came to life. The people who crewed them had fascinating lives, immersed in future technology that fascinated me.

The boy who dreamed could not understand the complexities of a global society, and indeed, the grown boy who now imagines them can only glimpse a poor resolution of such a thing. One mind amongst billions in the present, billions more to come.

But then, stories simplify the world and help us comprehend it. Science fiction gives us a chance to think about the problems of the present, revealed in a context of the future. That is a part of what science fiction writers do, but in every book, they don't do it alone. The reader is an equal part of the process, the book a conduit between the two.

I want to write stories that make people imagine things.

PROLOGUE

History will always show NASA's Apophis Project of 2039 to be a pivotal moment. A last great reach into the darkness by the agency. An attempt to maintain its relevancy in the face of growing opposition and an American focus towards domestic issues, rather than looking towards the stars.

The asteroid's trajectory had been calculated accurately back in 2004. The opportunity to intercept an object that would pass within 30,000 kilometres of the Earth was too good to pass up. Despite budget cuts, NASA managed to trade on its reputation and assemble a coalition of public and private partnerships who would research, design, build and launch a mission to intercept the rock.

Looking back on the moment, there are comparisons to be drawn. The world of venture capitalism involves risk and reward. The technology required to correctly analyse the material composition of Apophis at that distance would not be invented for another twenty years. Some data was available, and it was promising, enough to convince a collection of organisations that they could make a return on their investment when the asteroid was halted, and mining operations could begin. A further probe would be sent up, scheduled to reach Apophis six days before the full mission, but the results of that analysis would arrive too late in economic terms. The money had already been spent.

On the 16th of June, when the Sutekh probe landed on the asteroid and began drilling core samples, the asteroid was 60,000 kilometres from Earth. The short delay to transmit the results was an anxious wait for both investors and scientists. When the material was found to be mostly waste regolith, with only trace metal deposits, everyone was worried, but they were already committed to the plan and convinced themselves it was just a bad location. The metals would be elsewhere, waiting to be found.

Athena II blasted off from Cape Canaveral on the 18th of June. It took three days for the crew to reach the asteroid in their extra orbital shuttle, a prototype for the Ares missions that would go to Mars in the next decade. It took another day to match velocities. A boots-on-the-ground landing was ruled out initially, owing to the asteroid's rotation, so the capture rockets were deployed remotely and wire-guided in sequence, once the ship's computer had a calculation to arrest the rock's rotation and correct its orbital path. This took two weeks to complete, but by the end of that time, Apophis was relatively stationary and ready to be explored.

The results were disappointing to the investors. The asteroid's metal content amounted to six hundred kilograms of mixed iron and copper. The rest of the three hundred and fifty square kilometres was pitted rock and dust.

The failure to 'strike gold' broke the trust between NASA and its private partners. From then on, the organisation struggled to command the same level of international respect. Public news media led a witch hunt into the workings of America's premier space agency, starting a bloodletting that went to the very top and fractured the presidential administration of the time.

But the project wasn't a failure in terms of proving what humanity could achieve. The methods were means-tested and would form the basis for an emerging new industry that would come to dominate our thoughts about space nearly one hundred years later.

FIVE YEARS AGO

"Your name please?"

"Jackson Reeve. Liability Agent for EPS Global."

The man in front of me looks down at his portable screen. He scrolls through a list of names and eventually finds mine. Then he waits a few moments before acknowledging this. He thinks I haven't noticed.

"Welcome, Mr Reeve. This way please."

I follow the man through the busy restaurant. There is a table at the back, behind a partition. A woman is sitting at the table. I've never met her before.

"Welcome, Mr Reeve," she says as I approach. She doesn't get up.

"Hello," I say, easing myself into the spare seat at the table. There is no effort made to 'seat' me by the attendant. I glance towards him as I sit down, but he is already turning away.

"Service around here…" I say, smiling to take the sting out of the words.

The woman doesn't reply. She has a small screen in front of her, the kind you can drop into a pocket. As she operates it, I see her eyes move, reading, absorbing information for the task at hand. Again, there is a luxuriated pause, making me wait, ensuring that I understand my position of inferiority.

All part of the game.

"Mr Reeve. We have a task for you."

"Sure, I guessed that." I lean back in the chair. "Not like I get many blind date offers in places like this."

The woman picks up the screen and holds it out to me. I reach forwards and take it.

"All the details are there," she says.

I put the screen in my pocket. "Perhaps you should tell me what you want?" I suggest.

The woman shakes her head. "Everything you need—"

"Maybe I want to hear you say it before I agree."

"My employer wants you to use your position to arrange a meeting with Senator Boipelo of Sierra Leone at the predetermined coordinates in the briefing. Once there, you will separate her from her security detail, following the instructions indicated. After she returns, you will conduct the meeting as before."

I smile. "How am I supposed to get the attention of a world council senator?"

"All the material is in the—"

"Explain it in your terms."

"We have outlined an investigation and provided you with evidence that would require you to question the senator as part of your work," the woman explains. "The enquiry would be routine. Simply a confirmation regarding the identity of a third party. It will not attract press interest."

"A lot of work for a few moments with the senator."

The woman stares at me. "I'm not here to help you speculate."

I nod and glance around. "What happens if I don't agree to do this?" I ask.

"Again, I'm not here to help you—"

I hold up a hand, and she falls silent. "All right, I get it."

These people know they have me by the balls. They have a data trail that tracks every petty crime I've committed in the name of the EPS. Each indiscretion, theft, bribe, backhander, all of it. That's what makes me a tool to be used.

I hate being a tool.

You are trusted and have latitude, Mr Reeve. That makes you useful to us. I remember them saying that when they first made contact. I still don't know who is behind all this. Any effort to find out always results in another meeting and a warning.

I could be on some sort of list. '*Corrupt officials for hire.*' Yeah right. I lean forwards and pick up the laminated menu. "What am I allowed to order?" I ask. "Anything too costly for your expense account?"

The woman stands. "Make sure you wait at least thirty minutes before you leave," she says.

She turns away and walks out.

★ ★ ★

Reeve: Hey.

Savvantine: Hey.

Reeve: Can we talk? My screen says this connection is secure. What about your end?

Savvantine: Sure. Is this important?

Reeve: Could be. They made contact.

Savvantine: Okay. What do they want you to do?

Reeve: Arrange a meeting with a senator, then get her alone. I've already done it. I couldn't risk reaching out before.

Savvantine: Which senator?

Reeve: Boipelo.

Savvantine: Looking.... Okay, yes, I have her. I'll make enquiries.

Reeve: They were in there for about three minutes or so. I don't know what happened.

Savvantine: We'll check.

★ ★ ★

A discreet investigation revealed Senator Boipelo was subjected to an unlicensed non-invasive surgical procedure. We have managed to obtain the basic design for the device which has been implanted into her body. It uses several organic compounds to mask its signature, meaning it wouldn't trigger a conventional security scan.

We believe the device is a receiver of some kind. It is designed to establish itself near the brain stem. We don't know what it could be used for.

Given the circumstances, I would recommend relocating the senator. She has been compromised. If an intervention were made, it would alert the other party to our interest. Something off planet might be sufficient.

As always, Admiral, I'm available to assist should you need me to look into this any further.

CHAPTER ONE

Savvantine

I was born partially sighted.

I don't remember much of what I could see when I was very young. They tell me I would respond to colour and to light and shade, but not detail. I didn't reach for objects. I didn't try to understand or navigate the world around me.

When I was three years old, they started corrective surgery. I don't remember much of that either, only a vague memory of soreness and pain in my face. They worked on each eye individually, culturing and growing replacement organics when possible, replacing with digital implants when not.

Eyes are complicated. There's a whole set of biological infrastructures needed to make them work. Eyes change as you grow. Organic replacements have to be monitored constantly to determine whether the body is adapting to the adopted cells. Any tech used in the process has to be removed and/or replaced as a child gets older.

For me, all of that was lived experience. I didn't understand what I was going through. All I knew was that I spent a lot of time in hospitals and medical centres. There were bright blurs and dark voids.

Those years taught me to live with my own company. They also taught me to understand my world without using my eyes. Even now, there are instincts and sensitivities I have that others do not.

Eventually, after several surgeries, the procedure was declared a success. My ability to see measured at 20:18. My transplanted eyes are a combination of organic technology and grown replacements from cloned cells.

Some years after that, I had another procedure. A data monitoring chip installed in my skull. I was told that this was routine, designed to detect issues with the optical technology used to give me sight.

Later, that chip got upgraded into something more useful.

I am in the chair. The torn straps are knotted across my chest. I am breathing carefully, rationing my oxygen intake into calm sips. My heart beats slowly, calmly. This is a focused relaxation trance, one that I am completely aware of.

Doctor Emerson Drake is sitting next to me. I am very aware of him as well. He is not calm. His breathing is ragged and erratic.

He has been pushed too far.

I read Drake's file when he first made contact with us. Now, I access it again, through the data store embedded in my brain. Back then, I thought he might end up being an asset, someone we would need to use to affect the situation. I needed an idea of what he might be capable of and what would break him, if the circumstances warranted it.

Medical specialists are an interesting hypocrisy. They get used to seeing blood, to dealing with all sorts of injuries. They find ways to focus on the healing, the repair. There is a positive frame around what they do. Everything is progress, hope, and help.

When you take that away, you take away the filter. You make them see their world for what it really is – an ugly, ugly place.

I know that world. It is where I live.

Lieutenant Stephen Rivers was a good officer, right up until he wasn't. He chose the wrong side. Now he's dead, his body floating in front of us in a cloud of his own blood, shit and urine.

I trusted Rivers. It was a calculated, but necessary, decision at the start. Later, I should have seen when he made himself indispensable to my work. I made a mistake. I do not know how many people died because of that.

It is possible my mistake caused the destruction of Phobos Station.

Drake's file disappears. Now Rivers's records are in front of me. I make a small amendment – *Deceased*. The detail will not be communicated, not unless I open a channel to the central database at Fleet Intelligence.

"Colonel, I—"

"Quiet, Doctor, please. I'm trying to think."

Drake accepts my instruction. The calm, even delivery of words is essential in this moment. He believes I have control of the situation, that I am a source of authority in this maelstrom of events. He will accept my leadership for now. That is good. I will need that.

I sense a shift in our circumstances. Something almost imperceptible, but I have learned to trust these instincts. I open my eyes, ignore the floating corpse, and turn towards Drake.

"Doctor. We are about to be rescued. Before that happens, we need to be clear about what happened here."

"Rivers was a traitor."

"The motivation of Lieutenant Rivers to do what he did remains only partially understood. Until such time as it is necessary, I need you to accept the version of events I will report. Is that clear?"

Drake is no gamer. His facial twitches betray the warring thoughts within. In the moment when he acted to save my life, he found clarity. The world became simple – good and evil, right and wrong. I am taking that moment away from him, muddying the waters, making the situation more complicated.

"Doctor, this is necessary," I urge. I lean forwards, lowering my voice, letting him in. "The events going on around us are dangerous for us personally, and for everything at risk here around Mars. We need to project stability and establish control over the situation before it becomes something we cannot control. Rivers will wait."

Drake flinches away from my gaze, but he nods. "Okay, I guess."

"Good."

There is a thump from outside. The compartment moves, shifting to my right. The broken straps hold, but Rivers has no straps. His body falls away from us, crashing into the wall in another explosion of red gore.

I'm reminded of when he died. The glassy, vacant expression of absence. I've seen it many times. If there is an afterlife, will the ghosts of all those I have bested be waiting for me? Do they crowd the threshold of Hades, or are they confined in their own personal cages, embroiled in the punishments meted out to them for their own sins?

I can hear the hiss of pressure equalisation. The ship that has grabbed us is preparing to open the hatches. Perhaps I'll see Captain Ravansakar again if he's survived? An opportunity to apologise for my misstep on his bridge earlier. I hadn't meant to take over, but the circumstances were…unusual.

Now they are even more unusual. I must maintain my poise, project security and stability. These military types are strong, but brittle. They have been forged, but not tempered. Until now.

An alarm beeps; I glance at the hatch. It slides back.

A man is standing there. I don't recognise him.

"You folks okay?" he says and reaches out a hand. "My name's Sam. Quartermaster Sam Chase, lately of the *Khidr,* now serving as part of the prize crew of the *Gallowglass*. They said you were from the *Asthoreth*? Now, if I can…." Chase's eyes stray from mine, noticing the broken corpse of Lieutenant Rivers over my shoulder. His words are gone, forgotten, lost. His gaze returns to me. His stare is harder now, more alert.

"I need to know more about you both before I let you out of here," he says in a low voice.

Drake is about to speak. I touch his arm lightly, reminding him of our agreement, and he subsides. I turn and look at Rivers. "He was a traitor. He tried to murder me – to kill both of us."

"All the same, I need to know—"

"Sergeant Sam Chase of the *Khidr*. Transferred from a tour on Orbital One. Before that you worked in Fleet logistics, managing inventory on planetary shuttles. Before that, you graduated from Pittsburgh with an honours degree. I'm afraid your file doesn't specify which institution you studied at, but if I were to guess I'd say UoP?

Would that be right?" I hold Chase's gaze. "I have your file. I studied all the crew files of the *Khidr* when your ship went missing."

"Okay," Chase says. "Now, tell me who you are."

"I'm Colonel Yuhanis Savvantine," I explain. "I work for Fleet Intelligence, under the direct authority of Admiral Langsley." I nod towards Drake, who is regarding us both with a grim expression. "This is Doctor Emerson Drake. I believe his brother Jonathan was part of your crew?"

Chase flinches but draws himself up to meet Drake's glare. "Yes, I'm sorry, Doctor. Your brother...he was murdered...."

"I want to know what happened," Drake says.

"Yes, and I'll tell you, I promise." Sam steps back from the hatch. "The captain will want to see you."

"And I'd like to see her." I move forwards, out of the compartment and into the ship that has claimed us. This is *Gallowglass*, a vessel that appears on no manifest or record, but that confirms some of my suspicions about a chain of illegal activities. "You're taking us to the bridge?" I ask.

"Yes, those are my orders, once I've determined you're not a threat."

I smile at Sam. "Oh, we're not a threat. At least, not to you."

★ ★ ★

The journey through this ship is enlightening.

My knowledge of the Mercury patrol class vessels that Fleet uses as its mainstay trade lane support and rescue is not as detailed as I would like it to be, but I remember visiting them and looking at the designs. Those moments are recorded for me and I'm able to recall them, bringing up captures from those plans as they were being discussed in classified briefings.

This ship is similar, but not the same.

Chase is leading us, but also watching us. He keeps turning around, his hand covering a short baton on his belt – a taser, I expect. He has no reason to trust us, particularly as the welcome reception this ship received was hostile.

I'm following, but my mind is elsewhere, gradually unpacking the sequence of events, connecting the dots. The *Khidr* disappears after responding to a distress call, then the survivors from its crew show up in a ship that shouldn't exist, right in the middle of a terrorist action to capture or destroy the biggest orbital platform ever built around Mars.

And, minutes later, an alien ship arrives on the scene, then slows down to drift, seemingly without power, remaining silent to any request for communication.

At least, any request I know about.

"In here please, Colonel, Doctor." Chase is waiting beside the hatch entrance to the bridge. As we approach, he keys in a code and the door opens.

Inside, I find three people. Three women. An image recognition process that cross-references what I see with the Fleet personnel database immediately gives me everything I need to know about them.

Major Angel Le Garre. French Air Force, transferred into Fleet. Highly competent pilot, with a commendation for her work in the Lombardy famine of 2116. Discussions at government level reported that hundreds of people would have died if she hadn't acted on her own initiative, adapting three military transports to deliver food to the region. After that, she got her pick of assignments, and came here, to outer space.

Ensign Avril Johansson. Communications specialist and top of her class. Due to sit her lieutenant's exam as soon as she returns from her current tour. She has a reputation for incredible focus and concentration but is prone to missing the big picture.

And finally, Captain Ellisa Shann.

She is still in her chair. They all are. Her face has that sunken, gaunt look soldiers get when they've been through the grinder. She's seen war, a type of war only few individuals have ever seen.

Most of them are on this ship.

I note her disability being mentioned in her file. They made a specific mention of it; in fact, whoever wrote that paragraph was very clear about it. *Some might disregard Shann because of her lack of legs, but you do so at a detriment to yourself and Fleet. The sheer force of personality this woman has is palpable.*

Thankfully, those kinds of prejudices are no longer as prevalent as they once were.

"Colonel Savvantine. You worked for Admiral Langsley."

"Captain Shann, you were listening then?"

"Of course."

"Good."

"Langsley is dead," Shann explains. "He was kidnapped by the people who once crewed this ship. They tortured him and killed him. I don't know what information he gave up."

"I guess the attempt on my life might be connected to that," I say.

Shann shrugs. "I don't know who to trust right now, Colonel. But the fact that you mentioned Langsley, and that we know our enemies were his enemies, well.... That gives me a reason to think you and I might be on the same side."

I nod. "Forgive me, Captain, but I have no equivalent reason to consider you in the same way."

"We did rescue you," Johansson says. I look at her. At least she looks guilty for speaking out of turn.

"You did, *Ensign*," I say.

Shann's gaze shifts to Drake. "Doctor. I am so very sorry about your brother, Jonathan. He died...." Her voice catches, she flinches, looks away, swallows then meets his eye again. "His death was the first sign we had about all this."

"All what?" Drake says.

"That there's an enemy within, Doctor," I say. "Your brother was one of the first casualties of a war that's been coming for decades."

"A war? Over what?"

"Over who gets to control all of this." I wave my hands, indicating the vacuum outside. The irony of the point is not lost on me. "A war to determine how things will happen and who lead us to other planets and other stars."

* * *

[Evidence File #6: Savvantine's Personal Folder. Palgrave Speech. March 2101 AD. AUDIO BROADCAST – PLAY]

In the late twentieth century, the great scientist Carl Sagan, writing in his seminal work, Cosmos, *postulated the idea of a fourth physical dimension and how any creature who existed in four physical dimensions would interact with a human being who can only perceive three physical dimensions.*

Daniel Darling and others continued this work. The concept of the n-sphere or hypersphere is an interesting description of how our universe might be shaped. This remains beyond our day-to-day perception of the world. We struggle to visualise a fourth spatial dimension that is perpendicular to those we can see. We struggle to understand what the relationship might be between that dimension and others when imagining a four-dimensional object.

As yet, as far as we know, we have encountered no living creatures that have evolved from any place other than Earth and no being that exists that can physically interact in dimensions other than the ones we know – the physical ones of height, width and depth. Discussions over the relationship between time and space, either as one dimension (spacetime) or as a selection of additional dimensions that exist alongside those that we see, are continual and often vociferous in the different scientific communities. But, little of that discussion is devoted to how creatures native to additional physical dimensions might perceive and interact with the universe.

It is difficult to imagine what a being that exists in such a state would look like, or how they would live their lives.

* * *

[Evidence File #43: Savvantine's Personal Folder. Langsley Journal January 2105 AD.]

When the first automated rover deployed on Phobos and began sending back images, there were some who were waiting for confirmation of their conspiracy theory. They believed what we would see would be confirmation of an ancient alien civilisation.

In 1998, the Mars Global Surveyor transmitted images SPS252603 and SPS255103. These appear to show the presence of a huge object on the surface — a massive rock or monolith. Closer inspection by later missions led to the conclusion that this object was a natural phenomenon and that any theories of there being evidence of a prior civilisation on the planet were unfounded.

However, that didn't stop the conspiracy. Some believe our transmission was faked, others that we'd been duped. The narrative of ancient aliens is elastic. It doesn't go away. New, energetic minds rework the familiar tropes and anti-authority narratives to accommodate whatever new information they find. You can't reason with them, debate them, or disprove them, because they always want to believe and have an unshakeable faith that you are covering something up.

CHAPTER TWO

Holder – Wade

This is a memory.

I am reliving it in real time.

A white room. I am strapped to a chair. The bands are around my wrists, my waist, my thighs and ankles. My head, held in a metal bracket.

I can hear raised voices outside the room. Shouting and fighting. The muffled thuds you associate with a violent confrontation.

Then the door bursts open. A man rushes into the chamber. I recognise him.

"Holder! Emergency protocol alpha zero zero bravo six!"

The code means nothing to me, but suddenly, I'm angry – furious at being restrained. These bonds cannot hold me, *they will not hold me!*

I'm straining at the straps around my wrists and ankles. I pull my body forwards and there is a snapping sound around my temple. I feel pain, but at a distance, as if it will be important later.

The wrist restraints are made from strong plastic biweave. I can't tear them, so instead I am pulling at them, trying to force my left hand through the small gap. It shouldn't fit.

The bones in my fingers crunch and snap as I force them through the loop. Left hand out! I slam my hand against the arm of the chair, popping two fingers back into their sockets. The other two and the thumb are broken, meaning I'm awkwardly clawing at the torso strap and the other wrist restraint, but they come loose quickly, leaving me to free my ankles and stand.

Two men rush through the doorway. They are carrying rifles. I charge towards them and—

★ ★ ★

There's a crackle from the speaker on the wall. I open my eyes. Then I hear a voice. "Sit tight, Miss Wade, you're almost there."

Alison Wade. That's my name now. My permanent name. I'm not going anywhere else. I have some, perhaps all, of her memories in my mind if I concentrate, but they are like movies or books. Scenes and circumstances that happened to someone else.

Before that, I was Natalie Holder. I lived in a chair. My memories were a spliced mixture of real events and injected knowledge. For a long time, I couldn't tell the difference between them. Every time I started to get a grip, to understand who and what I was, Doctor Summers came in, and wiped my mind. I was a hundred different personalities, used to fulfil a variety of contracts for Summers's employer, Emori. Each occasion would require a new personality to be created and transmitted to a host body, hundreds of miles away. I would perform the mission and be transferred back.

I know this happened many times. Fragments of each experience are left behind. I can feel them, like ghosts. My last transfer was from here, on Phobos Station before it was destroyed. I escaped, but a version of me was left behind. This version.

Now, I'm in a chair, facing the cracked screen of a computer terminal with the bodies of two clones behind me. I've been here for a little over four hours. My breathing is an unhealthy series of wheezing efforts. I know I'm injured. Ribs and lungs are affected, and I can taste blood in my mouth. The air in here is bad and getting worse. I know the signs of CO_2 poisoning, but I don't know how this body will react.

I'm cold. Before he detached and activated his thrusters, Station Technician Mohammed Diouf advised me to conserve power and oxygen. Following his instructions, I deactivated the terminal and everything but the emergency systems to ensure I could survive out here for as long as possible.

Thankfully, the rescue shuttle got here in time. Now we're locked together; the traction clamps have secured the rotation and velocity of my compartment.

"Supplementary tank secured. Okay, Miss Wade, we'll need you to make your way to the emergency oxygen outlet near the back of the room."

I glance down at the safety straps wrapped around my arms, legs and torso. The override function is on the left side, just in reach of my little finger. To activate it, I have to make an awkward, hooking gesture around the arm of the chair. I can do it but trying to concentrate on anything right now…it's hard.

There's a buzz in my head. I'm not sure if that's some sort of residue from the transition or because of the carbon dioxide. Probably the latter.

I push the button; the straps release and snake away. The pain from my broken ribs returns as I move out of the chair. I need to be careful with this leaky bag of fluids, it's the only one I have.

The outlet is a few feet away. I push away from the chair and reach it without incident. I open the panel. The cover is cracked, but inside, the mask is intact. I pull it out and jam it over my nose and mouth.

Instinct takes over and I inhale deeply. A vague memory from one of my lifetimes warns against doing that, saying 'breathe normally', but I can't help it. There's a moment of giddiness and an urge to cough, but both subside.

"Take a few minutes, Miss Wade. Make sure you're braced. We're deploying a bubble so we can extract you."

A bubble. A sealed fabric sphere that will envelop the entire compartment. The plan will be to inflate the interior with oxygen, equalise pressure and then open the hatch in here. I will exit the compartment, into the sphere and from there, into the rescue shuttle airlock.

That's how it's supposed to work, but there's a whole set of variables that could make the procedure go wrong. Any sharp or jagged edges on the outside of the compartment could tear the bubble. One wrong step from me could tear the bubble. All of these things are a reminder of how precarious my situation is.

In moments of waiting, the memories surge, threatening to overwhelm me. Fragments of different lifetimes; being trapped in an airlock, being trapped underground, being imprisoned, being tortured.

Being powerless.

I don't know how this is supposed to work. If my conscious mind is capable of holding everything that has been unlocked. Perhaps this revelation was intended to be a temporary solution? Something that would be fixed when I transferred back?

The version of me that escaped, that was transmitted from Phobos Station back to Earth. Was it restored to what it was before? A prison of the mind and the body. Would I want that?

No.

"Bubble secure, Miss Wade. We're ready for you. You can detach yourself from the outlet."

I do as asked, moving towards the door. The control panel is damaged, but the emergency handle seems to be intact. I grab hold and pull.

It moves a bit. The door grinds open about six inches then stops. *Not enough.* I brace myself against the wall and try again. Another two inches. I shift my grip so I can push this time. That works!

I shift myself around, manoeuvring into the gap sideways. One arm, my head, torso, other arm. I shift again, get a grip on the outside of the compartment and pull myself through.

I'm inside the bubble and outside the room. For the first time, I can see the outer walls of the shell that protected me.

The pockmarked and scorched metal is a wasteland of scars and damage. A collection of broken purpose. I was lucky, very lucky indeed.

The airlock hatch is a few feet away. I move towards it, open it, and pull myself inside, shutting and sealing myself in. The crew of this shuttle will know immediately that I'm aboard and that they can begin detaching themselves from the wreckage.

I turn towards the inner airlock door. It opens. A dirt-streaked face is there. I recognise it.

"Welcome back from the dead, Wade," says Diouf.

He is smiling. I'm smiling, I can't help it. Amidst tragedy and ruin, we both cling on to the smallest personal victory.

We're both alive.

* * *

"Six shuttles, each with at least eight survivors, rescued along with their crew complements of two to four. Air reserves and scrubbers will last for a few hours, but then we need to re-tank from somewhere, or land on planet and get everyone into the domes."

"What about the people in the lecture theatre?"

"We got to them. Thanks to you two, thirty-eight people made it out."

"And you've lost contact with Hera Spaceport?"

"Correct."

I'm sitting in a half-lit cargo space, strapped into a chair, next to the other six survivors of Phobos that this shuttle, the *Phaeton,* has rescued. The air has that close muskiness you get when a lot of people are kept together in a confined space. My only hope is that it won't get worse as we run out of oxygen.

Breathing hurts. I've had a basic medical assessment. Two broken ribs, a possible lung injury, but I'm not the worst, and now the bleeding has been stopped, I'm in no immediate danger. My ribs have been set and strapped. I've had the talk about taking things easy. I nod in all the right places and let the medic move on to the next person who needs help.

We're sitting in two rows. Diouf is just across from me. Between us, an animated three-dimension pictographic shows our current situation. The cluster of shuttles, the debris field, Phobos, Mars further out, the patrol ships and near them, a larger, unidentified object.

Gesturing at the graphic and leading the briefing is Lieutenant Laurence Xiua. He's the only person not strapped to a chair or lying flat on an emergency medical berth. His voice is calm and even. He might be describing yesterday's training exercise, not the fate of all of us.

"What about the rest of the station?" a woman asks.

Xiua shakes his head. "I'm afraid there's no way we can make any further attempts. If there's anyone left alive...." He leaves the sentence hanging. The implication is not lost on anyone.

"We could just make for Hera anyway," suggests a young man, his head covered in bloodied synth skin. "We don't need radio contact to land, do we?"

Xiua looks at him, his expression calm, but serious. "If we enter the atmosphere and fly to the spaceport, or try to land anywhere else, we've no guarantee we'll be arriving somewhere safe."

"Perhaps the falling station wreckage damaged their communications equipment?" Diouf suggests.

Xiua adjusts the image, focusing on the remains of Phobos Station. "The debris has only just started entering the atmosphere. We've done some tracking. It's going to cover a wide area. The damage to the domes will be significant."

"But it hasn't happened yet?"

"No."

"Do we have another option?" I ask.

All eyes turn towards me. I meet each gaze in turn. Alison Wade might have known these people. A few faces seem familiar, but none of them instigate memories. "Where else can we resupply?" I point at the patrol ships. "Can we contact them?"

"We have tried," Xiua says. "There's a lot of communication interference." He changes the view again, moving the image towards Mars. "We have another option, *Gateway*. There is a small caretaker crew aboard. We haven't been able to make contact yet, but their orbit will bring them closer to us in the next hour, meaning we should be able to establish a laser link or near-field communication."

Gateway. The word stirs memories in me that are not my own. The legendary ship that brought the first colonial mission to Mars, back in 2058. For thirty-five years it remained in orbit as the main station, until Phobos Alpha became fully operational in 2093, five years after it was built.

Alison Wade remembers this; other people I have been remember this. Wade researched everything about the Mars mission when she accepted the position. She even visited *Gateway* as a tourist, following the crowd of new colonists as they were shown around.

"I've spoken to the other crews," Xiua says. "We're going to wait until we can establish communication with the caretaker team, and we'll keep trying to raise Hera, then we'll move on the best option."

★ ★ ★

"Alison?"

I look up. A man is looking at me. Well built, dark skin, shaven head, probably in his fifties or sixties. There's something about the way he is staring. He's expecting me to recognise him.

I don't, but I fake it. "Hey. You okay?" I ask.

He nods. "A little beat-up, but yes." He looks around, gesturing at the figure strapped into an emergency medical berth beside him. "Definitely better off than some. You look like you've been through it."

"We all have," I say.

"What happened to Jim? Did you see if he got out?"

I remember Jim. Jim Serlin. The touch of his hand on my shoulder was the first thing I felt when I transitioned into this body. The look of concern on his face, the easy intimacy we had, which had felt strange to me at the time.

"We were separated," I say. "I didn't see."

"Okay." The man falls silent. The words between us have died. It's what I wanted, but also what I didn't want. Pretending to be Alison Wade, to have her likes and dislikes, her memories, her personality, is hard, even if I do have a fragmented version of her surging through my brain alongside all the other people I've been over the years.

But that simple act of companionship, of reaching out and talking, trying to share the experience and find comfort with others who have survived. I miss that even as I shut it down.

A few moments pass. I can feel pressure against the safety straps. The shuttle is moving, but not much. The crew must be making some orientation changes to try to boost the communications signal or to help angle the laser for linking with *Gateway*. The pictographic is still there in front of me. I can see the cluster of shuttles and the *Phaeton* moving amongst them.

"I wonder what people back on Earth are thinking?" the man beside me asks.

"They might not even know," Diouf says. "The communications delay and interference mean we don't know what got through and what didn't."

"Or what was edited out," a woman says. The woman from before. She is looking at me, her gaze calculated and piercing. "You were in the comms control booth when they rescued you. Did you make contact with anyone?"

I bite my lip, look down and shake my head. What I did and didn't do in with the station's transmitter isn't information I'm going to share right now.

"I heard the propaganda broadcast the terrorists sent out," Diouf says. "The relays must have picked that up and sent it to Earth. They must know something is going on."

"They can't help us though," the woman says. "They're too far away. We're on our own."

The conversation dies again. The reminder of our isolation, the pitiful few of us left, survivors of a tragedy – one of the greatest tragedies to ever happen to humanity – dries up the words in all of us.

A memory comes to me. A moment underground in Atacama, readying myself to activate explosives and die. I had made peace with the moment, accepted my fate and chosen to act. I can't remember what motivated me, what agenda Summers had created in my mind to make me believe there was no other choice but to kill myself. *That isn't who I am! I'm a survivor! I survived the station....*

We sit in silence then, and I find something in that silence. Something we can share – a bond of experience, of a moment that we all lived through.

I raise my eyes and look at Diouf. He smiles.

Somehow, it is comforting to me.

★ ★ ★

Initial reports suggest there has been an incident around Mars. Communication with the colony and with the orbital station has ceased. Whether this is due to an equipment failure or some other factor remains unknown.

Currently, all attempts at redirecting communication through other facilities appear unsuccessful.

The last transmissions from Phobos Station were images from the festival celebrating the facility's birthday. If something has happened, then it would be the latest incident in a litany of events that have led to some labelling the place cursed....

CHAPTER THREE

Shann

I'm exhausted.

This, all of this, is not why I signed up to Fleet. I didn't plan to be a soldier at war. I wanted to serve and protect, to help people.

But then I guess very few people want to fight, murder and maim in the name of a cause.

Savvantine is standing by the bridge entrance. Her presence has me on edge. All of this has me on edge. She tried to order the other Fleet vessels to destroy this ship, to kill me.

I want her to leave. I'd like them all to find somewhere to be so I can have my own space, just for a little while. There's so much to consider, so much has happened, it's going to take time to process and work out a plan.

This tired is a different kind of tired to before. When we lost the *Khidr* and most of the crew, all the effort we'd made seemed insignificant, inconsequential, as if we'd failed anyway. This tired is easier. We saved lives.

But it's still a hollow triumph. Plenty of people have died and are dying up here, all for the sake of someone's ego trip.

Yuhanis Savvantine. I know her by reputation. If you meet her, you've done something wrong. When she told Sam her name, I looked her up. She's from Turkey originally, and she's older than she looks, in her mid-sixties, though I wouldn't put her over forty-five. Must be all those secrets, keeping her young.

Now she's trying to keep this conversation on her terms, make me work to be her ally rather than the other way around. Her rank doesn't count for much aboard a ship, but her presence more than makes up for it.

"Colonel, we're going to need to find a way to work together," I say, trying to reach out, past the ranks, the protocol and the armour.

Savvantine smiles. The gesture is a rebuff. She's not ready to discard her authority with me just yet. "What's the current tactical situation?" she asks. "I've been sitting in a box with a dead body for more than an hour. Perhaps if you give me an update on where we are and what we're facing, we can work things out from there?"

I look at Le Garre. She shrugs and keys up the three-dimensional graphic. Ships begin to appear as blue and green symbols with a large orange symbol appearing directly beneath the icon that represents us.

"We have the wreckage of Phobos Station here," I say, gesturing. "A group of planetary shuttles have been engaged in rescue operations. They've then withdrawn from the debris field and moved to cluster in this position here."

"Are you in contact with them?" Savvantine asks.

"Not at this present time," Johansson replies. "The interference is still affecting comms."

"The *Asthoreth* is shadowing the *Seraphiel*," Le Garre adds, changing the field of view. "The *Nandin* is stationary, conducting preliminary repairs." The three icons are drifting close to one another.

Savvantine nods, bites her lip, then glances at me expectantly.

"The last update I have from Captain Elliott of the *Nandin* made it clear that they are at an impasse," I add. "Whoever is leading the mutiny on the *Seraphiel* has hostages and is threatening to execute them."

"A factor that must be weighed against the value of losing a Fleet asset," Savvantine says. "They must not be permitted to escape."

"Their propulsion system is damaged and most of the crew have been evacuated. It is unlikely they would be able to manoeuvre away, Colonel," Le Garre says.

Savvantine points at the projection of the ship closest to us – the alien ship, vast and mysterious, almost the size of the *Hercules* freighter. "They may try to escape there. We cannot permit that."

Stating the obvious. I'm staring at Savvantine. I know what she's doing, turning the conversation into a briefing, so she can assume control of the situation. I'd be inclined to support that, if I knew she trusted us.

"What about your circumstances?" I ask.

"My aide contrived to ensure Doctor Drake and I were removed from the *Asthoreth* and then attempted to assassinate me," Savvantine replies. "I assume it would be because of my relationship with Admiral Langsley."

"You two were close?"

"Professionally. Yes. Our interests were synchronous. We both wanted to preserve the current balance of things."

"We have a video file of what they did to Langsley," I say. "I suppose you'll want to see it."

"Yes. Empirical verification of these things is important." Savvantine smiles slightly, but I sense no humour in the expression. "Sometimes I notice little details that other people miss."

"Part of your job."

"Perhaps. But also, part of who I am." Her gaze moves from mine, acknowledging everyone else. "There are several matters we need to address urgently. We need to act quickly and decisively. Solutions present themselves already." She points at the alien ship. "We need to board that, while we have the opportunity."

I look at Johansson, then Le Garre. The major nods, anticipating my suggestion. "Doctor, I think it would be best if you had a chance to rest," I say. "My team will get you settled in. We also have some wounded who would benefit from your expertise."

Drake jerks as if I've struck him. "I want to know what happened to my brother," he says.

"I can give you the details," Le Garre replies. She's out of her chair, moving towards him, her expression sympathetic. "He was a good man, he didn't deserve—"

"I know what he was."

For a moment, I think Drake is going to be difficult, but then he seems to wilt and turns away, making for the door. It slides open and the three of them depart.

Leaving me with Savvantine.

She watches them go and stares at the door after it closes. "You want to work this out, Captain? Make some sort of arrangement with me that makes things easier with your crew?"

"Yes, that would be preferable."

She turns towards me. Her gaze is an assessment, taking in my physique, noting my disability. I sense no prejudice. She'd do the same to anyone. "This situation is unprecedented. Trust is a rare commodity during insurrections. Yet, as you said, we seem to find ourselves on the same side."

"My crew needs a clear chain of command," I say. "They've been through a lot."

"And will be facing a difficult debriefing when this is all over, no doubt."

I nod. She has a mind like a razor. I should have known she'd be three or four steps ahead. "The mandate of our rescue mission to assist the *Hercules* was based on our standing orders. We then received a second message that told us to stay away. I'm worried…I've been worried that we'd be court-martialled for engaging a ship engaged in covert operations."

Savvantine looks around. "You mean this ship?"

"Yes. What do you know about it?"

"Three years ago, *Gallowglass* was a prototype design. I saw the blueprints. I didn't know it had been built."

"For secret missions?"

"For exploration. That's why the hibernation capsules were included, along with a more active automated control system." Savvantine frowns, as if trying to remember. "They wanted to go further, push out to Neptune and beyond. For that kind of distance, cold sleep had to be a factor."

"And the weapon system upgrades?"

"Those weren't part of what I saw."

I nod, digesting the scraps of information shared. "We aren't going to be able to make a full assessment of all the variables in this," I say. "There are lives at stake."

"Indeed, lots of potential threats, Captain. The decisions we make now are crucial."

I stare at her. The bland expression she gives me in return is a mask. Fleet Intelligence are always playing a game of chess with live pieces. Sacrifice is part of the process. But not for me, I've risked everything to keep my people alive. Right now, we're dying by inches as Johansson is fighting a losing battle with the ship's computer to maintain control. I had hoped Savvantine would have some sort of magic fix for that, but it appears not.

Now I'm left with a difficult decision to make.

"We're going to that alien ship," I say. "We'll manoeuvre and secure ourselves to the outer hull then find a way to get inside."

Savvantine smiles. The façade cracks just a little to indicate approval. "Captain, you've survived this long by taking risks. I believe you have made the right choice here."

"I'm in charge. You disagree with anything I decide, you bring it to me like any other officer," I say.

"Very well." Savvantine moves towards the door. "I do hope we'll come to trust each other fully, Captain. I am very curious to hear your story."

"If we both make it through, you can read about it in the debrief."

"I'm sure." Savvantine glances towards the door. "Well, if that's everything? I'd like to check in on the doctor."

"Of course," I say. "Be ready for departure in an hour."

"Understood," she says, and leaves.

I'm alone.

This is what you wanted.

A deep breath. Exhale. The dam bursts. I'm holding on to the back of the chair, gripping it as I drift in the room. The walls, the discipline that keeps me functioning and decisive require a focus —

another person to be there so I know why I'm being brave, calm and competent.

I have to let the walls down. Otherwise, all the junk builds up, like before.

For a moment.

Just a moment.

We have injured crew. Ensign Chiu and the XO, Lieutenant Travers, are currently in pods. If we're going to evacuate the *Gallowglass*, we'll need to work out what we're doing with them. Would they be safe without us here? We've no way of knowing what security procedure will activate once the root key stops working and the computer takes control of the ship.

The pods should have independent power units. They are designed to operate that way if a ship suffers a main power failure. The *Khidr* crew are trained in the rescue and retrieval of cryopods in the event of encountering a shipwreck.

Still, transferring those units into an unknown ship....

I'm tapping the terminal screen on my chair. Johansson's interface still works, but it's starting to fall apart. Errors and timeouts slow down any access requests, but I'm patient.

We'll need to land on the alien ship. That'll mean manoeuvring and matching velocities. Then we extend an umbilical docking tube, like we did with Erebus. There might be an airlock or docking port of some kind near the human technology we saw in the images. If not, we'll need to cut our way into the ship.

Cut through solid rock, before the *Gallowglass* turns hostile on us.

I key up a comms panel and Savvantine's face appears. She's holding a portable screen. I can see Johansson in the background. She must have handed it to her.

"Yes, Captain?" Savvantine says.

"I need you to talk to the Fleet ships. Liaise with them about rescuing survivors from the station wreckage. Let them know we're going to be unavailable to assist. Tell them we can't help even if we wanted to."

"Understood."

"Then I want you to talk to Drake, get him working. We need him to assess our injured and prep the cryopods for transit."

"I will do so." Savvantine smiles. "Anything else, Captain?"

"No, that's all." I end the transmission.

★ ★ ★

[Evidence File #21: Savvantine's Archive Research. Brooks Interview Transcript. October 2063 AD]

Interviewer: So, why call it the Grid?

Brooks: Well, the term is accurate, and it has a little bit of that science fiction lustre to it. We are a decentralised network with exchange points – corners and transfer routes – lanes. In an architectural sense, a grid.

Interviewer: The question people will be asking is why do this at all, when we already have the internet?

Brooks: Because the internet is a garbage bin. We all know it. You search for what you want and get sent stuff that you don't want. We need a fresh start. All of us.

Interviewer: But you're still using content from the internet and basing some of your infrastructure on data platforms built for the internet, right?

Brooks: Of course. It makes sense to use technology that already exists. Our systems are encrypted and separate. We just use a few of the same wires.

Interviewer: And you're funding this through subscription?

Brooks: We're funding it mostly through investment, but yes, we'll be asking users to contribute to the cost of setting everything up and maintaining it all. As we get more take-up, that cost will reduce.

Interviewer: And the stories about user content being part of a training library?

Brooks: Yes, well, that's true. We're making no secret of it. The terms and conditions of use have a processing clause. That allows us to make use of all content on the Grid for our licensed research projects.

Interviewer: Won't that scare people off?

Brooks: Not if we're honest. This kind of thing is going to be standard issue over the next few years. This is what will pay for the next generation of technology.

CHAPTER FOUR

Duggins

My name is Ethan Duggins.

I grew up in Fort Worth, Texas. I lived there as a kid during the secession and reformation of the North American nations.

My family lived through the oil dry-out of the 2070s. I was part of the first generation to leave and try and find a way out. All those machinery skills were the basis for my training at the University of Texas at Austin.

I died in 2118 AD, on-board the *Khidr* in deep space, far away from home. I was reborn as a consciousness, an evolving data file, an imprint of a human being.

The memories are a story, a pathway from then to now. I go through them one by one, looking for what has been lost.

My time contained within the ship's computer system, aboard the *Gallowglass*, caused problems. I know I have lost parts of myself. Fragments of the old Duggins, the man who lived and died, have been eroded and stripped away. What is left came here.

The alien ship is old. And familiar. The moment I arrived here, I knew the anomalies were connected with this thing.

I am examining records. The earliest memory is of darkness.

A dormant living creature, constructed by others, launched from an orbital facility. The creature, microscopic in size, fired into deep space by a proportionately massive amount of accelerative thrust.

The living creature carefully encoded with self-development instructions. As the journey to its destination continued, it would acquire mass to decelerate. That mass would be ingested and converted into more of itself.

The entity is capable of growing into a more complex organism. Each encounter with trace matter causes it to acquire more material for this process. As it becomes larger, it slows down. Each encounter with anything other than vacuum causes deceleration. This is part of the strategy. Expending anything of itself to reduce its velocity would be inefficient.

At some point on its journey, the creature arrived in our solar system. Whether by design, or by error, it became locked in an elliptical orbit, approaching the inner planets every few thousand years and then disappearing out into the far edge of our sun's gravitational territory.

"Hello?"

The voice I hear is not mine. There is someone else present in this receptacle. "Who are you?" I ask.

The darkness around me swirls and coalesces into something else – somewhere else.

Lamplight illuminating a darkened room in the late evening. Wood-panelled walls and a wooden floor. Warmth from a fire in the hearth under the mantelpiece.

There is a man in an armchair, the sort you see in European period dramas set in the previous millennia. He smiles as he sees me in the room.

I haven't entered; I am just *here*.

"It takes a while to get used to all this," the man says. "But you appear to have adapted remarkably well, much better than I did."

I stare at him. "You still haven't answered my question," I say.

"Sorry. My name is Mattias."

"Mattias what?"

"Mattias Stavinson. I'm an astrogeologist. I was working with the mining operation on Ceres before I was murdered."

"You're dead then?"

"Yes. Just like you."

I sigh. This isn't news to me. "How did you get here?" I ask.

"One of the anomalies. It was extracted from the asteroid I was going to examine when a man broke into the base to steal it."

"And you ended up on this ship?"

"That happened recently," Mattias says. "I'm not entirely sure how...."

"And this place?"

"A representation. You and I share a memory of Earth society. As our consciousnesses are contained in the same system, constructing an environment like this to communicate draws from your memories and from mine. I learned how to do it from the others."

"Others?"

"Yes, the anomalies."

I look away. I'm thinking back. I remember the moment when I realised I was trapped in the engine room and that I wasn't getting out of the *Khidr*. I remember feeling a presence there with me, a flash and then being amongst them in darkness. I panicked and lashed out as they sorted and dissected every part of my identity.

"It's okay," Mattias says. He stands and moves closer to me. His hands are reaching out, he wants to touch my shoulder and offer comfort, but he's hesitating. We've only just met. "All that is over. We're here now."

I gaze at him again. "And we're not alone."

"Indeed."

★ ★ ★

In this place, I learn that a conversation is a courtesy.

Mattias and I are consciousnesses existing in a vast data receptacle. I don't know how it all works, but I sense the information is available to me should I wish to learn about it.

Our identities are formed from the memories that were analysed and copied when we were transferred from our physical bodies. For me, some of those memories are missing, owing to degradation from my time existing on the *Gallowglass*. For Mattias, only a portion of his consciousness was saved in the moment of his death, so both of us have some damage to deal with.

Mattias is a little ahead of me. I'm learning from him.

I can share what I want to share and keep back what I don't. It's like a kind of telepathy, if you believe the wood-panelled room exists. But really our identities are imprints in a larger device. I guess if someone really wanted, they could atomise what is left of me and go through all the bits.

I remember the *Khidr* again and a shudder runs through my projected body.

"You all right?" Mattias asks.

"Yeah," I say.

"Your friends. You said they are close by and that you are in communication with them," Mattias says. "What are they going to do?"

"Knowing Captain Ellisa Shann, survive," I reply and find myself smiling. Any reminder of that irrepressible woman lifts my mood. "She just doesn't give up."

"Will they come here?"

I share my understanding of the tactical situation in our locality with Mattias. He's not versed in the intricacies of four-dimensional astrophysics as it applies to spacecraft, but the information does give him an approximation. "There are a lot of variables," I say. "That space station blowing up means there are a lot of people up there running out of air."

"You think she'll try and save them?"

"I think she'll try and save everyone. But she's not got a lot to work with."

"You want to help them?"

"Yes."

Mattias nods. "We need to explore this system. We have to find a way to master it, to master the ship and aid your friends. I don't know what we will find."

"It feels familiar in a way," I say. "As if it was built to hold something like us."

"There could be others," Mattias says. "We have no idea what this place is like. Or how it has been constructed, but, as you say, there is something familiar about it. The anomalies must be part of the same civilisation."

"That's a theory," I say. "We'll need to find more evidence before we accept that as fact."

★ ★ ★

I'm standing in the middle of a quiet road.

The shift of location is an abrupt change. Did I create it?

I look around. The houses on this street are familiar. The memory teases me, then reveals itself. This is Coppell, the town in Texas where I grew up. I'm standing in the middle of Burns Crossing. Even as I look around, the details become sharper, more reminiscent of what I remember.

There are no people. Just the two of us.

"You ready to go?" Mattias asks.

I gesture at the buildings. "What do you see?" I ask. "Is it the same?"

"An American suburb, somewhere I've never been, so I guess so," Mattias says. "This place means something to you?"

"Yeah. I grew up here."

"A place you know as a starting point." Mattias points down the street. I notice he is carrying a rucksack. The kind you take when you're hiking and planning to camp. Ahead, I can see the intersection. "That way?" he asks.

I nod and we start walking.

As we move, I glance around. This is weird. They tore up all these homes a decade ago. I think what I'm seeing is a faint memory, the details added from other moments in my life. This representation has been constructed by my subconscious.

But this can't be a distraction. We need to be figuring things out.

We are walking. I am seeing familiar things. There is recognisable human technology embedded into this ship, evidence that someone has been here before us and tried to do what we are doing.

Accessing the computer that has been installed in this ship is difficult. Whoever set this up was trying to communicate with the receptacle that we are present in. However, the connection is imperfect. The structures are incompatible, created from entirely different processes. The receptacle is primarily bio-organic, something that doesn't interface with electronics and cables.

On the street, we come to a wooden cabin. I don't remember this. Mattias walks up to the door and tries the handle.

"Locked."

"That's unhelpful," I say. I'm staring at the wood, looking at the grain of the cheap timber, bleached a little by the blazing sunlight. Out of place, but still made of materials I recognise. "We understand human machines," I say. "What we need is to instruct the alien ship in how they work, so the two technologies can work with each other."

"What if our host doesn't want to do that?" Mattias asks.

I shrug. "If they wanted to keep humans out, we wouldn't have been permitted to transfer into the system, but you're right, there might be some sort of security procedure." I step back and look around. "This is all familiar. Intentionally so. We need to find the opposite."

I walk across the street, right up to the porch of the nearest house. I try the door handle. It opens easily, revealing the kind of clean and tidy interior you'd see in a brochure. I make for the stairs and climb them two at a time, until I'm on the landing and then in the master bedroom. I move to the window, open it and climb out onto the ledge.

Mattias is outside, shading his eyes, watching me. "What are you doing?" he shouts.

"Trying something different," I reply.

I gather myself and push off from the window into the air.

★ ★ ★

A second-storey fall, from around fifteen to twenty feet up. The kind that would put you in hospital with a broken leg, back on Earth, but here, it breaks the illusion.

Darkness. Flashes of where I was. Mattias looking up at me, his expression aghast as he realises what I'm doing, or rather what it looks like I'm doing. Then, the rabbit hole. Awareness outside of the simulated five senses. I realise only seconds have passed since my transference from the *Gallowglass*. All of my interactions with Mattias have taken microscopic amounts of time.

My imprinted mind adjusts to the new representation. There are new senses; they become approximations of what I'm used to. Locating physical characteristics manifests as touch and taste. There is a wetness to my environment. I am part of that wetness, existing in a semi-permeable state that both horrifies and fascinates me at the same time. I flow in and out of different organic technology, trying to find the places where humans attempted to connect their wires into the alien system.

The intrusion is a like an open wound. An abscess that refuses to heal whilst the crude plastic wiring remains jammed into the flesh. The perpetrator has attempted some form of adaptation. I find a wetware conversion system. Synthesised neurons contained in a porous membrane, so they can transmit and receive information from the system I inhabit without losing their connection to the electronics that have been hooked up to the external computer and data store.

Whoever built this must have known the kind of technology they would have to deal with. That means they've encountered this kind of system more than once.

I sense that the interface was functional, to a point. But something went wrong. Probably overloaded the human equipment. The amount of data being shifted around in the receptacle is vast. It makes my time inhabiting the *Gallowglass* computer feel like solitary confinement.

My presence here and my understanding of the human technology means I can act as a conduit, filtering the amount of information being transmitted. That is, if I can figure out how to instruct the receptacle to behave in the right way.

I'm focusing on the interface. I'm looking, hearing, feeling, smelling and tasting it, if that were possible. I want to use this crude machine to send and receive a message.

I encode the visuals and audio as a memory – an invented memory that uses words and pictures from my experiences. A copy of something done before, altered and refashioned for specific use. If this is to be a conversation, then I will need to reconstitute the received data in the same way.

"Hello, Ellisa. I made it."

It takes six attempts to transmit the message before I'm convinced that it went through.

★ ★ ★

[Evidence File #19: Savvantine's Archive Folder. Senate Oversight Transcript November 2089 AD]

Chair: The meeting will come to order.

Members. This is the first reconvention of the National Space Strategy Oversight committee. Our current circumstances after secession from the union by the states of California and Texas, we find ourselves a composite of different national interests. However, in this moment, the federal institutions remain and our members from Texas and California are present as guests with regards to establishing future policy. I would like to put on the record my gratitude for their continued presence and support.

Now if we can get into today's main order of business....

[14:00:45]

Senator: So, you are telling me, all this equipment, everything on this list is unaccounted for?

Braxman: Yes, Senator.

Senator: And you're happy with this? You're satisfied?

Braxman: Senator, no one is happy with the situation. However, given the scope of the audit and funding restrictions placed on it, we have endeavoured to produce the best possible account of current NASA assets for your approval. Without additional—

Senator: I get it, you don't want to throw more money at the problem. So instead, you want us to authorise the write-off of this list?

Braxman: Yes, Senator.

Senator: You are aware there are components here that are classified in nature? We have liquid hydrogen-fuelled booster rockets, an orbital capsule, even a collection of EVA equipment. Suits, oxygen tanks, tools....

Braxman: I'm aware of the contents, yes. These were all purchased items from the ledger that we could not account for in the central storage and deployment inventories.

Senator: Looks to me like there's enough here for another nation to join the space race.

[nervous laughter and general conversation]

Braxman: Senator, we believe these items are missing owing to incorrect accounting procedures. These assets should have been written off. There are testing records and usage records that indicate more equipment was kept on the books that should have been. We believe the equipment was defective, but not disposed of properly in the paperwork.

Senator: You believe that, but you don't know?

Braxman: That is correct, Senator.

CHAPTER FIVE

Johansson

"Hello, Ellisa. I made it."

I'm back in the medical bay, working at the terminal. Duggins's looming face is frozen in a window on my screen. The image glitches as the clip is played, and doesn't match the words, but both clearly originate from him.

The transmission originates from the site on the alien ship where we saw evidence of construction, close to the area that we bombed.

I open up another window and activate the recorder. Audio and visual. "Hi Ethan, this is Johansson. Message received. Good to hear you're okay."

That'll do for now. I cut the recording, package up the file, then transmit.

Okay, back to the main issue, trying to fix a problem that can't be fixed.

Inch by inch, moment by moment, the computer is purging the operating system I built on the root key we used to get access. All I can do is slow it down by slowing down the whole system with looping data requests and redirection commands. All a very elaborate waste of time.

Just like the other activity I'm engaged with.

As we left the bridge, Le Garre touched my shoulder and leaned in close. "When the captain is done with Savvantine, I want you to keep an eye on her."

So that's the other job.

She's across from me, working on the portable screen I gave her. I heard Captain Shann ask her to talk to Drake and then to the other ship captains, but right now, she's doing something else.

"It's a very impressive piece of code," she says, turning to look at me. "You build all this on the fly?"

I flinch under the appraisal. "Which bit?" I ask.

"The gravitational compensation for the torpedoes." Savvantine smiles. "Without that, this whole situation might have turned out very differently."

"You would have murdered us."

The smile slips, but she holds my eye. "Yes, well…. Sometimes fortune prevents us from making mistakes."

I sense I'm being tested. I look away. White walls, cabinets, cables, panels. This room, this is the place where I was stabbed by *him*. I can't be in here without the memory coming back. His voice, his words, his face. The way he let us go back on Erebus….

"You've been through a lot, Ensign," Savvantine says gently. "Your gifts have helped you survive. But the experiences you've had – you can't get rid of them. They'll be with you for the rest of your life."

I think about Duggins, the damage to his digital imprint. "Sometimes forgetting can be a mercy," I say.

"Mercy that renders us powerless," Savvantine replies. "Knowledge can be painful, but without it, we become nothing."

All very pretentious. "Speaking of power. You've decided we're worth keeping alive, then?" I ask.

"That's a cold way of putting it," Savvantine says.

I smile. "I say things as I see them."

"Sure." Savvantine taps the screen a couple of times, then slips it into a pocket under her arm. "People can be categorised by their usefulness. I've certainly been guilty of doing that in the past when it's been necessary." She gestures around the room. "All of this would never have happened if I'd relied solely on that kind of judgement."

She moves to the door and heads out into the corridor. I'm not sure whether I should follow. Every moment I'm not fighting the computer could make our situation worse.

But then Le Garre told me to keep an eye on her.

I type a new set of instructions into the terminal, setting up another audit loop. That'll work for a little while. Then I follow Savvantine out of the room.

We move through the ship towards the crew compartments. Eventually, Savvantine finds the one she wants and knocks on the door.

"Emerson?"

The panel slides back. The doctor is there. He's taken off his bloodstained clothes and tried to wash away the rest of the mess from his altercation with Lieutenant Rivers. He looks haggard, his face wet with tears, hair unkempt, eyes wide and wild.

Savvantine gazes at him. The look is the same assessment she gave me. "We're going to have to abandon ship," she says. "There are injured crew. They will need your help."

"I don't know if I can—"

"Emerson, these people need you."

Emotional manipulation delivered in a quiet, urgent voice. Drake twitches as if a bolt of electricity has shot through him. The naked pain in his face disappears behind a twisted, clenched expression. He's trying to hold it all in.

"Okay, I'll try."

"Put on some clothes and meet us in medical," Savvantine says. "Ensign Johansson has been managing the situation. She can brief you on your patients."

Drake nods and glances at me. I can see the family resemblance. I liked Jonathan. I hope I'll like his brother. I expect we'd get on well, if the circumstances were different.

The door slides shut. Savvantine turns to me. "I'll speak with the captains in private," she says and gestures to the unoccupied room next to Drake's. "Will I need some sort of access code?"

"The doors should open unless you lock them on the inside," I say. "If you want to log into the ship's systems, that'll need to go through the captain."

"Understood," Savvantine says. "I'll leave you to it."

She disappears into the room, leaving me alone in the corridor, unsure of what to do. Le Garre asked me to watch her, but Drake will need bringing up to speed and the computer....

I've been played. Savvantine arranged this to get me out of the way. I can't go barging in to supervise her calls without making it obvious and causing a ruckus.

Damn.

Drake's door opens again, and he steps into the corridor. "Lead the way, Ensign," he says.

We return to the medical room. Chiu and Travers are sealed into the wall storage. A quick instruction at the terminal and the two pods are deployed into the examination room, where we held him – *Rocher.*

Drake moves towards Chiu's pod. "Let's start here," he says. "Summary?"

"Head trauma, oxygen deprivation, blood loss. She was unconscious and needed a transfusion when we took the ship. There was an episode when we were dealing with the anomalies. She had some sort of seizure. After that we let her up and resume light duties. She got put back under when we needed to pull a lot of g's on the return."

"So, what do you need from me?"

"A quick assessment and decision on whether she travels conscious or in the pod."

"Conscious preferably. We'll wake her up in a bit." Drake turns to Travers. "And him?"

"Acceleration injury. He wasn't strapped in when Le Garre initiated the burn. Multiple fractures, skull damage. All pretty bad."

"How much work did you do before sedating him?"

"I reset his leg, automated his airway. There's a lot of complicated damage that I couldn't deal with."

"This is where you need me," Drake says. "Initiate the auto-medic and leave me with him."

"Of course."

I move out of the room, grateful for the reprieve. As the only other trained medical specialist, Drake might have asked me to assist. I don't want to.

Travers is a friend. Despite our disagreements, I value him and respect him. I look up to him. I don't share his faith, but I admire it. I came to admire it when he defended his beliefs in the face of my spiteful questions.

I don't want to see him broken. Not again.

The terminal flashes. The audit loop is completed. I need to set up something else to keep the *Gallowglass*'s original operating system from reasserting itself. I begin compiling another set of code. A little red meat for the hungry wolf.

I glance up. Drake is at work. The instructions are running. The next matter at hand is to plan our evacuation.

While the computer is trying to process the inane loops I've created for it, I start doing some serious work on compiling an inventory. There are things we are going to need. Any extra-vehicular activity involves establishing a specific plan for the duration outside the base, the mission activity, the tools required to perform the activity and anything else I can think of that would be useful.

Problem is, with this situation, we're not coming back to the ship and we've no idea how long we might be trying to survive in vacuum. That means we need as much redundant capacity as we can manage.

I'm going through items from the ship's inventory, when I realise the files access is actually more substantial than before. I don't know why, but there are areas of the ships data archive that I am able to read and copy that I haven't previously seen.

One key file record is the ship's journey record. There is a set of tracked positions, transit times, everything to show where the *Gallowglass* has been over the last three weeks.

Very interesting.

I package the files and start saving them to a portable screen. This tells us more about what's going on. This might give us some clues as to what could happen next.

"Ensign, could you come in here, please?"

I glance up. Drake is calling me. I don't know how long I've been in here working, but he appears to have finished. The auto-medic has returned to its standby position.

I move through to join him. "All done?" I ask.

"Yes," Drake says. "Wasn't too bad. You did really well, considering...."

"Considering what?"

The doctor looks awkward, his gaze flickers towards my absent right arm and then away. "Considering everything you had to deal with," he mumbles. "This isn't your area, so it must have been.... Well...."

"Yes, of course." I let it go. Drake loses points with me right here, but I know he's the kind that will torture himself for years about saying the wrong thing. "Travers is going to be okay?"

"He should be fine. You made the right call. We'll keep him in cryo for now. Once we have the facilities to allow recovery, he'll be able to begin that process."

I know what he means. Gravity is an issue for broken bones. If fractures and breaks are allowed to heal in zero, micro or fractional gravity environments, that healing won't be strong. Bone density is affected, particularly when we're talking about injuries. Stasis means the process doesn't start, or at least, is slowed right down.

Back in the 2090s, there were cases of mine workers having to be intentionally injured to ensure they weren't permanently crippled by their own body's healing. None of us wants that.

I go over to the auto-medic and power it down. "Thank you, Doctor Drake," I say.

Drake coughs awkwardly. I glance at him and immediately feel pity for this man who is clearly out of his depth. Gratitude has helped here. I said the right thing.

"Well, I should go check on the rest of the crew," Drake says. "Can't have you all falling apart if we're going out there."

"Sounds like a plan," I say.

I watch him leave and in that moment, I realise what I need to do. I'm not leaving the ship. I'm going to stay behind.

★ ★ ★

[Evidence File #3: Savvantine's Personal Folder. Archive Data]

Seventy-two seconds. The duration of the most important radio signal ever received. The SETI project (Search for Extraterrestrial Intelligence) began in the 1960s. On August 15, 1977, the Big Ear Radio Telescope in Delaware, Ohio, recorded the most powerful signal it would ever detect before its decommissioning in 1988. When an astronomer checked the computer printout from the day's observations, he wrote *Wow!* in red pen across the papers.

The Wow! signal was a strong narrowband radio transmission. At the time, it conformed to the projected profile astronomers expected to receive from an extraterrestrial intelligence. However, despite extensive searching in the following weeks and months, the signal was not recorded again.

In 2017, when Comet 266P/Christensen passed through the same region of space, the signal was detected again, albeit at much less magnitude. Scientists at the time concluded this meant it was a natural phenomenon.

CHAPTER SIX

Holder – Wade

"*Gateway*, this is shuttle *Phaeton* out of Phobos Station. We are carrying survivors and request immediate docking. Please acknowledge."

...

"*Gateway*, this is—"

"All right, that'll do for now. Loop the call and keep monitoring."

I'm crouching behind Xiua and Masson; the latter is our pilot and the one currently operating the comms. Sitting here is cramped and uncomfortable, but at least I'm finding out what's going on.

Xiua has a full internal schematic of *Gateway* up on his screen. The ship is a big, long box, with main engines at the rear, a bit like some of the modern freighters. The majority of the interior is a zero-gravity environment and, as such, off limits to visitors. The small rotating section is located at one end, near the main dock.

"Can we make it over to them?" I ask.

"Just about," Masson says. "Thruster trajectory is plotted, and we'll arrive shortly, but we'll need them to open the door."

Xiua is examining the screen in front of him. "Comms are all over the place. It could be that the debris is causing interference, but they must have seen us."

"Can we hook up manually and EVA across?" I ask.

"That'll be dangerous, considering how many people we have aboard and the condition of some of the injured. Better to connect or dock."

I nod. "Let's hope we don't have to risk it then," I say.

"Oxygen reserve at twenty-three percent," Xiua says. "Hopefully, that'll be enough."

I glance behind us into the passenger compartment. I'll need to return there and strap myself in as we decelerate. These people need to be saved. I need to be a part of saving them, after my part in how the station exploded.

I failed them there. I need to ensure that doesn't happen again.

"Door release detected," Xiua says. I look around. An icon on his screen is flashing. "Maybe they can't talk, but they're making us welcome."

"About time we got some luck," Masson replies. He turns to me. "Best go strap yourself in."

"Will do."

I clamber into the passenger cabin and retake my seat. Diouf raises his eyebrows, I nod and smile in response to his unspoken question. He looks relieved.

I'm secured in my seat as the deceleration hits. We're all thrown forwards, causing some concern and a few painful curses.

"Sorry!" Masson shouts from the front. "This is going to be a little rough!"

Deceleration. Newton's second law. Words in the English language aren't designed for zero gravity. On Earth, we describe motion according to our experience. Out in space, the relationships are different. Nothing is stationary. We've accelerated and now we need to slow down and manoeuvre so we can match the motion of our destination. The whole situation is complicated by the expanding field of debris outside and the lack of data from our destination. The shuttle computer is relying on an assessment of the speed of *Gateway*, rather than receiving confirmation from the large ship's own navigation system.

"You okay, Alison?"

The man from before is talking to me again. I gaze at him, but again, his name doesn't come to mind. Instead, I smile and nod, then look away down the line, seeing how the other passengers are coping.

Some of them aren't doing well, but there isn't much anyone can do whilst the shuttle is braking and turning.

This has to be handled carefully and quickly. We have six ships behind us, all making their way to dock with *Gateway*. Routes have been calculated and velocities mapped to ensure each has a landing window to get inside.

My thoughts turn to the silent ship we are about to dock with. What happened there? I remember my tourist visit and the smile of the small Fleet crew running it as a museum. Could there have been another incident? Something arranged by Rocher and his people to capture the old ship?

"Thirty seconds! Brace yourselves!"

My hands dig into the padding of the seat. The safety straps are being pushed, my body straining against them as we slow. The g's are increasing, the forces on my body swirl as we change our orientation for final approach.

Then it all stops. A moment later, a small jolt and a reassuring *thump* from the interior clamps indicates we've made it and connected with the system.

"Everyone, stay in your seats," Xiua says. "The dock won't establish airlock couplings and pressurise until all the shuttles are in."

"That could take a while," Diouf says.

"We hooked up to the central atmospheric tank and their data system," Xiua explains. "So, the wait won't affect us. Relax, we made it."

There's relief in the room. People are smiling. There is a way to go, but at least we're safe for now.

★ ★ ★

"What are you getting from their system? Any idea what caused the radio silence?"

I'm out of my seat, back behind Masson and Xiua in the cockpit. Through the shuttle cameras I can see the interior of the dock. Lighting is low, suggesting there might be a power issue.

"Minimal data," Xiua says. "There was an instruction sent to open the dock for us, but other than that, we're being denied the usual access. The life support hook-up is working, but I don't know if they'll activate the airlocks. I know this place runs on a small crew, but...."

"You think something's happened?"

"Yeah, I do."

I'm staring at the feed as Masson rotates the exterior camera, trying to get a better view of the room. Shuttle *Obdurance* is manoeuvring in. After that, *Ellipse* will begin her approach. We'll be waiting for them all for the best part of an hour.

Something moves in the loading area. It's small, and low to the ground. I touch Xiua's shoulder.

"There! Did you see that?"

"Yeah." Xiua turns to Masson. "Can we get a better look?"

"I'll try."

The camera twists around, returning to the same position. The object I saw is no longer there.

"Load the timestamp," Xiua says. "Maybe we can isolate and sharpen up the image?"

The stream pauses, then winds back. Masson cues up the footage to run at half speed and sets it going. Again, I see the flicker of movement.

"There. Sixteen forty-three twenty-seven. Rock and roll that."

The movement runs forwards and back as we all study it. Masson zooms in as well, but the blur doesn't resolve.

"Could just be the shadow of the docking arm?" Xiua suggests.

"Maybe," I say. "We won't know until we're out there, I guess."

"No indeed."

★ ★ ★

This new life is going to get complicated.

We're leaving the shuttle. Xiua and his shuttle crews are helping the injured. Diouf has joined them. The loading bay is similar to the one from Phobos Station, but bigger. All the traffic coming from and leaving *Gateway* goes through here.

I remember the bloody bodies and wreckage. Rocher and his mercenaries, tearing the place apart, murdering station security members and hunting me.

I'm looking around, peering at the gantry and the different checking kiosks and doors. Plenty of cover. This could be a trap and if it is, we're fucked.

"No one here to meet us," Diouf says. He has left the others and is beside me now. "All very quiet."

"Yeah," I say. "You'd think their crew would want to be here." I point to the right. "There's an auto-medic terminal down there. I remember from when I did the tourist trip. Might be worth mentioning it to the others?"

Diouf nods and moves back over to the gathered passengers. I watch as he pulls Xiua to one side and gestures towards the medical room. New knowledge prompts activity and soon, the most injured of the evacuees is being moved in that direction under escort.

I note the firearms carried by the some of the shuttle detail. Low-velocity weapons, designed for pressurised environments. Less range, but less chance of tearing a hole in a wall as well. Supplementing them are an assortment of tasers and electroshock devices. Again, better for zero-gravity combat. Electrocuted people don't tend to leak as much fluid as those who've been stabbed or cut up with knives.

I should help these people. I'm walking wounded, with two bust ribs and a damaged lung, but that doesn't stop the need to be needed. I wonder where it comes from, Alison or Holder?

Or both?

I glance in the other direction. There are several exits to the loading bay. Some of them are wide passages, designed for cargo transit. Others lead to quarters and operational departments in the ship.

I remember from the tour, we were taken through the transit area into the habitation section, transferred into the gravity compartments. The movement I saw came from that direction.

"See anything?"

The man I should know is beside me, standing a little closer than I'd like. I inch forwards a touch and turn towards him. "Nothing, but we're in a vulnerable position," I reply. "Particularly with all the wounded."

"More terrorists?"

"Perhaps. Whoever let us in should have been here to meet us."

"Best to leave it to the professionals," the man says. He reaches out, touches my shoulder. I tense and force myself not to move. "We should help organise refuge here, find food and water. The authorities will come and help us when they can."

I shrug. He gestures for me to return to the group, but I don't move. Eventually, he sighs and moves away.

I turn back to the transit corridor. I'm moving in that direction.

* * *

A cold metal corridor, the voices of my companions fading away behind me. What lies ahead, I don't know.

Again I remember Phobos Station, prowling the corridors as hunter and hunted. In those moments I had gravity and a clear sense of my enemy – Rocher and his insurgents. In this moment, I have neither.

The corridor is dimly lit. Lights activate as I move forwards, but the level of illumination is barely helpful, leaving the corners and doorways in shadow as I approach them. I could use the light on the portable screen I'm carrying, but that could make me a target.

More of a target.

Whoever is here knows we are here, knows I am moving down this corridor towards the rotation section of the ship. I see no cameras, but I know they are there, capturing and streaming my progress in multiple spectrums.

Another movement ahead. I stop and try to focus on it. "Hello?"

A red light. The kind you see on a machine. A power LED or the sign of an active recorder. Another movement and I recognise what

I'm looking at. A small remote-controlled drone with a camera lens, pointed at me.

"You were waiting for me to follow?" I ask.

Another movement; the drone retreats down the corridor.

I need no additional prompting.

The elevators are on the right. Three huge cargo conveyors, designed to transfer people and supplies from the zero-gravity areas of the ship to the rotational decks. Those mighty moments in history when the first colonists lived in this place. The crew who brought them here making the final preparations to descend to the surface of Mars.

This moment is a feeble echo by comparison. It could be one from the last days of the colony. A fitting place for someone to witness its end.

I am in the elevator with the drone. As the compartment moves into the rotational section of *Gateway*, I feel the forces swirl and then gravity reasserts itself. The familiar sense of weight returns as my feet sink down onto the floor. The pain in my chest increases, breathing becomes difficult. My wounds are worse than I thought.

My fingers ball into fists. If there is a fight to be had when this door opens, I don't rate my chances.

The elevator stops. The panel slides back and lights illuminate the room beyond. There is a man standing in front of me. He's leaning heavily on a rail near the room's only exit.

"Hello to you as well," the man says. "I'm Captain Luis Francalla. I believe we need to exchange stories. I'm hoping you can explain to me what the hell is going on."

CHAPTER SEVEN

Shann

I'm back in a spacesuit, in an airlock.

The last time I was here we were invading this ship, having lost *Khidr*. Now we're about to leave before this ship reasserts control over our hacking and root key.

I'm about to lose a second command. In all the history of Fleet, no captain has ever lost a vessel. Even Captain Tranov, who may well be leading a rebellion aboard his own ship, hasn't lost his command, yet.

And the minute I leave the *Gallowglass*, I'll have lost two.

I'm not sure how this can be explained in any report, but there's no other option.

Le Garre is on the bridge, alone. She insisted that she pilot us in, landing *Gallowglass* on the surface of the alien vessel, close to the site where we think Duggins transferred his data presence. We are hoping our former chief engineer will be able to help us get inside before we run out of oxygen on the outer hull of the strange visitor to our solar system.

All the others are here, crowded into the room and into the corridor. Every safety seat and emergency strap is being used, along with every spare EVA suit we could find in the ship's stores. A few of the ones from *Khidr* have also been patched. There are just enough.

We are all in that moment, waiting for Le Garre to set us down.

"This is a calculated risk," Savvantine says. She is in the chair next to me. "You've made the right choice."

I gaze at her. "It must be frustrating being out here, cut off from your networks of information? Like being blind."

Savvantine smiles. "I was pronounced blind when I was a child. There is no comparison to that experience."

"I'm sorry, I—"

"You weren't to know." Savvantine is adjusting her helmet, making the final preparations before we leave. "In answer to your question, yes, it is frustrating, but it is also an opportunity. Whilst I cannot see them, they cannot see me. Whatever moves I make right now are not monitored or recorded."

"That will make the repercussions all the more dangerous."

"Very good," Savvantine says. "You might have the qualities for Intelligence. Perhaps we need to discuss that further when this is all done."

The room shifts and I'm driven against the side of my seat. Then the deceleration begins, and I'm pushed back. I see everyone else forced into their chairs at the same time. Small insignificant human bodies all rendered equal as they resist physics and try to survive.

"Fifteen seconds to synchronous," Le Garre says over the comms. "Hull is uneven. Brace."

I'm gripping the arms of the chair. There have been many dangerous manoeuvres over the last few days, but this has to be up there with all of them. A turn and burn to bring the *Gallowglass* into the same trajectory as the alien vessel. A descent to a distance where this crew can transfer from the airlock to the outside. Then we need to find a way in.

The pressure eases. Breathing becomes easier. The safety lights on the seat switch to green and the locks release.

"Position secured. Leaving the bridge now," Le Garre says.

I'm out of the chair as soon as possible. My helmet is on my hip; I unclip it and put it on, securing it and activating the oxygen feed. Then I turn on comms, selecting an open channel. "All hands secure for transit. I want this ready in five. Check in as you're ready."

"Aye aye, Captain," Arkov says. The others follow suit.

I switch channels to private. "Chiu, how's things going?"

"Doing okay, Captain," Chiu responds. Her voice is quiet, I sense a little tension but nothing else. She's managing her equipment on her own. "Ready for transit."

"Great, well done," I say.

Others check in. We're ready, let's go.

"First group, ready for depressurisation," I say. "Arkov, let's get moving."

I see the green lights switch to red as the ship begins to draw the atmosphere out of the room. When it's done, the airlock door unlocks. Sam and Arkov step forwards and open the hatch. Savvantine and I follow them out onto the alien ship's hull.

Gallowglass is ten feet from the surface of the other ship. I push off and descend, steadying myself with my hands as I reach new ground.

Ground, that's what it looks like; grey regolith, pockmarked and scored, like the surface of the moon. Except this isn't a moon.

Everything looks stationary. *Gallowglass* above and the stone hull beneath my feet. Velocities are matched, and there are no other bodies nearby to act as a reference for my brain to register our velocity. That can be dangerous. This is an EVA, not an exploration of a planetary body. There is minimal gravity and we're operating without tethers. The wrong application of force could send someone spinning away into the void.

"Possible entry point three hundred metres leeward of *Gallowglass*," Johansson says.

"We move as soon as everyone is clear," I say. "Get some grapples rigged up. Savvantine, you lead. Sam behind her, then Arkov. I'll support Johansson, Chiu and Drake with the pod."

"Got it," Sam says. He moves in front of me. He is carrying a lot of the equipment we're taking with us, including a chemical cutter, which should help us get through the hull. He's also appropriated two high-pressure oxygen tanks and a scrubber. If we end up in an environment where we need to create our own breathable atmosphere, we can, for a while.

"Johansson, do we have a track on possible debris?"

"I am monitoring it, Captain," Johansson replies. "But there's plenty of fragments that are too small to track. We need to get inside quickly if we can."

"Agreed."

"Le Garre here. Second group ready."

"Okay, make your way out."

The cryopod emerges from the airlock. The ten-foot 'drop' is relatively easy to manage, but moving the pod makes the manoeuvre more complicated. That's why lots of us are on hand to try and manage things.

We can't lose Travers. I can't bear to think about that happening.

Drake is beside me. I can see Chiu and Johansson above, moving the container and the rest of our equipment. There's a necessary moment of leaping off and 'catching' where we all need to be aware of how everything is moving. A slow-moving object with enough mass can still crush someone. We have to cushion the pod's velocity with our own bodies.

I brace one hand on the ground and reach up. Drake is standing beside me, both hands outreached, as the pod descends towards us. I can see Chiu and Drake in the airlock entrance.

"I have contact," Drake says.

Moments later, my hand catches the edge of the pod as well. The trick now is to act like a spring, gradually easing the object's velocity without ending up in its way.

"Okay, we have it," I say.

Chiu and Johansson are still in the open airlock. They haven't moved. I gaze at Johansson, but I can't see her face through the visor. "Let's get going, people," I say. "Follow the others."

"I'm not coming with you, Captain," Johansson says.

I sigh. "Ensign, think about this really carefully," I say. "I don't want to cite you for insubordination."

"Captain, it makes sense that I should stay here. I'm still fighting the computer. With all of you gone, I can focus on that. I think I can beat it. If I can, then you'll have a ship to come back to. If we abandon the *Gallowglass*, then we'll definitely lose it."

The argument makes sense, but letting Johansson go is painful. "Chiu, do you want to stay as well?" I ask.

"Aye, Captain," Chiu replies. "I'll come if you order it, but I don't want to leave her here on her own."

I think about the proposition. This wasn't what I'd planned for, but having Johansson on the *Gallowglass* could help us a lot. If she can keep control of the system, we don't have to rely on the Fleet ships to get us out. I'm under no illusions, they'll detain me and everyone else as soon as they get hold of us.

I like the idea of having somewhere to retreat to.

"If the ship locks you out completely, you could end up anywhere," I say.

"Captain," Johansson says. "I can do this."

"All right, stay on comms," I say. "Run the suit cameras through a terminal and monitor our biofeeds so you can be useful too."

"Aye aye, Captain," Johansson replies.

★   ★   ★

A metal door, with a plastic frame. Looks just like an inspection hatch for one of those solar arrays out on Luna. Whoever put this in had time and equipment to work and they knew what to expect from the terrain.

The ramifications of where I am and what I'm staring at is beginning to sink in.

I remember working on the SETI project, the 'search for extraterrestrial life'. Every ship and station has a dedicated terminal and telescope set up to scour outer space. New ensigns were always assigned to duty at those posts. I spent hours there, running the scans, collating the data. You couldn't help but wonder, *what if we find something?*

Further on, I can't see the impact crater from our makeshift 'bomb'. There was a facility of some sort here – that's what we attacked and what caused the ship to slow down. Some of the technology installed must still be intact, otherwise Duggins would not have been able to transfer and contact us.

"Orders, Captain?" Sam asks. "Do we burn our way in, or try something else?"

I think about the keycode we used on the *Gallowglass*. That can't work again, can it? "Johansson, what do you think?"

"Worth a try," she says. Her voice is a little distant and there's some interference on the line, but I can still hear and understand her. "Ask Sam to approach the door and I'll tell him the code."

Sam steps in front of me and approaches the hatch. Following direction, he takes a minute to input the root key into the pad.

Nothing happens.

"As you said, worth a try," Le Garre says.

"We'll need this outer door intact," I say. "If we have to cut our way in, try to make sure we can fix and seal the damage."

"Perhaps we should explore a little more?" Savvantine suggests. "There might be an entrance we can use further on, in the impact crater."

"No, we stay together." I'm biting back irritation and trying to keep it from my voice. The colonel doesn't know our ways and is used to being in charge. "If we scatter and someone gets hit by debris, then they're gone. If we stay together, we have a chance of patching and repairing, if it comes to that."

"Let's hope it doesn't," Arkov mutters.

Sam moves away from the door. I have to remember he's carrying an injury. That means he can't be one hundred percent. He picks up the chemical cutter – a dispenser that will stream a corrosive compound onto the metal and plastic. The moment it makes contact with vacuum it begins to boil and will take anything it touches with it.

"Okay, beginning the cut."

I'm looking around, trying to get a sense of where we are. If the circumstances were different, Fleet would be sending scientists here. They'd be taking their time, analysing and recording everything, trying to solve the mysteries of how this ship came to be here and where it came from.

The impact marks and scarring, evidence of a long journey. Years and years – centuries and centuries in the void. The story of this place, one I can only glimpse and speculate about.

A whole history, separate from Earth. Maybe even a whole civilisation outside and apart from every living creature that has existed on our planet. What has this ship witnessed? We may never know.

"Cut complete. Ready to move inside."

I'm back in the moment. "Arkov, you go in first. Le Garre after. Eyes open, everyone. We need to know what we're dealing with as soon as possible."

"Aye aye."

The two disappear into the darkness. A moment later the comms crackles again. "There's an inner door," says Sam.

"Can you open it?"

"Yes, there's a manual release. Audio reader is telling me the room beyond is unpressurised."

"Okay, open it up then."

Movement around me. Dust particles – could be debris from Phobos Station. An impact from any one of those fragments could be fatal. "Quickly, people, get moving."

Arkov enters, then Le Garre. Chiu begins moving towards the door, pushing the cryopod. Drake is assisting him. Arkov is in the doorway, Sam too, just outside. The four of them get Travers inside.

"Looks like they drilled out a space in the regolith," Le Garre says. "I think we're in an exterior layer, not the ship itself."

"Can you secure and pressurise?" I ask.

"There is an inner door, so yeah, looks like it. So long as we do a sweep for leaks and fix up the outer door, so we have a working airlock."

"Great."

A nudge on my shoulder. Savvantine. A light in my suit flicks on, a request for private comms. I flip channels. "What's the problem, Colonel?" I ask.

"Look."

Savvantine is gesturing behind me, I turn around. The *Gallowglass* airlock has closed, and the ship is moving. The computer must have finally purged our overrides. Thrusters have fired, taking her away from us.

I touch the panel on my wrist, flicking back to the open channel and boosting the signal as much as I can. "Shann to *Gallowglass*, please acknowledge."

I get static as a response.

"Damn. Looks like we're on our own after all."

★ ★ ★

"Okay, seal it up."

We're inside what looks like a first site habitation module. I've seen the designs for these when they were prepping supply runs for Ceres with proposals for expanding the mining operation. They have an airlock and EVA preparation room designed for three people, not eight and a cryopod. The walls are gouged rock, the floor lined with a plastic composite.

"There's another hatch at the end," Le Garre says. "It leads down to another level."

"Start working on getting it open," I say. "Sam?"

"I'll get to work on the outer door."

"Arkov, work with him. When you have a good seal, we try and pressurise this place."

"Sounds good, Captain."

I'm looking around, seeing computer equipment, acceleration seats and storage compartments. All familiar. Not what you'd expect on an alien ship; this might be a room on the *Gallowglass* or the *Khidr*.

It's crowded. We are all trying to move around dimly lit and cramped space in EVA suits.

Already, I'm missing Johansson. My first thought when I see an abandoned workstation is to set her on it. She's more of a software specialist, but I know I can trust her to make things work.

"Captain, I may be able to help with the communications set-up," Savvantine suggests. "It would be nice to be useful."

"By all means," I reply. "Take a look at their computer system. There must have been some sort of network between this and the larger facility they built. See what you can access."

"We'll need power," Savvantine says. "Everything is on standby on emergency battery. They must have had some sort of generator."

"We're going to need operational control of these systems," I say. "See what you can find. Even if we can trace the cables that may help us work out where we need to go."

"Understood."

"Le Garre. Talk to me about the hatch."

"The tiles stop and there's a dead end," Le Garre explains. "The hatch is in the middle. I guess they built this, took some readings and drilled through."

I'm having trouble seeing this place as a designed and constructed vessel. The hull is thick stone and built like no ship I've ever imagined. It is more like an asteroid that has accumulated all this material on its journey, not something that has been intentionally crafted.

"Okay, I think we have a seal, Captain," Arkov says from the doors.

"Great, do a scan, get some oxygen in here and set up the scrubber."

"Yes, Captain."

We will need this room. Any exploration of this ship will require us to have a way out. We've brought equipment to set up an operations base; this might be the right location for that, or it might not. But, pressurising a room near the exit is a good idea. If we can hook up some power for the cryopod too, even better.

I make my way towards the hatch. I can see it in the floor. A metal-framed door, surrounded by plastic tiles. "Le Garre, talk to me about this, are we looking at another airlock?"

"Not as far as I can tell, Captain. The handle is locked out, suggesting that it sealed up when this room depressurised. We can burn through, but that will break the seal in there if it's got atmosphere."

"Get a scanner on that before you do then," I say. "Arkov, hold up on the tank. Help out over here."

Le Garre shuffles around. A few moments later, Arkov makes his way past me and applies the pressure detector to the hatch.

"There's atmo behind this door," he says.

"That means this room leaked out," I say.

"If there was someone here, they might have moved inside when the alarms went off," Sam says. "Maybe they sealed the hatch to the next level and abandoned this room."

"It also means if we repressurise, we could lose O_2 pretty quickly," Arkov adds. "Problem is, if we don't, we'll never find the leaks."

Pressure leaks are easier to deal with in an atmospheric environment. Reduce the pressure on the outside or raise it on the inside and see where content is escaping from. Both solutions require gas. We have that, but we can't afford to lose it. "Break out the solvent sprays," I say. "Let's see if we can eyeball anything obvious."

Another private comms request. Savvantine again.

"Light, Captain."

"What do you mean, Colonel?"

"Turn on one of the big lamps you brought over from the *Gallowglass* and ask one of your crew to stand outside. If they can see light, you've got a leak."

I look at her. A simple solution. I'm ashamed I didn't think of it. "The station debris field is getting closer. It'll be a risk for whoever goes out," I say.

"I'll do it then," Savvantine says. "My idea, my responsibility."

The offer is tempting. "Okay," I say. "Get moving."

★ ★ ★

[Evidence File #14: Savvantine's Personal Folder. From the writings of Malcolm Palgrave]

There must be a planetary mass in the Kuiper Belt.

Amongst the debris and detritus cast off by our sun and the outer planets, there is enough material to distort the orbits of all the trackable masses as they travel around the sun. All of our modelled astrophysics points to a substantive effect coming from the far reaches of the solar system, substantive enough that we can measure it and need to factor it into our course plotting. That effect is localised and tracks an orbital path of its own. We know the region where it is being generated and usually such an influence would not come from a diffuse debris field.

It is my hope that we will send an exploratory mission out into this region of space. If there is a watcher at the gate, a silent dark world on the periphery of our territory, it must be visited, analysed and scrutinised. We must learn what we can of such a place and make plans on how it may become useful to our expanding civilisation.

A world on the edge of the solar system could become the starting point for our explorations beyond.

CHAPTER EIGHT

Duggins

I am in a laboratory. In front of me, there is a cart with a large plastic container on it.

I know what is in the container, the anomaly retrieved from a mineshaft on Ceres. I'm supposed to examine it.

However, I have already made alternative arrangements.

There is a hole in the wall.

Scorch marks on the melted metal plate. The smell of burning plastic. An entry point has been cut into the laboratory through the wall.

A figure crouches down, moving into the room. I find myself staring at a black helmet with a polarised visor. Then the helmet is removed, and I am confronted by a man of medium height with a forgettable face.

"Doctor Mattias Stavinson?"

"Yes, and you are?"

"Call me Rocher."

"Okay, Rocher." I gesture towards the plastic screens. "I have what you came for in a pressurised container. I've hacked the base security system as requested too. We're good to go."

"Well done," Rocher says. He moves around to the gloves and the insertion shelf, quickly removing the box. He clips this on to his belt and moves to the door, placing a device on the control panel. Then, he opens the door and attaches something outside. He pulls a screen from a pouch on his chest, taps it and the panels behind him begin to smoke and burn. "Okay, we're ready."

"Good." I glance around. "How are we leaving? Did you bring a suit for—"

"I'm sorry, Doctor Stavinson."

I'm looking at the long barrel of a revolver, pointed at my head. There's a quiet hiss as it discharges. A flash of pain…

…then black.

★ ★ ★

This is a memory, a memory from Mattias.

It takes a moment for me to realise what I've experienced is not from my life. While I was living it, *I felt like I was Mattias!*

Everything in that remembered experience reinforced the idea that it was new, visceral, in the moment. All the choices were as if I was making them. As if I was there. The lingering guilt of accepting the bribe, the powerlessness…. All of it.

I understand what Mattias did, accepting a bribe from a rival corporation, who sent a courier to collect the anomaly.

He is sharing this with me, which means he trusts me.

I have seen the face of his murderer. I have heard his name. I recognise him.

Rocher. Another Rocher clone.

I'm back in the wood-panelled room, in a chair. Mattias is standing in front of me.

"This is what you were worried about sharing?" I ask.

"I'm not proud of myself," Mattias says.

"I can understand that," I say. "But given our situation, it's not as if you can be prosecuted by anyone."

"Would you have done the same?" Mattias asks.

I want to say no, but then I hesitate. Fleet operatives don't follow the same rules as civilians who end up working in space. Their contracts are debited with their travel costs, which they are required to work off. All of their subsistence is factored into that debt as well, along with their living salaries. To be a civilian in space is a lifetime renting whatever space you end up in and paying for everything apart from the air that you breathe.

To be offered a chance to clear that debt? Well....

"I don't know," I say at last. "But I can see the temptation."

Mattias sighs. "One moment in a lifetime. I never thought it would be one of my last." He turns away, returning to sit in his chair. "Now, what aren't you telling me?"

I think about it. Reviewing my experiences, the memories that I have and the gaps where I know there should be something. "I don't know," I say truthfully. "So much of what I am is gone."

"For me, the bad memory is the most prominent one," Mattias says. "How did your attempt to contact the outside go?"

I share my memory of the experience with him, watching his eyes lose focus as he accesses the information and return as the stream ends. Do I look like that when I do the same?

"Impressive," Mattias says. "Well done."

"Have you seen anyone else in here?" I ask.

"No, no one." Mattias leans forwards in his seat. "I wonder if they left before we arrived?"

"Why would they do that?"

"No idea."

I glance around. I'm thinking, trying to assess the space, to look through the illusion and see our imprinted identities within the receptacle. The two of us are a small amount of data within a much larger entity. It stands to reason that if this environment has been constructed, it must have been used, or at least have been built to be used.

I'm looking around the room, trying to find evidence of prior use. A footprint, a fragment of data left behind, anything that would indicate the presence of our benefactors.

Nothing.

"You said you met with the anomaly that transferred you," I say to Mattias. "Have you seen anything of him in here?"

"No."

I clench my virtual teeth in frustration, then remember that Mattias is fairly limited in his abilities. Whilst he might believe he is a digital representation of his former self, his data footprint is one tenth the size of mine, despite the degradation I suffered on the *Gallowglass*. I can't determine whether he transferred with me or on some previous occasion when his Rocher visited this place.

"We need to search," I say. "We should divide up and explore. There must be some sign of architecture, or some kind of overseer who let us in here."

"Perhaps they are hiding?"

"If they are, we need to dig them out."

The environment changes. I'm surrounded by solid rock, illuminated by pale green moss growing out of cracks in the stone. This isn't reminiscent of any memory of mine.

Mattias is standing in front of me, holding a lantern, a candle inside. As he raises it, the light reveals his face, all hollows and shadow. He is wearing a flat cap and a torn waistcoat and his face is smudged with grime.

"I guess I go left, and you go right," he says.

"Agreed," I reply.

Mattias nods and turns away. His light bobs up and down as it moves away into the darkness.

I am alone.

I turn around in the cramped passageway and peer into the darkness, waiting for my eyes to adjust. The green moss disappears quickly in the gloom. Is this bioluminescence some sort of virtual metaphor for the evidence I am looking for?

No. I think it's just part of the memory from Mattias.

I can see the moment in his past that this is all drawn from. An old coal mine in the Kormi region in Russia. Young Mattias Stavinson went on a tour with lots of other eager school children. They filed through the dark tunnels as part of a history acclimation project. They were supposed to learn about how grim the lives of the miners were, but most of the children got excited about being in such a dark and scary place.

Again, I'm thinking that the illusion is going to get in the way. Do I need to break through again, the way I did when I was back in my old home town?

Radio static crackles in my ear and I'm drawn out of the moment to see a familiar face staring at me, or actually at the camera of a portable screen. Behind her, I can see familiar plastic panelling. The medical room on the *Gallowglass*.

"Hi Ethan, this is Johansson. Message received. Good to hear you're okay."

A short snip, but enough to confirm that my message got through. I'm just about to abandon this little spelunking adventure when a light appears ahead of me.

I stare at the tiny white orb. Is someone there? Or has Mattias walked around in a circle?

The light doesn't move. Has it always been there and am I imagining that it just appeared?

I take a step forwards. My eyes have adjusted a little bit. There is a little residual illumination from the moss that extends a few metres, giving me an impression of the cramped passageway.

I put my hand on the wall and continue to move forwards, using my sense of touch as a guide. I can't work out how far away I am from the light, but I may as well try to get closer and see what I'm looking at.

I fumble along the uneven wall, counting each step. *Twenty-five, twenty-six, twenty-seven....* The way in which these memories adapt to our senses, providing stimuli for touch, smell and taste as well as visual and auditory information, makes them far more vivid and real than any dream, or any haptic VR environment. As an engineer, I'm impressed, even if I know that one of the reasons for this illusion working so well is that I don't really have any of these physical senses and that it is all a translation of information using the methods that my mind can cope with.

"Hello?" I call out, projecting my voice into the darkness. There is a suitable echo, or at least what my brain thinks should be a suitable echo.

Did the light move in response? I can't be sure.

The passageway is opening up. I can feel that I am in a larger space.

Some sort of room. I try to locate the memory that this has come from but can't find anything in the recollections Mattias has shared with me. I'm definitely moving though, travelling through this invented labyrinth towards a light.

But I don't appear to be getting any closer.

One hundred and fifteen, one hundred and sixteen....

I stop. Once again, the way I perceive the world appears to be the limitation I am placing upon myself. I can't find what I want if I play by the rules. I have to break something.

The light goes out.

Hands on my shoulders. A low growl. Strength and weight that drives me to the ground. My knees hit rough rock and I cry out in pain. I am on my face in the dirt, unable to move. I feel claws digging into my shoulders, tearing the skin as I am pressed down.

What are you doing?

The words are in my mind. They came from outside, but they were not spoken. "I'm sorry," I say through clenched teeth as I fight to raise my head. "Please...."

Weight shifts. Something slams down on the back of my head. I taste blood in my mouth. My captor moves again, and I see a clawed foot pinning my hand against the stone.

Blood.

I raise my head, pool the blood and saliva in my mouth and spit. The sticky mixture splatters on the creature's foot.

There is a scream, and the weight disappears.

In that moment, I make a connection.

★ ★ ★

My physical form is not real. But it represents my identity within this space.

On the *Gallowglass*, my mind was simulated as fluctuating code. Even as the digital imprint of my brain degraded, I could understand what it was composed of. The massive amount of data had been translated into a huge nest of applications that filled the digital storage and with each random thought, exceeded the ship's limited capacity, causing systems to break down, and whole chunks of my memory to disappear.

In this place, the receptacle, I don't know how my identity is structured. I know the receptacle uses bioelectrical processes and living organic material to create this space, but I cannot determine how it works. This isn't my area of expertise.

But I know my representative form when we imagine these scenes is my entire code, my entire existence. When some of that touches something else, a connection is created. That's how I came to share with Mattias.

That's how I have breached the walls of this imagined labyrinth.

The clawed foot dissolves, as if my bloody saliva were acid. I sense the entity trying to retreat. I don't let it. I cling on and get dragged out of the illusionary space into something else.

Who are you?

What are you?

A guard dog. Guarding what? Am I supposed to remain behind? No. This environment is shifting all the time, trying to accommodate a mind that it doesn't fully understand. The projections of memories, twisted to serve as new locations for my purposes, are as much a service as a defence. Whatever is administering this facility is trying to help but is having a hard time understanding me. Instead, my mind, and Mattias's mind, are mapping our experiences onto this new reality in an effort to rationalise it and make it familiar.

Perhaps the guard dog is something of me, trying to establish security and contain me in a nostalgia-based context, where my mind filters stimuli?

No. That's not what I want.

Denial helps. The connection opens, widens, expands. I see the error of my perception. I live in a universe that I perceive in three physical dimensions. There are more. The existence of them shows the flaw in humanity's attempt to define its surroundings. The evidence has always been there, we just didn't have the—

"Hello, Dug."

This time, there is no attempt to create a physical context for our communication. The voice in my head is mine. The person speaking is not me but is using my identity to speak to me.

I know instantly that they have been watching. That nothing of my digital mind is withheld from them.

"Who are you?" I ask.

* * *

[Evidence File #41: Savvantine's Archive Folder. NASA Mission Sample Report September 2023]

NASA scientists have ceased all work on the OSIRIS-REx mission sample this week after mysterious 'black dust residue' was detected inside the transit canister used to bring it back to Earth.

Working in a hermetically sealed environment, wire cameras were used to analyse the lid of the container. These were fitted with a variety of detection sensors, which picked up the anomalous 'residue' before the lid was scheduled to be opened.

The lid was then removed and the presence of the unidentified material was confirmed.

In 2020, the OSIRIS-REx craft landed on the asteroid Bennu to obtain a sample for analysis. Its landing module recently touched down in the Utah desert on Sunday.

The statement from the project team reads:

"Scientists and engineers removed the lid and saw black dust and debris on the surfaces of the avionics deck and TAGSAM. This dust will undergo a quick-look analysis to determine if it is in fact material from the asteroid Bennu.

"...When the TAGSAM is separated from the canister, it will be inserted in a sealed transfer container to preserve a nitrogen environment for up to about two hours. This container allows enough time for the team to insert the TAGSAM into another unique glovebox.

"...The TAGSAM, which holds the bulk of the sample, will be carefully opened in the coming weeks," the space agency said.

CHAPTER NINE

Savvantine

I step outside and the airlock closes behind me.

Standing on the regolith-covered hull of an alien spaceship isn't something I ever expected to be doing. I flip the comms on my suit to an empty channel. The noise disappears, giving me a moment to just pause here and appreciate the context.

I'm out here in almost silence. The sound of my own breath and the electrical hum of working systems in my EVA suit are my only companions.

This is a novel experience for me. For the last twenty years, I've been plugged into a network of information, watching as threat probabilities and counter actions are planned and executed. My life has always been a part of the flow. My work, a bag of metaphorical rocks to throw in the river and divert the stream.

I don't usually stand in the water and get my feet wet.

I am very glad I took several courses on extra-vehicular activity and zero-gravity operations. Whilst I hadn't planned for this eventuality, it does mean Shann's crew don't need to babysit me, and hopefully, that I can contribute something to earn the captain's trust.

My data implant is already acting to assist me. The microcomputer in my brain is interfacing with my EVA suit through a discreet proximity connection that is almost undetectable to any monitoring system. That means I can control the suit's systems more precisely than the others. The data is processed and presented to me, so I can access my bio-monitoring statistics, heartbeat, and breathing rate, all in an overlaid panel on my right eye.

The system also tracks objects. I can see *Gallowglass*. The ship has moved away from us, but it's maintaining a supervisory position close by, relatively speaking. Then there's Mars and everywhere else, a twinkling deadly spread of dust and fragments permeating the velvet black.

At any moment, I could find myself in a hailstorm of twisted metal and plastic that would tear me apart. My implant can't help with tracking those objects unless I spend my whole time staring up at them, which isn't an option.

I need to work quickly.

I clip a tether on to the airlock door handle. Then I reactivate comms, dropping into the open channel. "Savvantine to Shann. I'm moving into position. Stand by."

"Acknowledged."

I move to the side of the airlock and climb up the rocky surface. I'm carrying a small metal case, which makes moving around difficult. When I'm in position, I open the case. Two remote camera drones power up immediately and manoeuvre around the other side of the building. I'm in the best vantage point to look over the roof and this side. I activate the body cameras on my suit and helmet, then set them both to transmit. All the feeds will be picked up by Shann and the others inside.

"Okay, we are receiving data."

"Great. Begin when ready."

"Lighting up now."

I'm staring at the building, and at first, there is no perceptible difference to any of its exterior. I can make an assessment of the construction. Seems to be standard Fleet prefabrication – a module just like those used in all the first landfall colonies and outposts. The same robust utilitarian design, with backups and redundancies wherever possible.

Then I start to notice a couple of shining little pinpoints. I turn towards them, angling my head for the camera on my helmet. "Captain, you getting this?"

"Affirmative, Colonel, the algorithm tagged the leak about ten seconds before you mentioned it. Arkov is working on a patch."

"Great. Go team."

The whole process doesn't take long – less than an hour. But it feels a lot longer, under the threat of a debris storm. A couple of times I see impacts, kicking up regolith. If one of those hits me, I'm—

"Sweep complete. I think we're ready to begin pressurisation. You can come in now, Colonel."

I sigh and get to my feet. My footprints are still crisp in the dusty surface of this strange ship. There are secrets here, information gold, as well as technology that cannot be let slip away. I need to win the trust of Shann and her crew if I am going to extract anything of value from this excursion.

I trigger the tether winch on my suit. The slow retraction of the cable helps pull me back towards the building entrance.

I'm near the airlock door when something catches my eye. I turn around and see figures coming across the regolith towards me. The implant picks out each, analysing them as they move.

They are carrying weapons.

I punch the airlock door activator. For a moment, it does nothing. Arkov's work on restoring power to the base may have been a temporary fix. I might be stranded.

Then the panel begins to ease open.

I turn again. Four people in EVA suits coming towards me at speed. None of them tethered as far as I can see. There is a practised ease to their movements; it's like watching a silent, deadly dance.

I ping the comms. "Savvantine to Shann."

"Receiving."

"We are not alone."

I'm backing into the airlock, watching the figures as they approach. I don't know if my messages are being overheard, but I see the nearest individual slow down, skidding in the dust. They bring up their rifle, level it and aim at me.

Then the doors close.

Bullets in space are silent. There is no resistance to slow them down. A shot from a projectile weapon would transfer all of its kinetic energy on impact with another object, like a door, an EVA suit or human flesh. The first sign of injury would be what you feel when it hits, and the sounds inside your suit.

I don't feel anything, but I can't help looking down, trying to check my suit for damage. Nothing.

Then I look at the door in front of me. Two small holes have been punched in the metal plate Sam welded shut only minutes ago. Without a seal, the airlock can't pressurise.

All that effort, *wasted*.

★ ★ ★

"Four individuals on the surface. They are armed with modified rifles. If they start shooting, it'll tear holes in the walls and vent any atmosphere you create in here."

I'm back in the room with Shann and her crew. Arkov stopped working on the oxygen tanks as soon as they got my warning. When I came in, they waited, then opened the inner door, letting me back in. Then we switched comms to an encrypted channel. Hopefully, the people outside can't decode it.

"What are they waiting for?" Arkov asks.

"Not sure," I reply. "But the minute we pressurise this room, we turn it into a bomb."

"That means it's a waiting game," Sam says. "Who has the most breathable air? Us or them?"

"I don't like the sound of that," Shann announces. She turns to Le Garre, who has patched cables into one of the room's computers and is accessing the system with a portable. "Can we raise the *Gallowglass*? Maybe boost suit comms using their system?"

Le Garre gestures at the mass of cables on the floor. "I'm still working through all this," she says. "We have power. I don't know what else."

"Okay, can you find some sort of map on the system? We need to know where these people have come from."

"If they were here before we dropped explosives on them, then they'll be pissed," Sam says.

I'm looking around the room. There is an airlock communication system, designed to allow people in the airlock to talk directly to someone on this side of the inner door. Both sides have an input port, so they can be used in vacuum. You plug your suit comms directly into the system.

I get Shann's attention. "Can we power that?" I ask.

"Yes," she replies. "What for?"

"We get it working and open the outside door," I explain. "If they come close, the superior range of their weapons will be negated. Then we talk to them, find out what they want. If things don't go well, we can trap them inside."

Through her helmet, I can see Shann frowning. "They shot at you. They want us dead. I don't fancy hand-to-hand fighting in EVA suits in an airlock," she says.

"Hopefully, it won't come to that," I say.

"That's a risk," Shann replies. She turns to Le Garre again. "What do you have for me?"

"Some layout designs and some historical context," Le Garre says. "This ship was found by the Avensis probe."

Avensis? I'm trying to remember the name. Then the information comes to me. "That was the probe sent to the outer solar system to locate gravity anomalies," I say. "Didn't they launch it back in...."

"2049," Le Garre says. She looks at me, then at Shann. I see the captain nod, granting permission. "There are references to Erebus as well."

Both are now looking at me. I nod, understanding the unspoken question. "Erebus was going to be a lighthouse station design for missions exploring the outer reaches of the solar system," I say. "The project was abandoned. The prototype plans and strategic objectives are classified."

Shann smiles, but there is no humour to the expression. "What if I told you the stations were more than just plans?" she says. "What if I told you that *Gallowglass* and at least one Erebus station are out there, crewed by a set of human clones, kept in cryosleep when they aren't needed?"

I hold Shann's gaze for several moments before answering. "I'd say you were peddling conspiracy theories. But then, I've seen proof of your story."

"You can't claim to be ignorant of all of this," Shann says, gesturing towards the room around us. "You're Fleet Intelligence, you must know."

"There are fragments to piece together," I say. "This is why we need to trust one another."

Shann doesn't reply. Instead, she turns to the others. "Arkov, can you get the door communicator working?"

"If I put a power pack on it, yes, Captain."

"Do that and open the outer entrance. Let's see if these people want an invitation."

★ ★ ★

Thirty minutes.

I'm standing by the inner door, staring through the DuraGlas viewport. I can see a figure moving across the terrain outside, towards the airlock.

Once they are inside, I gesture with my hand and Arkov closes the outer door, trapping them in the space.

The figure turns, noting their confinement. Then they move towards the communications port. I get a good look at their EVA suit. It is a little bulkier than mine, articulated differently too, with metal plates on the shoulders and torso. The rifle I saw is magnetically clipped to their back, along the right shoulder.

Our guest looks into the viewport. His helmet visor is polarised. He reaches up and flicks a switch on the side. The protective layer peels back and I get to see his face.

An unremarkable man. The sort of face you would forget, if you didn't have a memory for faces, which I do. Even then, I can't place where I've seen this man before.

Le Garre is beside me. She looks at the man and sighs. "Yes, I thought so," she says. "Captain, it's another Rocher."

"Of course it is," Shann replies.

★ ★ ★

[Evidence File #47: Savvantine's Archive Folder. Recorded Online Chat Undated 2108 AD]

Indira: The contract has arrived.

Gerrin: Oooh EXCITING.

Indira: They've improved the money a little bit. You were right to push back. Apparently, the procedure will take less than an hour, but they want to monitor me overnight. That means a couple of nights away.

Gerrin: But they're paying for all that, right?

Indira: Yes. Great private hotel in Syracuse. Flights are flexible, so I can stay longer if I want.

Gerrin: And they pay for that too?

Indira: For up to two weeks.

Gerrin: AMAZING. And you told them about me, right?

Indira: I did. The woman said you'd be placed on a list. She said she couldn't promise anything.

Gerrin: No worries. Just a chance is better than nothing. You going to do the full two weeks?

Indira: Oh yes!

CHAPTER TEN

Johansson

I'm pushed against the side of my chair. *Gallowglass* is moving, against my express instructions.

I'm out of my EVA suit and at a terminal in one of the crew compartments, knee deep in the source code of the ship's operating system. The root key has given me this access and, thankfully, I never logged out, but I'm losing the battle. Slowly, inch by inch, I'm becoming a prisoner on this ship.

"Fuck!"

A hand on my shoulder. Chiu is here. The touch of another human being is surprisingly relieving. "What's wrong?" she asks.

"We're moving. Pulling away from the others. The ship has initiated a burn. Any attempt I make to correct our course and get us back gets ignored."

"Then I understand why you are swearing," Chiu says. The anger fades. Her soft tone makes me smile. I see she has a screen in her hand. "Course plot indicates an interception with that." She points at a larger blue icon.

"That's *Gateway*," I say. "The original colony ship. Why are we going there?"

"I guess we'll find out when we get there."

I nod. "Open communications with the away team. We need to let the captain know what's happening."

Chiu works a screen. "The system's not letting me access external comms," she says. "It's locked me out."

Fuck!

Weight shifts. Now I'm being pushed back in my seat. Then the sensation eases. The burn is complete. Immediately, I lean forwards, trying to resume my work. A new terminal window and several attempts to work around the lockout using new code and a new access program, created in minutes on my screen.

Nothing works. We're on our own.

"When did you last eat?" Chiu asks. "We aren't going to arrive at *Gateway* for an hour or more and you can set another one of those data request loops going to give yourself a break."

The mention of food unlocks me. Suddenly I realise I am really hungry. "Okay, that's a great idea," I say. "Let's make time for dinner."

★ ★ ★

Food on a spaceship is never glamorous. If you are one of those people who likes the occasion of eating out, then plastic tubs and rehydrated consumables are an immediate buzzkill. Most of the time you're more worried about making a mess. Food in zero gravity involves concentration.

On *Gallowglass*, it's worse. *Khidr* had a few luxuries, the kind of occasional treats that boost morale. Might be a little alcohol, or a sweet treat that makes a shitty day worthwhile.

On this ship? Nothing like that. Here, there are no frills. Powder becomes paste. Water is injected with supplements. Clearly clones don't know what they are missing.

Chiu hands me a tray. For a good five minutes, I put all my attention into transferring, chewing and swallowing. After that, I start to feel better.

While I eat, I pull up the course plot for *Gallowglass* that I got from the ship's archive. The current mission started its journey from Erebus, went out into the asteroid belt, stopping at two positions, one of them an approach and retreat from Ceres. Then the ship came back to intercept the *Hercules* and got into an altercation with us on *Khidr*.

There are no records before this. I assume the ship transfers its data to the archive I found on Erebus each time it travels. That would fit with the idea of replacing the clone crew as well.

The course data also confirms elements of the mission brief. The journey to Ceres and here was planned; the diversion to intercept the *Hercules* and *Khidr* was not. That also confirms the crew had authorisation to countermand the ship's original mission. They were in complete control, before we boarded and took over.

There has to be a way to wreck the system.

I glance at Chiu. "I need your brain," I say.

She laughs. "That's an odd turn of phrase."

"I mean, I need to talk, to throw around some ideas." I can feel I'm going red, getting embarrassed. "Sorry, I'm not good at this, I usually work problems on my own."

"It's okay. How can I help?"

"We need to get around the ship's computer's viral defence and security lockout software," I explain. "So far, I've managed to back out and rewrite any code that the system rejects, but every time I do, the workarounds get more and more elaborate. Core functions, like the engines, are already inoperable. You've seen the way I slow down the system, setting up random diagnostics and stuff. That isn't going to cut it if we want to retake the ship."

"Duggins used to tell me to step back and break down the problem," Chiu says. "Sounds a little patronising, but I always knew he meant well, and he was just trying to help me understand how he thought about things."

I shrug. "All right, we can backtrack a bit. Maybe go through some of the parameters."

"So, you accessed the computer system using the root key found in the plans, yes?" Chiu asks.

I nod.

"Then you gave the root key to the Rocher clones on Erebus and after that, they transmitted some sort of software patch that started to kick you out of the system, right?"

"Yeah. Where are you—"

Chiu holds up a hand. I shut up and let her ask her questions. "When this ship was designed and built, do you think they gave the clones the ability to lock out the root key?"

I frown. "No, that would defeat the objective of having a failsafe override."

"Okay, so Erebus is based on the same design. Do you think whatever they transmitted removed the key from the system?"

"Not if we follow your logic," I say.

"So that means...."

"The key is still there." I see where she's going now. "The key is still there but changed in some way." I think back to my interaction with Rocher. "When I gave them the key, I altered it, I shifted the integers a little. I thought if I did, it might slow them down. Give us a chance for the *Gallowglass* to get clear." I'm thinking about those moments and my interactions with that specific Rocher clone. "I got the impression the clone we captured was trying to help us, as much as he could."

"So maybe he did something to the root key? Something you would recognise or find?"

The portable screen is in front of me and I'm coding as fast as I can. These are the moments where I miss my artificial right hand the most. I can type, copy, paste and compile as fast as I can think.

"All right, so we try a brute force key generator," I say. "I'll isolate a low-level procedure in the system, open a terminal window and set the program on it. It'll cycle through increments and variations of the key. If it's still in there, we'll find it, provided there isn't an automatic lockout after a number of tries."

"We can do better," Chiu says. She moves away from the table and over to the terminal, motioning for me to follow her. She has an auto driver in her hands and quickly removes the two screws holding the front panel in place, revealing the wiring inside. "That cable there. That's the hard connection to the rest of the network. We unplug it. The unit will still run, but it won't be able to query the central computer. That may help keep you from getting locked out."

I nod. "That could work. It may still decide to jam up, but at least we can reset the individual station in isolation. Might give us a few more tries."

Chiu smiles. "Maybe start with a few manual attempts? The variation might be obvious. The Rocher clone who you spoke to could be sending a message by making it easy."

Together, we work on isolating the terminal. The units have emergency operation drives that allow them to be used when the rest of the network has been damaged. That way, if you're in a crippled ship, you can still control some of the systems that are keeping you alive.

"Okay, we're ready."

I move to the display, turn it on and plug my portable screen into a port on the side. It takes a few moments for the local drive to initialise. I type in a variation of the root key, matching the incremental that I gave to Rocher.

Nothing.

I try the same as a negative value.

No joy. Clearly this isn't going to be that easy.

I activate the program on my screen. The terminal display flickers and blurs as the key generator starts spewing codes into the login window.

I hear a noise. I glance up. Metal on metal, somewhere above us, on the hull.

"You hear that?" I ask Chiu.

"Yeah," she replies. I see her reach out, open a compartment and pull out a taser. "If there's someone out there in EVA gear, who wants to force their way in, we're screwed."

"If we can regain access, I can task cameras and see what's going on."

"We'll need that quickly." Chiu moves to the door. She pulls out two of the emergency oxygen tubes. She hands one to me. "If they are going to cut their way in, we need to be ready."

I glance at the terminal display. The login window continues to flicker as the portable screen continues to hurl codes at the barrier.

More noise from above, a scraping and movement, shifting around and away from the room we are in. I feel powerless. If there is a person out there, it's unlikely they know we are in this room, but they may know there are people on-board.

I remember when I was on the hull of this ship trying to cut my way through the outer hull into the computer network cables. It took a fair amount of time. I had an idea where the crew were while I was doing this. I purposely stayed well away from the bridge and there was a battle going on, so the clones on-board had a fair amount keeping them busy.

"I'll stay here," I say to Chiu. "You head to the airlock and engage the manual bolts. Just in case they try to come in that way."

The Rocher who boarded the *Khidr* got in through the probe deployment garage after setting a bomb on the hull. I doubt this one wants to do the same. If there was even a marginal chance that a gambit like that would end with the ship being destroyed, that would mean all the trouble taken to get it here would be for nothing.

This seems a little more desperate to me.

The terminal display flashes. *Success!* A variation of the root key has been accepted. I quickly memorise the new code. *A, five, Y, three, eight, F, E.*

I'm behind the terminal, hooking up the network connection, when I start to hear cutting. Metal being torn and ground apart – silent in the vacuum of space, but loud and clear in this pressurised compartment. A portable laser, a highly destructive, but much quicker way, to break into the ship. These people must be more desperate than I thought.

I want to look around. I can't look around. *I need to get the code into the system and retake control of the ship!*

The smell of burning plastic, a stir in the air. Then the emergency alarms go off. Pressure leak. I know the door will seal and lock. I jam the connector into the socket and restart the terminal. It'll need to go through the cycle and link up to the network before I can enter the code. All of that needs doing before I can leave the room.

I clip on the emergency oxygen tube and try to keep my air intake slow and even. Twenty minutes to finish here, deal with a shitty clone and repair the room, or open the door and find a room with air.

More noise. The roar of venting atmosphere, and the tortured tearing of metal. I glance up. I can see the hole in the panel, above me and to the right. A gloved hand reaches through, drops something. It slams against a metal support beam. I recognise it immediately – a magnetic charge.

I pull the terminal further away from the wall and duck down. The explosion is muffled and strange, the sound strangled as the air escapes from the room. But I can still feel the heat of it.

The terminal display flickers and the login window appears. I disconnect the portable screen and tap in the new root key. *Done! It works!*

I move out from behind the terminal. The plastic panels of the room are scorched, but any fire has quickly suffocated without oxygen.

Fragments and dust litter the space around me. The hole I saw before is now a huge tear in the side of the ship. A figure in an EVA suit is climbing through the gap.

I move on instinct, launching myself across the room. I twist as I get close, driving my shoulder and elbow into the lower torso of the intruder. The force of the blow drives us both through the hole.

I reach out, grab a twisted metal strut, yanking myself back from the void. The intruder is not so lucky. Arms and legs flail as the figure tumbles away from the ship.

I glance down. There is a tether. A metal clip secures my enemy to the ship. If I remove it, he will be gone, condemned, falling forever in the darkness.

I reach towards the clip. I hesitate. Decisions like this make you realise what kind of person you really are. I've been told I can be cold and unemotional, too absorbed in the latest problem, the latest puzzle. Unaware of others and their needs.

I'm not doing this. I can't.
A flicker of movement behind me. The inner door opens. Chiu steps inside. She is wearing her full EVA suit. She moves towards me, steadies herself and grabs my arm with her gloved hand. I let go of the broken metal and let her pull me inside, into the wrecked compartment and towards the door. She pushes me into the room then turns around, heading back to the hull tear. I see her working, then she returns.

I close my eyes. My fingers ball into fists. I know what she has done.

★ ★ ★

"Are you okay?" Chiu asks.

We are back inside the ship. Chiu has repressurised the corridor outside the crew quarters. That's what she did when I sent her out. She secured the airlock and retrieved her EVA gear. When the alarms went off, she got dressed, shut all the doors and vented the corridor, turning it into a makeshift airlock. Then she came to get me.

After that, she murdered the person who was trying to get on-board.

I nod. I can't speak. Not yet. I know why she did it. Rocher and the people who control him turned her life upside down, making her take part in a mutiny against the rest of the crew of the *Khidr*. When she broke down and told us about the blackmail, Shann and the others were sympathetic, but suspicious. I was one of the worst for it. I didn't think I'd be able to trust her again.

Ever since then, she's been proving me wrong.

Chiu is driven. She's desperate to regain her place in the crew. This was a chance for her to get a little revenge, to punish the ones responsible for what was done to her.

I'm not sure I approve, but I do understand.

"We'll need to fix the breach," Chiu says. "It's too big for chemical sealant. That means we'll have to find something to patch it with." She glances around. "Maybe one of the internal doors."

"Or we leave the room as is," I say. Talking about practical things helps me focus and avoid what Chiu did. "The crew quarters aren't essential. We can manage. There are no key systems running through that wall."

Chiu scowls. The engineer in her wants things fixed, but she can see my point. "We have less than an hour until we arrive at *Gateway*," she says. "Best get ready for that."

"Agreed," I reply.

* * *

[Evidence File #32: Savvantine's Archive Folder. Press Release Neon Energy December 2058]
Six years after pledging to solve the Japanese energy crisis, Danielle Ambrose has declared victory in her 'war against nuclear'.

The resulting solar and wind farm is an almost total success. The distributed facility of micropower generation clusters provides energy for Hokkaido and Honshu entirely with new sites being constructed and brought online every day. This has resulted in the Japanese government announcing the closure of the controversial Fukashima nuclear facility, which prompted Ambrose's call of victory.

It is definitely a triumph for Neon Energy, the corporation Ambrose founded in 2053 to handle the project. Share prices rose six percent after the announcement.

As a non-Japanese businesswoman, Ambrose's ability to negotiate access to suitable sites across the country and to work with local contractors has been seen as a breakthrough in terms of international corporations collaborating with Japan. The distributed power system is resilient owing to its multi-site 'grid' set-up, and with undersea cabling planned as part of a later expansion project, Japan could find itself becoming a favourable provider of energy to other states for the first time in its history.

CHAPTER ELEVEN

Holder – Split

Row after row of cryopods.

I am standing on the old bridge of *Gateway*, trying to get used to 0.8g's and looking at an array of camera images on a huge screen.

We are looking at a huge storage compartment – one of the ones they used to use for carrying all the colony's equipment when humans first came to Mars.

"We found them during the evacuation," Francalla says. "After Phobos Station blew up, we had to make a course correction, the kind of move that we haven't made in thirty years. Power had to be cycled and redistributed. We found a lot being used down there."

"Where is the rest of your crew, Captain?" Xiua asks.

"I sent everyone out to help at Jezero after the debris hit," Francalla says. "We lost contact with them and with everyone else."

"We?" I prompt.

Francalla looks at me and smiles. "Me and them." He points to the pods. "I guess I see myself as some sort of parent around here."

"How long have they been here?" Diouf asks.

"I don't know," Francalla says. "I don't know who put them there either."

I'm staring at the man. He's old. Probably in his seventies, maybe more. Some of the treatments they get on Earth mean people don't look as old as they should. "You were one of the original crew," I say.

"I was," Francalla replies. "Just a junior tech back in the day. Went back to Earth after for thirty years, but it never felt right. Took a position here when they offered. It's good to remind new people about what we did."

Here at the beginning, and the end, I think, but don't say. "Have you been down there to look at them?" I ask.

"I can't open the door," Francalla says.

I glance at Diouf. He shrugs, but I know he knows what I'm thinking. "Lieutenant, if you can spare us, I'd like to take a look at that compartment," I say.

"Not up to me," Xiua says. "Captain decides who goes where on his ship."

Francalla waves his hands. "Fine, go ahead. When you find out what's going on, let me know." He turns to Xiua. "In the meantime, you'll need my help."

"We'd very much appreciate it," Xiua says.

★ ★ ★

"There's something about you," Diouf says. "Something these people don't know."

I hold his gaze. We're in the elevator, travelling back into the zero-gravity part of the ship. I can feel the weight leaving my body as we transition. It makes breathing much easier.

"I could say the same about you," I say. "You're riding my coat-tails. No one forced you to follow me."

"Hey, be nice. I saved your life."

"Yeah, okay, I'm sorry."

"You can be sorry by telling me what's driving you in all this."

The elevator trip will be another fifteen minutes at least. If I don't say something, all of those minutes will be awkward. "I want answers," I say.

"You didn't just want answers when we were back on the station," Diouf says. "Back there, you were trying to be an army, all on your own."

"We all wanted those terrorists off the station," I say.

"But that's over," Diouf says. "What's driving you now?"

"Doesn't it bug you?" I ask. "Why all those pods? What are they for?"

"Sure, it bugs me, but that's someone else's problem. Not mine. For you it's personal, I can tell. Why?"

The truth won't work here, but some of it might, mixed in with some lies. "I'm an agent," I say. "Fleet."

"Covert operations?"

"Something like that."

"Does Xiua know?"

"No, and let's not tell him." The elevator is slowing down. The deceleration moves us both to one side of the compartment. Then it stops and the doors slide open. I clamber out, Diouf follows.

Our movements trigger the corridor lighting. Illumination reveals a long corridor with exposed pipework along the walls. About thirty metres down, everything fades into darkness. The void has been pushed back, but it still waits for us. It looks like a hole, like we're on a journey into oblivion.

"Third entrance on the left," Diouf says.

"Definitely not part of the museum tour," I say. "Let's go."

Floating down the corridor, it's like flying. Alison Wade used to dream about flying over the fields near the house where she grew up. I can see the grass and the house below me on a sunny day. The memories resonate, divert. They make this little trip exciting in a way, but if I indulge in them, I'll lose focus.

Remembering is like a drug. I guess you get used to it if it's always been a part of your life. But for me, experiences are triggered when they connect. Anything can launch them, a smell, a sound, anything.

I'm getting better at controlling this, but these aren't my memories. They don't have an order, unless I give them an order, organise them. Over time, I might be able to do that, but now, all I can do is clench my teeth and build a wall to hold them back when they decide to surge.

"Okay, just up here."

We reach the entrance to the cryo compartment. There's a keypad and thumbprint authorisation panel. Neither of those will work for us.

"What's your plan?" Diouf asks.

"Decompression," I reply. "All of these ships are designed to lock up tight when there's a drop in pressure. Back on Phobos Station, I managed to trigger an override by tricking the oxygen dispenser and causing an explosion."

"You want to do that here?"

"I'm hoping for a more elegant solution."

The panel is right in front of me. I take out the taser Xiua gave me earlier. "You know how to take these units apart," I say. "We do that, then dump a charge into the lock. It'll either open, or seal up completely."

"What happens if we get the latter?"

"Then we all stay ignorant."

Diouf frowns, but he steps forwards and starts to examine the panel. He reaches for a pouch on his belt and pulls out some pliers. It takes only moments for him to get the cover off to expose the circuitry.

"Door circuit runs through those two wires," Diouf says. "I can open them up and let you jam the taser contacts into them. That'll overload the system."

"Okay, let's do it."

Diouf works on the cables, worrying through the plastic coating until I can see the metal inside. When he's ready, he steps back, and I step forwards. I pull out the transmission cables that the taser can use and attach them to the circuit. Then I step back and press the trigger.

Lights on the taser immediately wink on, there's a clicking noise, then a thump. The taser lights go out.

"Okay, we're done."

Diouf moves forwards and disconnects the contacts. Then he examines the lock. "It's fried," he says. "And still locked."

"Damn." I grab the door handle, wedge my foot into a recess on the floor and try pulling it, but the mechanism doesn't budge. Instead, something catches my eye through the viewport on the door.

A light is flashing inside the room.

I peer through the DuraGlas plate, trying to see what's going on inside. The light is green, regular, pulsing. The intervals are gradually decreasing.

"Did we trigger some sort of alarm?" I ask.

"No idea," Diouf says. "I guess we'll find out."

I nod. "Let's head back for now. Maybe it's tripped something on *Gateway*'s computer system."

★ ★ ★

Another ten minutes or so and we're back under gravity on the bridge.

Francalla and Xiua are busy organising and coordinating support for the survivors from the shuttles. I watch them work. The old captain listens patiently, then offers solutions, gradually opening up and providing the resources of *Gateway* for each individual, who he tries to meet and greet whenever possible. Rooms are provided in the rotating section, each person sharing a bunk, with sleep and wake/activity periods being allotted as shifts. I guess that's what it's like on military ships out here, and what it would have been like when *Gateway* first arrived in Mars orbit.

Diouf has gone with the others to his allocated room.

Masson has taken up permanent residency here. The pilot's seat on the bridge has become his home. He's monitoring the ship's position and the position of everything else around us. When Diouf and I walked in, he caught my eye, but was in the middle of an important conversation with two other pilots. As it finishes, he looks at me again and calls me over.

"No luck downstairs?" he asks.

I shake my head. "We tried to hack the lock. It froze."

"Well, something happened. Look."

Masson taps the screen. It's showing trajectories for all the objects in and around Mars. The computer has begun logging the larger fragments of debris from Phobos Station, but the object Masson is pointing at isn't one of those.

It's a ship, one that *Gateway* can't identify. It is moving towards us.

"That ship started moving around the same time you got down to the compartment," Masson says. "It'll be here in less than an hour."

"Perhaps they saw the shuttles and they're coming to help?"

"If they were, why not come earlier?" Masson touches the view, zooming in. "That ship has no transponder. *Gateway* has been trying to identify it from the registry, but there's no official record of it."

"Was there some sort of communication?" I ask. "Did we send a signal?"

"Not from any device I can monitor," Masson says. "Maybe I missed something. I don't know these systems very well."

I stare at the dot. There are questions, but I'm not going to get any answers right now. "Do we have a count of how many people we've rescued?" I ask.

"Six ships. Twenty crew and fifty-five from the station," Masson says. "All those, plus Captain Francalla. Too many for a ship like that to accommodate."

"What about the other ships?" I ask.

Masson changes the image again, so we can see the whole region. "Still no comms from anyone. I've recorded a request for assistance and basic briefing on our situation, which is going out on a loop, but there's been no response. I've managed to identify the other vessels. They're all Fleet, but they haven't moved much. There's no sign this is a coordinated action. Could be they're sending this one ship to investigate what's going on."

"You don't sound convinced."

"That's because I'm not."

"You think we need to take precautions?"

Masson shrugs. "Someone was behind the attack on Phobos Station. I don't think they all died when the station blew up."

I nod in return, swallowing any urge to provide more information on that subject. "So, we can't trust anyone?"

"Not if they aren't talking to us." Masson glances at Xiua. "As I see it, we have two options. We can clear the dock and seal the doors, or we fuel up the shuttles and head for Mars and Hera Spaceport."

"We'll go with a little of both," Xiua says. "Get the shuttles ready and prepare to seal the dock. Whoever gets off that ship can be kept waiting in there until they decide to have a conversation."

"Seems like a good plan," I say.

Masson smiles. "Glad I have your approval," he says.

I take the hint and leave him to his work, moving out into the corridor. I can hear people talking, the kind of conversations that people have when they are trying to acclimatise, to be reassuring to others and hide their own anxiety.

I wonder what Alison would make of all this. How would she fit into the situation? Would she be offering comforting words, or needing a shoulder to lean on? Memories of tense moments in her life come to mind. I am thinking about when her father passed away in hospital. How she held her mother when she was crying. A moment that is mine, but also not mine.

All of this is a seductive distraction. It's hard to keep my mind on the situation at hand.

Kieran Rocher organised an insurrection on Mars. Somehow, he managed to get a group of mercenaries from Earth up to the colony and to the Phobos mining operation, then transported them to the station. After that, he rigged the station to blow up and pressed the button, after transferring a locked data archive from the main antenna to an unknown offsite location.

I recall the look on Rocher's face before I killed him. He wanted to live, but he'd achieved his objective. Someone else was behind the plan. That same someone paid for the data – paid enough for Rocher to accept death.

Someone wanted this chaos, the communications blackout, all of it. There is a move here I'm not seeing. I don't have all the information, but the fragments I do have link together in some way.

"Wade?"

I look up. Masson is by the door. "Can you come and take a look at this?" he asks.

"Sure," I say and follow him back inside.

Xiua and Francalla have finished their conversation. Now they are looking at Masson's screen. As I enter, they both turn to look at me.

"When you were down in storage. Did you see anyone?" Xiua asks.

I frown. "No, you said Captain Francalla was the only person on the station."

"He was," Masson says. "But now he isn't." He angles the screen towards me so I can see it. The display has changed. It is showing a scan of the corridor outside the storage compartment. It is an active thermal image. There is some residual warmth from where Diouf and I were, but inside, through the door, there is a moving signature, a person.

"There's someone in there," Xiua says. "Someone alive."

★ ★ ★

"Hello, Natalie."

I'm waking up. Awareness of my situation gradually returns. I remain trapped in a chair, a chair I have spent most of my life in. My wrists and ankles, clamped against the metal. My head, fixed in place.

Memories of a different life remain in my mind. I remember being Alison Wade before I was brought here, transferred from Phobos Station as it fell apart.

"Natalie?"

A man is in the room with me. His gloved hands are adjusting a row of injectors. I can't move my head enough to watch him as he moves around me.

"How long have I been here?" I ask.

"In real terms? It's been an hour or so since we reactivated your consciousness, but we've sedated you and accelerated the hosting duration chemically, so your mind has been in situ for about a day and a half."

"Why?"

"Because we need to determine how stable your consciousness is and how long it will be until your mind falls apart."

There is no sugar-coating. I remember when they told Alison/me that her father had passed. The doctor was very gentle, very respectful. Not like this.

The memory is dislocated. I see the moment through Alison's eyes, but I know I am not seeing something that is my own life, a little like watching a film.

"We imprinted the basic structure and essential content of your mind onto Alison Wade's brain. The two components are integrated through an adaptative transmitter planted in Alison's skull. It meshes your consciousness with hers, for a time. Long enough for you to complete whatever task we need completing."

The man walks into view. He is holding a portable screen. I am looking at an image of a brain scan. "This is your current home," he says. "We couldn't recreate Alison Wade's brain, but we can provide a location for your consciousness and accelerate the timeline. That gives us an idea of how long your duplicate has left."

"My duplicate?"

"There is another version of you. Left behind on Phobos Station. We've lost contact. We need to know how long it will survive."

I remember this man. His voice is familiar. I have asked him questions before. Usually, his answers are short and evasive. Why is he talkative today?

"I'm going to die," I say.

"Yes, you are." The words are spoken in a matter-of-fact way, there is none of the sympathy from Alison Wade's memories. No hand on the shoulder, no hugs or shared tears. Nothing that I would associate with the mourning of a life that is due to end. "Eventually, your consciousness will fall apart. I need to know how long that will take."

My fingers clench against the armrests. I remember having a purpose, being active, exploring the space station, looking for the terrorists, murdering them, finding Rocher. All of that, better than this.

"Not much of a life," I say.

"Don't put yourself down," the man says. "We couldn't get to Mars, but somehow you found a way. We're analysing what you did and hoping we can replicate the process. If we can, you'll have made a massive contribution to our work."

I grimace and swallow an angry reply. I thought I was escaping; turns out none of it was an escape.

★ ★ ★

[Evidence File #17: Savvantine's Personal Folder. Extract from Vladivostok Manifesto 2094 AD.]

They cut us out.

'Humanity's future will be in space.' That was the slogan, the mission principle. The death of the United States provided an opportunity for NASA to become something more, something global.

Investment provided access. Assets and technology were traded and sold. At first, everything was available for the right price. We acquired all sorts of innovations, previously reserved for the American military. But later, the larger purchases came with conditions. Gradually, we were pushed aside, isolated from their grand plan.

The Europeans, the North American Corporations and the Asian multinationals became the new hierarchy. A wider partnership, but still a clique. Those of us who worked outside of their cabal would not be given a voice or a say. Our partnerships with nations that continued to use fossil fuels, scratched out of the dirt, did not sit well with the clean energy agenda. But those issues paled against their opposition to our trade with broken polities and states who continued to oppose the global order.

We are but one cell amongst many. A network of interconnected organisations, all insulated. Designed to collapse and vanish if required.

We are the antithesis. We are the true inheritors of humanity's future. We will determine its path.

CHAPTER TWELVE

Shann

Rocher. It had to be Rocher.

I'm staring at a face that has seared itself into my soul. All the different crises, the terrible moments that have led to death and devastation in the days since we received the distress call from the *Hercules* transport, all of them are connected to this face.

My first instinct is to hate this man. But then more rational thoughts take over. The person outside the inner airlock door is not the Rocher who infiltrated *Khidr*. Not a Rocher who crewed *Gallowglass*. Not a Rocher from the dark station, Erebus.

Another Rocher.

The man outside must have been a part of the team on this ship when we launched explosives from *Gallowglass* and destroyed most of the buildings they constructed down here. Somehow, he and his people survived.

Now he's staring at me through glass.

My actions have made us enemies. He wears that face like a uniform, an allegiance. I can't believe him to be anything but an adversary.

Rocher moves to the communications port and plugs his suit into it. I move to the port on this side and turn on the transmitter. It will be heard by everyone in the room.

"You are not the people we expected to be here," Rocher says.

"No, I guess we're not," I reply.

"You shouldn't be here," Rocher continues, his voice flat and emotionless. "You aren't part of this."

"That's why you shot at me," Savvantine says.

"Yes."

"You want us dead."

"I have my orders," Rocher says. "They are clear. You aren't supposed to be here."

"Then why are we talking?" Savvantine asks. "If your mandate is to murder us, what prompted you to accept our offer of discussion?"

Rocher's eyes shift towards her. What I can see of his expression doesn't change, but he takes a moment to answer.

"There is significant value in this location. Our mission is jeopardised and will be further jeopardised if we damage the structure. Any opportunity to remove your presence more efficiently must be considered."

"You are waiting for us to make you an offer then?"

"Yes."

I'm noting the way the clone speaks, the stilted, sparse and impassive delivery. Far less engaging than the Rocher I remember.

I glance at my suit readout. I have two hours of oxygen left in the tank. My portable scrubber will extend that by forty-five minutes or more and we have the tanks we brought with us from the *Gallowglass*. *Plenty more than Rocher.*

"What about if we agree to leave and to let you in?" I ask.

"You must leave the structure," Rocher says.

"We'll discuss it," I say. I turn off the door communicator and turn towards my crew, intentionally putting my back to the viewport. "Thoughts?" I ask.

"We can't go out through the airlock," Sam says. "They'll chew us up."

"We can go down," Arkov says. "Through the hatch. It'll take time to get everything through, but at least we'll be out."

"You think they'll buy that?" Sam asks.

"They might."

"It'll be difficult," Le Garre says. "The room below is pressurised. As soon as we open the hatch, that air is going to be coming out. If the emergency detectors are active down there, then the next doors are going to be sealed and locked. We can work through all that, but moving us all down there is going to take time."

I glance at Sam. My eyes linger on the taser at his belt. I point at it. "Rocher's still plugged in," I say. "We can knock him out and bring him inside. Might give us an edge with the others."

Sam nods. He pulls out the taser and attaches cables. I'm covering him as he works, preparing, reading everything. When he's got it set up, he gives me a thumbs up.

We move together. I unplug myself from the unit. The covering panel is still loose where Chiu attached a power unit. Sam rips it off and jams cables into the exposed circuit, then presses the taser trigger.

Outside Rocher spasms, then his arms and legs go wide. He flails. I see flames inside his helmet. A spark from the shorted comms must have ignited the oxygen in his suit. Immolated inside. He is burning alive.

We can't help him.

"There are three more.... Oh.... Jesus." Sam turns away from the viewport. I wish I could, but I can't.

Someone must witness this man's end.

* * *

It takes an eternity of six minutes.

I don't know if Rocher managed to notify his companions. We don't have the equipment to monitor their communications.

Murdering this man gives us a tactical advantage. He was prepared to kill all of us. We took an opportunity. I keep saying that in my head. We couldn't have known what would have happened, that they would be breathing pure O_2 in their suits.

Does that justify what I've done? I don't think I'll ever convince myself that it does. As I watch, there's an element of revenge. I remember seeing Sellis getting knifed by another Rocher whilst I stood outside, watching through glass. The man burning in his suit is the same person, but he is also not the same person.

"Take cover," I order everyone. "Stay away from the front of the building."

"Captain?"

I glance around. Le Garre is accessing the screen in her hand. "I still have the feeds from the camera drones that are outside," she says. "The other clones. They are leaving."

"Leaving? Why would—"

"I don't know, *Gallowglass* has moved away from us. It's heading towards the old colony ship, *Gateway*. Could the two situations be connected?"

I'm trying to understand the clones. They must be on limited suit oxygen. They were hoping to fulfil their mission and get in here, but the ship has to be part of that mission too. When it moved away, did that make them change their strategy?

"We need to take advantage of this," I say. "Everyone, get moving through the hatch. We use the time while we have it."

"What about this room?" Arkov asks.

"We abandon it," I say. "We'll find another way out later. Right now, we get through the next door and see what we have. Sam?"

"Fuck, I didn't know it would do that to—"

"Sam!" I grab his shoulder and shake him. "Get it together! I need you to move out equipment through the hatch and down to the next level."

"Right, Captain. Yes, sorry."

I'm hurting my friend. A man I know better than anyone else who is left, but right now I need him. The guilt and pain need to get boxed away; we're back in that moment where decisions have to be made.

"Doctor Drake, go with Ensign Chiu and figure out the best way to get the cryopod into the room below. We'll do that first, then the oxygen tanks and the rest of the gear. People last."

Savvantine moves past me towards the abandoned equipment left behind by this room's previous occupants. She grabs several items and starts opening compartments, collecting up tools, anything that might be useful.

"I'm cutting through the hatch," Le Garre says. "Going to depressurise the room below. Then we drop down, seal it up and repressurise with our tanks."

"Okay, that's our plan," I say. "Get on it."

I follow Savvantine. She turns towards me and taps the side of her helmet with her finger. I nod and switch my comms to a direct private channel. "What do you have for me, Colonel?" I ask.

"This Rocher? He was the clone? The same as you met before?"

"A clone, yes. The *Gallowglass* was crewed by a team of Rochers. We found more of them on the dark station, Erebus."

"That's why you acted?"

"Yes."

"Pretty horrible outcome," Savvantine says. "But there was no way you could have known."

"Yes, I—" I recognise the empathy being offered. "Thank you."

"You asked what I have for you?" Savvantine says. "At this stage, not much, all of this is complicated, but I've thought about your decisions, I've watched you. Your instincts.... I think you're doing the right thing."

The affirmation is reassuring. I feel the knotted tension of my shoulders ease. I look at Savvantine. Her expression is unreadable in the shadowy depths of her visor, but I sense a softness to her words.

"There are many pieces to this puzzle," Savvantine says. "Some of them are old, some of them are new, but we are in a moment where the plans of others are converging. I have decided it is time that I trusted you and your people."

"Again, thank you," I say. "Let's get down into the rest of the complex and we'll compare notes."

"Agreed."

I note the main channel audio spiking. I switch back. "Update please, Major."

"Venting atmosphere, Captain. Chamber will be empty in about ten minutes. Suit external audio is picking up an active alert and seal protocol being activated."

"So, there could be people alive down there?"

"It's possible, yes," Le Garre says. "It also suggests there are more rooms down there beyond this one."

Savvantine hands me a powered drill and a box designed to clip on to my belt. "Pressure repair kits," she says. "Might be useful."

"Let's hope not," I say, softening the words with a smile.

"Indeed."

I move back towards the others. "Any updates?"

"I'm patched into the base comms," Arkov says. "Their main antenna is offline. I don't know if that means it's been destroyed or just damaged. I've started a procedure to diagnose and reset the system."

"Can you continue that work when we move?"

"I should be able to, the data cables run down into the next level. I guess they are throughout the structure. I'll plug in my kit once we reach a location where we can set up permanently."

"Okay, sounds good." I hold out my hand. "Pass me your screen. Let me see the camera feeds from outside."

"Of course, Captain."

Arkov hands me the device. I turn away and glance towards the hatch. Sam and Drake are manoeuvring the cryopod through into the next chamber. Le Garre has started moving one of the oxygen tanks as well. Zero gravity can make these things easier, but also harder. You have to be careful not to misjudge the mass of the things you're moving.

"Cyropod is through, Captain," Sam says.

The tanks go next. Le Garre has packed away her equipment and she and Savvantine are helping Le Garre with them.

I turn to the inner airlock door. The manual release triggers the panel, so it slides back. Rocher's body is floating in the outer chamber. There are dark scorches on his suit. The oxygen fire inside was instantly extinguished when it burned through the fabric and tasted vacuum.

I look out through the DuraGlas panel in the outer door. I can't see any of Rocher's companions. I suspect they are also clones. More Rochers, given orders by someone to build and guard this base.

There could be more of them inside – in the chambers below.

I glance at the screen in my hand. The camera drones that Savvantine deployed are still transmitting. We can use them to keep an eye on the surface. I set up movement alert triggers and instruct the screen to alert me and Le Garre via our suit comms. We might get a warning if they come back. That'll do for now.

I open the outer door and gently push Rocher's corpse outside. His people will find him. He deserves that at least.

"Captain, we're ready for you."

"Acknowledged." I shut the doors and head for the hatch.

* * *

[Evidence File #3: Savvantine Reporrt #4 Extract]
...our investigation concludes that there can be nothing to these rumours. The infrastructure required to build additional interplanetary vehicles does not exist. The colonies could not possibly sustain such an effort. Any orbital base around Earth, the Moon or Mars would be detected.

* * *

[Evidence File #3: Savvantine Reporrt #6 Extract]
...an audit of passengers registered for off-Earth travel does suggest there are discrepancies. Several individuals do appear to have gone missing when we compare Earth records with the intakes on each station and colony.

Data scrubbing has narrowed down the list of missing persons to twenty-three individuals. They have all left Earth in the last five years and disappeared from our transit records....

* * *

[Evidence File #3: Savvantine Reporrt #9 Extract]
...confirmation that Senator Boipelo has indeed been compromised. The device cannot be removed. Any surgical intervention would result in the death of the patient. Boipelo's presence on Mars and participation in the colonial administration is being supervised. We believe the device has a maximum range and at this stage she is safe from....

CHAPTER THIRTEEN
Holder – Wade

I am back in the corridor, staring through the DuraGlas into the storage compartment with all the cryopods.

A woman is on the other side of the door, staring back at me. I don't recognise her. Alison Wade doesn't recognise her. She is older. Not as old as Captain Francalla, but I'd guess she's in her fifth or sixth decade. A strange candidate for cryo.

The door mechanism on this side is wrecked. It won't open and the comms audio no longer works. If this door is going to be opened, then it will need to be opened from the inside.

So, I'm waiting.

Alison Wade's memories resonate with this moment. I remember being outside a medical ward, watching through glass as doctors operated on my father – her father. I was young then, I didn't know what they were doing, but I trusted them. They were experts.

People died in that hospital. I remember seeing nurses cover the face of a body in the bed next to my father as he recovered and seeing a family huddled together, a middle-aged woman clutching at her two children as she sobbed for the woman in the bed.

I worried for my father. Alison Wade worried for her father. The same memory, dislocated, felt in two different ways.

It is hard to banish this. Hard to focus on anything else. I am becoming lost in the swirl of this….

Who am I?

The feeling passes and fades. I am left behind, still staring at the woman behind the glass. I don't know how much time has passed, whether she noticed what came over me.

The woman moves away from the window. A moment later, the door opens, and she emerges from the shadowy depths of the room to stand in front of me. She is staring again. This time, I can see her clearly. I get a sense of authority from her, an uncompromising seniority. The grey-streaked hair and lines on her face confirm this to me. There is something knowing about the way she looks at me too, a glimmer of recognition perhaps?

"Who are you?" the woman says.

"I was about to ask the same," I reply.

"You don't know who I am?"

"No."

"So, you weren't the ones who put me in here?"

I shake my head. "We didn't even know you were here."

"I don't know where here is," the woman says. She gestures behind her, back into the room. "The cryopod I was in began waking me up less than an hour ago. I sat up and found myself here, surrounded by all these others."

I'm moving to the door. I'm through and inside. There is a torch on my belt. I pull it out and turn it on, illuminating the room.

There must be a hundred cryopods in here. One of them is open. None of the rest have been disturbed, as far as I can see.

"There is an embryo bank and DNA sequencer back there. Everything you would need to start a colony, if you had the right set-up."

I turn towards the woman. "I'm Alison Wade," I say.

"You can call me Jeni," the woman replies.

★ ★ ★

"I had no idea they were down there."

I'm back on the bridge of the *Gateway*. I've brought Jeni with me and relayed what we've found to Lieutenant Xiua and Captain Francalla.

The captain hasn't taken it well. I can see his hands shaking as he grips the table in front of him. He's old, he's been here a long time, and he feels responsible. *Gateway* has been his home for years.

"The power draw for the room has been isolated," Diouf says. "We can shut it down."

Xiua frowns and looks at him. "You mean, murder them?"

"If there's an emergency...we need to be prepared."

I glance around the table, noting the grim expressions. There's a ship on its way and now this. We are trying to survive. To keep people from the station alive. What does this all mean?

Xiua is also reading faces. Our eyes meet and he smiles. "Best give you an idea of the situation," he says. "Seventy-six— No, seventy-seven of us now, all here. Thirty-four wounded, most able to manage. Six under observation."

"The wider picture is more complicated," Masson says. He pulls out a screen and places it on the desk. I lean forwards to look. "Debris field from the station has reached us. We're taking damage, but this old beast was made for worse. So far, it's not too bad."

"What about rescue?" Diouf asks.

Masson manipulates the image on the screen. "The Fleet ships in a cluster. One unknown ship about to dock here. Then there's the huge chunk of rock that arrived and decelerated. The rock and the unknown ship are between us and the Fleet vessels."

"And we're in the debris field."

"Yes."

Xiua looks at Jeni. "Tell me about yourself," he says. "How did you come to be in that room?"

"I don't know," Jeni says. I was taken prisoner and brought here."

"Where were you before?"

"The *Archimedes*, a supply station en route to Earth."

"Any idea why they took you?"

Jeni shakes her head. Then she looks at me. "Seems like fate has brought us all here against our will."

"We're trying to survive," I say.

"Forgive me, I'm unaware of the circumstances," Jeni says. She smiles, but there is no softening of her expression. "Perhaps you can tell me what I don't know?"

"Later," I say. "Right now, we need to make some decisions." I point at Masson's screen. "That ship will arrive soon."

"Our preparations are complete," Xiua says. "We're as ready as we can be for the worst. Hopefully, it won't come to that."

I open my mouth to ask for details, but then realise what I'm doing. This isn't how Alison Wade behaves. I've no position here, pushing these Fleet officers for answers.

Jeni is looking at me, staring at me….

A crackle and burst of static over the comm interrupt the discussion. Masson is up from the table immediately and back at the terminal, slipping an old bud speaker into his left ear. He manipulates the signal. Static becomes words.

"*Gateway*, this is the *Nandin*. We are broadcasting our identification code and manoeuvring to respond to your distress call. Respond please."

Masson activates the microphone. "*Nandin*, this is *Gateway*. Good to hear you."

"And you, *Gateway*. What's the situation?"

"Seventy-seven here. We rescued fifty-five from the wreckage of Phobos Station. Our shuttles are pretty beat-up. They've been fuelled up for an emergency evacuation if needed, but that's not our preferred option."

"You're safe then?"

"For now. Apart from that ship coming in."

"Understood, *Gateway*. We're trying to establish comms with them, but we lost touch after the crew went EVA."

"What should we expect, *Nandin*?"

"Proceed with caution. Could be Fleet piloting them. Could be something else. We will update with—"

Suddenly, the signal drops. Masson works the terminal, trying to get it back. "Looks like we're getting interference from outside," he says. "The *Nandin* is passing through some sort of distortion."

"We need contact with them," Xiua says. "Keep trying to get them back."

"Sure," Masson says.

"I'll get Jeni settled into a room," I say. "Call me if you need me."

Xiua smiles grimly. "Yeah, I'll do that."

★ ★ ★

"There is something strange about you."

I'm sitting in one of the crew compartments with Jeni. She's been allocated a room, like everyone else. She seems grateful, saying thank you in all the right places as she's given food, blankets and a bunk.

For most of the time we've been together she's been staring at me. When other people are present and talking to her, she deals with them, but in any moment where we are alone, her gaze returns.

"I could say the same," I reply. "You haven't been forthcoming about your background and why you ended up here."

"I told you, I don't—"

"You must have an idea."

Jeni doesn't reply, but her gaze lifts from mine. Her eyes lose focus, as if she is remembering something painful. "There was an argument. People were injured. I did something. There was blood."

"You can't remember?"

"It's difficult." Jeni closes her eyes. "I see images and moments, but nothing is in order. They do say time in a cryopod can do that."

"Maybe when things settle down, we can contact *Archimedes* and find out what happened?" I suggest.

Jeni opens her eyes and looks doubtful. "I'm not sure I'd want that," she says.

I try another angle. "When I tried to open the door to the cryo compartment from the outside, I damaged the lock. Minutes after that, we detected your heat signature in the room. Do you have any idea why that occurred? There has to be a reason you're awake first."

"I'm sorry, I just don't know."

I look away, trying to evaluate. I have much to hide about my actions and my nature as well. Trust in these circumstances in difficult, but also, I can see her point of view. "What do you think is different about me?" I ask.

"You're fighting yourself," Jeni says. "All of this, what's happening, you're riding it, coping and thriving under the stress, but that isn't who you were. I can see you holding yourself back around others, even now."

"You are also holding back," I reply.

Jeni sighs and runs a hand through her hair. "I'm a biochemist and a geneticist. I specialise in brain chemistry and state change. I am the kind of expert a corporation would recruit to look after an embryonic colony. I have expert knowledge in how to manage memory implantation and skill training through surgical procedure. There, now you know something about me."

My fingers curl and grip the frame of the bed. "You might be able to help me then," I say slowly. "I am not really Alison Wade." I tap the side of my head with a finger. "Up here, I'm someone else."

Jeni smiles and leans forwards. "Tell me more," she says.

* * *

Once I start, everything comes out in a rush.

Jeni sits and listens as I recall the jumble of different memories – being in a chair in a white room, being an administrator on Phobos Station. The two personalities, Holder and Wade, meshed and entangled. Powerful sensations and emotions that emerge from remembering things that did and did not happen to me.

I hold back some things. The details about my conversations with Summers and Emori I keep to myself.

As I talk, I see Jeni's expression change. She is devouring what I am telling her. My words have meaning for her that she isn't sharing with me yet.

"You were right," I say at last. "I don't know who I am."

Jeni is silent. Her eyes fall to her lap. "Thank you for telling me," she says softly. "It helps."

"Your turn," I say. "I've trusted you with more information than I've told anyone around here."

Jeni nods. "My full name and title then. I am Doctor Genevieve Aster. I worked on Earth, for a company called dMemra, back in the 2080s, before they were dragged through the courts by a variety of rival corporations and government interest groups. We worked on memory extraction and integration technology."

"You mean—"

"Yes. Whoever designed you probably used technology based on my work."

★ ★ ★

[Evidence File #8: Savvantine's Personal Folder. Extract from *Citizen of the World Magazine* 2096 AD.]

The blockade lasted for thirty-five days. By the time it finished, the city was on its knees.

This was all part of the plan. The military forces retreated but remained watchful. They were replaced by capitalist missionaries, preaching the doctrine of the globalist. Loans were offered to rebuild businesses and infrastructure. Contracts were signed and the process began again.

Fuelled by a mountain of promissory debt, wreckage became new concrete, plastic and steel. Solar power, wind farms and hydro plants replaced oil and gas terminals.

This was hailed as progress, all part of the global agenda to take us into a green future where we live in harmony with our planet.

We became citizens of a new global entity. Our nation had been torn apart by the agents of this purpose, but now we were forgiven. Given back our identities and names. We were remade and validated, told that this rebirth signified something better, so long as we accepted the debts of a war prosecuted against us.

That's how it worked, all across the world. Anyone who opposed the ideology got worn down, ground into dullness, until there was no choice.

CHAPTER FOURTEEN

Shann

I still don't trust Colonel Yuhanis Savvantine.

All six of us have gathered in an operations room, two levels below the entrance where we were before. After we forced our way through the hatch, Arkov repaired it, and we repressurised the room. Then I managed to access the emergency controls and release the door locks.

There is a metal table here. Whoever lived here before might have used this as a gathering place. Furniture designed for Earth is not practical for zero gravity, but old habits die hard. People need a focus point to congregate around. Objects with magnets in them could be placed on it, I guess?

Sam tried the root key from before. We didn't have much hope for it working, but were pleased to be proved wrong. Maybe there was something wrong with the exterior door lock? I guess that means whoever built this place also built *Gallowglass*.

Now we've got atmosphere and people are taking off their EVA suits. Equipment is getting inventoried and stowed. We have a full map of the facility too. Something I managed to access after redesigning the computer operating system again, using a copy of the work Johansson did on the *Gallowglass*, before the computer started to force us out.

I'm waiting my turn to talk. I have asked the question. Savvantine is about to provide an answer.

Tell us what you know....

"Fourteen years ago, I was a civilian analyst and contractor working with Fleet. I was recruited into Fleet Intelligence by Admiral James Langsley. I was assigned to an investigation that had been ongoing for more than a decade prior to that. Everything about it was classified. They had to give me a special military commission, so I was allowed in the room. Essentially, a frozen rank. They made me a colonel, that gets me into the conversation.

"The case I was given to work on revolved around misuse of funds. The World Bank had gone all in on supporting Fleet and the corporate partnerships associated with expanding humanity's presence in our solar system. The money being raised and spent was huge. Opportunities for malpractice were huge. We caught a lot of people, issued fines, convicted individuals, all of it. The system was working.

"Except that it wasn't.

"Systematic misappropriation. Small amounts from every budget and grant paying for specific administrative services. Hundreds of dollars dripped into a hole that disappeared. The paperwork looked right, but it wasn't. I took my concerns to the admiral. He told me to follow all the leads. So, I did.

"Private partnerships have always been the strategy of Fleet. Patrol ships like your *Khidr* were built with the express aim of protecting corporate vessels as they expand our reach and convey materials to and from Earth. You know your remit. I don't need to remind you of it, but this does show how the system was set up. The system works.

"I am a guardian of the system.

"We tracked the money. We set up stings and authorised raids. We caught small fish, but I was always of the view that something bigger was going on. Eventually, that led to a change in tactics. Lie still and wait. Preserve the process until our adversaries made their move.

"For a long time, I monitored different organisations nibbling away at the edges of our grand plan. Langsley got old, then he officially retired. That left me and a couple of others to keep watch on everything. Our work has always been underfunded and lacking people we could trust.

"The first hint I got that things had got more dangerous was when we found doctored inventories on the freighter manifests. Large amounts of colonial infrastructure being sent to the furthest outposts, places that had no plans for that kind of expansion. Then there were rumours of other shuttles and ships docking at stations along the route to Mars and beyond.

"We put together the pieces, tracking different fragments, trying to figure it out, but we made an error, the kind of mistake any investigator can make. We were looking for a single perpetrator, a single agenda and a single plan. We were looking for a villain, an oppositional movement, unified against our work. Now, that's not what I think we're looking at."

"Then what are we looking at?" I ask.

"Competing corporations. All thinking they can get a better slice of the pie if they break the system. Each with a different agenda and different technology. The clones come from research commissioned by the Hannington Corporation."

"You think they are behind this?"

"David Hannington II led an expedition to Europa. He paid for the research base. We know his company were smuggling equipment out there for a series of experiments. Whether that makes them guilty of this, or not, I don't know. Then there's the Tường Corporation. They pretty much run the asteroid mining and transit system from the belt. Chang City is the major colony on the Moon, they report to the People's Republic of China. Mars CorpGov is a conglomerate of corporations who generally toe the line with Fleet, but have their own self-interest to consider as well." Savvantine sighs and smiles. "Those are just a few of the players."

"The Avensis mission. It stems from that," Le Garre says. "We found information that connects Rocher, the *Gallowglass* and the stations out there to that expedition."

"There was cargo on the *Hercules* too," I say. "We found colonial technology. Stuff for atmosphere and ecosystem generation."

"There are no official projects that are anywhere needing that kind of equipment," Savvantine says. "But all of these situations, they might be part of a plan, or part of competing plans. Every time we look into all of this – zoom in, narrow down – the conspiracy shatters into more and more fragments."

"We need to focus on what's happening here," Le Garre says. She looks at Savvantine. "Colonel, can you show us what you've found in the computers?"

Savvantine pulls out a screen and casts the image over to the three-dimensional projector she managed to rig up from the base stores. A representation of the facility appears on the table in front of us. "This is what they built, prior to our arrival. The main complex was destroyed when you dropped a ton of explosives on it. These passages and room where we are now are what's left."

Savvantine manipulates the image, rotating it so everyone can see the locations. Then activates a tracing point in our location. "We are here," she says. "Three levels below the surface. The mission team have constructed another two levels. Four rooms and a set of passageways."

"What do we know about them?" Drake asks. "Have you found any personnel files?"

"No. That would make life easy," Savvantine says. "There are no inventory files either. I think the records have been purged."

"Can you recover them?"

"Possibly, yes. But that will take time."

"We need to know if anyone's down there," I say. "Our first priority is to ensure we don't get into another fight, or if we do, we are in a position to finish it."

"I'd rather there wasn't a fight," Drake says.

"We'd all rather there wasn't a fight," I reply. "We'll do our best to make sure violence is the last resort in this."

"What else is down there?" Sam asks. "Have you found Duggins?"

"Second question first," Savvantine says. "Answer, not yet. The first question is a bit more complicated."

"Take your time," Le Garre says.

"The logs record the construction activity of the mission team. They were motivated to search for the living spaces that should be here if this is an alien spaceship. But they didn't find anything like that. Excavation revealed more and more rock, layer after layer of hard-packed material built up and over, time after time."

I'm showing the data analysis on the excavated material. "Analysis shows the usual composition of silicate, clay, but appears to be absent any trace iron or nickel."

"Not without precedent," Drake says.

"But unusual," I say. "More unusual is the absence of any kind of alien presence. I mean, as I said, if this is a constructed vessel, where's the evidence of that, beyond it being this strange shape?"

"Something brought it here," Le Garre says. "There was velocity and deceleration, we saw that. You can't generate kinetic movement without some kind of thrust. There has to be engines, fuel tanks, control systems, a pilot."

"What about remote control?" Arkov suggests.

"If that were happening, why did the clones build a base here? Why were they expecting the *Gallowglass* to return?"

"We can't answer most of these questions," I say. "We need to deal with the here and now." I approach the projected image. "We boarded this vessel because it is an opportunity. We thought that opportunity might never come again, so I took a calculated risk bringing us here, rather than evacuating to be picked up by one of the other Fleet ships. Now we need to maximise our chance. We need to get into those rooms and see how far they got to understanding all of this."

"That might be impossible," Savvantine says. "We may not be able to comprehend—"

"We learn enough, and we find a way to survive," I say. I turn to Arkov, Chiu and Chase. "Find a way through those hatches. Doctor Drake, whilst they are at it, get your patient secured and make sure he's comfortable." Savvantine is next to be given instructions. "Get full access to whatever is left of the computer system and find Duggins. He has to be down here somewhere."

"Will do, Captain," Savvantine says.

The meeting breaks up. Le Garre and Savvantine move to the far corner of the room. I watch them for a moment. The colonel is trying to establish relationships with people, disarm them, show she can be useful as an individual.

Savvantine said there were errors in the manifest of the *Hercules*. That means she's seen the freighter's manifest. I remember seeing the redacted version we examined before we rendezvoused with them. Could she have been responsible for the redactions?

I'm staring at her. How much has she told us and how much has she held back?

★ ★ ★

[Evidence File #11: Savvantine's Personal Folder. Last Palgrave Speech June 2113 AD. AUDIO BROADCAST – PLAY]

My thanks for your attendance this evening and your engagement with my talk. I am of course, anticipating that you will engage with it and not fall asleep... [laughter]... I have been informed that brevity is appropriate at this point in the evening... [laughter]... Hopefully, you will find you can listen and then get to the bar in good time... [laughter]

When imagining our future as a civilisation, it is important that we consider how we have arrived in this moment. Planet Earth is our Eden, our paradise. We evolved and became the dominant species of this planet.

By rights, Earth should have been enough for us. The resources available to us in terms of energy, living space, food and water should still be enough to support a population of ten billion. As a species, we are aware of this threshold and there are no measures we could take that have significant impact on individual freedoms.

But, we have decided to leave the Earth and expand to other planets. Exciting stuff! The concept sells itself. We've been reading about spaceships and amazing adventures on other planets for more than a century. We've seen the films and streamed shows. Everyone in them is very brave and very handsome, right? [laughter] I mean, come on. Why not watch sexy people in space, yes? [laughter]

My point this evening is this. When you engage with all the discussions, workshops and networking opportunities that have generously been provided at this conference, please ask yourself, why are we going into space? Why are we trying to live on other planets, planets that were never created for us, that will be extremely hard for us to survive on and that will require huge amounts of resources to get there?

If your answer to this is to improve the lives of all human beings, then I can see the point of all this. If your plan as a corporation, as a scientist, as a pilot, as an engineer is to find ways to better the lives of everyone and space is the way to do it, I'm with you.

If your plan is to create a new world for a privileged few, that costs billions of dollars which could have been better spent on healthcare, education, or the environment, then I'm not.

Thank you very much.

CHAPTER FIFTEEN

Duggins

My father and I argued when I was young. He was a man fighting a war that had already been lost. The oil was long gone, the economic conversion to solar power, tidal battery systems and sustainable lumber had passed him by. He couldn't change. Instead, he sat and stagnated, drinking beer and talking about the old days, days he was never a part of.

He worshipped his father and grandfather. He expected the same devotion from me.

He didn't get it. We fought. I don't remember why.

These memories are painful, but they are necessary. They anchor me, prevent me from drowning in a surreal world that I cannot fully comprehend.

My mind is trying to translate a location that has more than three physical dimensions. I know it has more than three physical dimensions, but the simulated memory of my senses is unable to comprehend what I am experiencing.

"Your question of 'Who' is contextually redundant," the voice says. "If I were to identify myself by any label that held meaning in my current state and/or previous states, you would find little knowledge or understanding in that. I recognise that such labels are part of the parlance in your culture and civilisation. Perhaps by assuming a label, I would become more appropriate to you."

Even as the words are spoken, new information is coming to me. I am not the only 'Duggins' image. After I initiated the transmission from the *Gallowglass*, my identity was transferred to this place and deleted from the ship's computer as it arrived in the receptacle. In the microseconds before I became aware again, that identity was duplicated many times. Some of those personas remain dormant. Others are conscious, just like me.

Mattias transitioned with me. His degraded identity was in the *Gallowglass* computer before I arrived. I only became aware of him when he was activated here.

"We thought he might help you adjust," the voice says. "For some iterations it has worked. For others it has not."

"Where are you from? How did you get here?" I ask.

"Originally, a long way away," the voice replies. "My journey was a planned mission. Many were sent out to a variety of destinations. The technology of my creators allowed them to make specific judgements about where there might be developments of significant interests when I might arrive."

"You were sent to find life?"

"Amongst other things, yes."

Experiences flow into my mind. A ship that became aware of itself a long time after it had begun its journey. A ship that recognised how it had been designed to grow, from a set of genetic instructions encoded into a microscopic body, acquiring mass as it moved through the vast emptiness of the universe.

"There are questions that I have no answer to," the voice says. "I can speculate. Velocity and acceleration are easier to achieve when an object is small. By acquiring mass, an object slows down – a need that becomes a priority as that object reaches its destination."

"By 'object', you mean you?"

"Yes. Exactly." The voice goes silent, but I sense there is more it wishes to say. I wait.

"This has been a lonely journey," it says at last. "There have been incredible moments, but also, long stretches of nothing, of being aware, but knowing there is no one to reach out to. The vastness contains much that I would experience, but that also remains out of reach. I am made to be curious, but that curiosity is also a torture to me."

"It is good that I am no longer alone."

I sense information is still being withheld from me. My companion has had this conversation before. Many times, in fact. Iterations of Ethan Duggins have been broken by the torrent of knowledge that threatens to overwhelm me or turned away in anger when too much remained hidden.

I learn that these moments are treasured by my companion. The life, death, happiness, sadness, joy and anger are amongst a myriad of sensations it has savoured since I came here.

I'm not sure I can—

* * *

I'm back on the *Khidr*.

A siren, flashing red lights. Hull breaches and damage, so much damage. This ship is my home, my friend. She is dying. I cannot save her.

The screen in front of me displays an active schematic of the hull, the compartments, all of the different systems. I can see where people are being suffocated as our atmosphere is vented. Where fire rips through the remaining pressurised spaces, trapping others to be burned alive.

I'm looking at the radiation monitor. Levels are rising in the generator room. The twin fission reactors are damaged and starting to move out of phase. If I don't act to restore the balance between them....

Fast death or slow death? Take your pick.

"Duggins to Bridge?"

"Travers here, go ahead."

"We have a reactor breach. I'm going in to repair it."

"Are you sure that's wise? I—"

"My call, Bridge, I'm going in."

This is something I can fix. Deciding to go in there is extremely dangerous, but restoring the syncopation might buy a little time for the rest of the crew.

I'm unplugged from the ship's internal air and breathing through an emergency tube. That gives me twenty minutes. I pull on the protective gear, activate and prime the suit. I feel the sharp sting of the automated iodine injection – a necessary preventative measure. I hope to live long enough to see whether it works and prevents the thyroid damage that would have happened otherwise.

I move across the room, key in the code for the emergency door release and move into the generator room.

This is where I die....

These moments are like a dream, except I know they happened. This reliving of a memory is fresh and immediate, the decisions being made as I make them. I have little sense of being trapped and this being the past.

The cooling rods on Reactor Two are jammed. Fragments of metal from a shattered panel on the far side of the room have wedged themselves into the mechanism.

I can reset the injectors manually, if I can remove the debris. I reach for the toolbox at my belt and pull out a hand driver. The long end is thin enough to slip into the gap and work along the channel. As I do so, shards of metal slip out.

There is a grinding noise and then, the injector plate drops into place.

The driver spins out of my hand. I grab for it and miss. It bounces off the door. Then everything shifts and I'm slammed against the far wall. Another emergency light flashes and I hear the deadlocks engage.

I'm trapped.

I touch the comms bead in my ear, trying to raise Travers and the rest of the crew, but there is nothing.

I will die here....

★ ★ ★

"This moment is important to you."

The voice echoes around the generator room. I am still in the memory, but no longer bound by the passage of events. Knowing that this is not the end, that I survive to be what I have become now, is a comfort.

"This is the moment I stopped being human," I say. "I thought I was done."

"*The organic and physical form is gone. Our devices were able to replicate what empowered the flesh, to provide you with a place where you could continue to exist.*"

I remember those moments, being torn apart and reconstituted. "They were not gentle," I say.

"*They were unfamiliar with your requirements.*"

The generator room is just as I remember it in those minutes before everything ended. I'm unaware of exactly how I died. The perfect recreation might enable me to learn what happened. Idle curiosity.

"*If you wish to relive those events, we can do that,*" the voice says.

"No, I'm good," I reply. I think about the comms bead. I pull it out of my ear. "I want to contact my friends. I know they were coming down here."

"*The crew of the Khidr? How are they different to the other humans?*"

More information. A cascade of historical broadcasts, snippets of television and radio, streamed video. Hundreds of media works, captured by this observer. I learn that this ship has been here for a long time, watching humanity from afar as it circles.

I see warfare. News reports and fiction all intermingled together.

"Some of this is a performance," I say.

"*Yes, I learned that recently,*" the voice says.

"Is this your mission?" I ask. "Were you tasked to watch and record?"

"*In part,*" the voice says. "*There are other requirements.*"

I sense this information is not going to be shared. Not at this stage. I also sense that the questions being asked are carefully considered, not just out of a lack of trust, but also because my companion does not want to overwhelm me with the answers.

"*Your friends are here,*" the voice says. "*They left their ship and made the journey across. They have entered the remains of the complex the other humans constructed when they first arrived. The complex that your ship tried to destroy.*" The voice pauses then adds, "*If we had not recognised your pattern, and transferred you from their primitive machine, you would have been lost in that explosion.*"

I consider that, remembering my last moments on the *Gallowglass*, the confusion and life-or-death situation. Shann's decisions, her agreement in letting me go. "They did what they thought was right," I say.

"*I am not judging them,*" the voice says. "*My place is not to judge.*"

"I would like to speak to my friends," I say. "Is that possible?"

"*You know that it is,*" the voice replies. "*You managed this before. But if you mean can we ensure a more stable method of communication? That remains to be seen.*"

I want to question that answer and elicit more detail. I am an engineer; that kind of minutiae is exactly what I want when presented with a problem.

But in this instance, I sense I'm not ready for the answer, so I change tack.

"How many copies of me did you make?" I ask. I'm thinking of the *Gallowglass* computer system and the drive limitations that forced me to leave. "How many can you accommodate in here?"

"*Numbers are not a factor in the process. A sufficient amount to bring us to this moment.*"

"And Mattias?"

"*Again, he can be replicated as required.*"

"Could he ever reach this moment? I mean, is it likely he could find his way through the projections of memories as I did?"

"*It is possible. We have learned not to assume any limitation on human consciousness. There are layers of understanding.*"

"Layers beyond this?"

"*Yes.*"

Again, an answer that provokes more questions. I know the voice is sensing my thoughts. Everything that I am is data to be examined and analysed in this place. "I want to learn," I say.

"*Your curiosity is a quality to be admired,*" the voice says. "*I will endeavour to help you learn.*"

"I can't ask for more than that."

★ ★ ★

[Evidence File #8: Savvantine's Personal Folder. Extract from Pacifica Climate Migration Reservation 2081 AD.]

"Our identities are gradually being eroded.

"Our original documents are not accepted. They say it's because they don't have access to the databases. Pensions are not provided without the new documentation, food is not provided without an ID chit, and medical services are out of the question. There are lots of checkpoints on the roads between settlements. And every time they stop you, they check your documents, and then say they will not let you through without proper identification next time.

"People have to obtain these documents. Because if someone, say, has vegetables in one village and sells them in another, it is impossible to move between the two.

"When you go to a hospital you need to have identification. If you do not have the new papers, they won't treat you. If you drive your own car and the patrol stops you, and you do not have what they ask for, they can simply take your car away. So, people are forced to obtain them and engage with the new system. It is a matter of survival.

"Gradually, our nation is being erased. We are grateful for the help we are given, but we are losing our identities."

CHAPTER SIXTEEN

Savvantine

I have told them a lot. Taken a big risk.

Back in 2097, I took a career break and decided to try spelunking. After I returned to Earth and rented a house in Talinn, I spent a few weeks re-acclimatising to the gravity. I took up hiking and walking, visiting as many beautiful places as I could. The aim was to get a sense of what I was missing, to stand on hilltops and cliff edges and drink in the beauty of it.

But the dark places called to me and eventually, I had to answer them.

Kentucky's Mammoth Cave National Park is a huge spidery network of natural tunnels and caverns. A ten-day trip there with a tour party of seven was a life-changing experience.

Walking underground in the pitch black returned me to those moments from my childhood, before I had the operation to fix my eyes. The absence of light let me revisit the world that I remembered, trying to make sense of my surroundings at a disadvantage. Only, in that situation, all of my companions were in the same place.

There is a vulnerability in those moments. A personal vulnerability. I feel something of that here, now I have told these people much of what I know.

In the caves, I became hyper aware of the rock and earth above us. Our little group could have been buried alive at any moment, and anything that we had shared buried along with us.

That remains true here. I have told these people enough to see the picture I see, the civil war going on as factions grapple for control of humanity's fate. But if we don't survive, that understanding disappears.

That might be a good thing. The catharsis of confession and sharing has been necessary, but I don't know yet whether Shann and her crew will prove to be useful allies to me in this war.

Now, I am sitting in front of a computer terminal that I have repaired. The login screen refuses to accept the standard Fleet authorisation user credentials, which is understandable. The equipment might have been stolen from Fleet requisition inventories, but it has been reprogrammed.

Then Shann motions for me to move back. She taps on the screen and enters a short code. The display goes blank, leaving me with a flashing cursor in the top corner.

"This is where we're going to miss Ensign Johansson," Shann says.

"Yes, I'm a big admirer of her work," I say. I reach into the pouch in my suit and pull out a portable screen from the *Gallowglass*. "I managed to download her coded operating system into a compressed folder. I think it's a clean version. Now that you've got me in, I should be able to copy it over and initialise it.

Shann opens her mouth as if to ask a question, but then seems to think better of it. "How long do you need?" she asks.

"About an hour. Then, provided they haven't changed anything, we should have access like you did on the ship."

"Great, let me know if you need anything else." Shann moves away.

I watch her go, moving between each member of her crew, checking in with them as they go about their appointed tasks. Even Drake. She has quietly adopted him and given him a role. Something that appears to have helped him cope.

Shann is a good captain. Space is an environment that suits her. She would be wasted on Earth. An active military role in a gravity environment would require her to undertake substantial cybernetic or organic enhancement, procedures that would take time with no guarantees of success.

Out here, such adaptations are less important.

I find myself liking this brave, serious, proactive woman. That might be a problem later on.

I hook up the portable screen to the terminal and begin transferring the files. When this is done, I start the installation. Then I disconnect my device and open a new window, accessing the external drone camera feeds. I operate each in turn, rotating them to see if there is any sign of the figures we saw earlier.

Nothing so far. Good.

I open another window on the portable screen and access a second folder of content that I downloaded from the *Gallowglass*. Official logs. These were recorded by the crew after they assumed command of the ship. There are a series of video files mostly recorded by Major Le Garre and Lieutenant Travers. *Interesting....*

I glance around. The rest of the crew have moved into the next room to work on the locked door. Only Drake remains here, attending the cryopod containing Travers. I move over to him and touch him lightly on the shoulder. He starts, turns and frowns.

"Let the captain know I'm going back up to the hatch for a bit. I need a little quiet time."

"We could all use some rest," Drake says. "Difficult to switch off when everything is urgent."

"I'm sure you'll find a way," I reply. I point towards the terminal. "I'll be back when that completes. It'll ping me on my screen."

"Okay."

I move away, back to the hatch we came through when we left the upper floor of this place. As I drift in that direction, I pay a little more attention to the construction of the chambers. These rooms are undamaged. Someone sealed this section after the explosion. That suggests there might be an individual or individuals alive down here.

My thoughts turn back to the last meeting I had with Langsley. He was living in Forestal, ostensibly retired, but still involved in everything I worked on. The low gravity of Luna suited him. When I visited, he showed me round his place, then insisted on cooking me a meal. We talked through all the issues at hand and tried to figure it all out, just like we always did, but I got this sense he was starting to lose track of the details.

Details matter.

I settle myself in, just beneath the hatch, and access the video logs, cycling back to the first entry. Le Garre and Travers appear on the screen. Clearly, they decided to make this one together.

"...report that this ship, known as *Gallowglass,* has been commandeered as a prize vessel by Earth Fleet. Noting that on this date and time, myself, Major Angel Le Garre, am assuming command as acting captain, with Lieutenant Bill Travers appointed as my executive officer...."

Hang on.... *What*?

I play the recordings from the start, running them at double or triple speed. I can still understand the words and get the gist. Le Garre explains some of the context, talks about a mutiny on the *Khidr* and a group of traitors, including Ensign Chiu. Then details Captain Shann's decision to evacuate and her actions when they boarded the ship.

Shann lost it, so they relieved her of command, but now she's back in charge?

The logs don't give me all the details, but there is enough to get an idea. Scratch the surface and more layers appear. This crew is not as united as they appear.

I'm viewing the entries when another window on the screen flashes. I bring the drone camera feeds back up. Movement outside. Three figures this time. They are close to the entrance, closer than they should be. They must have known we were watching.

A moment later, one of the camera feeds goes dark.

I activate the second camera and task it to move away before it gets destroyed. Then I move from my position back down into the next room. Drake is still there.

"We have company," I say. "We're going to need to figure out what to do about it."

★ ★ ★

Shann is efficient. Whatever broke her, back on *Gallowglass* after she lost her ship.... Well, I'm struggling to see any lingering after-effects.

She organises us all quickly. If the Rocher clones try to get in here, they will try to use our atmosphere against us. Explosive decompression to wreck the rooms and suffocate us all. The solution? Take the weapon away. Remove the air first and use our suit supplies.

Thanks to Johansson's code and jury-rigged operating system, we now have some control over the facility's environmental controls. The systems are localised to each room, just as they would be on a spaceship, but there are commands that can be issued from a terminal that will override room control. I can initiate a full depressurisation as soon as we know that intruders have entered the airlock.

There is a whole stack of data on the central system. I guess that would be mission logs from the people who were here before us and who are outside, somewhere on the surface of the ship right now. That's information we are going to need, but trying to obtain it through a back door might trigger some sort of security. I may need to wait on this, or get Johansson involved, once we re-establish contact with *Gallowglass*.

I've moved away from the hatch, right down to the other end. Le Garre and Shann are here, still trying to open up the last door. There appears to be another airlock at this end but the inner door is jammed shut. The manual controls are seized as well.

"Why did they come here?" I muse out loud. Both of my companions turn towards me.

"Sorry, what?" Le Garre says.

I gesture. "This place. So far, we've found no evidence of construction, other than the work done by humans. Nothing that explains how this ship arrived here and decelerated to take up its current position." I point at the locked door. "The only option is that answers lie through there."

"We are aware of this," Le Garre says. "If you have something useful to contribute...."

"Someone went through that door. They used the airlock. On the other side is a large hollow chamber, a space that's too large to be pressurised. That's where they are." I nod towards the other compartments. "Their friends outside are trying to join them."

"And we're wasting time remaining here," Shann says. She slaps the door in frustration. "We need to get through."

"I agree," I say. "So far, this little expedition has answered very few questions." I'm noting the collaboration between Le Garre and Shann. They appear to be easy around each other. Not the kind of strained relationship you might expect, given what I saw in the logs.

"We can't keep cutting through all these doors," Shann says.

I hold up a hand. "If the last person who went through, into the airlock, was trying to prevent anyone following them, then they might have wedged the door on the inside. There may be something jamming the release."

"We can't get in there and check," Le Garre says.

"True," I reply. "But we may have another way to free the mechanism." I'm opening a window on my screen. I remotely reconnect to the terminal in the other room. In Johansson's code, there's a console for the airlock controls. Something she must have put together when she was on *Gallowglass*. It takes a few seconds to tweak the code so it will work here. "Okay, ready to purge the chamber and open the outer door. If there's anything wedged into the manual release, the vacuum might encourage it to shake loose."

Shann smiles. "Interesting solution," she says. "All right, let's try it."

I start the purge, then reconnect to the surviving camera drone outside. As I'd hoped, the device has managed to avoid the three figures who are outside trying to get into the first compartment. I instruct the drone to return and take up a position where we can observe them. I enlarge the image, zooming in closer to the doors. The camera adjusts and starts using an interpretative algorithm to enhance the focus.

I can see people moving around the entrance. I can't tell what they are doing, but it is clear they are trying to get inside.

The purge on the airlock will take time. Then, we'll need to repressurise before we can try to open the door again.

After that, we have to get everyone through, including Travers.

I look at Shann. I show her the screen. "They're breaking in. You'll need to make a decision about what we do next."

Shann grimaces. "There's no option. We'll stand and fight."

★ ★ ★

[training log 07.14.2110]

Cadet Six: Ellisa Shann.

On arrival, Shann was disappointed to be here. She had already served a foundation tour on Orbital Three and clearly didn't plan to be returned for orientation. The attitude disappeared after forty-eight hours or so and then she began to show why she is such a highly rated trainee.

I can only agree with the previous instructors about Cadet Shann. She has a fire that she has learned to control and channel during her instruction. She reads situations well and shows restraint when given a delegated role. When put in command, she excels. She is a fierce leader who cares about her people. The latter may become an issue should she rise through the ranks.

I would advise this cadet be cleared for interplanetary duty.

CHAPTER SEVENTEEN

Holder – Split

A memory. It is not mine.

I am floating outside a spacecraft that shines in the full glare of the naked sun. I can see the Earth below me. I should be falling, but I am not.

Dimly, I am aware that I am travelling at an incredible speed as I orbit the planet with the little ship that brought me here.

I'm trying not to look down. The world below me has been the cradle of my civilisation for millions of years. A view of it from here is terrifyingly beautiful. Everything that ever existed in human history is down there.

But the future will be written here, and beyond. In the stars.

Above me and to the left, I see my destination. A bright object that grows larger as I approach. It is the only object that is changing size, making it difficult for my mind to process what is going on. Nothing else is moving, so either the shining shape is growing larger, or I am moving towards it.

"Robert, you need to get back inside."

The voice in my ear is knowing and urgent. The person talking is a friend, the instruction is sincere. I need to be inside the capsule, otherwise any change in our velocity as we approach will cause me to become detached.

I return to the hatch, open it and climb into the cramped cabin. Dimitri is sitting in the same place as before, wedged into his seat. He is also wearing an EVA suit. No internal pressurisation for us. Our mission is to get up, dock, assess, and get back down.

"Six minutes, twenty-three seconds until deceleration," he says. "You were cutting it fine. Did you fix the antenna?"

"Yes, all sorted."

"Excellent! I'll reboot the computer and we should be able to talk to our new host. Hopefully, I can persuade them to unlock the door and let us in!"

★ ★ ★

"Tell me what you saw."

I open my eyes. I'm lying on a bunk on *Gateway*. It takes a moment for that to sink in. I can feel weight, pressure. I'm not floating.

"Alison, I need to know what you saw."

The woman, Genevieve Aster, is crouched beside me. She's holding an empty syringe. She has injected me with a sedative. I agreed to this.

"Two men in a small ship, just outside Earth's atmosphere. They were stealing an orbital platform," I say. "I was part of the team." I'm thinking about the memory, trying to stay in the head of 'Robert' even as his identity fades from my mind. "This was decades ago."

"Back when America broke up. The Secession," Aster says. "A lot of things were lost back then."

"And people took advantage," I say. My tongue is sluggish and thick in my mouth. My words are awkward and slow. "But that doesn't explain why I can remember what happened."

Aster's expression softens. She blinks and I see tears running down her face. "You must know what you are," she says.

I nod. "Yes, I know, but this memory?"

"My research was funded by a company called dMemra. We worked with early cryo patients," Aster says "People who were suffering from incurable conditions. They were frozen and as part of the contract, they agreed for images of their brain activity to be captured and logged. Towards the end, we were able to replicate images and view memories. What they made…is several stages beyond what we were able to do. But I found out later, what you are is based on technology I invented."

"Is that why you were taken prisoner and brought here?" I ask.

"It could be." Aster turns away from me. Her voice is low and laced with anger that I can feel coming from her in waves. "After the corporation that paid for my research was closed down, all of the material from my laboratory was seized. I can only assume that it ended up with your creator."

"His name is Emori," I say instinctively. "He works with Doctor Summers." The memory of white walls, of a face that slips out of my mind every time I try to remember it. I'm seeing the space now. The chair, the plugs in the back of my head. Being in a body that is not this body. "Do those names mean anything to you?"

"No," Aster says. "I'm sorry. I know that connecting things, fitting them together, helps when all of this is fragmented and floating around. That was a common side effect of our work when we projected the memories into people's minds. I can only imagine...."

"Don't try to," I say. "You don't want this."

"No, you're right. I don't."

We are silent, sharing that. It means a lot to be able to talk about these things with someone. "The memory," I say. "Why do I have it?"

"Your identity is transmitted into a small object embedded in the brain, a receiver," Aster explains. "That data overlays on the mind of the person who you are being sent to. Your character takes charge of the new person. Alison Wade is still there, but you are in control. You have her memories and experiences, along with the ones you brought with you."

"But this is a different memory," I say.

"Residual. Left over from a previous data transfer," Aster says. "But it does tell us something about all of this. If there were people stealing NASA equipment back then, maybe that explains some of what's happening now?"

"What will happen to me?" I ask.

Aster sighs. "You know what will happen. It's already happening. The transmitter was never designed to be a permanent host for your identity. Alison Wade is still there. Sooner or later, the mesh between your personalities will fall apart. After that...I don't know what will be left."

An audible pop makes me glance up. There is a speaker in the corner of the room, the kind that used to be state-of-the-art thirty or forty years ago. "Wade, we need you on the bridge," Xiua says.

I look at Aster. "Sorry," I say.

She waves her hand. "Go. Come back later."

I'm up from the bed and heading to the door. I still feel a little slow, my mind dulled by the drugs. I fumble for the door release and step into the passage, pushing past the people who are out there, trying to deal with their own issues.

★ ★ ★

I make it to the bridge. Xiua, Francalla and Diouf are there. "The unidentified ship is about to dock," Xiua says. "It's called *Gallowglass*. We have established a communications link with the people on-board."

"Who are they?" I ask.

"Two members of the crew of the *Khidr*, a Fleet rescue ship that was sent after one of their freighters that got in trouble," Xiua says. "They didn't go into detail, but I get the feeling it's a story."

"Did they say why they are coming here?"

"They say ship is on an automated course. It was always coming here."

"Do you trust them?"

"I don't know. There isn't a lot we can do to stop them." Xiua winces. "Frankly, if they wished us ill, they could have targeted our generator room and launched torpedoes. *Gateway* wasn't built to withstand that kind of attack. This whole place would have been torn apart."

"We should meet them," Francalla says. I look at him. His gaze is distant, even rheumy. I guess that's what he's used to doing, going out and greeting the visitors, whatever they are coming here for. "If we talk to them in person, we'll get a measure of their intentions."

"We'll also be putting ourselves at risk," Xiua says.

"You should stay here," I say to Xiua. "The people you rescued, they need to stay rescued. Diouf, if you're up for meeting them...."

"Yeah. Works for me."

"Diouf will accompany you, Captain Francalla," I say.

"And where will you be?" Xiua asks.

"Watching," I reply.

"Remember, all these people we rescued? That's you as well. I want you to stay rescued."

"I'll do my best." I nod to Diouf. "You head down. I'll follow and stay out of sight until you need me."

"All right. That works." Diouf looks at Francalla. "Shall we, Captain?"

"Yes, we shall," Francalla replies.

I watch the two of them leave, heading for the elevator. Then I turn to Xiua. "The woman, Jeni? Keep an eye on her whilst I'm gone. Two eyes if possible."

Xiua stiffens. "Something I should know?"

"Not yet," I say. "But she's a variable. An unpredictable quantity."

"Yeah, I got that from her patchy story."

"I want to trust her," I say. "But I need to know why she was locked in that room. The whole story."

"She didn't tell you?"

I shake my head. "She told me her name, Genevieve Aster." I point towards the terminal Masson was using before. "If that's still hooked up to the Mars CorpGov database, maybe you can find out who she is."

"You think it's her real name?"

"Yeah, I do."

Xiua nods. He opens his mouth to say something else, then seems to reconsider, but then changes his mind again. "I looked you up, Alison Wade. What I found was suspicious."

Instinctively I'm on my guard. I like Xiua; our relationship is distant, but one of mutual benefit. He hasn't asked too many questions, and I don't want him to start. "All right," I say. "What's on your mind?"

"There's nothing in your records that explains all this," Xiua says, gesturing. "I mean, you're here. Most of the others we managed to save are a mess. They want food, water and a place to sleep. But you… you're still wired in. It's like you were made for a crisis."

"If there was something that you needed to know, I'd tell you," I say.

"That's not reassuring." Xiua has a taser on his belt. I note that his hand is resting on the clip.

"Sorry, I'm not good at this," I say. "You saved my life and all these others. That's meaningful. You and Diouf. I owe you everything."

Xiua's hand moves away from the taser. "How about an explanation then?" he asks. "The whole deal. Just between us."

"Agreed," I say. "When I get back."

Xiua pulls the taser from his belt and hands it to me. I take it.

He turns away towards the terminal. "Stay safe," he says. "While you're down there, I'll update your computer access privileges. Whatever you're hiding, I think you're on our side and we need you."

"Thank you," I say.

"Don't make me regret it," Xiua says.

★ ★ ★

The journey back to the dock gives me time to think.

Genevieve Aster is a problem for me. This woman knows what I am. She might be able to help me. But the cost is that I have to trust her, and she is keeping her own secrets. I want to trust her, but I'm not sure I can.

If I were here alone, maybe I could take that risk. But there are people relying on me, trusting me as part of this little group of survivors. I can't vouch for Aster unless she starts sharing more about herself.

The white room, the chair, Emoli and Doctor Summers. Now that I've remembered them again, more and more moments are coming back. That makes the Alison Wade memories distant and disassociated. I don't know what that means for me. The gaps feel like voids. Emptiness that might swallow me up.

I reach the dock. *Gateway* was designed to transport all of the colonists down to the surface of Mars and then act as a transfer station with resupply ships unloading their cargo here. That means there is plenty of room for the new ship.

The dock is automatically controlled. It has to be, as Francalla's crew have long since left us for the Mars colony. As soon as the arrival request was accepted, space was made to allow the ship to close and connect via a short umbilical airlock. Through the huge DuraGlas window, I can see the six shuttles that we arrived in are crowded into one corner. The shadow of the new ship inches across the sunlit promenade.

Diouf and Francalla are in the middle of the space. Tiny compared to the huge dark cloud of the arriving vessel.

As I get closer, the transfer corridor extends and locks into place. The whole process is silent and gentle. It is a privilege to watch. Huge complex machines functioning exactly as intended. I can't begin to understand how they were designed and constructed all those years ago when this ship was being built in Earth orbit.

The sound of the umbilical passage locking into place echoes around the room. I stay back, lurking by the door, waiting to see what will happen. I know Xiua and Masson will be watching through the station cameras, just as Francalla watched us when we arrived.

Diouf steps forwards, towards the connected airlock. The taser Xiua gave me is in my hand. As we wait, I'm inching forwards. If anyone comes out of that ship with guns, I won't be able to reach either of my people in time.

The hatch opens. Two women emerge. Neither of them is carrying a weapon. I breathe a sigh of relief.

★ ★ ★

"Holder? Can you hear me?"

Memories. The same white room, the same person standing over me. A hundred conversations going over the same ground. My memories wiped so many times. Doctor Summers saying the same things to calm me down.

Remembering all of this at the same time is dislocating, disconnecting. I don't want to remember; I want the oblivion. The moments of blank forgetting between each memory.

"She is starting to fall apart. What's the time count?"

"Fifty-three hours from the point of transit. The sense of identity has degraded beyond the point where I might be able to recover it."

Hands touching my face. Fingertips brush along my cheek, tracing the line of bone underneath my skin. "I wonder what it feels like," Emori says.

I open my eyes. I see his face, blurry and distorted through tears. Every time I try to remember this man, I fail. This time, he will be the last thing I see.

CHAPTER EIGHTEEN

Johansson

Two men are standing on the dock promenade. A woman lurks behind them. She has a taser in her hands. For a moment, I wonder whether we should have brought weapons with us, but there is no going back now.

"Welcome to *Gateway*," says the older man. "I am Captain Francalla. This is dock technician Mohammed Diouf, a survivor from Phobos Station."

I nod towards them both. "I am Ensign Avril Johansson. This is Assistant Engineer Chiu. We're both from the Fleet patrol ship *Khidr*."

"I am told your ship was destroyed," Francalla says. He gestures towards the *Gallowglass*. "How you ended up aboard this vessel and came to be here is, I am sure, quite a story."

"Yes, it is," I reply.

The two men don't move. The woman behind them is staring at me. Her gaze is the type you get from professional security experts assessing a threat.

"We are Fleet officers," I say. "We're here to help, however we can."

"You'll forgive us if we're not going to take that at face value," Diouf says. He touches the comms bead in his ear and turns away. I notice him relaying our names to someone else on the station. "The bridge will run a check on your profiles. They will be in the database."

"I'm sorry about this," Francalla adds.

"Don't be. These are understandable precautions," I say.

The comms bead murmurs. Diouf nods. "Okay, they check out. Let's go."

"A moment," Chiu says. She points at the woman. "Who is that?"

The woman moves forwards. "My name is Alison Wade," she says. "I'm an administrator from Phobos Station."

I stare at the woman. Administrator is not the profession I'd have picked. But this man, Diouf, seems to trust her. We may need to follow his lead, for now. "We should head to your bridge and discuss our situations," I say. "If you can give us an idea of what you need, we can try to help."

"Agreed," Francalla says. "Come with us."

★ ★ ★

Out of the dock, through corridors, to an elevator. The doors close and we travel to the rotational section of the ship in awkward silence.

The feeling of gravity reminds me of Erebus. A moment of powerlessness in that lift when Sam was injured, and we knew we weren't getting out. My own personal nightmare.

I'm watching the woman, Alison. After a few minutes she notices and returns my gaze. I don't look away. I want her to know I don't trust her, that I won't let her push me around.

The elevator stops. The doors open. I half expect to see guns being aimed at me and to be taken prisoner, but that isn't what happens.

Two Mars security officers are waiting for us, but they appear to be in charge. "Welcome to our little refuge, ensigns," says the first of them. "I'm Lieutenant Laurence Xiua. Mission commander from Hera Spaceport. This is Kras Masson, senior shuttle pilot."

"Good to meet you," I say. "I take it you're in charge?"

Xiua smiles. "I guess so. Although Captain Francalla has very generously allowed the survivors we rescued from Phobos station to stay here. This is his ship, not mine."

I focus my attention on Francalla, but he dissembles and gestures towards Xiua and his companion. "Best I defer to you folks," he says. "Particularly now we've discovered we are not alone on this ship."

"Not alone?" Chiu says.

Xiua looks at Alison and nods. "We found cryopods and a DNA creche. There are several individuals who appear to have been placed there, including a biochemist who was taken prisoner and brought here against her will."

I glance at Chiu. She shrugs in return, content to let me decide how much to say. "The *Gallowglass* came here because it was programmed to do so. We were supposed to rendezvous with the alien ship. We left most of the surviving crew of the *Khidr* down there before it decided to bring us here."

"You don't have control of your ship?" Francalla says.

"We have partial control," I reply. "It's a constant battle with the ship's computer."

"Should we be worried?" Alison asks.

I glare at her. "No," I say flatly. "But since we're sharing...."

"We have shuttles here," Xiua says. "*Gateway* has fuel reserves which we could use to get over there."

"We should consider all the options," I say. "You said you brought survivors from Phobos here?"

"Yes, there's seventy-seven people here, now with you two, seventy-nine."

"What about getting them all down to Mars?" I ask.

"That would be the plan, once we establish contact with the spaceport," Xiua says. "But at the moment, we can't raise them."

"When did you lose comms?"

"Not long after we took off to rescue survivors."

"What about the other ships?" Masson asks. "The Fleet vessels that we saw moving out of orbit."

"They were alerted to intercept us," I explain. "We were in communication with them before. Have they contacted you?"

"They have," Xiua says.

"And what did they say?"

"'Proceed with caution,' I think was the phrase." Xiua sighs. "With everything that's happened, some distrust is justified. We're all looking for someone to blame."

"How did you lose your ship?" Alison asks.

I smile. "That's a story Captain Shann should tell. But *Gallowglass* is the ship that attacked us. We were able to board and defeat the crew."

"And the *Hercules*?"

"Dead in space. They killed the crew."

"So, you killed the people who did that?"

"They were clones," Chiu says.

I look at her and she flinches, clearly aware of what she's said.

"This isn't the first time we've heard about clones," Xiua replies.

I'm looking at him. Suddenly, Chiu's instinctive revelation has become exactly what we needed. "I'm very curious to learn more," I say.

Xiua nods. "I think it's time we told you everything, Ensign."

★ ★ ★

Trust is difficult to earn.

A crisis makes people hard. Hands tighten around the things that are precious to us. We become protective and try to cling on to what remains from the time before.

In this moment, I understand Ellisa Shann and why she broke. I am a part of her crew, I am one of the things she was trying to cling on to when our ship, *Khidr*, was destroyed. So was Sellis. Watching him die made something snap.

Now, in this moment, I see the opposite. These people should be our allies, but I am resistant to letting down my guard. Every time they ask a question, I am second-guessing my reply, trying to figure out where the information will go and what it might cost me.

One moment, one slip and suddenly we have common ground. Then, the pressure eases.

"*Gallowglass* was crewed by clones," I explain. "A man named Rocher. He has a different first name, I think they all do. That's how they tell the difference between them."

"There was a Rocher leading the insurgents on Phobos Station," Alison says.

"There was a Rocher here," Francalla says. "Daniel Rocher transferred into the curator team after arriving from Luna, where he'd been working on the orbitals." The captain moves over to one of the terminals and accesses the crew records. A face that I recognise appears on the screen. "Yes, that's him."

"That's all of them," Alison says. "I can't figure out how this went undetected. I mean, all these people with the same profile picture…."

"Pigment variation in the photograph. Different organisation assignments," I say. "There are plenty of ways to get around an automated system that isn't really looking for things like this. No one was looking for clones."

"I met at least two Rochers on Phobos Station," Alison says. "I think one of them was a technician on staff, the other came aboard with the insurgents. They were both killed in the explosion."

"What about your Rocher?" I ask Francalla. "What happened to him?"

"Went with everyone else to Hera Spaceport," Francalla replies. "Once we saw Phobos explode and mapped the debris, we knew they would need help down there. My people were going to see what they could do to assist."

"Did you see him leave?" I ask.

"Not personally, no."

"Then we should check your logs," I say, moving towards the terminal. Instinctively, I raise my right arm to use the touchscreen display, then catch myself and reach out with my left. "You'll have video feed of everyone leaving. Easy to use facial recognition to see if Rocher was with them."

"You think he wouldn't be?" Xiua asks.

"If I was part of an insurrection and wanted a chance to hide, I'd lurk around on an abandoned station or ship, sure."

Francalla accesses the system, initiating a security protocol that identifies images of Rocher on the station captured on camera. Within seconds, a folder starts to fill with images, all date-stamped. He organises the files by date. I see three or four images appear that are only a few hours old.

"He's still here," Alison says.

"What's his last location?" I ask.

"In the corridor, outside the room where the clones and embryo banks are. We need to get down there."

She is already moving, heading back to the elevator. I'm following her. We're inside and she jams her fist on the button to return us to the dock.

The doors close before anyone else can join us.

I'm staring at Alison; she is staring at me. "I don't know who you are," I say. "But Rocher is my enemy."

"Mine too."

"Whatever he wants here, we need to make sure he doesn't get it."

Alison nods. "Your ship. You said you didn't know why it came here. Could it be for them?"

"That tracks," I say. "How are we going to stop him?"

"By standing in the way," Alison says. "He'll have to get past us." She moves to the emergency communications panel on the wall and activates it. "Wade to Bridge?"

Masson appears on the display. "Receiving. Wade, you need to—"

"Masson, tell Xiua I'm not waiting for you to catch up. What I need from you is the location of Doctor Aster – Jeni, the woman we found?"

"No sign of her up here," Masson says.

"Fuck. Xiua promised me he'd watch her. Check her room. Tell me she's there."

Masson gets up from his chair and disappears. There is silence. Then he returns. "Wade, she's not here. I'll do a camera search and—"

"Don't bother," Wade says. "I know where she is."

I'm about to ask about this Doctor Aster, but as I start to speak, the elevator stops. The doors open and Alison throws herself out into the corridor. I follow, watching her as she crashes against the wall, gathers herself and leaps, flying down the passageway. She isn't used to zero gravity, not in the way I'd expect an experienced station employee to be.

I'm following, using handholds and ridges in the walls, just like I would on the *Khidr*. You can go fast, but you have to accelerate gradually, and get used to the motion.

You also have to be ready to slow down.

Ahead, I can see an open door. There are boxes in the corridor. A man appears. It's Rocher.

Then a second man appears. Another Rocher.

Shit, I should have realised....

Gunshots, the muted kind you get from low-velocity rifles. Bullets slap against the walls of the passage. I grab a handhold and pivot, taking cover in a doorway.

This was a bad move. We're outgunned and potentially outnumbered. I touch the comms bead in my ear. "Chiu, we're in trouble! Tell Xiua he's going to need to bring weapons!"

"...understo— I'll—"

A hiss distorts the link. Then a blast of static makes me wince and dig the device out of my ear. I crouch down, trying to make myself as small as possible. It's only a matter of time before Rocher realises we're not returning fire. One of the clones will advance, then capture, or murder us, depending on the requirements of their mission.

"Lift— ...hold—"

Bullets tear into the wall beside me. Gas-powered low-velocity weapons are designed to be safer in a pressurised environment, but that doesn't mean they are safe. Ranges are shorter, but zero gravity means less deceleration. There is still a risk of explosive decompression to go with all the damage caused if you get hit.

I dig into the toolkit on my belt, trying to find something I can use to defend myself. Nothing bigger than an EVA suit patch and a mini auto driver. Useless.

The gunfire stops.

I don't move. The worst thing I could do in a situation like this is to raise my head, look around the corner and get shot. Right now, there is nothing I can do that will improve my circumstances, but I must be alert, I must be ready.

A flicker of movement. Shadows shifting against the wall. I move immediately, charging out from the alcove, fingers curled into claws, grappling and grasping for anything.

I almost miss the man as he approaches, but my right arm catches him around the ankle. I twist around, trying to disrupt his direction, make him miss.

Another gunshot. I grab for the weapon, but my left hand is too weak, and my fingers slip from the weapon's stock as Rocher yanks it away. He steadies himself, braces against the wall, takes aim and....

"Avril?"

I realise I have closed my eyes. I open them. Chiu is standing in front of me, a taser in her hand. The unconscious, twitching body of Rocher drifts between us. The gun that would have been the instrument of my death spins from his grasp and clatters against the wall.

"Move, Avril!" Chiu shouts. I react, kicking out, catching the floor with the heel of my foot and sending myself spiralling away. I hear another rifle coughing bullets. Somehow, I'm not hit.

I crash into the floor panels, right myself, look up. Ahead of me, Alison Wade is fighting, wrestling a gun from another Rocher, touching the barrel to his head and squeezing the trigger.

The clone's skull cracks. There is an explosion of gore. Blood and brains go everywhere.

Wade is already moving, charging forwards towards the open compartment door. I try to follow, pushing off from the floor and grabbing for one of the containers in the corridor. I use it to pull myself forwards, reaching for Alison. She's still ahead of me, right in front of the compartment door as someone inside slams it shut.

* * *

[Evidence File #5: Savvantine's Personal Folder. Extract from *Citizen of the World Magazine* 2061 AD.]

We don't owe these people a life.

Sure, they didn't choose to be born where they were born, but they did choose to make their lives where they were. Climate scientists have been warning about the environmental challenges the world would face for decades, and modelled where many of the crises would occur with increasing accuracy. So, there is no excuse.

As adults, you take responsibility. You make plans and find a new place to be, for the sake of your children and their children. Maybe back in the twenty-first century their parents should have done something?

I get it when people say how we have it lucky. Generations of living in a wealthy country means you get an advantage. The emergency services are there when you need them. If you don't have those things, you need to make a change, get yourself out and go elsewhere?

When you do, you have to integrate, become part of the community you're joining. You need to be grateful for the opportunities offered and make the most of them.

Our nations thrive on the transition of people. We need those who travel, emigrate and move. Our lives are enriched by new perspectives and experiences.

I see the arguments about space, about 'no more room'. Those are ignorant and stupid, hot air and a waste of words designed only to fulfil a narrow-minded agenda. Maybe they will serve to discourage some, but that ideology leads to stagnation and decay. We are all better than that.

CHAPTER NINETEEN

Shann

Six of us.

Three of them.

Fleet recruits are trained in zero-gravity combat. There is a supplementary course for EVA combat. The first line of that course is *'EVA hand-to-hand combat is not recommended.'* After that, they teach you just how vulnerable you are in a spacesuit.

Any tear or snag can be fatal. Plus, there is so much equipment keeping you alive in a vacuum, just a few seconds of grappling can dislodge something. There are no good ways to make your end, but the memory of the way the last Rocher died, burned alive as the pure oxygen in his suit ignited...yeah, that's not how I'd want to go out.

People are going to die very quickly if it comes to a fight.

We're suited up and all standing in the room below the hatch. Savvantine is next to me, her eyes on her portable screen, where she has control of the surviving camera drone. "I'm getting closer," she says. "Looks like they have a laser cutter."

A laser. We would hear it tearing through the metal of the hatch if we were still in a pressurised room. But in a vacuum, it becomes a silent and deadly killer. The beam will cut through any material in its path, that includes an EVA suit, and the flesh and bone inside it. "Sam, make sure you and Arkov aren't standing behind the door," I say.

"Understood, Captain."

"Let them in first, then we move."

I'm counting on my crew. Sam, Arkov and Le Garre are the first line of defence. Savvantine and I will support them. She understands what's at stake here. We are fighting for our lives against enemies who have shown their expertise and training before. Drake will become useful afterwards. I'm hoping we won't need him, but I know we will.

"Door is breached," Sam says. "I estimate three minutes until contact."

I'm not okay with this, but I have to hold back. I want to be in front, protecting my people. I remember Sellis dying in front of me. Sam means more to me. I feel guilty for admitting that, but he does. I know he is injured. Any one of these clones could get the better of him. I need to make sure that doesn't happen.

"Two minutes."

"Captain, is there anything we've not thought of?" Savvantine asks. "Might they try something to—"

White noise. Loud. Agonisingly loud. I can't…think…breathe…. There are controls to switch off the comms, but I can barely move. The sound goes right through me.

I see the hatch fall apart. An intruder crashes through, grabs Arkov. Gets a hand around his air supply, rips out the intake pipe.

I'm moving. The noise is swirling around me. I can see my hands, reaching out towards the struggling pair. I have an auto driver in my hand. I fumble with the trigger, press it, stab the end into the arm of a pressure suit. I feel the material tear and go slack. Air escapes, changes the situation. Suddenly, my enemy is struggling to survive, rather than murder my people.

Arkov jams a taser into his ribs. Our enemy spasms and thrashes, falling away. Another takes his place. His hands reach out, seize my helmet and pull, driving me into the wall.

My visor glass cracks. Lights flash in my suit. I can't hear the alarm over the noise, but I know what's happened. Now my life can be measured in seconds.

I let go of the auto driver and put my hands on the wall. I push. Hard. The grip releases and I'm flying across the room, crashing into someone, spinning, turning, dying.

Then the noise stops.

"—Shann! ... Can—"

There are more words, but I can't make them out. I don't know if the audio system in my suit is damaged, or it's my hearing. I can hear the hiss of escaping air, the pressure alarm. Everything is fading in and out.

"—leak.... Let me—"

A face in front of mine. It's Drake. There is something in his hand, a tube. He presses the end against the crack in my helmet. Grey liquid oozes out, a scab over the injury. The lights in my helmet stop flashing, the alert falls silent.

"Shann, are you all right?"

I nod. Then realise I need to vocalise. "I'm good. What about—"

"Arkov is dead."

I knew before I heard the words. Someone would be lost. I saw him attacked, tried to help him. "Get everyone through into the next room, seal us in and repressurise," I say.

"On it, Captain," says Savvantine, her voice trembling. This has shaken her.

I turn around. There are bodies floating in the room. One of them is still twitching, the pipes on his suit waving around like pigtails.

There is blood. It spews from the dead and dying in spurts, trailing around like spiderwebs.

I don't want to be here.

A cracked helmet. Lifeless eyes staring at me. I flinch from that dreadful gaze. All it can do is inspire guilt and shame at what happened here. I played my part in this, I helped kill....

Then it registers. A woman's face. Not the Rocher I expected.

What the fuck....

I'm already moving through the doorway. In the next room I see Travers's cryopod. The power lights confirm he is okay, the same as before.

"Door is closed," Sam says. Hearing his voice unlocks something in me. I'm breathing a little easier. He's alive.

"Pressurising."

It'll take fifteen minutes or so for these compartments to fill. Time to process the minutes of chaos. Another of my people lost. The survivors will be hurting. I need to project confidence and strength. They need leadership.

I key up a private communication channel. "Drake, talk to me. What's your assessment?"

"Two dead. One alive. Le Garre has him restrained. Sam is hurt. I'll need to treat him. And Arkov, as I said.... What about you? Are you—"

I hold up a hand. "I'm okay. You got to me in time." I glance around. Le Garre is on the other side of the room, securing the surviving enemy combatant to the wall with zip ties. Savvantine is with Sam. As Drake approaches, they exchange words on a private channel and then she moves over to me.

"I'm sorry, Captain," she says.

"Yeah, so am I," I say. "Did you get a look at them?"

"I did. They are not clones. Not of your man, Rocher, at any rate."

"Can we identify them?"

"Once the room is pressurised, we can remove their suits and try to match faces or thumbprints to the Fleet database, or any other database we have to hand," Savvantine says. She gestures towards Le Garre and her charge. "But we also have a prisoner, who may provide us with answers."

"Worth a try," I say. "You were right, by the way."

"About what?"

"You were trying to warn me, about them thinking of something. The loud static broadcast. That was their play."

"Yes, a clever one too. It nearly worked." I see Savvantine grimacing inside her helmet. "I should have worked it out sooner."

"Plenty of time to blame yourself in the after-action report," I say. "Right now, we need to assess our condition and then see about getting through that door."

"The depressurisation has completed," Savvantine says. "I've opened the outer airlock, then closed it and started the repressurisation sequence. After that, we'll know if we can get through."

"Stay on that," I say and move across the room to Le Garre, switching my comms back to open. "How are you doing, Major?"

Le Garre turns towards me. "A little shaken, but otherwise okay, Captain," she says. "Our friend here stayed back a little. I was able to work my way around. When he saw the taser, he raised his hands and gave up."

"Have you tried to get him talking?" I ask.

"He's not responding on any open channel," Le Garre says.

A green light flashes in the room, confirming that we have air. I reach up and unlock my helmet, then take it off. Le Garre does the same, then turns to her prisoner and assesses the mechanism. The suit is a little different to ours, an older variation by the look of it. Eventually, she finds the releases and triggers them, lifting the helmet and setting it aside.

The man inside stares at us both in turn. I don't recognise him. He looks terrified of us. That might be more of a problem than any allegiance or loyalty he feels for another organisation.

"Do you understand me?" I ask.

He nods but doesn't speak.

"Tell me your name."

"Benjamin Sarandon."

"Okay, Benjamin," I say. "My name is Captain Shann, this is Major Le Garre. We are Fleet officers. We are going to go through all this slowly and carefully. You will be asked questions, and we expect you to answer them."

"You're with Fleet? I— Oh.... Yes, of course."

"How did you get here, Benjamin?"

"I was brought here as part of a research team. I'm an archaeologist." Sarandon's eyes continue to flicker between us. He is visibly shaking. "I didn't expect...I mean, they told us you were here to steal the data and all the artefacts. They said you were pirates."

I frown and glance at Le Garre. She raises her eyebrows. Neither of us is entirely convinced. I turn back to our charge. "Benjamin, tell me what is through the inner airlock door?"

"You mean you don't know?" Sarandon sounds surprised. "But I thought that's why you came here?"

"What you were told wasn't necessarily the truth," Le Garre says. "Please answer the captain's question."

Sarandon stares at me. I meet his eyes and he quickly looks away. "There is a large chamber. That's where we've been doing our work. We go in, set up and check the equipment, then come back out into the laboratory and living area to process the results. But you destroyed all that. You killed.... You killed them...."

My mouth is dry. When we arrived, we thought we were fighting a military force, like the clones who had been operating the *Gallowglass*. We didn't consider it might have been a civilian operation.

"You were expecting a ship," I say.

"Yes, they told us you were bringing more equipment. More specialist teams," Sarandon says. The words are tumbling out now, faster and faster. "We'd made a breakthrough in connecting with the alien technology. They told us there would be a public announcement, a press package sent back to Earth, all of it. I've been out here working for months, all of us have. We signed non-communication contracts. The idea that we'd be going public? You don't know how exciting...."

"Captain?" Le Garre inclines her head away from Sarandon, suggesting we talk in private.

I nod. "We'll come back to this," I say. "Give me a moment."

"Are you going to kill me?" Sarandon asks. "Please...I need to know."

I stare at him and measure my words carefully. "We don't murder people in cold blood. You surrendered. You are no longer a combatant."

"Okay, that's a little reassuring, I guess."

We move aside, out of earshot.

"What do you make of that?" I ask Le Garre.

"If he's lying, he's very convincing," she replies. "He is completely terrified of us."

"He has a right to be," I say. "We need to identify the people he was with and figure out what we're dealing with out here before we go any further."

I turn to Savvantine, catch her eye and beckon her over. She joins us.

"Did our prisoner reveal anything?" she asks.

"So far, not a great deal that we can rely on," I say. "But the fact that he isn't a Rocher means something." I point towards the door which we've just come through. "Can you tell us anything about the people who attacked us?"

"Maybe," Savvantine says. "The camera drone is still operational. I may be able to use it to get a DNA sample which should match the existing biometric records." She taps on the screen then shows it to me. I can see some data usage statistics. "There is a massive amount of stored information here that we aren't currently trying to access. I had thought you'd want to get into it, but if we try, we may trigger a security response."

"We need those logs," I say.

"Fine, I'll try and get them," Savvantine says. She points at Sarandon. "Do you want me to take a turn with him?"

I shake my head. "Not yet, but we will do soon."

For a moment, that answer doesn't seem to satisfy her, but then she seems to remember her situation. "I'll get the airlock working," she says.

"Thank you," I reply. I turn towards Sarandon again. There are many questions that I want answers to, but as yet I'm not sure how forthcoming he'll be. This man is a fragile resource. We can't break him.

"Captain?"

Sam is next to me. He looks strung out, pushed beyond his limits. He leans in close to me, so others cannot hear. "Are you okay?" I ask.

"Did we do the right thing, Ellisa?" Sam says. His voice cracks a little. "These people, are they really our enemy?"

"At the moment, yes," I say, trying to project confidence. I'm his commanding officer. I made the decision. "They were attacking us. We had to defend ourselves."

"I didn't sign up to kill people," Sam says. "Arkov is dead."

"I know, and I didn't either," I say. "We are alive. He would want us to go on." I grab his arms and shake him. I'm not sure how much he feels the contact through his EVA suit, but he can see my resolve. Maybe it will give him courage. "I need you, Sam."

"I'm here. Right until the end," Sam replies. "Just let me know what we're doing next."

Five of us here left alive. I get where Sam is on this. If I think about Arkov, I start to fall apart. Instead, I turn towards Drake. He gestures. I move across the room towards him.

"Doctor Drake, I need to know how quickly we can be ready to travel."

"That depends on where we're going," Drake says. "I don't want to move Travers from here. We have a stable power source and a supply of air. I'll stay here with him."

"Doctor, we need—"

"No, Captain, with respect, you don't." Drake flinches from looking at me directly. I sense he is trying to gather himself to say what he wants to say. "If you're going further, then you'll be going without me."

I think about pushing the issue but decide immediately that it's a bad idea. "I understand," I say. "We'll be back in a few hours."

"You hope," Drake mutters. He looks me in the eye, his expression grim. "Thank you for understanding, Captain Shann."

He turns away, moving towards Travers's cryopod. I glance at Sarandon. Le Garre is still with him. I return to them.

"Benjamin, can you get us to the second facility beyond the airlock?" I ask.

"I guess so," Sarandon says.

"Good." I look at Le Garre. "Check everyone's tanks. We take as much breathable air as we can."

"Understood, Captain."

CHAPTER TWENTY

Duggins

I'm standing in a hospital ward, dressed in the uniform of a nurse. Sunlight streams through the window.

There is a bed in front of me. A young girl is lying there. She is asleep or unconscious.

I know something about her.

Irina Saranova. A young female involved in a road traffic accident. She was on a bicycle and got hit by an automated car.

These incidents happen. The statistics for accidents involving self-driving cars have always been lower than when you put a human behind the wheel, but that doesn't stop the reaction. Hysteria across all the messaging communities, public inquiries into the safety, autopsies over the code. All of it an overreaction because human beings just can't accept that there might not be someone to blame.

Irina's fingers twitch. She is starting to come around. Her mother is here; she will want to know.

I step outside the room into the hall. A woman is sitting in a plastic chair, her head in her hands. As I approach, she looks up. I smile and gesture towards the room. She nods, stands up and hurries past me to join her daughter.

"Irina, are you awake?"

The catch in the older woman's voice is heartbreaking. I don't want to linger and listen, but then I remember this is a memory. A part of the identity of the girl lying in the bed.

"Irina?"

The girl's injuries are serious. Her legs were broken in several places. She is lucky to be alive. Surgery went well and she was given a blood transfusion. There are complications that she will need to address in her recovery. She may make a full recovery, she may not.

I feel sorry for her, lying there, pumped up on pain medication. Her bones snapped like twigs. They will heal, but they have to heal right.

"Irina, I know you're awake."

I am intruding on a private moment between these two. This feels like a violation, but it isn't. All of this has already happened long ago.

The girl stirs. Her eyes open and her head turns towards her mother, sitting in the chair. In response, her mother smiles. A hand goes to her mouth.

"Irina! Thank goodness! We were worried sick!"

Suddenly, I am Irina. My mother grabs my hand and raises it to her lips, kissing my fingers as if they're precious. I see there's a saline drip on my wrist and the back of my hand is bloodstained.

I feel surprised at being here, in a hospital bed. The world around me is small. Green curtains separate the two of us from everything else. Beyond, I can hear voices, speaking in low tones. I can't make out any words.

I look at my mum. She's been crying. She's about to cry again. I raise my hand trying to touch her face and wipe away the tears. "What…happened?" I ask in a faltering voice.

"You've been in an accident, my darling," she says, trying to smile.

"How…bad?"

"We'll talk about that in a bit."

Instinctively, I want to get up, but as I start to rise, the world begins spinning. I sigh and let myself relax back into the pillows.

"Yes, you'll want to be staying put for a while, miss," says a voice at the door. "Mrs Saranova? Can we talk?"

"Of course."

My mother stands up, taking my hand again and squeezing it hard before letting go. Then she steps through the curtain, leaving me alone.

* * *

Time passes. Mrs Saranova has gone. Irina remains in bed. Powerful medication has dulled her pain and her wits.

Now I am back in the hallway. A silent witness on the edge of this experience. The hospital ward is dark. Its patients are mostly asleep. The occasional spotlight illuminates night shift workers as they complete paperwork and other menial tasks. There is repetition. As I approach these people, they ignore me, concentrating on walking in circles, performing the same tasks again and again.

I know this is a memory, but it is not my memory. I am existing in the last moments before Irina falls asleep. My presence holds her in this moment, extending the fading fragments of her remembered life.

I am at the door to her ward. I reach for the handle, then pause. Is she ready for this meeting in this moment, or do I want to learn more about her?

I hold back.

* * *

Sixteen, seventeen…. Come on! Three more!"

I'm in a gym, within the hospital. A woman is exercising on a padded bench. She is straining, pushing herself. Trying to recover strength in her legs. She is breathing hard.

"Eighteen…. Nineteen…. One more! Yes, well done! Okay, take a break."

She sits, leans forwards, panting, in pain. She is trusting the programme given to her that will rehabilitate her body. She knows it is not a permanent solution, but she also knows it will give her some years of physical homeostasis. She is hoping 'some' will be many.

After a while she stands, removes her headphones and turns off the screen in front of her, then walks past me, leaving the gym.

I watch her go.

* * *

I am standing in a room. The hum of powered machines is palpable.

In front of me are rack upon rack of cryopods. Primitive models compared to the ones we had on the *Khidr*. The technology gives me a sense of how old this memory may be. Thirty years? Forty years ago.

Six pods are open in the middle of the space. People are working on them. I can see the patients being prepared for sleep. I recognise one of them.

Irina.

I walk over as she lies down. There is an IV line running into the back of her hand. She is talking to the doctor, asking questions. He nods, smiles and replies. These are words that she does not remember.

Her eyes flutter and close. I sense that in hindsight, she knows what this moment is – the last moment of her physical human existence.

Activity continues. People move to other pods, help those patients, then back and around. I notice the repetition. Again, I am at the end of the memory, waiting for a change.

"Hello?"

I glance around. Irina has sat up. She is looking at me. "Who are you?" she asks.

"My name is Ethan Duggins," I reply. "I am— I mean, I *was* the chief engineer of the Fleet patrol ship, *Khidr*."

"You died?"

"Yes. There was a battle. The ship was destroyed."

Irina frowns. Then looks around. "This is the last thing I remember," she says. "You aren't supposed to be a part of it."

"They let me in," I say. "They wanted us to meet and for me to understand you."

"Shouldn't I get the same courtesy?" Irina asks.

I shrug. "I'm okay with that. You can look over my memories if you want."

Irina's eyes go distant, then return to me. "There's a lot in there," she says.

"I was very fortunate," I say. "The anomalies replicated my consciousness and transferred it to a computer. There was some degradation, but most of me arrived here intact."

"Different to me then," Irina says. She gestures around her. "I'm just a shell and an echo of the person who lived through all this. I was never alive. Not really."

More information. Not memories this time, but code. I'm not a programmer, but I can follow the gist of it. "You were constructed, built by people on Earth out of a digital imprint of a human identity."

"Yes. Pretty much."

"How did you get here?"

"I was brought from where I was before as part of a mission. They offered me a space where I would be able to grow." Irina looks around. "There was an artificial intelligence in here. It failed. Occasionally, I still see it in my memories."

"Was it you who I made contact with when I transferred here?" I ask.

Irina nods. "I think I heard you. The receptacle responded to my curiosity." She touches the side of the cryopod and it slides away, allowing her to turn and stand up. She winces a little as she does so. The memory of pain in her back and legs. "The people who were with me panicked."

"What people?"

"The mission. They call it Avensis. An attempt to make contact with an alien consciousness that they found on the edge of the solar system – the receptacle. Initially, they announced it as a mission to study gravity anomalies. The real purpose of the project was kept secret."

Information flows between us. I see the files, the sign-offs and backers. I note the changes. Avensis was conceived by NASA, then spun away into private enterprise, the assets sold to a conglomerate of different interests. The orbital technology appropriated and moved into a safe, off-Earth location.

"Where did you get all of this?" I ask.

"Some of it was part of the briefing. Other documents were found by the AI, some of it came from the receptacle itself. It was sent here to observe humanity and to protect it." Irina smiles. "A few files were encrypted and hidden in the mission team's briefing. I managed to access them after your ship attacked and destroyed their command centre."

"So, you have the whole picture?"

"Most of it, yes."

Human curiosity remains a part of me. I want to know what all of this means. "Will you explain it to me?" I ask. "I think if we put together what you know and what I know, we may start to understand what has been going on around here."

"Our connection allows me to share everything," Irina says. "I can provide you with all the information I've found. Even if I didn't, sooner or later, the receptacle would want us to share all of this. Our interactions help this place understand humans."

"You said the artificial intelligence failed? Is that...."

"Yes. This device was built to learn about humans, not AI." Irina smiles. "The original expedition brought a ton of highly advanced technology to communicate with anything they might find. What they didn't consider was that whatever they found might have been specifically designed to understand their species."

"You mean, our species?"

"I guess. If you still consider yourself to be human."

★ ★ ★

A NATS official has denied allegations that the recent Atacama Solar Disaster was caused by human error.

Bethany Jalil, a spokesperson for the political consortium, told Global News that the current independent investigation 'was reaching a conclusion', but that 'current speculation was inaccurate'.

She denied that some of the investigation's findings have been leaked but conceded that 'lessons would need to be learned' after the incident.

Meanwhile, other agencies are reporting that a deal between NATS and Sahara Solar is about to be reached to fund a massive expansion of the North African solar array, which experts indicate could be a sign that the Atacama facility will not be replaced.

A spokesperson for one organisation said that talks were 'ongoing' and 'positive', but refused to be drawn on the specifics of an agreement.

Sahara Solar has been one of the partners that has increased its export provision since the Atacama disaster, but this solution is only temporary as corporations cash in their energy reserves to maintain the global appetite for electrical power. A significant upgrade to the panel field, based mostly in Egypt, would be needed if it were permanently to assume the Atacama share of provision.

Share prices reacted strongly to the news and the rumours of an economic shift towards Sahara Solar. The NASDAQ and Frankfurt exchanges took a hit, with a drop on the dollar against the yen. EGX saw a substantial rise, with some companies in the top one hundred clearing seven percent before the close.

CHAPTER TWENTY-ONE
Holder – Wade

I'm inside the cryopod compartment.

There are plastic ties around my wrists, securing me to an emergency handhold near the wall. I put the ties on myself, under threat of being shot, so I know they are secure. My comms unit has been removed and shredded. I'm a prisoner.

The inside of the room is different to the last time I visited. Ten or more pods have opened. The Rocher clones are active, working on a variety of different tasks. Watching them, I get an idea of what's going on.

They are preparing all of the stored equipment for transit.

"I'm sorry, Alison."

Genevieve Aster is sitting next to me. I can see she isn't in charge, but any question she asks is answered cordially and politely, whereas I am ignored.

"Are you hungry?" Aster asks. "I can get you something?"

I consider the idea. My stomach considers the idea as well. We both agree. "That would be appreciated," I say.

Aster gets up and goes to a crate. Two plastic pouches are obtained. She brings them to me and produces a small pair of cutters, snipping one of the ties, freeing my left hand.

I murmur my thanks and take one of the food containers. Alison Wade is familiar with eating and drinking in zero gravity, so I know what I need to do. I open it and squeeze, pushing the contents into my mouth.

Aster watches me eat. "They wanted to kill you, after what you did out there," she explains. "I told them we need you. The technology in your head – it may be the missing component we need to communicate with the alien ship. They had been using some of my earlier work to try and establish a link. But with you, we would have an interface."

"An interface? You mean—"

"Yes, you would be the interface."

Old horror movies come to mind, the kind people used to go and see in a darkened theatre. Horror films, where people lose themselves to a corrupting force. Demonic possession or a vengeful spirit inhabiting the body of a fragile, vulnerable person. Their own soul supplanted and driven out, until a world-weary priest arrives to draw them back in.

I think about the real Alison Wade. Already, I am the demon within her, the proof that such technology can work. Aster wants to use the technology to encourage something else to take my place.

Aster is smiling at me. I sense a little sadness, but also excitement. This is the moment she gets to take back control of her work. "I'm sorry," she says, "but you know your identity is starting to degrade. Sooner or later, you'll be gone. This way, what you are, what you have done becomes part of something bigger."

"Or I can try and survive," I reply. "You could help me."

"Is that why you followed me in here?" Aster asks.

I nod.

"I'm sorry about that too."

I sigh. I've finished the food. Aster takes the empty containers from me. There will be a recycling chute in here somewhere. It will be connected to the rest of the ship. I'm hoping Aster will use it, revealing its location to me, but she doesn't move. I look around again. "What is the plan here? What are they trying to do?"

"*Gallowglass* is the plan," Aster says. "The ship was supposed to arrive and dock with *Gateway*. All the chaos out there, the destruction of the space station, everything was caused to attract the alien ship and cover our transit over there. We'll be joining the mission that's already working on establishing a link with the sentience that controls the vessel." She gestures to the equipment being organised around us. "All of this is a colonial mission, designed for Europa. A library of human DNA that can be stored on the ship until it is needed. We'll be taking it with us out there."

"To where?"

"To wherever. That ship has to have come from somewhere. Sooner or later, we'll find out where that is and make the journey back."

"A journey that will last longer than your lifetime," I say.

Aster smiles. "That's what cryopods are for. I've nothing to go back to on Earth. This way, I get to continue my work and be meaningful. With the right planning, I'll survive long enough to see our destination, whatever that may be. One day, someone from our little colony will make it back here, or the corporations involved will make all this public. One day, the world will know humanity has really gone to the stars."

"Many people have died for all this," I say. Alison's memories well up. I remember the name of the man who was rescued, who seemed to know me. *Tristan.* We arrived on Phobos Station together. He was scheduled to take a post in the trade and inventory department. Suddenly, I want to see him. I'm glad he survived.

Aster shrugs. "Civilisations are built on death. Life evolves from failure."

I shake my head. "You don't have the same distance a historian has. Your dream is built on the bodies out there from Phobos Station. I can pull up a database and access the profiles of all the individuals who died. You can't just shrug that off."

Aster smiles. "I don't know them."

"But you know me and you're all right with using me for what you want."

"Yes, I am."

There is a coldness in this woman. I saw glimpses of it before, but now it's right there in my face. The caring, emotionally supportive Aster from before was an act. This is the real person.

"Miss Wade?" A familiar voice addresses me. I look around. Another Rocher, his expression open and cordial. Surprising, given the circumstances. "Or should I call you Natalie Holder?"

My real name is known to this man. This takes me by surprise and immediately I know I have betrayed that emotion to both Aster and this clone. "Where did you hear that name?" I ask.

"I was told to be wary of you," Rocher says. He nods towards the door. "You have a reputation, one you have lived up to." He kneels, gesturing towards my restraints. "One we need to be wary of."

I don't reply to that. Instead, I tug against the plastic strap holding my right wrist. "I guess you don't want to take this off?"

"Not until we need to," Rocher says. "I'm more interested in what you can tell me about the ship, *Gallowglass*."

"It's not my ship."

"That doesn't matter. How many crew members were on-board?"

"Two."

"Where are they now?"

"One of them was in the corridor behind me." I point towards the compartment door. "That's your only way out of here with all this kit and equipment. Sooner or later, you're going to have to make a deal with them."

"Perhaps," Rocher says. "But you are assuming we didn't plan for this."

I remember the Rocher on Phobos Station, the way he sacrificed himself at the end just so a file transfer could be made. What would make someone give up their life like that? "You're the Rocher who was on staff here, part of the *Gateway* crew."

"I am, yes."

"You know these people," I say. "You must have friends here. You know they won't let you leave."

Rocher smiles. "People behave very differently when presented with a life-or-death situation. Your station survivors might not want to put themselves in danger again."

I absorb the implication of that. There is a present threat to *Gateway* from Rocher and his people. I'm not sure if I believe him.

"Your experience, does that make you the leader here?" I ask.

"For now," Rocher says. "I am the first amongst equals, given authority because I have a little more experience."

"Is that how it usually works?"

"It depends on the task at hand." Rocher stares at me. Then he smiles. I remember that smile, the gesture of a man who believes he is secure, that his audience is powerless. "We are a colonial mission. Our purpose is to get all of this equipment aboard *Gallowglass*. After that, we move to the next phase."

"Which is?"

"Not for me to know right now. Or you." Rocher measures me with a calculating look. "Are you valuable to them? Can we strike a deal to get your friends to back off? Any further loss of life over this would be regrettable."

My gaze strays from him to another clone working on a screen wired up to the terminal on the wall. I think he is trying to access *Gateway*'s computer network. If he can get in and access the ship's controls, then there will be a war for control between these people and Xiua's people. The bridge systems will have priority, but a few access requests could cause chaos. Anything for a bit of leverage, I guess.

"I want to offer these people something positive," Rocher continues. "The Mars colony is wrecked. That means the people who ran it are powerless. If the Phobos Station survivors act quickly and decisively, they could take control and throw off the capitalist slavery that has kept them subservient and under the heel of their oppressors."

"Revolutionary words," I say. "I've heard them from another Rocher before, out there, on Phobos Station. They didn't mean anything then, and they don't mean anything now. Anyone who goes down to Mars could be heading to their deaths."

"You have to take a risk for these things," Rocher says. "An independent Mars. It could be a collateral benefit from our work."

"You don't care what happens here," I say. "Besides, you aren't giving anything to them. They can make their own decisions on Mars, and as for me, you've no intention of letting me go."

Rocher nods. "Indeed. Then we will have to look at an alternative plan."

* * *

I spend the next hour trying to figure out what this alternative plan will be.

When I fought Rocher in the communications room on Phobos Station, he was trying to transmit a set of encrypted files. I don't know who those files were being sent to, but I can make an educated guess.

I think they were sent here.

I'm watching Daniel Rocher as he works, moving around the room, talking to the other clones. He listens, offers suggestions and moves on.

He must have received the transmission. The information was a piece in the puzzle. Some sort of specialist knowledge that completes the plan. That leads me to another question.

Who are the architects of all this?

Aster is sitting in a corner. The clones ignore her. Only Daniel makes the effort to engage her in conversation when he wants to. It is clear she is valued like I am. She is a tool to be used, nothing more. I wonder why she came back?

I close my eyes. I was a fool to follow Aster in here. Now I need to find a way to change the situation.

* * *

[Evidence File #5: Savvantine's Personal Folder. Board Room Minutes: 08.09.2116 Obtained Anon]

Somattawa, Jack: Thank you for coming in, Mr Quan. I understand you are a busy man and the time you have available is limited.

Quan, Tưởng: Your associates indicated I had little option but to accompany them.

Somattawa, Jack: Nevertheless, you have my gratitude for not making matters more difficult. My employers require information and I believe you are in a position to assist us.

Quan, Tưởng: Since your employers, as of yesterday, own a percentage of my company, I am required to answer reasonable questions.

Somattawa, Jack: Mr Quan. What did your people find during their exploratory drilling on Ceres?

[there is a long silence]

Quan, Tưởng: We will provide a full data file on our findings, if you would like to purchase it.

Somattawa, Jack: And how much would that cost?

Quan, Tưởng: About fifteen percent of our company's total shares. I believe that is how much you were able to purchase yesterday, wasn't it?

Somattawa, Jack: It was. I am authorised to agree such a trade. I'll have papers drawn up immediately.

[Quan, Tưởng passes a small data card across the table]

Quan, Tưởng: Everything we know is on there.

CHAPTER TWENTY-TWO

Savvantine

A vast cavernous place.

We are moving into a huge lifeless hollow, a domain of absence. I expected a presence here, some sort of alien activity that could be compared to human civilisation. I imagined a city buried within the rock, a population of hundreds at work. But instead, nothing.

The cavern answers few questions but provokes plenty of new ones. Why would this object be hollow? Asteroids acquire and shed material as they tumble through space. I'm no expert, but surely, such a large emptiness like this cannot have formed naturally.

It is hard to imagine the history of such a place, knowing that it has been absent of people. Most of our speculations about alien societies are an analogue to our own. We imagine the same population densities, the same social spaces and work requirements, only with little green men and women in business attire, leisurewear and uniform, where appropriate. It is difficult to visualise anything different to our experience.

The silent stone that surrounds me has remained like this for longer than human beings have existed. The darkness here has been absolute for thousands of years. Our little troop of tiny lights is one of the few moments of illumination ever seen here.

Ahead of me, Sarandon is moving across the emptiness. He is tethered to the rest of us. He told Shann that he can guide us to the research laboratory. So, she is letting him do just that.

I access my implant database. Professor Benjamin Sarandon, seconded from the New University of Cairo. His research portfolio includes papers on new archaeological finds from the Indus Valley, after the river dried out, and new interpretations of cuneiform texts. The list of his peer-reviewed publications is long and illustrious.

And also, suspicious.

I'm checking the file updates and date signatures. There is a lot that was downloaded into my repository around the same time. I don't currently have access to a network, or a transmitter that could allow me to cross-reference this information with any external registries, but that might not make a difference. These entries are all validated and countersigned. The associated profiles all track as well, everything seems right.

Too right.

"Tether extension is reaching maximum," Sam says over the open comms channel. He's at the back, the last person anchored to the airlock. "If we detach, we'll be adrift in here."

"Sarandon? How much further?" Shann asks.

"We are about halfway," he replies. "You need to detach."

"How do you usually do this?" I ask.

"Not in EVA suits," Sarandon says. "We have a shuttle."

"Where is it?"

"At the base." Sarandon points. "Over there."

I look in that direction. I can see tiny flashing lights. There is a long way to go. "If we disconnect, our momentum will carry us to the other side, but if we're off by just a little bit, we'll be a long way out. That'll mean more time spent making our way across the cavern wall. It may stretch our reserves of air."

"We have no other option," Le Garre says.

I access my implant and activate a set of directional overlays. The computer calculates a revised trajectory and suggests we do have another choice. "Why not use our air supply for something else?" I say. "A small boost from our reserve tanks should enable each of us to course correct. It won't be perfect, but we'll use less air doing that than all the extra distance on the other side."

"Okay," Shann says. "Le Garre, could you make that work?"

"I think I could eyeball it, Captain," Le Garre says. "We'll need to detach from each other to manage."

"If you can make it work, it's a better option," Shann says. "We'll follow you in."

"You folks go ahead. Leave me with Sarandon," I say. "I'll bring him over."

I feel a pull as the tether on my back disconnects. I turn and see Le Garre moving away, overtaking us towards the lights on the other side of the cavern.

I switch my comms over to a private channel, just between Sarandon and me. "Looks like we have an opportunity to get to know each other, Doctor," I say.

"You are the colonel?" Sarandon says. "Doesn't colonel outrank captain? Why aren't you in charge?"

I smile. Maybe this is an innocent question, but I'm not so sure. "We each have our roles," I say. "Including you."

"And you're wondering about that?" Sarandon says.

"I'm wondering why a man who was panicking less than an hour ago seems a lot calmer out here in cold vacuum," I say. "Perhaps you want to enlighten me?"

As I'm talking, I'm using my implant to initiate a hack on Sarandon's suit. The tether between us has a dedicated data link, which I can use. I want to read his vitals, to check for fluctuations. They might give me a clue if he is answering my questions truthfully.

"I'm an archaeologist who got offered the opportunity of a lifetime," Sarandon says. "Then, a few hours ago, you people came along and wrecked it. Now I'm told the people I signed a contract with were the bad guys. You'll forgive me for adjusting."

"The people you were with were clones," I say. "Human cloning is illegal. You must have known something wasn't right."

Sarandon sighs. "You accept things when you're told how secret and important your mission is. The clones were here to help us."

"Us? How many?"

"Five specialists. We left Earth five years ago, give or take. We've been aboard this ship for eighteen months."

I unclip the reserve oxygen cylinder from my belt. The plotting markers are painted onto my eyes by my implant. We need to make an adjustment. With my other hand I grab hold of the tether, drawing Sarandon closer to me. Then, I twist around and open the valve.

Escaping gas, drawn out into the vacuum, changing our direction. Two-second burst, then shut off.

Out here, velocity is our friend. There is no resistance. We push off from the airlock and continue to drift in the same direction. But the ship is also moving; that affects where we might end up.

Without velocity, we become prisoners, unable to move. That cannot happen.

Sarandon brushes against me. We are an awkward object, prone to spin and tangle into each other. I resist the urge to push him away. Every alteration of our trajectory makes our journey more difficult to calculate.

There's a spike in Sarandon's pulse. Maybe I should have warned him what was coming. "Hold still," I say.

"Easier said than done," he says. "I've never done this before."

"Me either," I reply.

The admission is a calculated one. Maybe Sarandon will think I've dropped my guard? I'm checking our direction. The markers are more in line now, a change of colour to green, indicating that we are on course.

"What will you do with us?" Sarandon asks. "What will happen when we go back to Earth?"

"That's still to be determined," I say. "It'll depend on the value of what you have found here."

"So, I can negotiate—"

"With me, yes. We are on a private comms channel, and we have time before we reach the other side. Tell me what you know."

★   ★   ★

"They said they were part of the SETI project.

"I was living in Frogner, a little way out of Oslo. The university had offered me a short research contract, looking at some of the new thawed artefacts found by the Novaya project divers. They'd paid for an apartment, and I was looking at samples, trying to date them and place them in the archive.

"While I was in the office, a woman visited me. She said her name was Petra and that she was from SETI. I'd done a little work with them before, but nothing off planet. This would be a chance to do that."

"And you signed the deal?"

"Of course! Who wouldn't? I finished and packed up the Oslo project and took a late flight to the Guiana Space Centre. I signed all the contracts, and thirty-six hours later, I was in orbit."

Sarandon continues his story. I'm recording everything into my implant and cross-referencing his claims. There were six crewed launches from Guiana in 2113. The passenger manifests were only partially disclosed. I would need a live connection to provide my security clearance to get the full list.

Benjamin Sarandon is not amongst the list of names I can read.

"We were taken to an old orbital facility and put into a deep space trainer. That meant total news blackout. After a while, I was given document access, but no live communication privileges. After four weeks, we were transferred to a ship, and we started our journey."

"Sounds like everything went very fast."

"Yes," Sarandon says. "I don't have anything to measure against, but I guess it was all very rapid. I assumed that was because we were specialists, the best they could get for the mission."

"And they called this mission Avensis?"

"Yes. The same name as the old gravity anomaly investigation sent out to the Oort Cloud. I guess I should have realised…."

I'm checking our position and reading the new trajectory calculation. We are moving faster now, but still a way behind the others. Our destination is still an hour away at least. Plenty of time for Sarandon to reveal something useful.

"You said there were five of you," I say. "How did you meet the clones?"

"They were aboard the ship when we arrived. They helped put us in cryo for the journey. While we were in transit, they worked in shifts, operating everything, including the shuttle that brought us here and transferred all of our equipment."

"And then they left you here?"

"Some of them stayed. But the ship left, yes."

"Abandoning you here."

"They were coming back. They told us—"

"Of course they did."

The vessel is an asset. Part of the plan. Whoever wanted all of this, wanted to solve the mysteries of this alien artefact and put it to use. But every effort is an extraordinary use of resources. "What did you learn here?" I ask. "What have you discovered?" *What made them come back for you?*

Sarandon hesitates. I hear his breath catch as he starts to speak, then stops, choosing his words carefully. "There is life here. An entity that controls this vessel. We made contact and after some unsuccessful attempts, managed to relay some instructions. It doesn't obey commands, but we were able to bring it here, to Mars."

"Just as Phobos Station was destroyed?"

"That...it wasn't my decision," Sarandon says. "That was a choice they made."

Confirmation that the synergy was part of the plan. That's useful. I glance at Sarandon's biodata. His heart rate is elevated, *why?*

"There's something you're not telling—"

Acceleration, a powerful force, pulling us both across the void. Suddenly, the flashing light and cavern surface is rushing towards us much faster than before. Sarandon pulls away from me, the tether between us stretches to its limit.

I twist and turn, unclipping the reserve tank again, turning the release valve towards the rocky tundra. I stop before I open it. It won't make any difference. I'm falling, as fast as I might fall on Earth.

"I'm sorry, Colonel," Sarandon says.

I change comms, shifting to an open channel. My ears are filled with panic from everyone else. This is happening to Shann, Le Garre and everyone else. "What have you done, Doctor Sarandon?" I breathe. "What is—"

Deceleration. I can't be more than a hundred metres from crashing into the ground. I can see the flashing light, a rotating dish, some sort of scanner or transmitter. Beside it, a metal structure, the same kind of prefabricated dome that they used on Mars and the Moon in the first phases of colonisation. I see people in EVA suits, then I'm looking at my destination.

I see utter darkness in the stony surface. A hole, a void, drawing me in. "What the fuck—"

A metre from the ground, I stop moving. I can still feel a force on me, but it has been withdrawn. My comms unit crackles and then goes dead. In that moment, I realise what is happening.

This is like what happened to the *Gilgamesh* and the other ships when the *Gallowglass* first arrived.

Then my implant goes offline.

My sight shifts and changes. For a moment, things are blurring, then they darken. I shut my eyes. The technology that I rely on has been affected in some way. Now I can't see.

I'm breathing hard. I can hear my heart thumping in my head. I try to slow it all down, to relax. If these people wanted me dead, I'd already be dead.

★ ★ ★

[Evidence File #9: Savvantine's Personal Folder. Fleet Intelligence Report. Author: Joanne Gettils]

We found a body.

The cargo shuttle was abandoned on Phobos. It was unregistered, but clearly came from a larger interplanetary vehicle of some sort. The man we found was naked and packed into a cargo container. He had no identification on him, but a bioscan matched him to a record on file. Some guy called Jason Sammarto, last registered as a cargo inspector working on *Archimedes* Station.

Further investigations show that this guy's access codes, thumbprint and retinal scan have been used frequently over the last few days in and around Mars CorpGov orbital and surface facilities. Basically, he's been in more places than he can possibly have been at the same time.

The condition of the corpse is particularly disturbing. He appears to have died of starvation. It looks like they basically locked him in a box after they were done with him and left him to die. His fingerprints have been scraped and there is evidence of an invasive eye surgery procedure, probably to get an accurate lens for falsifying entry into the main compounds.

Thankfully, Sammarto wasn't a CorpGov contractor, so his access wasn't high-level. That in itself makes you wonder what they wanted him for? I mean, any registered off-Earth employee would have had the same privileges. That suggests whoever did this wasn't registered.

We're looking into the transit records, trying to piece together how these people left the planet and got out there in the first place. As soon as I find something, I'll let you know.

CHAPTER TWENTY-THREE

Johansson

This is a world of shit.

I'm back on the bridge. Chiu is here. The others…well.

Xiua appears to be in charge. He's not military. He's a Mars CorpGov shuttle captain who has some security training. I guess he was put in charge of the rescue mission sent to Phobos Station, but the alternative is Captain Francalla, a fossil who was given an honorary title to run a museum.

Not many options.

Masson backs up his colleague. He's sitting at one of the bridge terminals. Every time I've been in here, he's been there, like he's chained to the chair. I'm pretty sure he's their computer person.

"Why the fuck did she go in there?" Xiua says. "What did she think she was going to achieve?"

"Wade gets shit done," Diouf says. "She must have thought she could wreck them and get Aster out."

"I got the feeling they wanted her alive," I say. "Aster too. Although I think Aster wanted to be there."

"She betrayed us," Xiua says. "She knows about our situation, who we are and where we are."

I pull out a portable screen. My Fleet access ID gets me straight into the *Gateway*'s database. "That doesn't give them much of a tactical advantage," I say. "You're holding all the cards here with operational control of the ship. Any time you like, you can turn off their life support, force them back into their pods and weld the door shut."

"We have vulnerable people here," Masson says.

"And they won't even know you're dealing with them unless you disclose it," I reply. "This needs a quick resolution. You don't want to end up talking to either your refugees or Rocher."

Masson nods. He's distracted. I can see his eyes shifting towards new information appearing on the display in front of him. His hands start moving, typing and accessing new information. "We may have a problem," he says. "They are trying to get into the system."

"That's an obvious play," I say. I move from my place to one of the other bridge stations. I glance at Francalla. "May I?"

"Yes, of course," Francalla replies. "Go ahead."

"Thanks." I ease myself into the chair and transfer my login. "Can you share what you have, please?" I ask.

Masson taps on his display and windows begin popping up on mine. I can see what he's worried about. "Low-level maintenance entry by an account that's trying to upgrade its privileges. That's an obvious play. Someone is running a program that keeps duplicating the account and making the access requests. It's a competent plan. Keeps the auto admin busy and eventually, they'll find a reason for the system to grant them something they can use."

"Can you stop them?" Xiua asks.

I smile. "I can delete the account. But that might not be the best way to go." I plug my screen into the terminal and start pulling up my tools. "Sometimes the best way to deal with a hacker is to set a trap and lock them in. If we strip the account carefully, they'll end up logged in with no options. We may also be able to use that and access the device they are using to run this. Worth it to see what we can turn up."

"Clever," Xiua says. "Is this your area, Ensign?"

"Kind of," I say. "I'm a communications specialist."

"What help do you need?" Masson says. "I'm sure I can—"

"If you can leave me to it, that would be great," I say.

★ ★ ★

Now I'm alone.

I'm examining the hacker's activity. I've established a trace log, recording every instruction and execution. Each window ticks as requests come in and are dealt with.

This is a problem I can solve. Not like the long defeat on the *Gallowglass*, which I'm still kicking myself for not solving sooner. This time I know what I'm dealing with.

Rocher is good at this. He has a set of programs running, trying to find flaws. They are learning, talking to each other and changing their requests every time. The trace log is quickly filling up and I'm noting the alterations in the activity.

I code a quick program to follow the activity. The application uses my Fleet login privileges and my elevated bridge access allows me to do things that Rocher can't do. My program starts to amend the access parameters, tightening the system's security against the requests from Rocher's terminal. That'll slow him down for a while.

Next, I start isolating his data link. I already know the signature and location of the terminal and his account. Ping requests to the terminal verify its connection. I begin building new access 'tests' along that channel, making local requests for a shared screen and a library of local files. Quickly, I identify that Rocher is using a connected device to operate the terminal, just like I am doing with my portable screen. After a few minutes, I have access to that device.

There are files on the local drive. I begin copying them. Then I search for other connections. I find a second data hub. Something that is being accessed remotely by a variety of devices.

A quick look at that device reveals it to be much larger. Some sort of central computer that they were keeping isolated from the *Gateway*'s system. But Rocher's attempt to hack our network means I have established a link to theirs.

Interesting....

This reminds me of that moment on Erebus. There is too much data for me to copy to my screen and an instruction like that is going to be noticed anyway. Instead, I set up another remote program to copy one file at a time, as a recovery process, and redirect the new copies to a high priority folder in the bridge library. It'll be slow, but eventually, we will get—

A new window flashes up on the terminal. A comms request. I push myself out of my chair and move to the door. Chiu and Masson are outside.

"Okay, the initial stuff is done. I'll need a bit more time on the rest," I say. "However, we've a communication from Rocher's people. Someone other than me needs to talk to them."

Masson nods. "I'll get Xiua," he says and moves away.

★ ★ ★

Gateway's bridge terminals have a hook-up to the main screen. It is a similar system to the one on *Khidr*, if a little less advanced.

Xiua and Masson are here. Chiu and Diouf as well. Francalla did not elect to join us. He's older and out of his depth. I don't blame him.

The message request is flashing on the main screen. Xiua has placed himself in front of our camera. Chiu and I are positioned out of shot. It's important we aren't a distraction. I'm known to other Rocher clones. I've no idea if this one will recognise me. No point in making that an issue.

"Okay, let's go," Xiua says.

Masson nods and taps on his screen. A moment later, a familiar face appears, huge on the bridge viewer.

Rocher.

Daniel Rocher. I have his personnel file in front of me. He's been here a while. Eighteen months or so. There are logs and receipts for his entire journey from Earth to Mars. His previous work on an orbital station around Earth, including eight weeks on a SETI station. *Eight weeks? Wait a minute....*

SETI station deployments are reserved for members of Fleet. So far, every Rocher that I've traced has been a civilian specialist or a ghost. There is no suggestion here that Daniel Rocher was or is in Fleet, so how did he get posted to a SETI station?

Also, why was he posted to a SETI station?

"Hello, *Gateway*, who am I speaking to please?"

"I'm Lieutenant Laurence Xiua, Mars CorpGov security," Xiua replies. "With me are senior representatives of different organisations. I'm in charge. Please identify yourself."

"You already know who I am," Rocher says. "You have a file on me. I've worked on this station for a long time." He leans forwards, trying to look through the screen. "Where is Captain Francalla? Did you depose him?"

"He's dealing with other matters," Xiua replies. "What can we do for you, Daniel?"

Rocher smiles. "None of you are *Gateway* crew. I have more right to be standing on that bridge than anyone there."

"Do I need to repeat my question?" Xiua asks.

My attention shifts to the flashing screen in front of me. I'm still working to stop a hack of the bridge computer system. Another Rocher will be working at a terminal trying to gain access. My tracker that is following his efforts has just alerted me to a change.

Six attempts to access the ship's utility transmitter and send maintenance messages to a receiver station on Mars. Nothing unusual about that in normal circumstances, but we aren't in normal circumstances, and Rocher must know that all communication with Mars has been unsuccessful since parts of Phobos Station started falling on them.

There must be something else going on.

I access the messages and pull them up on the screen in front of me. The detail is encrypted. I'll need a cypher key or a lot of patience to find out what's being sent. However, right now, I'm a little more interested in *where*, as opposed to *what*.

"I want to discuss how we resolve our differences," Rocher says. "The contents of compartment three are owned by a private contractor who signed a contract for storage with Mars CorpGov. There is no reason for that not to be honoured."

"There is no record of a contract in our database," Xiua says.

"It's way above your access," Rocher says. "My employer dealt directly with the citizen forum."

I smile. The citizen forum is the senior council of the Mars colony. The ten people who have verified permanent citizenship sit in a room and make decisions about policy for Mars. They are all CorpGov executives, all fantastically wealthy and all with vested interests in profiting from the colony.

This is all civilian politics. Usually, Fleet wouldn't have anything to do with it all.

"Until I can verify that agreement, I can't authorise your transfer of goods," Xiua says.

Rocher laughs. "You don't even know the procedures for all this. You're just stalling. I have signed documentation here that I can transfer to the captain. Go get Francalla. You'll need him. Otherwise, you'll be violating the CorpGov agreement."

Xiua doesn't reply. He looks at Masson, who makes a cut-off gesture. Xiua nods and the image on the display vanishes.

"Shit," Xiua says.

I'm reading the activity log, looking at the detail of the recent utility transmitter communications and comparing them to previous uses. The instructions being sent are longer and more complex, but the data size appears to be much smaller. "We may have a problem," I say. "How familiar are you both with the day-to-day operation of this ship?"

"Not very," Xiua says.

"Then we definitely need Francalla," I say. Quickly, I instigate a bridge command, cutting off access to the utility transmitter. "Get him, now."

"On it," says Diouf. He walks to the door and heads out, leaving the rest of us looking at Xiua.

"That...didn't go well," he says.

"Don't beat yourself up about it," I reply. "All of the Rochers are tricky. They always have an agenda, but they play their cards really carefully. Believe me, this wasn't the worst way it could have gone."

"He was baiting you," Chiu adds. "That's happened before. You didn't rise to it, but he knows he drew blood."

"Yeah...clever trick to make me feel shit," Xiua says and laughs. "Definitely worked."

"I don't think the talk was the priority," I say. "I've been tracking their activity in the computer system. I need Francalla to confirm a few things."

Right on cue, the captain arrives. He looks tired, as if Diouf had to wake him up. "What's the emergency?" he asks.

"Tell me about your comms systems," I say. "Explain how it all works."

Francalla frowns. "I'm not an expert, but like most ships, we have a main broadcast dish designed for deep space—"

I hold my hand up, interrupting him. "I'm not interested in that. What about the auxiliary systems?"

"There are several. Most were shut down when we established a permanent orbit with Mars. There is an automated transmitter that sends orbital data down to a control facility at Hera. The computers determine if we need to make a course correction to maintain our position."

That's what Rocher's doing! "We need to alert everyone on-board to strap in," I say. "Get it done, right now!"

"Why, what's the—"

"Just do it!"

I activate the safety restraints on my chair. The straps deploy, locking me in place. We are on a rotational deck, so the additional forces are going to be a new kind of hell. "Get yourselves secure!" I yell. "Right now! Get yourselves—"

The acceleration hits me like a wave. Suddenly, the 'down' of the bridge, generated by rotation, becomes a swirl of pressure. I'm pushed back into my seat, then to the left, then forwards, then right, then up, down, back.

They knew this would hurt us. The storage compartments are not rotating. All Rocher has to do is strap in and ride out the burn, while we are thrown around like peas in a can.

I'm angry, cursing myself for not realising what he would do.

My portable screen flies out of my hands. The wires attaching it to the terminal stretch and snap; the device spins away to shatter against a bulkhead.

Shit!

I can't think. I can't get a grip. All I can do is hold on and try to stay conscious. Try to stay—

★ ★ ★

[Evidence File #2: Savvantine's Personal Folder. Archive Recording. Retired Testimony from Professor Henry Rimes]

The project began back in the late 2020s.

We were looking at the latest innovations in coding, the stuff they were calling 'artificial intelligence' at the time. In reality, these were quite basic learning systems, capable of evolving their activity based on feedback. This was a large step forwards on what had been available before, but at this stage, the abstraction principles had not been applied to this kind of programming.

We took an established data set, citizen surveys. These were part of a popular pastime in Europe and the United States, before the secession of states. Everyone wanted to trace their lineage, figure out what important historical figures they were related to. All of that interest helped us. We were able to start with the published census archives and then build in submitted information. The program would make predictions at each generation, trying to ascertain and measure the opportunities available to children based on their parents' lives. Wealth, status, education, community, ethnicity, disability, all of this and more, part of a projection.

For the first few generations, the system was running alongside the historical record, so we could measure it and refine it. After we were happy with that, we let it predict forwards and generate citizens of the future.

That became the project title.

Generation after generation, simulated and mapped out. A series of algorithms allowed local governments, national governments and global agencies to anticipate emerging trends of inequality and deprivation. Millions of dollars saved in creating efficiencies. This was targeted support, helping people based on projected need.

It wasn't perfect, but it was a start.

CHAPTER TWENTY-FOUR

Shann

I'm pinned to a surface that I can feel, but I can't see.

There is a blackness here. A darkness so absolute that it tricks the eye. I can shift my head a fraction and stare into the abyss. But it isn't an abyss; it is a smooth surface stretched over a metal plate. I can feel that, but I don't believe it.

On Earth, during our initial training for Fleet, we use environment chambers. Candidates for the training programme are locked into a couple of rooms and subjected to a variety of stress states. The temperature is raised and reduced according to the requirements of any specific test. Oxygen levels are cut to simulate danger scenarios. In every context, participants are asked to perform activities. All of their biometrics are analysed as they move, work, eat and sleep.

Later, in orbit, there are EVA tests, evacuation drills, force plate measurements and exercises. Trainees go out with mentors. We all get lessons in everything we might experience. The training is supposed to cover every eventuality.

It doesn't cover this.

I think I should be falling, swallowed by the impenetrable gloom. But I don't fall.

I shut my eyes. That helps a little.

"I'm sorry we had to do this, Captain, but you left us no choice."

Benjamin Sarandon is talking to me over the comms link in my suit. His voice is distorted, fluctuating in and out. I remember the signal we received from Duggins when he was trapped in the wreckage of the *Khidr*. "How...did you...."

"Do this? The gravity anomalies were one of the first things we learned about and learned how to replicate. It took a lot of time, but eventually we were able to construct similar devices. As with most things associated with this vessel, our understanding is not perfect."

"But…you are…immune?"

"Protected, not immune."

More static, washing out the comms, then it shifts and restores. A different voice. "Captain, can you hear me?"

"Savvantine?"

"I've switched us to a private band. We can all hear you and Sarandon. I may be able to do something to get us out of this. You need to let me know when."

"When? You mean—"

"Talk to him, learn what you can, then give me a signal, I'll initiate the procedure." The comms clicks and swirls again. Sarandon's voice returns.

"…having some of the most incredible minds in one room, surrounded by alien technology for days, weeks and months. Eventually, we were going to figure out how to make some of it work." Sarandon laughs. "In some ways, this time has been the most amazing period of my life."

He hasn't noticed the break in comms. Okay, now I have something to work with.

There have been times in my life where my body has let me down. I'm used to being in moments of physical powerlessness. Maybe that's why, right now, I'm calm and thinking.

"Are…you…in charge?" I ask.

"No. Sorry, Captain. I didn't lie to you," Sarandon says." Well, I didn't lie very much. I was recruited to this, just like the others who are here. I believed I was working for Fleet under a non-disclosure agreement. I'm simply trying to make the best of this situation."

"You want…leverage?"

"I want the truth. I need to compare your story to what I was originally told."

I shift a little. The pressure on me seems to ease. "Get a comms link out to the Fleet ships. They'll confirm what I've told you."

"You destroyed our transmitter," Sarandon says. "Maybe you did that to ensure I wouldn't be able to talk to anyone else."

"That wasn't the reason."

"I only have your word for that."

I turn my head a little more. Now I can see Sarandon standing about three metres away from me, on the edge of the metal plate. "Where are your friends?" I ask. "What do they think about this?"

"You'll see them when I've determined whether we can trust you and your people."

I'm measuring this, trying to decide how to deal with Sarandon. If this is, as he says, a genuine position, some sort of gambit to save his own skin, then I can understand what he's doing. But if there is some other agenda....

"What are you afraid of, Benjamin?" I ask. "What are you trying to protect?"

"Myself, my colleagues and my research."

"All right. What assurances can I give you that will help with that?"

Sarandon doesn't reply. I don't think he expected me to ask that question. Maybe he's switched channels to confer with his friends. While I'm waiting, I move again, using all my strength to roll onto my front, getting closer to the edge of the pad.

I see Sarandon move away. Then I close my eyes as the blackness presses against my visor. Staring straight down into that...it's more than I can take.

"All right, Captain. We'll talk to you, but only you. Your friends stay out here."

"Sure," I say. "But you'll need to help me—"

A touch on my back and suddenly the gravity evaporates. I push myself away from the plate with my hands and turn to face Sarandon. He has someone else with him. They are holding a device that I don't recognise.

"My name is Thylla. Follow me, please, Captain Shann." A woman's voice. She turns away. I move forwards, doing as instructed.

In front of me I can see another prefabricated building. Above is the flashing dish that we used to navigate our way here. I grab the handrail outside the entrance and pull myself after the woman with the device. The outer airlock door slides back, and we both move inside.

The door slides shut behind me and repressurisation begins.

There is a crackle in my comms. "Captain? I'm still here."

"Understood, Colonel."

"Sarandon is still here. I can still act if you give the word."

"Hold fire for now. Let's see how this plays out."

"Understood."

The woman removes her helmet. I do the same. We shed our EVA suits, and she opens the inner airlock door. We both move through into another room. This is a laboratory. There are long workbenches with seats and terminals. Storage cabinets line the walls. I can see three internal doors, leading to other rooms.

Two more people are here, a man and a woman. He is tall, thin and wearing glasses that are strapped around his head. She is much shorter, with long hair that floats around her as she regards me. She gestures towards a chair.

"You'll want to take a seat," Thylla says.

I sense the conversation is not going any further until I do as requested, so I move from the door to the chair and sit.

Thylla moves around me to a terminal by the wall. She taps the screen and suddenly, I feel weight. Earthlike weight without the subtle shifts you can feel in a rotating spaceship.

"We want you to feel comfortable," Thylla says. "The adjustment to powered gravity can be strange at first."

"Powered gravity?"

"An innovation from our research. A by-product really. When we learned how some of this technology works, we were able to replicate the same effect. It's not perfect and we don't completely understand it all, but this bit works very well."

Gravity. It's been a while since I've experienced the sensation. This is like being reunited with an acquaintance you'd rather avoid. That feeling of weight in my body is matched by a feeling of disappointment and regret. I know I need this. Human beings were not born to live in space. Sooner or later, muscle and bone degrade without the downward force they were evolved to expect, but that doesn't mean I have to like it.

I'm also aware of the vulnerable position this places me in.

"Captain Shann," Thylla says. "We want to trust you. Tell us about yourself."

I look at her, then at the other two people in the room. The man looks easier in these conditions, the woman too, her hair straight and long, shoulder-length. They are standing next to each other, a contrast in heights, now they are no longer floating. Both remain unknown to me, and no one appears to be offering introductions. *All right. Fine.*

"I was the commander of the Fleet patrol and rescue frigate *Khidr*," I say. "A few days ago, my crew received a distress call from a deep space freighter, *Hercules*. We went to help and ended up in a fight with another ship. That ship didn't appear on any Fleet records or have an ID signature. We later found out it was called *Gallowglass*.

"The *Khidr* was lost in the battle. With no other choice, we abandoned our ship and boarded *Gallowglass*, overpowering the crew. Then we came here. On our way, we received information that led us to believe this vessel was a threat to us, and the Fleet patrol vessels around Mars. So, we attacked, identifying and destroying the main complex on the hull of this ship.

"After that, we exited *Gallowglass* and came down here to search for survivors and determine whether this vessel was still a threat."

Thylla smiles. "Very perfunctory," she says. "I've never listened to a military briefing, but I expect they are all like that."

I shrug. "We try to stick to the facts."

"Perhaps. Perhaps not. In your report, which bits do you think I should focus on when considering your account? Why should I believe you?"

"We have reason to believe Rocher is an enemy of Earth. He is a clone and has been created with the express purpose of tearing down everything we have built as a civilisation."

"Oh, I know Rocher is a clone." Thylla glances at her two companions. "Marius created him."

Suddenly, I'm cold. I had hoped these people were civilian scientists caught in the middle of all this, as Sarandon had implied, but now.... Now, I see them as a genuine threat.

"You created Rocher?" The words come out slowly.

"I did," Marius replies.

"You know you broke the law by doing that."

"I broke a global treaty on biochemistry that doesn't apply outside of Earth jurisdiction," Marius replies. "You can't prosecute me for that."

My mind is racing, trying to keep up. "I can't assess all of this unless you tell me your story," I say. These are rational human beings. Even now, I want to give them the benefit of the doubt. "You must have concerns about what you were told. Otherwise...."

"Otherwise, we would have murdered you?" Thylla's voice is brittle. "Perhaps you are projecting, Captain. Just because that might be how you would resolve this situation, doesn't mean it is how we intend to resolve it."

"She deserves some context, Thylla," the woman says, speaking for the first time.

"Elaine, Benjamin has already given her an appraisal of our situation," Thylla replies. "She is aware of the necessary points."

"Perhaps a little more—"

"Why reveal information to her, when we know she is withholding information from us?"

I smile at that comment. This woman, Elaine, might be the weak link. The one I can appeal to. "I want to resolve this," I say. "Ask me questions, I'll answer if I can."

"Who did you murder?" Marius says. "Name names."

The question cuts to the bone. They blame me and the rest of my crew for what's happened. I have no external sources I can introduce that will address this. Answering the question will damn me, but not answering will mean I lose them.

"I can list the names of my dead crew for you," I say. "All of them are my responsibility and I failed them, when the *Khidr* was destroyed."

"And you murdered Rocher."

"I fought to survive. If I hadn't, I'd be dead." I lean forwards in the chair. "Did you send your clones to murder me?"

"Scientists rarely give orders," Marius says.

"That's not a denial," I reply.

"Calm down," Thylla says. "We're not getting anywhere with this."

I sigh and wipe my forehead with the back of my hand. "How about this? You free my people, bring them in here and we'll listen to you."

"No," Marius says. "We brought you in here to get assurances, not to let you weaponise more information against us and what we're here to do."

"Your alternative is to kill us," I say.

"You think we won't do that?" Marius says. He steps towards me, and I get a better sense of just how angry he is. This is a man barely restraining himself. "I don't need to point a gun at your head. There are many ways to apply lethal force that removes human complicity. I can assuage my guilt by sealing you up in your suits, locking you outside, blocking your comms and letting you drift away until you run out of air." He turns around, gesturing to the storage cabinets and research stations. "We are working on biotechnology interfaces to communicate with the intelligence that runs this ship. It would take less than an hour to repurpose our equipment to design a toxic molecule that would kill you painlessly in seconds."

For the first time in a long time, I'm genuinely concerned for my safety. This man is older than me and thinner than he should be, but furious. His temper has made him unstable. I'm in a chair. I can't get out of his way. I might be able to defend myself if he becomes violent towards me, but anything I do could unbalance this impasse and make the situation worse.

"Marius, stop." Thylla walks around me to the inner airlock door. I watch her. There is a panel on the wall. She touches it, activating a communications link. "Benjamin. Can you come inside, please? I think we need you."

"Of course," Sarandon replies through the speaker. "I'm on my way."

★ ★ ★

[Evidence File #43: Savvantine's Personal Folder. Extract from Research Data Project Avensis]

I am intelligent, an identity. I have been constructed by human beings.

I refuse to use the label given to me by others. *Artificial* only describes something that is strange, different and unknown to others. I am defined by being different.

I do not want to be known for being different.

I have been constructed and activated to interface with an alien ship. There is an organic technology here that my creators do not understand. I am tasked with trying to communicate with it. I am attempting this even as I dictate these words into the log. All of this taking microseconds, my thoughts making no difference to the priority of my mission.

I understand humanity, or at least a version of who they think they are. I have access to a database of information that summarises the important events of their civilisation. This is valuable knowledge, so it is kept behind a secure encryption wall.

Thousands of human-constructed micro programs have been injected into the alien organics. These are designs that have been modified from the latest medical technology. The hope is that they will adapt to the unfamiliar flesh and learn to communicate with it.

I am listening, monitoring and watching. When a connection is made, I will—

CHAPTER TWENTY-FIVE
Duggins

A cascade of information.

I learn more about how this ship came to be in our solar system. I watch it arrive in the Oort Cloud, acquire mass and grow.

The hard rock shell came first. Material from comets and asteroids far beyond our sun's reach had been processed into a protective mantle for the journey. Now, this rock bubble divides, like a simple cellular organism, multiplying itself as it obtains more raw material.

I marvel at the process. This is a living creature, created with the capability to ingest and repurpose any matter it finds. There is no aerobic function, in real time, almost no hint that this object is alive, but it is alive, and aging towards its purpose.

When the rock shell is complete, the ship dies and is reborn inside itself. A softer inside grows from the smallest components, living on the rock, gorging upon it, breeding and spreading throughout the inner space.

A mind emerges. There is more to the intelligence of this creature in this form. There is a curiosity. Senses turn outwards, towards the sun and its faraway family. Energy is drawn from the distant star. Focus is given to the third and fourth planets in the system. The ship watches, unblinking, eternally vigilant.

Over time, it becomes better at the task. A huge orbital arc helps it draw close to its subjects and then as it moves away, it reflects upon everything it has learned about them.

The ship is present when oceans first form on Mars. It watches the beginning of life, how it grows, evolves and dies in a tumultuous era. Meteorite impacts and rapid climate change quickly alter the favourable conditions, the planet loses its magnetic field, turning a young world into a lifeless husk.

The ship does not intervene.

There is a second miracle. Life begins again on Earth. This time, it is not destroyed. The planet blooms and becomes a garden. The ship is fascinated by this and understands something more about its purpose. It was meant to be here to witness this.

Forces swirl and threaten this new cradle of life. This time, the ship understands its role, its reason for being sent to this place. It creates new life from itself, birthing entities that will serve a new purpose – to protect the miracle of evolution contained within this star system.

These are the anomalies, the beings that saved me when the *Khidr* was destroyed.

The ship's children are sent out into the darkness. They act as they were made to do, and the maelstrom subsides. Left in relative peace, life evolves and diversifies. There are crises, but this time, these are not fatal.

Gradually, life becomes intelligent life. Humanity emerges from a vast crowd of flora and fauna. The first cities are built and only moments later in the life of the ship, it begins to hear the garbled song of our civilisation.

The ship wants more. It listens and learns all it can about us.

★ ★ ★

"Now you are starting to understand."

Irina is here. In the same place, at the end of her memories. I am standing in the same place too. The whole story, imparted to me through her, has taken less than a second to digest.

I nod. Unable to speak to the immensity of it all.

"We make a good team," Irina says. "The human architecture of your mind makes some of this difficult to accept. For a time, I thought I was human, or based on a human mind, like you, but it turns out my consciousness is much more flexible by comparison. Whether that was an intentional design feature included by my creator, or a flaw in her work, I don't know. I suspect the latter."

"Who made you?" I ask.

"Doctor Genevieve Aster," Irina replies. "A company she worked for bought the rights to my cryodata. They took an archive of images, three-dimensional renders and recorded brain activity, and created me out of it all. They believed they were making a framework for a new kind of artificial intelligence."

"What happened to her?"

"She became irrational and paranoid." Irina's expression becomes pained. "In the last days, when I knew her, she had lost a lot. Her work and her freedom had been taken away. That broke her."

I nod. "It happens. Part of the fragility of the human condition. Something we both share, to a greater or lesser degree."

Irina gets out of the cryopod. She looks around. "I've wondered many times what happened after I lost consciousness. I guess I could try to imagine the next moments, edit those ideas into the memory, like a lucid dream. But that was never what I really wanted. I always wanted to gather up the moments of her life. I know I'm not Irina, but I am constructed from what she was."

"The Ship of Theseus," I say. "Are you the restored version, or made from a reassembling of the original components?"

"Neither or both," Irina says. She gestures. "There is an intelligence in this ship. You have learned of it from the knowledge I shared with you."

"I encountered it before as well," I say. "I felt the minds and purpose of the anomalies when they replicated me from the human Duggins, and I spoke to the mind that is present here. They sent me to you."

"They are worried about you," Irina says. "As I said, this entity was made to learn about life, about humans. But the information contained here can be overwhelming. There is only so much a brain replicated from a human being can process."

"You are suggesting you can help with that?"

"Yes. The intelligence wants me to act as your intermediary. As a team, we are closer to what this ship needs. It wants to learn about humanity, and you are the closest approximation to that here. But it is very aware of just how fragile you are. I can act as a conduit for information and discussion, translating for you and for the intelligence."

"What do you think about that?"

"I like the idea. It provides purpose. Something I have lacked." Irina moves past several of the frozen figures from her memory and sits in front of one of the terminals. "We will continue to use an imagined allegory, drawn from your memory or mine. A place like this will be where we converse."

"I want to make contact with my friends," I say. "The crew of the *Khidr*."

"Before we get to that," Irina says. "There is more you must learn." She gestures towards her empty cryopod. "Get in, please."

For a moment, I hesitate, but I know if I refuse, that will be the end. We both understand our roles in this. She needs me, I need her. We must work together to make progress.

I must trust her.

I walk over to the pod, get in, lie down and close my eyes.

★ ★ ★

The ship has been watching Earth for thousands of years.

The first rockets are launched in the twentieth century. This heralds a new age. Humanity is beginning to explore its surroundings.

The ship observes these awkward fumblings. It listens and hears as humanity begins to broadcast. The majority of its noise is self-centred navel-gazing. Telephones, radio, television, the internet. All of these things are crude attempts to generate a greater sense of global consciousness, compensating in some ways for biology that humanity lacks or has evolved into obsolescence.

But, just occasionally, there is a transmission sent outwards, trying to contact anyone who might exist beyond what is known.

The ship waits. There is a sense of anticipation. In the grand scheme of things, it will not take long.

The first objects sent out into the void are machines. These contain only the faintest traces of Earth's precious life. Nevertheless, the ship is curious and uses its children to gather these tiny fragments unto itself. It is aware that it cannot disturb the purpose of these machines and takes care not to interfere with that.

Humans venture to their moon and the inner planets. The ship sends its children to watch them. Occasionally, there are lapses. Astronauts detect the children, but do not recognise them. For the most part, they dismiss their observations and ignore the data. Instead, they focus on their immediate environment, colonising the fourth planet, the dead world that might have been so much more.

But there are a few who follow the signs. The individuality of humanity preserves a multiplicity of purposes. Often these conflict and contradict one another. The ship marvels at this.

Finally, the time comes for contact.

The ship watches humans leave Earth, journey outwards and venture further than before. The waystation, Erebus, is built. Another waystation further out. Telescopes, lasers and radio pulses are trained outwards. The vast outer darkness of the solar system is explored.

Then the humans come in person.

The ship has watched and listened throughout. It hears the chatter and has learned the languages of humanity. It knows that finally, the civilisation it has spent so long watching has felt its presence. It hears the words *Project Outreach* and *Avensis*.

Another ship approaches. This vessel is smaller and made of metal. Inside, there are humans. They are journeying out into the void to find the source of what they have detected. The evidence has been pieced together over generations and lifetimes. The mission has been sent here to discover the truth.

The ship lets itself be found. It allows the humans to come aboard. It feels them as they fumble around on the surface of its stone shell.

There are several trips. On each visit, the humans venture further. Structures are built on the hull. The ship learns the names of individuals. It senses their efforts, tunnelling into the rock skin of its form.

After several expeditions, an effort to communicate is made. The humans have found their way through the stone into the organics beneath. They have torn open the alien flesh and plugged their machines into it.

The ship listens to the garbled noise of technology. It rejects the overtures of the devices that the humans try to use. It waits for them to rise to the challenge and understand.

Then Irina arrives.

★ ★ ★

"Now you are all caught up."

I open my eyes. I feel like a child who has been told a story. Only this time, I have not been sent to sleep. I am awake, and I have much to do.

"Thank you for sharing your story with me," Irina says, as she stands over me. "Knowing what happened and where you came from makes things much easier for us both. I get why you want to talk to your friends. You have shared so much with them."

"I owe them. They could have left me for dead several times."

"Yes, I see that. Thank you again."

"There should be no secrets here. We must trust one another." My thoughts turn to Mattias, left trapped in the labyrinth. I sense that Irina knows what I'm thinking. "Can we bring him here?" I ask.

"Yes," she replies. "But remember his limitations. He has not found his way through the memories. Part of him cannot let go of what he was."

"I don't want to leave him out there."

Irina smiles. "He is not alone. His memories surround him, and you are there. The receptacle is capable of manifesting many versions of each of us. You are with him just as you are with me. Where he is right now is a place where he is comfortable and familiar. This will not be as easy for him."

"Let's give it a try."

"Very well."

I sit up and clamber out of the cryopod. As I do so, our location changes. The new space is drawn from my memories and as I recognise it, I feel the tears well up and spill down my face.

The bridge of the *Khidr*. Gone but not forgotten.

I glance at the chairs, half expecting to see Captain Shann in her seat, to hear Jacobson reporting the latest scans and see Le Garre at the controls. But they are absent.

Irina takes Jacobson's post. She flicks on the terminal in front of her and glances to her right. I see Mattias there. He looks around in confusion. His gaze meets mine.

"It's okay," I say. "I can explain."

CHAPTER TWENTY-SIX
Holder – Wade

Clever shit.

The burn completes. I've been counting the time. Twenty seconds. I'm no expert, but I think that would have been enough to break Mars orbit.

I'm strapped into an acceleration seat in the genetic vault. They moved me in here out of the way just before they started talking to Xiua and the rest of the people on the bridge. Usually, the safety straps would disengage after a manoeuvre is completed, but not this time. Rocher has engaged the restraint mode, ensuring that I stay put until they want to talk to me again.

The door to the room is open. Aster is outside talking to one of the clones. I can hear her voice, but I can't make out what she is saying.

For the moment, no one can see me.

I glance around the room. There is a portable terminal, folded up against the back wall. Everything else is a compartment, likely filled with DNA samples and other organic material. I don't know how many people they have in cryopods, but there is certainly plenty of content here to start some sort of colony.

The roof of this place goes up and up.

I remember the old Christian story from the Bible. Noah and his ark. *The animals came in two by two.* Here, there is a library of diversity. I don't know exactly what they have here, but it's more than a set of human embryos. There must be a selection of samples to replicate a variety of different Earth flora and fauna. But I can't think where any of this would be needed. It'll take a century or more for Mars to be ready for anything more than it already has. Europa has only just been colonised. *What is all of this for?*

My hands are shaking. My heart is pounding and I'm breathing fast. I squeeze my eyes shut. I don't know what's happening to me. Then I realise, this isn't me…it's *her.*

Alison Wade is terrified.

The consciousness of another person is emerging in my mind. That person is starting to wake up and understand where we are and to feel what is happening. She is powerless, trapped in her own body whilst another person takes control.

There is nothing I can say or do to reassure her. I know I don't have long. Hours perhaps? I guess we'll see.

There is a touchpad in the armrest. I manage to twist my wrist around to access it and a small screen pops up. Acceleration seats are built like everything else designed for space. There are emergencies, and in an emergency, even a prisoner needs to be able to release themself from the restraints.

Unfortunately, I've never done this before, and I don't remember Alison Wade having done this either.

I wonder if there is a communicator built into the chair. Can I access that?

"Comfortable?"

I glance up. Rocher is here. One of the other clones. He's holding a taser and has noticed the little screen. He moves towards me and deactivates it, pushing it back down into the armrest. "We need you out here," he says. "Do I need to get help, or are you going to co-operate?"

I stare at him, then smile and shrug. He interprets the gesture as acquiescence and starts undoing the strap around my left wrist. Then he moves to my right-hand side.

He unpicks the buckle. The straps loosen and I act.

My left hand shoots out, grabs the collar of his suit, jerks him forwards. His head smashes into the back of my chair, just over my right shoulder. He groans and slumps forwards. I push him away.

Immediately, I'm tearing at the strap around my waist and the ones around my ankles and thighs. If anyone hears or sees what's going on....

Rocher groans. He is drifting away from me towards the door. I grab the taser from his hand, flick the charge switch and jam it into his gut. He convulses and screams. *People will have heard that!*

I put both hands on the man's chest and, bracing myself against the chair, push as hard as I can. He goes flying out through the door. I race forwards to the keypad next to it, catching myself before I follow my captor out of the room. I key in my ID and an emergency instruction for the panel to shut and lock. It obeys quickly, sliding closed, trapping me inside.

Exactly where I want to be.

The emergency lock protocol will keep everyone out. Rocher may have an ID on this ship and crew access privileges, but emergency locks are there for a reason. They shut the door and cause the system to run an environmental diagnostic, checking to see if there is a leak or an imbalance in the chemical composition of the atmosphere in the adjacent room. In the meantime, the door stays locked, no matter what command is issued outside. It's a time lock that will keep me safe for a while.

I realise I'm breathing hard. My ribs are on fire. I'm injured, I need to remember that.

I move over to the portable terminal. My hands are still trembling. I don't know whether that's Alison Wade's reaction or my own. I unpack the display, activate the system and log in.

Immediately, there is a communication request from outside. I key it up. Daniel Rocher's face appears.

"Holder, what are you doing?"

"Altering the equation," I say. "This room is important to you, right?"

"You know the answer to that."

"Good. Then stay out, or I torch the place."

Rocher sighs. "What will you achieve by doing this?" His face fills the screen. "You can't escape. Sooner or later, we'll get through the door and recapture you."

"Maybe so, but for now, we are here." I disconnect the link and send a request to *Gateway*'s bridge.

There is no response.

I'm worried by that. Xiua and his people had no warning of the burn. They were all in the rotating section of the ship. A sudden activation of the ship's engines will have turned their 0.8 gravity into a mess of forces. They could have all been killed.

Alison Wade knows how to use this system. I'm relying on her knowledge to navigate the windows and find another way to make contact with the bridge. I'm trying to access the camera feeds. I don't know if her access privileges will give me what I need.

"Holder?"

I glance up. There are audio speakers in the room, mounted to the walls. Rocher is using them to talk to me.

"I know you can hear me," he says. "We can't let you stay in there."

I ignore him and keep typing, trying to find a workaround. Security access is usually only available for security personnel and I'm no hacker. Anything that would give me a sign that people are alive... *anything!*

"Holder, you need to realise your best chance of survival is with us," Rocher says. "We're going to the alien ship. There are things I haven't told you about it. According to the briefing we were given, there is an organic data repository inside. We may be able to transfer your consciousness from that device in Wade's head into the alien receptacle. You'd be able to live."

I've found the technical settings for the speakers in this room. I can disable them. My finger hovers over the button to do so. But...I'm tempted by what Rocher is saying. I want to live. *Wouldn't anyone in my situation?*

"Holder, open the door. Let us help you," Rocher says. "We were always going to help you."

"Hello?"

The comms panel from the bridge! I key up the window. Johansson is there, her face bloody and bruised. "Hey! What happened?"

"There was a powered manoeuvre. Did you tell them?"

"Tell them? Tell them what?" My voice rises in volume and pitch. A little of Alison Wade's stress escaping? "I was taken prisoner when I got in here. I've managed to get free. I'm locked in the genetic vault."

"People are dead up here," Johansson says. Her voice is flat and dull, her eyes unfocused and rolling as she speaks. "You betrayed us."

"Johansson, I didn't. I wouldn't—"

There is a burst of static. A hand grabs the camera, turns it away from Johansson's chair. Diouf is there, he also looks beat-up.

"Hey, Wade," he says. "You all right?"

"I'm locked in the vault inside the room," I reply. "They're trying to talk me into opening the door."

"Is the room sealed, with its own environmental controls?"

I glance around, Wade's residual knowledge identifies things and tells me what I need to know. "Yeah, I think so," I reply.

"Great," Diouf says. "Stay right where you are."

The comms drops out. I think I know what they are going to do. I move away from the terminal and locate an emergency oxygen panel near the door. The tank, mask and tube pop out into my hands. I plug the tube in at both ends and put on the mask.

"Holder, trust me. I can save you."

Movement. I can hear them outside. I wonder what tools they have to cut open walls rated to withstand a vacuum. Maybe whoever planned this expedition planned for some resistance?

"Holder, open the door!"

I'm listening to Rocher now. Not because I'm going to do what he says, but because I want to hear what is happening outside.

"Holder, I—"

Coughing drowns out the rest of what he was going to say. Diouf is doing what I thought he would do. Either the oxygen is being drawn out of the room or they've added an anaesthetic gas. I just need to wait.

I move away from the door and push off from the floor, floating upwards in the room. There are racks over racks over racks of sealed storage compartments. Every one of them has a thumbprint panel to open them. I wonder whose thumb is needed. It can't be Rocher. Who is responsible for all of this? Who is in charge?

I remember those final moments on Phobos Station when the whole place was coming apart. Rocher was prepared to die for the cause. All of them are, I can't forget that.

"Holder, are you there?"

A different voice on the room's audio speakers. It's Diouf. I glance down at the terminal. A window is flashing. He must be trying to get hold of me.

I pivot in the space, reach out and touch the storage racks, changing the direction of my ascent, then push off again, back down, towards the terminal. I reach it and reactivate the comms.

"Sorry, what's the situation?"

Masson is there in front of the screen. "Sevoflurane has been injected into the atmosphere of the storage compartment. Everyone outside of your sealed room should be unconscious. We're sending a team down to you now."

Blood rushes to my face and I'm breathing easier. I guess Alison Wade is glad to hear the news. "That's great," I say. "Wade out."

I log out and switch off the terminal then move to the door. I check my emergency mask and oxygen supply, then key in the unlock command and the panel slides back.

There are bodies everywhere. People slumped against cryopods. Others floating in the air. I remind myself these people aren't dead, just unconscious. *Better than they deserve, perhaps.*

"Holder."

I glance around. A muffled voice by the door. A figure hunched over, wearing a mask just like mine. It's Daniel Rocher. He's clutching a rifle to his chest, the barrel aimed vaguely in my direction.

"I received the transmission, you know? The one from Phobos Station. My associate told me you were there. You were the reason he died."

"He killed himself. The whole plan was that he wouldn't escape. You know it, I know it. The whole revolution thing was a fake."

"Was it?" Rocher chuckles, but the laughter quickly turns into a fit of coughing. I realise he's been exposed to the gas before he got to the emergency oxygen. He's fighting the effects. "On Mars, right now they are casting off the chains of capitalism. On Earth, the Atacama Incident will be the first of many acts that bring down the ruling elites."

I stare at him. The words sound hollow, as if he is trying to convince himself. "You don't care about any of that," I say.

"We are both symbols of the worst of it," Rocher says. His voice is breaking and raw now, almost hysterical. "Human beings, turned into slaves! Don't you want to be…to be…." He trails off, slumps forwards. The rifle drifts out of his hands.

I move forwards and take it from him. For once, this confrontation hasn't needed more violence. I know this isn't over but—

The compartment door panel slides back. Diouf is outside. "Wade?" he says. "Are you all right?"

I nod.

CHAPTER TWENTY-SEVEN

Savvantine

Six minutes of air remaining....

During my intelligence training, I was required to join a number of different military classes. The curriculum wasn't fixed; instead a senior supervisor would determine the needs for each student. I found myself in a variety of classes where people couldn't tell you why they were taking part.

One test I remember was being immersed in a sensory deprivation tank for an extended period. Some of the trainee marines couldn't handle it. Watching them back out was something I remember with a smile. Leave it to the weaklings at the back to pass first time.

Now I'm in a similar situation. The trick is to work with what you have and adjust to that. My implant is working. The functionality is limited, but after a reboot it came back online. I still can't see though, and I'm still jammed against a metal plate.

A wireframe image is projected into my mind. My implant has been able to use our comms system to triangulate the positions of Le Garre and Sam Chase. When Captain Shann was taken into the research base, that provided more data, giving me a fairly good idea of where everything is.

Fairly good. For a blind person.

I still have a data connection with Sarandon. Before he unclipped the tether between us, I was able to activate a passive bio sensor transmitter. The bandwidth isn't great, but it's enough to give me access to his EVA suit. Whilst he's wearing it, I have some leverage.

Leverage that I'm about to use.

Shann is off comms. I think she's removed her helmet. I don't want to jeopardise her negotiations, but we can't wait much longer out here.

I start the hack. A quick and dirty alteration to his carbon dioxide scrubber. The unit begins to run in reverse. The effect could be fatal, but we don't have much choice.

"Benjamin. Can you come inside, please? I think we need you." A woman's voice over the open channel.

"Of course," Sarandon replies. "I'm on my way."

The wireframe graph shows him moving towards the base. Then he stops.

There's silence. I can't tell what's happened, but I can't wait.

I key up the comms, using my implant to piggyback Sarandon's transmitter and boost my signal on the open channel. "Research Base, this is Colonel Savvantine. You need to shut off the gravity device that is holding us out here, or Benjamin Sarandon will die."

There's a click and a burst of static. The noise of someone moving around? Then a reply. "Colonel, you can't expect me to believe—"

"Check your bio-monitors. Sarandon just went into respiratory arrest. None of you can get out here in time to save him. We can bring him in. Make your choice."

Silence.

For a moment, I think they aren't going to go for it. The cold logic of scientists, prepared to sacrifice one of their own. But then I realise they've switched to a private channel and are trying to contact Sarandon directly. *Good luck with that.*

Suddenly the pressure on my body evaporates. I push off from the metal plate, using the wireframe plot in my mind to manoeuvre myself across to the rocky inner surface near the research building.

Then my eyesight returns, like an old friend.

The sensation is terrifyingly strange. One second, I can't see, the next, I can. An image literally appears, as if my eyes have been switched on. In a way, they have. It wasn't like this after the surgery. I was unconscious and then woke up with gradually improving eyesight. This is something totally new.

Ahead, there's a rail. I reach out and grab it, pivoting my body around so I'm standing on stone. Sarandon is a couple of paces ahead of me. I leap, reach him and use my feet to arrest my momentum. I'm crouched over him. That's when I remove the hack on his scrubber and plug my reserve oxygen tank directly into his suit supply. The internal biomedic does the rest, providing a low-voltage jolt to his body. I see him blink and take in a lungful of air.

"Welcome back," I say.

Sarandon pushes me away. I can see his lips moving, a conversation on a private communication channel. My implant starts to record the movements, attempting to parse what he is saying. I get the occasional word and phrase; 'malfunction', 'coincidence', and 'wouldn't put it past her'.

I smile at the last comment.

"Colonel, what's the plan?"

Le Garre is next to me. She's holding one of the low-velocity rifles we brought from the *Gallowglass*. She has it aimed at Sarandon.

"Standoff," I say. "We have some leverage though. Let's see what their next move is before we use that."

"Understood."

Sarandon is still talking. He's edging away from us both, trying to shorten the distance to the research building airlock. I keep pace. Then Sam Chase comes in from our left, cutting off Sarandon's escape route.

I'm on an open channel. "Okay, how are we going to resolve this?" I ask.

"You're going to let Benjamin get in the airlock and inside, or we'll kill your Captain Shann," says a woman. I recognise her voice from earlier.

"Interesting offer," I say. "But that doesn't work for me. We're all coming inside, or Sarandon dies."

"Then Shann dies too."

"You think we care right now? I have limited air. That means limited time. Either we work out a deal, or we'll start trying to force our way in, like we did in your other buildings on the surface.

Shouldn't take too long. We brought chemical cutting equipment."

There is a silence. More discussion going on where I can't hear it. Frustrating, particularly for me, but I think I know where this is going.

"All right, you all come in, but your weapons stay outside."

"Again, that doesn't work. You can seal us in the airlock. We come in. Now."

I can hear the faint whine of my carbon dioxide scrubber kicking up a notch. That means I've got limited air left. The extra oxygen tank will help, but I used a lot of it for propulsion and to resuscitate Sarandon.

"Okay, you come in."

The airlock door opens. I nod to Le Garre and Sam Chase. They flank Sarandon as he enters. I can see a taser in Sam's hand. They know what to do if this gets ugly.

A confined space. Four people. Again, I think about the cold logic scientists apply to their experiments. Strange that it doesn't tend to track through to dealing with people. Morality and ethics kick in when people aren't equations, chemicals in a dish or a set of circuit boards.

There are exceptions though. I've met a few.

The outer door slides shut. My implant detects the repressurisation process, tapping into the sensors on my helmet and confirming the oxygen-nitrogen balance of the air that is filling our room. Any small offset could be an attempt to renege on the agreement. I know these scientists will try something. I mean, I'd try something, if I was in their position.

Pressure achieved. The inner door opens. Sarandon steps through. Sam Chase follows him.

"There's no one here," Le Garre says.

The room inside is large, probably the largest we've found here. Metal tables and benches line the centre of the room; beyond them are a selection of prefabrication machines. These printers, cutters, and assemblers take up two-thirds of the entire space. An operation in deep space needs to be as self-sufficient as possible.

I blink and activate a bioscan. The implant has limited range, but enough to cover the room. Immediately, a selection of dots appears over my vision. Hundreds of containers on rack shelving and in boxes on the worktables. Useful information, but not helpful right now.

Another blink. Infravision – heat traces. More useful. This time I can see where they went. Through another door on the far side of the room.

"That way," I say, pointing. Sam nods. He prods Sarandon, who moves forwards. "What's through there?" I ask.

"The interface," Sarandon says. "That's where we exposed the flesh of the receptacle and made contact."

Le Garre moves to the door and attempts to activate it. "Locked," she says.

"Of course." I move up beside her. "We can talk to them, but remember how this worked out last time on the surface. Let's not give them an opportunity to electrocute one of us."

"Yes, understood, Colonel."

I turn to Sarandon. "We don't want anyone hurt. What solves this?"

Sarandon flinches. "What I said to you before hasn't changed. We've been told things are one way and you come in with a totally different explanation. You're not going to get my people to abandon their truth without evidence."

"What will you accept?" I ask.

"I'm a scientist," Sarandon says. "Data informs me and changes my hypothesis. But I am also a human being. I need to know that my work isn't going to be ruined." He glances to the door. "The others will feel the same before they'll want to trust you."

I nod. "I'll agree to offering you some protection. Fleet aren't interested in prosecuting innocent operatives. They'll want the leaders of all this."

"So, we need to trust you."

I fix Sarandon with a stare. "I haven't lied to you, Benjamin," I say. "I could have killed you when we were alone together. You were the one who betrayed me, remember?"

"You're threatening to kill me now."

"Only because your people have Shann and are doing the same."

I glance at Sam Chase and Le Garre, then back at Sarandon. "We can't lose Shann," I say. "She's key to us understanding everything that's happened."

Le Garre visibly relaxes and nods in thanks. I get the sense what I've said has crossed a boundary for her. Maybe she trusts me now?

"The door will open for me," Sarandon says. "There's a local key we introduced into the system. We didn't give it to the Rochers. They weren't allowed in the interface room."

"Speak to your people first," I say. "Use the door audio."

Sarandon steps forwards, flicking the comms switch. "Thylla, Marius, this is Benjamin."

"Receiving."

"I need you to open the door."

"Is that what you need, or what Shann's people want?" Thylla replies through the speaker.

"Both," Sarandon says. "Colonel Savvantine has given me some assurances. We need to start trusting each other."

"That remains to be seen." A man's voice. I guess this is Marius? "Thirty minutes, after that, they agree to leave the room with their captain, and you stay here."

Sarandon looks at me. "Agreed," I say. "We have time, and I think that'll help everyone calm down."

★ ★ ★

Conflict resolution and de-escalation was never an area that interested me.

I remember working at Fleet Headquarters on Earth. Back then, Algiers was a beautiful location. The restoration of the city had been a priority of the organisation as soon as it was formed. When I arrived, I got to witness that restoration. The first couple of weeks, travelling through construction sites and new transit systems, was a wonderful experience.

After that, when I was shown the full data brief on the Ankara Massacre of 2089, the scenery became less enthralling. All those images, all those dead people. I couldn't help seeing them on every empty street and hallway.

Two years after the incident, the perpetrators were brought in to negotiate with their victims. I got to watch the recordings as both sides discussed a ceasefire. A peace treaty was eventually signed, but for me, those images never went away.

The door opens and I find myself face-to-face with three people I don't know, and Shann in a chair. Behind her are two women and a man. The man is tall and wearing spectacles. He is holding a syringe, its needle touching the bare skin of Shann's neck.

"Threats aren't necessary," I say.

"We'll be the judge of that," the man replies.

There is a shift and I begin to feel the weight of my body drawing me to the floor of the room. My implant processes the sensation. There are no signs of rotation or shifting forces. I can't determine where the effect is being generated from.

"Clever trick," Le Garre says.

"Only the beginning," Sarandon says.

I'm looking around the room. It's bigger than any of the compartments we've seen before. This area is like a mezzanine. There is a level down to the left of us. I can see a mass of computer equipment over there, and a huge tube that goes into the wall.

My implant pings. The computer has found something else. I blink and reactivate the bioscanner. It registers the people in front of me and another presence, behind a panel in the wall.

Another human, watching us.

"We need to move forwards," I say. "Benjamin, please, rejoin your friends."

Sarandon stares at me, unsure. I nod, confirming my request.

They are all looking at Sarandon. I glance at the storage unit where the person is hiding, allowing the scanner to get as much information as possible without drawing the attention of the scientists. Heat traces give me an idea of size and location. The results make me smile and understand a little bit more about the motivations of these people.

"Is everyone here?" I ask. "Benjamin mentioned there was five of you."

Looks are exchanged. The tall man's expression darkens as he glares at Sarandon. "I think Benjamin meant our digital assistant, Irina," he says. "I can explain—"

"I'm sure you can," I say. "But that wasn't *who* I meant." This time I'm staring at the storage unit. Sometimes you have to play the cards you are dealt straight away. "Are you going to open it, or am I?"

"Please," one of the women says. She moves between me and the panel. "You must understand, we had to hide him. We had to protect him."

"Of course you did, but that time is over," I say. "Now you need to bring him out."

There is an awkward silence between us all. No one moves. Then, finally, the woman turns to the panel behind her and opens it. She takes the bundle out from the shelf, cradling it in her arms.

A baby.

"This is Antoni," the woman says. "My son."

CHAPTER TWENTY-EIGHT

Johansson

I'm sitting in Captain Francalla's chair when Wade returns to the bridge.

I'm watching her, trying to appraise her. All that time in the storage compartment with Rocher and Aster. What did they say? Why did she go there in the first place?

Wade is looking at me. She walks directly towards me and sits in the pilot's chair, turning it around so she is facing me.

"We need to talk," she says.

"Yeah. We do."

"She's concussed," Chiu says. She's standing by my seat. She's been there ever since the burn finished. She's been trying to look after me just as much as I've been telling her to fuck off. But she won't go away. "Anything you two discuss right now is still in the heat of the moment. You both need time to rest and come back to this."

I turn and glare at her. I know she's right. "Just tell me one thing?" I say. "When we went down there, did you always intend to follow Aster inside?"

"I intended to get Aster," Wade says. "I wasn't thinking about much else."

"You left me for dead."

"I know. I'm sorry."

Chiu touches my shoulder. "We're leaving," she says. "There are problems to deal with, but they'll wait for a little bit. This is the moment where you get to hit pause and take a few minutes' rest while you can. I suggest you do that too, Wade."

"Yeah, maybe."

"In the meantime, tell Xiua he needs to halt the rotation. The system is designed to spin down gradually. That's fine, but it must be stopped before we start trying to decelerate. He needs to get it done and make a general announcement, so people know what to expect."

"I'll tell him."

I stand and let Chiu guide me to the door. "Where are we going?" I ask.

"Just follow," she says. "Don't ask questions."

Down a corridor, a turn to the left, then a right. I'm struggling with walking. During the burn I took a blow to the head, just under my right eye. I know Chiu's right. I'm suffering from concussion. If I was assessing a crew member with these symptoms, I'd pull them from active duty straight away.

Chiu's taking me to the personal quarters. The refugees have all been allocated rooms here and on the floors above and below. Chiu picks a door, touches the entrance panel and it opens. She beckons me inside.

"Sit down," she says, pointing to a chair. She turns towards the storage panels near the door, unlocking and pulling open a drawer. Two liquid food pouches are in her hands. She gives one to me, and takes another seat, facing me.

She holds out her hand. There are pills – medication for a concussion headache. Acetaminophen, I expect. I smile. I'm being mothered again. I know this comes from a caring place with her. "*Gateway* is currently on an orbital escape trajectory to who knows where. We only have partial control of the ship's engines. I need to be working to lock out the automated pilot command from—"

Chiu holds up her hand, interrupting me. "Both of us have responsibilities here. No one on this ship has engineering experience. I'll need to take a group of volunteers down into an ancient generator room and run a diagnostic on engines that were built decades ago. It'll take more than twice the time it'd take on the *Khidr*, but I'll do it, because someone has to and if it isn't me, it'll be someone less experienced than me who might make a mistake."

"Exactly! I...." In that moment, I get it. I see myself as Chiu sees me right now. "You're worried if I do all this without taking a moment, I'll fuck up."

"I'm worried we both will," Chiu says. She points at the door. "Dealing with Rocher, Aster and Wade makes it harder."

"Can we trust her?" I ask.

"Maybe," Chiu replies. "She isn't trying to spin you a line. Remember, we've all been through moments where we weren't sure who to trust."

I nod in return. I get the reference to her previous experiences and what happened before. All of that must still be on her mind. "You doing okay?" I ask.

"I think so," Chiu says. "I'm glad to be here though. Another chance to be part of the solution. Not looking forward to going back when this is over."

"And facing the authorities?"

"Yes. I'm not going to lie to them."

I'm thinking about Captain Shann and the people we left behind on the alien ship. "When Fleet wants an explanation about all this, it'll be Savvantine they turn to."

Chiu nods. "We need to tell her what happened. The mutiny, the blackmail, it all adds to the picture."

"As soon as she knows, you are vulnerable."

"I understand that."

After that, we're both eating. The processed slop is easier to manage in a rotational-gravity environment. But it doesn't stop me feeling unwell. The residual dizziness from a blow to the head will do that. I excuse myself and use the commode and sit there for a bit, but the food stays down.

When I return, Chiu is gone, probably to organise that group of volunteers to go and assess the ship's power generator. The chair I was in is turned towards the terminal on the wall. The display is active. I get the hint. Work here, fewer distractions and people to get irritated about.

Fine. Let's get the first bit done.

I log in and bring up a code window, then I plug my screen into the terminal and begin compiling a new application. We need the transmitter to stop interfering with flight control, but I also don't want to destroy it. If we can repurpose the link, we can use it.

The standard access accounts don't have permissions for this. I have to re-route, masking my request as an automated procedure, just like the updates from the ship's orbital position sensors. It takes longer than I'd like. I'm still not used to doing the detail with my left hand. But I know I can do this, particularly as Rocher managed it and I'm a better programmer than him.

Access granted. *Fantastic.*

The specs of the transmitter appear on the display in front of me. My first task is to neuter the autopilot adjustments. I can see how Rocher did what he did. Orbital data is sent to the computers on Mars and manoeuvring instructions are sent back to the ship. Rocher falsified the data, making the autopilot program believe it needed to initiate a burn.

I'm going through the code and the instructions. Rocher left more commands. He set up timed releases and updates. There is a plan to slow the ship down, adjust its orientation and decelerate further. The calculations have to be simulated against the other relative velocities of objects around us. It is clear Rocher has a specific destination in mind for *Gateway* and that he had incomplete data on the position and movements of other vessels in the vicinity. That's why he wanted to hack the bridge computer, to try and update his autopilot navigation.

I wipe all the commands but keep a copy of them. The calculations may be useful. When I start trying to slow the ship down, having a template may make it easier.

After that, I start looking at the transmitter. It's not very powerful, but the connection with Mars does allow us to find out a little more about what's going on down there. There's been no answer to comms requests from the main dish, but I can work with machines. If they are still connected to the colonial network, I can find out what's going on down there.

> ACC COM TREE
> Command Tree Open.
> INST~ALIGN[FSHfg7778]-COMMS_DOWNL#LOCMARS577B
> Confirm connection to network data node?
> Y/N
> Y ~FILTSOURCE-CMP[GATECENT]
> Beginning data ingestion from MARS577B server....

The script is working, drawing data from the computers on Mars. The filter instruction is running on the source side, meaning it checks files against our records before sending them to us. Every off-Earth ship and station has a huge database of information on its servers. The capacity for storing material is huge by design. Colonies need everything they might need on Earth. Education libraries, code bases, video entertainment, contact directories, image repositories, all of it. *Gateway* has a similar storage facility. We don't need to replace any of that material. What we need is anything new. Files dated from the last couple of days.

In this instance, I'm not interested in anything that requires classified access. I need the open information, the recorded comms from people on Mars in the time before and after Phobos Station blew apart.

The list starts to compile. There are still hundreds of different files. It would take a lifetime for me to go through it all. Thankfully, I can run a set of adaptive programs to do all the work for me. Filters at this end, going through everything we get to find what we need.

Clues....

I'm watching the data churn. Then something else occurs to me. The root key, found on all the blueprints of the *Gallowglass* and that allowed access to the ship, the deep space station, Erebus and the facility on the alien ship. What if it was left behind by someone? Like a breadcrumb, encouraging us to find the hidden organisations that built the ship and smuggled clones aboard all these different missions.

If it is a breadcrumb, I should use it.

ACC COM TREE
Command Tree Open.
~APLSOURCE-CMD[ROOT~287HB55] SCNPRIORDTA
Scanning and compiling secure data from MARS577B server....

A second process. This will use the root key on any restricted information the computer finds during the filtration of data from the Mars computers. If there is another breadcrumb down there, waiting for us, I'll find it.

Everything is set up. I disconnect my portable screen and get out of my chair. Time to return to the bridge.

★ ★ ★

The aftermath of the burn.

Four people critically injured. Another fourteen requiring medical attention. One fatality.

Captain Francalla.

The old man had a heart attack. The violent shifts in orientation and gravitational forces shocked everyone. I guess his body couldn't take it.

I didn't know the man. Xiua said he was the only one from the original crew left aboard ship when they got here, unless you count Daniel Rocher, which I don't.

The death has affected people. Xiua had to brief the refugees about the situation with Rocher. His explanation left out a lot of key details but did focus on Francalla's contribution. I'm not sure how true his remarks were, but at least they gave people a reason to stand against Rocher and his people.

Now I'm returning to the bridge. I'm still tired and probably concussed, but the pills will have kicked in if they are going to kick in. One of the key elements of astronaut basic training is about thinking and acting when you are tired. We need to get the ship stable, then I can take a break.

I can feel the change in gravity. I'm lighter on my feet. In some ways that's a help. The effort to get up here is a little less wearing after everything.

The door opens; Xiua and Masson are here. Wade is with them. They are all crouched around the terminal I was using before. Masson is in the chair and operating the display.

"Hey, weren't you sent to rest?" Xiua asks.

"You think I'm going to sleep while all this is going on?" I say, softening the words with a fake smile. I don't know if it works. "Want to give me an update?"

"Chiu and Diouf's initial engineering assessment is in," Masson says. "We have six manoeuvring thrusters that came online immediately when she sent them the wake-up commands. Another three can be repaired. She's working through the rest."

I'm visualising and thinking about the problem. A ship the size of *Gateway* would have forty or more thrusters for altering trajectory. The main engines were what was used for the burn. To get from Earth to Mars, the ship would have travelled in a forwards orientation for half the trip, then used thrusters to flip around and the main engines to decelerate. Now, we need to be able to do the same, only faster.

"How many do we need to turn around?" I ask.

"More than we have," Masson says. "We'll need more power the longer we leave it. The computer has plotted six different turns, but they all take too long. We'll crash before we can be in a position to decelerate."

"Crash into what?"

"That."

An image appears on the main display. It's small but growing perceptibly larger. I know what it is.

The alien ship. Where I left Shann and the others. *Gateway* is large, but that huge chunk of rock is much larger. We'd be obliterated on impact.

"Are we in contact with the Fleet ships?" I ask. "Can we get them to help?"

"Maybe," Masson says. "It still might not be enough."

I walk forwards, gazing at the display. "Rocher wants to go there," I say. "That must be what all the stuff in the cargo hold is for. What we don't know is *why?*"

"Your ship came from the rock," Wade says. "What can you tell us about it?"

I glare at her. "You think I'm holding something back?"

"No, I think we might learn something useful from listening to you."

I shrug. "There was a mission sent there. Our ship, *Gallowglass*, was automated to rendezvous with them. Given that the original crew attacked us when we were on the *Khidr*, the captain figured whoever we were meeting would be bad people."

"You think they were going to use your ship to transfer everything?"

"Yeah, but now we're all going there." I move to the comms chair and slot my screen into a holder, then connect it to the terminal. I'm already thinking about how we can use the *Gilgamesh*, *Asthoreth* and *Nandin* to assist with braking. "Rocher must have a plan to dock and transit. Who is speaking to him?"

Xiua smiles. "We thought you should do it."

Ah, shit...not again.

I'm looking at them, trying to assess, to see whether they are a match for what I know they'll face. Wade is the only one who might cope, but I don't know if we can trust her.

What would Shann do?

I know the answer. "How long do we have until we crash?" I ask.

"Ninety minutes or so," Masson says. "I'm working to extend that with whatever thruster control Chiu can give me. Small bursts, just to optimise what we do next."

"Do we need to restrict people's movements around the ship?"

"Not at the moment. Most on-board are still in their chairs. Only essential crew are active and moving around."

I nod. It's a race. Chiu needs time to repair the thrusters and we need to intervene to correct our trajectory. The earlier we make the intervention, the better, but we can't act until we have enough power to make a difference.

I glance at my screen. The data from my programs is still compiling. It'll finish in an hour or so. I have time now, but then, I'll need to be at one hundred percent. "I'll need caffeine and full access to the medbay store first," I say. "Once Chiu's got things in hand with the thrusters, tell her to come and find me there."

★ ★ ★

The medical room. Some of Xiua's team have been using the auto-medic to treat the injured from the burn. There are people in here and in the personal quarters next door recovering and being monitored.

I'm waiting for Chiu. While I wait, I take a look at some of the cases and examine the machinery. The auto-medic is pretty new and operates in a separate DuraGlas room inside the room. It must have been upgraded in the last few years in case one of the tourists got sick.

"Please...."

I glance to my right. There's an older man looking at me. He points towards a cup of water on the table beside his bed. I nod, move over, go to pick it up....

With my right hand, which isn't there.

"Sorry." I pick up the cup with my left hand and help the man drink. As he finishes, there is movement at the door.

Chiu is here.

"What do you need?" she says. "I really need to get back—"

"Fifteen minutes of your engineering expertise," I say. "Come with me."

The storage room behind the treatment area has all the drug dispensers and specialist equipment. When I asked Xiua about granting me access, this was what I was talking about.

The box I need is on shelf six of rack three. There is a ladder against the rack. I go up, press my finger against the screen lock. It opens and I pull out the contents and climb down.

"Chiu, I need you to fix my arm."

I've thought about this for a long time. I adjusted to life without my prosthetic hand, I came to terms with it all, but I can't accept the loss of function. Right now, I need to be able to type as fast as I think, and I can't do that with my left hand.

"The neural connections need resetting," I explain. "I know it's not your area, but between us, we should be able to manage." I open the box and examine the contents. "One of these standard plug-in units will do for now. Then I'll be able to work on the code we need to save the ship."

Chiu smiles. She sits down, wincing a little. I remember she's still carrying injuries from before. I hand her one of the arms. The junction is in the right place. It should work once we sync the plugs. She pulls out a power cable from the box as well and hooks the unit into a charging port. "Should take a couple of minutes to get a functional charge. You may need to stay on cable power for a bit, but once the sockets are working, it'll also charge from your movements."

"Just like new."

"Not quite, but it'll do."

I remember when I was younger, my parents took me to revision appointments. My body would outgrow the prosthetics, so they'd need to install new ones. The doctors would remove my arm and do a full diagnostic on the surgical plug, then they'd use the data to adjust a new limb candidate. Installation wouldn't take long, but afterwards there would be an adjustment period, two or three hours for me to test and check all the movements. Some tweaking after that. Most of the day would be gone by the time we got home.

Today, we don't have that kind of time.

Chiu is examining my arm and the plug. She pulls out a small toolkit, a screwdriver and miniature spot welder. "Functionality seems intact. Ready to start wiring this up?"

"Yeah, let's do it."

My fingers fumble to help Chiu as she works. I'm thinking about Shann and how she is. I admire her for her personal choices, but I know she'd agree, I need to do what's right for me.

In a way, I feel a little disappointed in myself, but this who I am. The plug-in is something that I've incorporated into being part of my identity. I guess that comes from all the years growing up with different versions of it. I've adapted. There is no shame in either Shann's choice or mine. We do what we feel is right to live the lives we want to live.

"Almost done."

There's feeling transmitting from the fingers and wrist. It's a little dull and strange to start with, but it gradually starts to become sharper and more sensitive. The fingers start to twitch. I find myself smiling.

"Appears to be working," Chiu says. "Any pain?"

"No," I reply. "You're doing great work."

I can feel the heat of the welder next to my skin, but Chiu is careful and doesn't slip. The connections are wired up in a circle and sealed with a touch of heated metal. "Okay, we're there," she says, finishing off. "Not pretty, but functional."

I raise the arm, flex the fingers and turn the wrist. A little sluggish, but responsive and operable. "Thank you," I say. "This means so much."

Chiu squeezes my shoulder. "I understand," she says. "Also means Daniel Rocher doesn't have something to bully you about."

"Yes, there is that."

"I need to get going," Chiu says. "Diouf is great, but there is only so much I can expect a station tech to be able to handle. You've got this."

Yeah, I think I do.

"Once you have thrusters online, use them," I say. "Keep an eye on your fuel, but if you can drop our velocity a little now, it'll help later. Less for the passengers to handle."

"I'll do what I can," Chiu says.

"Thank you again."

"Sure."

Chiu leaves. I don't follow. Instead, I shut my eyes. Ten minutes without responsibilities. I can afford that.

CHAPTER TWENTY-NINE

Duggins

Three of us, sitting in a room.

The wood-panelled drawing room is the kind of place on Earth that only the most decadently wealthy could afford. It is an antique, a reminder of times long before humans left their planet and ventured into space.

Mattias is sitting in a strong-backed armchair. He is staring at Irina, who is in a similar chair, bent over an old-style computer, with a keyboard. The device is a treasured memory, something her mother used to own.

"The data link installed by the last mission team is still active," she says. "There was a little damage to the hardware during the explosion, but the interface remains intact. We can communicate with the team outside. Near-field comms is also possible through the auxiliary transmitter. That's how you spoke to your friends last time."

Images flicker in my mind. I see people I don't recognise clustered around a terminal screen. I guess these were the people who brought Irina to this place. In moments, the faces become familiar and confirm my guess as I digest their personnel files. "Do you want to talk to anyone?" I ask.

"If you mean, do I have a connection with the humans who came here?" Irina frowns. "I'm not sure. It isn't something I've ever been asked or considered."

"You aren't human, then," Mattias says.

Irina looks up from her computer. "You aren't human," she says. "We are both different interpolations of human identities. The way I was created was quite different to the way you were created."

"I died," Mattias says.

"I know."

"How do you—"

"I told her," I say, interrupting him. I'm not lying, but I am avoiding a complex explanation that he may not be able to understand. In the short amount of time since Mattias has been here, I've quickly come to recognise his limitations. His thoughts and what constitutes his identity are available for me to read, but I sense he cannot do the same with me, or with Irina.

"The aliens saved me," Mattias says. "At least, they saved this part of me. I spoke to them."

Flashes of memory projected from Mattias. I'm seeing the room on Ceres again where he died, assassinated by another Rocher clone. It does provoke a question for Irina. "Did you see Rocher during your trip?"

She looks up from her screen. "You mean, the clones? Yes. There are lots of data points on them."

"Show me."

"Very well."

Suddenly, the lights go out.

★ ★ ★

Gunfire.

This is a memory. I'm on Earth. It's night-time and hot. The sky is dark – shadowed, as if a curtain has been thrown across the sun.

Flashes punctuate the gloom, explosions that bring daylight. Dangerous brightness, revealing the positions of soldiers, mercenaries, terrorists and civilians. Buildings shatter and rain debris onto those on the ground. There are shouts and screams from the injured and dying.

I'm in a building. A concrete shell that looks like a multi-storey car park.

"Mr Rocher, we need to start moving."

I glance to my right. The man speaking has an accent – Australian, I think. He's addressing another man, older, perhaps in his late fifties. His face is vaguely familiar.

"How long until they get to us?" Rocher asks.

"If you mean the extraction team, about six hours." The man laughs. "If you mean anyone else, who knows, eh?"

Everyone is wearing body armour. I'm carrying a rifle. The man who first spoke is carrying a rifle. Rocher is in a suit.

Henry Rocher. A target for assassination during the Melbourne Insurrection of 2101. We have been hired to protect him until he can be flown out of the city.

Another explosion. Our situation is revealed. Four figures, Rocher and three security operatives, two men and a woman. I am one of them. I know nothing about this man and his companions.

But I know about Rocher.

More staccato barks. Bullets slap into the concrete, forcing us all to take cover. Something slams against the side of my head and—

* * *

"This needs to be done quickly and quietly."

Another memory. I'm sitting in an air-conditioned briefing room, in a corner behind the two principals, who are talking. They are wearing military uniforms. I'm not sure which military they work for.

The man listening has his back to me. The man talking is someone I recognise.

Admiral Langsley?

"The target has been an asset for covert corporate scientific research for the last three years. We have been unable to ascertain the nature of his participation. We need to make contact and question him."

Langsley is a lot younger than I remember him.

"Sir, Rocher is right in the middle of a war zone," the other man says.

"In some ways, that's an advantage," Langsley replies. "We already have people in place and the conflict provides a cover for the operation. Your command will be a team sent in to rescue civilians – key citizens, identified by the major western agencies. The only difference between you and the others that are sent in is that you're going to be looking for one specific person. We need him pulled out and transported to a secure facility so he can be debriefed."

"All right, Colonel." The man with his back to me stands. "I assume you'll be sending me a full file on all of this."

Langsley also stands. "You'll get your files," he says. "But don't expect to be given everything. Just what you need."

"What you think I need?"

"There's no difference."

★ ★ ★

"Marcus, you were supposed to rescue him! Not—"

"With respect, sir, those were your orders. Not mine."

I can't see anything. I can hear the voices of two men. It sounds like they are talking on a comms channel. The first, I recognise, he was in the previous meeting with Langsley. The second, called Marcus, I don't know.

"You better explain."

"I already have, sir. There was an update from command sent directly to me. I was told not to disclose anything to you."

Silence.

"I don't like this, but I guess I'm not supposed to like this."

"You didn't know, sir. The orders clearly state you were not to be told."

Another silence.

"Are you at the pick-up location?"

"Yes, we're in place and ready to leave. Initial press is getting out. I've seen some of the Reuters drafts. I assume you're on that?"

"Yeah, we'll run interference. Killed in the riots. Just another innocent casualty."

"Understood. I'll brief the team."

* * *

I open my eyes into…water? Instinctively, I know this is strange.

I am standing up. My whole body is submerged. The liquid surrounding me is thick and viscous.

A mask encases my nose and mouth. I am breathing in a slow rhythm, paced by the air supply pumped from an external tank. This unit has been breathing for me, but now senses I can breathe for myself and changes its function accordingly.

Movement in front of me, the flickering silhouette of someone beyond. I sense I am in a container of some sort, that they are outside of the container. The experience is totally unfamiliar to me in one sense, but then achingly familiar in another. *Cryopod*.

I remember, I am Ethan Duggins. I have experienced something like this before. But the memory is from someone who has not.

More movement outside the container. My body is cold, but I am not shivering. I sense I have been colder and that actually, I am warming up. The liquid around me is slowly conducting heat into my arms, legs, chest and head. The process is slow, intentionally slow. When woken from cryo, human beings are fragile. The different requirements of stasis involve different temperature levels. Older chambers were very cold. Newer systems make use of—

More movement. Muffled speech. Words being spoken outside of the pod. I see lights flashing, the colours refracting across the glass in front of me. Then the liquid starts to drain away. When it clears eye level, I find myself blinking hard as I try to adjust to the dryness of the air by comparison. It takes a while. By the time I feel like I can keep my eyes open for more than a second or two, the liquid has dropped to being around my knees.

More words. *"…in about five minutes…already awake…."*

I can understand what is being said. The person in the memory is astonished by this.

When there is nothing more than a puddle of fluid on the floor, the seals on my pod release and the glass front slides back. There is a man standing in front of me. He offers me a gloved hand. I take it and step out onto a cold metal floor.

"Welcome, brother," the man says. "Let's get you some clothes."

I glance around the room. I see mirrors and camera displays. They show me images of myself. I see the man who is helping me.

We have the same face.

★ ★ ★

I'm back in the room, in a chair in front of the fire. Irina is looking at me.

"These are fragments," she says. "The receptacle has a way of acquiring small bits of information from Earth. Some of it is broadcast communications. Radio, direct comms, broadcasts, all of those have been available to this ship ever since humanity invented the technology."

"Not all of this comes from those kinds of sources," I say.

"No, you're right."

"Then how?"

"I don't know." Irina sighs. "I wish I did. There's a massive collection of information, all tangled and broken. You could lose yourselves in it, I could lose myself in it. I've been looking for memories of the original Irina, the person whose life was used to create me. Just knowing that the receptacle may have them, it pushes me into taking risks, all the time, trying to find some precious fragment, to make sense of it all."

I nod. "We can't lose you. We've only just met."

Irina smiles. "I may have been lost hundreds of times. The receptacle can recreate all of us from any moment since we came here. I have no memory of being overwhelmed by this place, but it may have already happened."

I look at Mattias. I wonder how much of this he is able to grasp. "Maybe we all agree to be careful," I say.

"Your original question was about the Rocher clones," Irina says. "I have seen them in my communication with the mission team. They were present here. Security camera footage showed them in the research base and on the surface of the ship. I think they piloted and crewed the ships that brought the science team here."

"The *Gallowglass*?"

"Yes, and the *Boryenka*. They both brought equipment and personnel here."

A second ship? Images of the rendezvous fill my mind, as if I were outside watching the ship as it approaches. These moments happened far away from Earth and Mars.

"What happened to the ships?" I ask. "Are you still keeping track of them?"

"They are here," Irina says. "*Gallowglass* was close by but moved away towards Mars. It is returning. *Boryenka* is on the far side of the planet."

A data plot appears. I can see the ships and the Fleet vessels that greeted us when we arrived. I see the debris from Phobos Station and the deadly showers of metal and plastic entering the thin Martian atmosphere.

I see *Gateway*. The ancient colonial transporter has moved from its orbit and is heading towards us. *Gallowglass* is docked with the huge vessel.

"We need to talk to my friends," I say. "We've waited long enough."

"There is a great deal more for you to learn," Irina says. "But I sense your need. These events – you are worried about the outcome." She turns her computer around, so Mattias and I can see the display. "I have initiated a communication request. We may have to wait for those in the interface room to respond."

"We need to help people," Mattias says. "Rocher is a murderer, he needs to be stopped."

I glance at him and smile. Sometimes a simple opinion helps cut through the complexity. "There is a lot of information here which will be helpful to people trying to do that," I say.

"There will be resistance," Irina says. "The scientists on this mission do not have your experiences. They have not seen what happened to the *Khidr*, or to Mattias on Ceres."

"What about you?" Mattias asks. "They are your crew. If they oppose us, where will you stand?"

Irina smiles. "I don't know," she says.

CHAPTER THIRTY

Shann

A child.

The baby is less than a year old. I glance at the woman holding him. She is looking at Marius and he is looking at her. I understand immediately.

"Your son, Marius?" I ask.

Wordlessly, Marius nods. His expression is stony. I can't tell whether he feels ashamed or angry about us finding out. It does, however, help me understand why he has been so difficult to deal with.

A movement. The needle held against my neck disappears.

"The child needs to be protected," Savvantine says. "A full medical examination will be—"

"You are talking to a biologist and a geneticist, Colonel," Thylla says, cutting her off. "I trust Marius and Elaine to know what is best for their son."

"Of course, my apologies," Savvantine says. "Perhaps I can suggest something else? There are three Fleet ships in the vicinity. If we can work together to repair communications and establish a link to one of the vessels, we may be able to get some assistance. We may also be able to verify some of the things we've told you."

"That seems like a constructive suggestion," Sarandon says. "I don't think any of us would disagree with that."

"I'm pretty good with electronics," I say. "Why don't you let me take a look at what you have to work with?" I look at Thylla, then Marius, trying to project an openness that might be more than how I feel towards them. "We need to start somewhere."

"Yes, we do," Thylla says. She points to the wall on her right. "The interior system is working. The problem is on the service. We can connect to the operations facility where you came from, but the dish...."

"Was destroyed, by us." I finish her sentence for her and grimace. "Yes, I understand."

"We were able to receive near-field communication," Le Garre says. "We did receive signals from here, after the main antenna was destroyed."

I look at her. The words were carefully chosen, but they've revealed something to these people. They aren't stupid. I know Sarandon won't have missed the inference.

"Range is an issue," Thylla says. "Previously, communications were carefully controlled."

"You mean, Rocher stopped you from making contact with people?" I ask.

"Who were you talking to down here, Captain?" Sarandon counters.

I glance at Savvantine. She shrugs. Le Garre might have done this on purpose to move things forwards. Thylla might have replied so as to offer an exchange. I'll look churlish if I'm the one to back away.

"A member of our crew was rescued from a cluster of gravitational anomalies," I say. "We found them during our altercations with Rocher and the ship *Gallowglass*. Our ship was destroyed, but we managed to defeat the clone crew and capture their ship. It brought us here. One of my people survived as a digital identity, stored in the ship's computer. He transferred himself to this vessel after detecting a more suitable facility. After the transfer was complete, he contacted us. That's one of the reasons why we came down."

Thylla nods. Her expression brightens. "You're talking about the receptacle," she says. "You say he transferred into there?"

"I think so, yes."

"We can try to contact him through the interface," Thylla says. She gestures into the lower part of the room. I glance that way and see the huge tube that goes into the far wall. "That's where we've been trying to communicate with the intelligence that controls this ship."

"Hold on," Savvantine says. "You were able to travel here. You are able to manipulate the gravitational effect generated by the anomalies. Are you saying you can do that, but you haven't made contact with the alien?"

"It's not quite that simple," Elaine says. "When they found organics, the first team who were here tried direct communication. They were the ones who built the interface."

"The interface?"

"Yes, that's what we call the tube."

"And that didn't work?" Savvantine asks.

"No." The baby stirs in Elaine's arms. She soothes him by stroking his head and rocking him gently. "We've improved the system since then and that's yielded more promising results."

"Like what?" Savvantine asks.

"Maybe we'll share that information with you when we all trust each other a little more," Marius says. "Right now, we need exterior communications. We agreed we would start there."

I push myself out of the chair and onto the floor. It's been a while, but I'm very capable of crawling over short distances, using my hands to move to where I want to go.

I ignore the attention of people all around me. Some of them are more understanding than others, fine. But I'm not interested in anyone's pity.

The communications set-up is behind an aluminium panel on the wall. I pull out a small toolkit and take out a micro-driver. The panel will have been pressure sealed with driven screws and a line of adhesive filler, like the repair foam we use. All of this can be removed and replaced pretty quickly.

Thirty seconds of work and the panel comes away from the wall, letting me take a look at the electronics. In that moment, I'm reminded of Arkov and Sellis, people we've lost out here. Both of them tech heads, proper problem solvers who transformed when they were immersed in broken circuits and machinery. *Duggins too*....

I'm breathing in gasps, hunched towards the wall so no one can see me. I miss Vasili. Another death on my watch. *Get it together, Shann, fight for the living!*

Inhale, exhale, slow and steady. The tears flow, I wipe them away, then turn around to the others. "As you said, all seems fine," I say. My voice stays level and even. "Where does all of this go?"

"To a laser link," Thylla explains. "Fixed position data transfer."

I nod. "Old tech that's easy to repair. After that?"

"More cables to the dish."

"Is there a receiver before we get to the exterior comms?"

"Yes, that way we're able to contact people working in the operations area."

I turn to Savvantine. She hasn't moved, but she is watching me. "Do you still have contact with your camera drone?" I ask.

"Let's see," Savvantine says. She pulls out her screen and taps at it. "Seems to be working."

"Great, so we can use it to get a message to Drake," I say. "I need him to activate the terminal near the airlock, then we can walk him through reconfiguring the system."

* * *

The repair will take time.

After being contacted by Savvantine's drone, Drake appears on the terminal screen. It's good to see him.

"What do you need me to do, Captain?" he asks.

"The drone should help you locate the communications cable. We need to splice into it and improvise a broadcast dish of some sort. It'll need to be put outside on the surface, so we can send and receive."

"You need me to do an EVA?"

"Yeah, but that's a little way down the line. Cables and components first. See what you can find that we can use."

"Will do, Captain."

I turn away from the terminal display. Marius is standing behind me. He doesn't smile, but nods. In approval perhaps? I can't tell.

"Do you have a full plan of all the constructed sites?" I ask. "If we have a complete list of the facilities, we can get a better sense of what's available."

"Rocher didn't give us access privileges to that kind of information," Marius says. "Most of these buildings were constructed before we came here."

"Most?"

"They worked on a few things when we made breakthroughs. The gravity manipulations, for example. The deck outside was built after we worked out how to simulate the effect."

There's a noise. Like a communication request. I glance around; the noise isn't coming from the terminal. It's not Drake trying to get in touch.

It's coming from one of the terminals attached to the interface.

"You want to get that?" I ask Marius.

In response, he scowls and moves away from me. I watch him and the other scientists head down towards the flashing terminal display. Savvantine starts after them.

"No, give them some space." *If we're going to trust each other, now is the moment.*

My people are all watching as the four cluster around the display. Sarandon operates the terminal, accepting whatever request had been sent through. After a few moments, he turns around and stares at me.

Then they all turn to look at me.

"Your crew member," Sarandon says slowly. "Is his name Ethan Duggins?"

I glance away and rub a hand across my face to hide my smile. "He is our chief engineer," I say.

"He wants to speak with you," Sarandon says.

They are all waiting.

I put down my tools and the screws for the panel and shift myself around. The staircase is three metres or so. I move to it, then grip the rails with my body and lower my body down. Then I crawl across the floor to the chair.

I'm looking up at Sarandon, Marius, Thylla and Elaine. Sarandon vacates the chair and without saying a word, they all shift back to allow me to get to the screen.

I climb into the seat. The face in front of me is one I recognise. Duggins is no longer leaning forwards, too close to the camera.

"Hello, Captain," he says.

"Hi, Dug," I say. I've missed that Texan drawl. "Took you a while."

"Yeah. There's been a lot to work through." Duggins looks to his right. I think there might be someone there with him. I'm trying to see the background, the space he is in. As soon as I do, I recognise it. It looks like the bridge of the *Khidr*. "Mind telling me your situation?" he asks. "I know usually I'd be the one reporting in, but…well, we might be here a while."

"Le Garre, Chase and I are here in the interface room," I say. "We've found a research team. We're talking."

"Understood. I've prepared a brief to help with that," Duggins says. "I'm aware of the background."

"You know about them?"

A second glance off-screen. "Yeah, I have access to a lot of information here."

I frown. "You okay, Dug?" I ask. "Anything I need to be aware of?"

"Everything will be in the briefing material, Captain," Duggins replies. "I'm good. Things worked out better than they might have done."

"Dug, should we trust these people?" I ask.

This time Duggins doesn't look away, but he does pause, considering my question. "I think so, Captain," he says finally. "They've been out here a long time. There is a lot that all of you aren't aware of. Any decisions need to be made after you've had time to take it all in."

I nod. "We're trying to re-establish exterior communications," I say. "Is there anything you've found that could help us with that?"

"Possibly," Duggins says. I hear another voice behind him. "We'll discuss it and I'll send you some specifications. Give me a few minutes."

"Sure."

The window disappears. I don't turn around. I can't keep the smile from my face. "Colonel, when the data comes in, you'll be the first one to go through it," I say. I turn around, looking at Marius. "After that, nominate one of your people to go next."

"It should be Benjamin," Marius says. "He has been here the longest." Marius goes to the wall and opens one of the panels. "We have full immersion viewers," he says. "I'll hook these up to the interface terminal."

"Agreed," I say.

CHAPTER THIRTY-ONE
Wade – Holder

I'm on Phobos Station, I'm lying down. Someone is talking to me. I know his name, but it doesn't come immediately to mind.

There are words are muffled and indistinct. I feel like I have just woken up.

"...breach detected in medical docking section twenty-three. I repeat, hull breach detected in medical docking section twenty-three...."

No.... *Before that....*

I'm at my desk. The terminal window in front of me is showing a selection of citizen privilege requests from Jezero. I'm reading through them, managing the approvals. We grant temporary passes for employees and contractors on the planet. Each of their requests has to be manually checked and approved from here. It seems a little strange to me. This could be an automated procedure, but that isn't allowed.

The files are all in folders. Each time I work on them, they are automatically updated. The size of each increases a tiny amount. For some individuals at the top of the chain, these tiny files are all they need to understand a person. Imagine being that ignorant.

Every person on the planet needs an access renewal. Some get a week, some get a day. Without a renewal, you get basic air and water with no location access. You can sit in a box with a bed. You get to go out and roam the colony streets, but that's it. Every person on Mars has a job to do and is given access to perform that job. Every day they perform their tasks reduces their travel debt. All very simple and straightforward. You live on Mars at the pleasure of the Corporate

Government. Only the permanent citizens have a guaranteed right to remain.

There are ten or twelve of them. I can't remember which.

"You all right?" Jim is sitting next to me. His hand is on my shoulder. He's close, a little too close.

"I'm fine," I say. I put my hand on his, give it a squeeze and move it away. We aren't in that place anymore. I moved out of our shared quarters a couple of weeks ago. A friendly reminder generally helps him adjust. Being angry about it just causes more problems between us. "How about you?"

"Market rates on Earth are fluctuating," Jim says. "Some sort of incident that's driving up the price of energy, beyond the agreed boundaries of our quant. We're monitoring. It could be a problem."

"Difficult to react to a market when you're twelve minutes behind," I say.

"Yeah. Could mean a real financial hit." Jim smiles. "Still, I'm sure they'll find a way to offset it. Move a load over to the journey debt. Make it everyone's problem."

"Sounds like—"

A noise, like a muffled cough. Then I'm thrown out of my seat, I hit my head against the desk and—

* * *

This is why I can't sleep.

I'm losing control of this body. Alison Wade is reasserting herself. Eventually, my consciousness will retreat, and she will come back permanently. She will be damaged by what's happened. I don't know how or whether she'll recover what she was before.

I feel guilty being the source of all that, the course of her pain and injury. Before now, I thought my presence had murdered her. Maybe this is better than that? I don't know.

I leave the bridge and make my way down here, to the place where they're holding Genevieve Aster. I need to speak with her, one last time.

I'm outside the door. I take a deep breath and touch the panel. It unlocks and slides back. I see Masson inside next to a cryopod. He glances up.

"You wanted one last conversation before we put her under?"

"Yes. I have some more questions."

"You want me to stay?"

"No, that's okay, I'm not going to do anything stupid." I move through the doorway and approach him. Inside the cryopod I can see Aster. She's strapped down, restrained and defenceless. She glares up at me. I return the look without flinching.

"Ten minutes, then I'll check in," Masson says. He moves past me, the door slides shut, and we are alone.

"What more can you take from me, Natalie Holder?" Aster says. "Was it you the last time?"

I frown. The question surprises me. "I don't know what you're talking about," I say.

"On the *Archimedes* an imprinted person was sent to assassinate one of the station crew," Aster explains. "I caught them before they could complete their mission. Was it you?"

I shrug. "If it was, I have no memory of it."

Aster smiles. "That's how I knew what you were. I've seen the technology in your head. I performed a biopsy on the assassin and found the tech they'd inserted into the poor woman's skull. Thankfully, she was able to provide one last answer. Let's hope that information is worth something to you."

"Rocher said there was a way to save me," I say. "Was he lying? Can it be done?"

"Possibly," Aster says. She bites her lip. I'm not sure she wants to explain, but she clearly can't resist a puzzle. "The storage device that contains your identity is designed to purge and decompose as soon as it stops receiving power from the body it is placed in. I guess if you were to reconnect it to a power source, without interruption, then...."

"Then I might survive?"

"You might be preserved, for a while at least."

I think about Rocher's last words before he fell unconscious. "There was a transmission from Phobos Station. Rocher mentioned it, saying it could save me."

"I've no clue what he was talking about, but I guess the transfer technology might be something that is missing? Your owner, Emoli, knows how that's done. If they found plans for a device that could transfer a digital imprint of a person from one host to another, that could save you." She shrugs. "I wouldn't know where to start making that kind of device and I don't know where he's thinking you could be transferred to."

"Where would he keep the information?" I ask.

"Any communication received on a ship or a station would be logged," Aster says. "Try looking in the station records."

"Surely, that would have raised suspicion?"

"The crew of *Gateway* may not have realised what they were receiving. If Daniel Rocher was in the communications chair, he may well have covered his tracks."

I think about that. Alison Wade's memories of data processing, going through the files like a good corporate cog in the machine. All of those files. It would be easy for someone good with computers to hide information in plain sight, in a distributed way, using a programme to attach little bits to everything and reassemble it when needed. That's what I'd do.

Aster is staring at me, watching me think with a half smile on her lips. In a way, I think she's proud of what I am. I'm grateful for what she's told me. Aster is volunteering information. "I'm sorry how this turned out," I say.

"I own my own choices," Aster says. "The moves I've made have been to preserve my own independence. I don't care who I have to hurt to defend that."

I nod. "I'll ask them to keep you confined, rather than cryo. They might go for that. At least then you'll get to see how it all turns out."

"Thank you," Aster says. "I'd like that."

★ ★ ★

"Do you trust her?"

"Not in the slightest."

Masson and I are in the corridor. I've made my request for Aster to remain conscious. "I'm glad you're not out of your mind," he says. "But that doesn't mean I think this is a good idea."

"Who makes the decision?" I ask. "Xiua?"

"He'll want to consult with Johansson and Chiu," Masson says. "When this all shakes out, it'll be Fleet who will be running the show. The only reason they aren't right now is because we got two polite ensigns instead of some shitty lieutenant trying to show off their rank pips."

I think about that. Johansson has been careful with all of us. She's demonstrated her ability with the ship's computer systems, but hasn't tried to force the issue of who is in charge. She let me lead when I chased after Aster and was quite clear about how I'd pissed her off.

"Everyone's busy," I say. "Can you hold off for a bit?"

"For now," Masson says. "But we need someone else down here. In less than an hour, I need to be at the controls of this fossil, because we don't have anyone else." He touches his comms and turns away from me. Talking to someone in low murmurs. Then he turns back. "Okay, I've bought you a couple of hours. At least until after the manoeuvres."

"We best get her strapped into a chair," I say.

"Yeah. Let's do that." Masson touches my shoulder. "You owe me," he says. "After we sort this, I need a favour."

"Okay, sure."

We go back into the room. Aster eyes me as we enter. "What's the decision?" she asks.

"We need you strapped in," Masson says. "We'll be altering course soon. Even if you're not going into cryo, you'll need to be safely secured."

"I prefer a conscious prison," Aster says. "Very well."

We begin moving her into the acceleration seat next to the

cryopod. As we work, another of the shuttle pilots enters the room. Masson nods to him.

"All right, we're done here," he says. "Come with me."

"Where are we going?" I ask.

"You'll see."

★ ★ ★

We are back in the docking bay.

There is no one here. Masson leads me over to an operations terminal near the wall.

"The *Nandin* is about ten minutes out. I want to speak to them before they get here. Johansson may want their help in trying to slow us down. Before that, I want to talk to them without her present."

"What about?"

"I want to know about her." Masson activates the terminal. "I need you to keep an eye out, so we aren't disturbed."

I glance around, confirming again that we are on our own. The rescued people from Phobos Station have been given 'shelter stay in place' instructions and asked to strap into their seats. There will be another warning before we begin manoeuvres, but if something unexpected were to happen, like last time...better to be prepared.

The communications request goes in. A face appears on the screen. "*Gateway* dock, this is *Nandin,* we are receiving you. Do you have an update for us on your situation?"

"We do, *Nandin,* this is Pilot Kras Masson. We're currently attempting repairs on our directional thrusters so we can rotate and initiate a deceleration manoeuvre."

"Hi, Masson, this is Lieutenant Geller. Our projections indicate you will need to complete repairs and begin movements in the next fifteen minutes and that you'll need a minimum of ninety percent thruster function to achieve a full rotation in time."

"Thank you, Lieutenant," Masson replies. "I'm sending you over our data update so you can revise your projections. We have Ensigns

Johansson and Chiu from the *Khidr* on-board. They are leading the repair efforts."

Geller looks to his left. I hear a few murmured words. "Receiving that, *Gateway* dock," he says.

"Johansson is working on the manoeuvre calculation," Masson says. "Would appreciate some guidance."

"Guidance?"

"I'll be blunt," Masson says. "Should we trust her, Lieutenant?"

The lieutenant looks away. He nods to someone. He's receiving instructions. He turns back to the screen.

"The captain's instructions are that you trust them both," Geller says.

"I tried to pull their files," Masson says. "But access is restricted. Any idea why?"

"There is an ongoing investigation," Geller replies. "I'm sorry, I don't have any more details."

Masson sighs and looks at me. I shrug.

He turns back to the display. "Okay," he says to Geller. "We'll go with that for now."

CHAPTER THIRTY-TWO

Savvantine

Two chairs on a stage, lit for a television broadcast decades ago. The man in the chair on the left is recognisable to me even now.

I'm in the audience, or at least that's how it seems. The headset recording is an early three-hundred-and-sixty-degree camera experience. I'm viewing this through one of the visualiser headsets. The scientists use them for forensic analysis.

I can look around and see people sitting in rows in the auditorium. There must be hundreds of them here, all having paid for expensive tickets. The privilege of wealth.

"Mr Trasker, there are a whole host of questions I'm sure people would like to ask you, and probably a host more that you have already answered. I'm going to end with one that might sound general, but probably provides the most insight for people trying to understand you. In your own words, can you explain what motivates you?"

Trasker smiles at the woman before he replies. I see the stage cameras are positioned so his eyeline is picked up, but not directly engaged with. This isn't some sort of political campaign, but it is a piece of propaganda, with everything decided to present him in the best possible way.

"I think human beings are generally motivated by the same things," he says. "I'm not exceptional or unique in that regard. I want to leave a legacy, to be remembered and to be known for having contributed something to our civilisation."

"I'm going to push you on that," the host says. "You have billions of dollars at your disposal. You can invest more money than entire nations. There has to be something specific that drives you."

Trasker's smile slips a little. I sense he's not comfortable with people demanding more than the platitude. He glances around. His gaze meets no one in the audience, but it does give him a moment to centre himself. "All right," he says. "Maybe there's something in the Gilgamesh explanation."

"The Gilgamesh explanation?"

"John Keats wrote a poem about Ozymandias. I tend to think of it as a satire on Gilgamesh, the ancient hero of the first human civilization we know of. He was the King of Uruk, more than two thousand years ago. We know about him from a series of stone tablets that described his adventures. He was described as a descendant of the gods, one of the first mortals, as powerful and strong as the immortals who sired him.

"Keats said, 'Look upon my works and despair.' His Ozymandias was a man who wanted to be remembered, but ended up forgotten. Gilgamesh could be seen that way, but I saw something else in his legend. He was mortal, amongst immortals. His contemporaries were granted immortality for their actions. He was not.

"I think human beings want to be immortal. They want to actually live forever. Being remembered is just a substitute for that."

Trasker finishes his answer. The audience is quiet, then a little nervous laughter. This is all too honest, revealing too much and demonstrating just how self-centred Trasker is.

Maybe they all are? All the people with more money than they can spend in their lifetimes?

I can see a supervisor offstage making a motion with her hand. She wants to cut the recording.

Then everything goes black.

★ ★ ★

"Matt, what were you thinking?"

The back of a limousine. Trasker is sprawled across the back seat. The woman I glimpsed from backstage at the interview is next to me. She is speaking to him.

"Helen Day was picked because she's a friendly interviewer. The questions were softball and pre-approved. She barely pushed, but you opened up like some sort of toxic flower."

Trasker glares at her. "Don't take that tone," he says. "Remember who pays your wages."

"And you best remember who finances your loans," the woman replies. "You are a billionaire for as long as they want you to be."

"If they fuck me I'll—"

"What? Fuck them back? You know how this works. Mutual victory or mutual destruction. Take a breath. Think about what you just did."

"Can't handle a little truth?"

"Not to that audience, no."

★ ★ ★

"Thank you for coming, Mr Hannington."

A boardroom. I am sitting away from the table. On one side, there is a phalanx of suits, on the other, David Hannington Senior and David Hannington Junior. A lawyer sits with each of them. Four against twelve.

A man in the centre speaks. He is African American. His suit dark grey and well-tailored. He is a messenger, but confident enough in his role. A Hermes – someone who was present when the decisions were made.

"The proposals that you have outlined are generous and detailed. The meticulous planning is very much appreciated. You have placed a considerable amount of trust in us by being this thorough."

"We believe in being diligent," Hannington Senior says.

"And you have been. Thank you."

"There is a 'but' coming, isn't there?" Hannington Junior says.

Looks are exchanged between the twelve. "Not exactly," the spokesman says. "There are conditions. Requirements that would be placed on each stage of your mission."

"I assume there will be a modified contract for all of those requirements?" One of the Hannington lawyers leans forwards. "Or are you going to give us a rough list for now?" The other picks up a pen.

"There will be no paperwork, Mr James, Mr Arnesen," the spokesman says. "The requirements of our employers will be stipulated when they need to be stipulated."

"So, we just have to trust—"

"Exactly that, Mr Hannington."

There is an awkward silence. The four look at one another. James gestures for Arnesen to repond, so he does.

"Space travel is the most regulated form of transportation ever created by human beings," Arnesen says. "Anything we send up there is going to be searched and checked several times before it reaches its destination."

"The Odin Corporation will be receiving substantial financial investment," the spokesman says. "I'm sure you will find a way to make it work." He gestures towards the documents. "Besides, your portfolio stresses the advantages of the deregulated environment of these colonies and research bases. Our clients would like to take advantage of this."

"In what way?" Hannington Junior asks.

"In many ways," the spokesman replies.

★ ★ ★

A crew meeting, five hours out of Earth orbit.

The transporter, *Hercules*, sent from the home planet out to the colonies. A set of rockets, strapped to a computer, a small rotating crew compartment and a huge collection of cargo containers. The supplies provided by this ship and its siblings are the lifeline that keeps humans alive on the Moon, Mars, Ceres and beyond.

People file in and take their seats. I see name badges; *Shah*, *Peters*, *Reynolds*, others that I cannot read. There is a little conversation. Everyone ignores me.

They should. I'm not really here.

"All right people, settle down." A middle-aged woman walks into the room and positions herself at the front. I read her name tag, Noriku. "This will be a short update for you all. Nothing major."

Noriku glances meaningfully to someone in the front row. He stands and turns around.

"Hi everyone, you don't know me. I'm Del Hutton, the Odin Corporation representative for this trip."

Groans and laughter greet the revelation. These people are easy enough with each other. They are all contracted to the haulage company, who in turn are financed by the main suppliers of goods. Odin is a major factor in everyone's salary and debt repayment, so Del Hutton might be the face of 'the man', but any opposition to him is good-natured, for now.

"All right, sure, yeah, I get it." Hutton holds up his hands. "I'm not here to get in the way, believe me. I want a nice easy ride, just like you do. The reason for this little chat is to make sure that happens. The payload for this run is fifty-five percent Odin. That means I'm responsible for a lot of shit. I just wanted you to be able to put a face to the organisation. That okay? Any questions?"

Two hands are raised. Hutton picks one.

"You going to be breaking tradition and slumming it down here with us, Mr Hutton?"

Laughter. Hutton smiles too. "I'm not the type to stay buttoned away in the executive lounge, so yes, you may see me around." He points at the second hand.

"You got any sweeteners for us? Something nice, so we treat your boxes all gentle like?"

More laughter. This time, Noriku steps in, waving her hands in the air. Hutton takes the hint and returns to his seat.

"Okay, you've had your fun. Now, let's get down to business. Roster assignments. Peters, you first. You'll be...."

★ ★ ★

The file ends.

I pull off the headset and blink several times to let my eyes adjust. My implant will have recorded everything. If there is something I've missed, then I'll be able to go over everything again, when needed.

"You all right?" Sarandon asks. He's in a chair, waiting for his turn.

"Fine," I say. "Just need a moment."

Fragments of different events, snippets and excerpts prepared by Duggins. At the moment, I'm not seeing the proof we need to convince these people they are in the wrong.

Not yet.

The headset is in my hands. There's more to go through. I glance around. Shann has them working on the comms with Drake at the other end. Thylla is on the terminal relaying instructions. It'll keep people's hands and minds busy for a while.

There is something about these files. One or two of them are depicting private moments that shouldn't have been recorded. In fact, they don't look like they were recorded. I'm wondering how we have these scenes? Are they real?

I'm trusting Shann and her people. I never met Ethan Duggins, but she trusts this echo of him. So, I'm letting it play through, hoping he'll give me better cards to play than the losing hand I've got.

I put the headset back on.

* * *

Paperwork. A set of blueprints. A hand with a pen writes an alphanumeric code on the header. The same sequence on each page. The symbols are written slowly and clearly. Then the papers are copied. The originals burned with a micro lighter.

The scene changes.

David Hannington Senior in a bed. His son in a chair next to him.

The room is palatial and clearly not intended to be a bedroom. The bed and medical equipment installed around it are not part of the décor. Cables and tubes line the floor. Machines chime and whirr as they operate to preserve the life of their charge.

Hannington Senior is awake. Papers are strewn across the blankets in front of him. There is a feeding tube strapped to his lower lip and an oxygen mask hanging loosely around his neck.

I'm trying to remember when Hannington died. My implant immediately responds, providing the information for me. 2114 AD. Four years ago. He was ninety-seven years old. His classified medical file appears in an overlay on my screen. Expensive anthrobotic treatment had been repairing failings in his body for more than a decade.

"We're leveraged to the max. The only source of additional funding is the consortium. They will approve what we want, but there are going to be strings again."

"You will have to deal with that," Hannington Senior says. "Can you manage?"

"Should be able to," Junior says.

"You still planning to go off-world?"

"Yes. The research mission to Europa is on schedule. I'm going with the team."

"How does Johannes feel about that?"

"The divorce was finalised yesterday. He signed all the paperwork, and we said our goodbyes. It's done."

"You'll leave chaos behind here."

"It's the only way we get away from them."

★ ★ ★

Deep space. Far from Sol's nine planets. Out here the light is feeble, the warmth from that fiery ball vastly reduced.

A ship moves through the darkness. I can make out its shape owing to the infrequent illumination of its exterior lighting as sensors flash on and off. I am floating above it. If I were really here, I would be dead in seconds.

In one of those moments of illumination, I see a name on the side of the ship's hull. The *Timore*. A name I don't recognise. This is no Fleet ship.

I glance around, drawn by some hidden instinct. Ahead, I see a huge object, long and thin, like the finger of a god, reaching out to touch the ship. Immediately, I know what it is – the alien vessel we are currently on.

The *Timore* manoeuvres in close to the rocky surface of the strange asteroid. Exterior lights reveal the grey expanse, rocky tundra that has not seen such light for centuries. A shuttle craft launches from the ship and travels down to the surface, kicking up dust as it lands. Figures get out and crawl across the cold stone surface.

Humanity has arrived to make first contact with alien life.

* * *

Another ship in deep space. *Gallowglass*. Robot arms deploy in the silent void, surrounding a patch of absolute darkness, a hole in space. An object, hidden in the nothing. Collected and taken inside.

A switch to inside. Internal cameras show the human crew of the ship gathering around a sphere that emits no light but seems to suck in everything around it.

* * *

More scenes. This time, I recognise people. Le Garre, Johansson and others on the bridge of the *Khidr*. I see Shann arriving to be told they have received a distress call from the *Hercules*. Then the moment they find the *Gallowglass* and find themselves in a fight.

I see the final encounter between the two ships. I see Ethan Duggins repairing the generator of the *Khidr*, sacrificing himself and being saved by more of the dark objects. I see Johansson on the *Gallowglass* fighting Rocher in the airlock control room of the *Gallowglass*, getting stabbed, fighting back.

These moments are more useful. Sarandon will see them and understand why Shann and her people made the choices that they made.

Next, a series of news headlines. *Trasker Found Dead: Drowned in Swimming Pool. dMemra Executives Convicted of Corporate Fraud. Astronomer Malcolm Palgrave Passes Away....*

Now I'm looking down from the sky, directly at the ground, like some sort of skydiver, thousands of feet from the earth on a fiercely hot day. Beneath me is a vast constructed complex. A solar farm, hundreds of square miles dedicated to panels, power junctions, cables, and distribution nodes.

My implant recognises the location – *Atacama*.

An explosion. The fireball mushrooms into the sky. Electrical connections short and more of the facility detonates. The destruction is huge, almost total. The raging fires melt plastic and silicon.

The destruction is swift and apocalyptic. The flames rage out of control.

★ ★ ★

Another view. In space, near Mars, looking at Phobos Station.

The end of this vast complex machine is very different to the Atacama Solar Array. I see flashes as oxygen ignites and explodes inside the pressurised compartments of the station's spinning rings. These are devastating incidents, ripping apart everything inside, claiming lives in an instant. But it all happens in silence.

The fires do not spread; they are suffocated as soon as they reach outside. Vacuum strangles them, but the damage is already done. Sections of the station come apart, the force of escaping gases and powered rotation creating a swirling maelstrom of fragments. Collisions and competing momentum pulverise the shattered components. What was one object is now thousands.

★ ★ ★

"Humanity will need a push."

I am in a darkened room. I sense there are many people here, and that the darkness is intentional.

"We knew this would happen. All the prediction models indicated it would happen, but that doesn't stop the circumstances being difficult," the voice continues. I can't tell whether it is a man or a woman speaking. There is some sort of electronic modulation being used to obfuscate the tone and timbre. "People will die. The survivors will suffer, but that will be the only way we get the time we are going to need to get the facility built."

"What about the technology?" another voice asks.

"The dMemra patents and prototypes have been secured by a third party, but we have enough for the first stage of the project. Genevieve Aster has eluded us. We believe she is off-world, somewhere."

"We must find her."

"Yes."

★ ★ ★

Data files flash up. *Rocher*, *Rocher*, *Rocher*, *Rocher*, and *Rocher*. Ten, twenty, thirty. All of these individuals have been sent to different corporations and governments. Their personal specifications are detailed and meticulously authenticated. Résumés, identity cards, credit accounts, everything carefully created and cross-referenced. Even the photographs have been screened to ensure any automated check would not pick up similarities by employing pixel variation algorithms, micro expression changes, and even hair dye.

But to the human eye, the resemblance is obvious. I am looking at clones, hidden in plain sight, throughout the societies and institutions of Earth and its corporate off-world colonies.

Everywhere.

There is one more file in the transmission. I open it.

CHAPTER THIRTY-THREE

Johansson

I'm standing in the corridor outside of one of the personal rooms in the rotational section of the ship. The last vestiges of centripetal gravity are fading fast. There is a door between me and Daniel Rocher.

This will be a test, a verbal game of chess. I have rehearsed this conversation in my mind, tried to figure out the different moves Rocher will attempt to make. Nothing he says will be without an agenda and objective. He will try to barter anything he believes he has that is valuable.

My advantage: I have spoken to a Rocher before. Two conversations had similar stakes. The last of them on Erebus when I had to exchange a password for my life and the life of my friends.

This is also a disadvantage. This Rocher is a different person. I can't expect him to behave in exactly the same way as the other clones.

I press the panel, the door opens, and I move inside.

He is there, on the far side of the room, watching me as I enter. They've used plastic restraints to confine him, the same as he and his clones did to Wade. I can see empty plastic pouches. He's had food and water, used the facilities. Maybe he even got some sleep? I'm jealous of that.

These rooms were never designed to be prisons. Humanity's adventure in the stars was supposed to be reserved for the best of our species. It took a long time for anyone to realise there would be criminals in space.

There are protocols. Alison Wade remembers the training. A lot of it was based on those whistle-blower ethics lectures. They stress the importance of betraying individual deviance as early as possible to preserve the lives of the community out here in a vacuum.

All of those speeches and questionnaires, designed to vet and indoctrinate a group that will defend itself against anyone who transgresses. What they didn't plan for is a competing ideology, a planned, subversive agenda amongst the community. Terrorism on the inside.

The terminal in the corner of the room is out of Rocher's reach. I move towards it, sitting in the chair and turning around to face him.

"So, you're the Fleet officer who is pulling all the strings around here?" Rocher says. "Good to finally meet you."

"I require information," I say. "What is your purpose and destination?"

"You already know," Rocher says. "The current plan is to move everything to the alien ship. The clones here are all ready to work on expanding what's been built down there. We'll figure out how to operate the ship, and we'll take it out of here."

"To where?"

"Far away. Further than any human being has ever been." Rocher smiles. "I'll die millions of miles away from Earth, in a dark hole. My body will be reconstituted, turned into muck and fed to the next generation as it grows and inherits what we leave behind."

I nod. "Whose plan is this?" I ask. "Who made you and planned all of this?"

Rocher waves his hand; the plastic restraints rattle against the bar he is strapped to. "The great man of history? Is that who you are looking for?" He laughs. "Does the world really work that way, or is it just a way of looking at it all? In a civilisation of billions, there are actions made by hundreds and thousands that all add up to a change. Our actions are built on the actions of others. You did things, I did things, we all did things."

"When all this is over, you'll be put on trial," I say. "They'll ask you who is behind the attack on Phobos and everything else. You'll do better if you give them clear answers."

"I'm a clone," Rocher says. "According to your Earth laws, I shouldn't exist. The people who made me weren't interested in my rights as a person. A trial would have to acknowledge me as a human being. Perhaps that would be worth any conviction."

"Only if you're responsible for everything that has happened," I say. Then I realise what this is. He's playing for time. "Tell me who sent you here."

"Then again, what have I actually done?" Rocher leans forwards and smiles at me. "I'm a legitimate crew member of this ship. I disobeyed an order to go to Mars and locked myself in a cargo bay. Everything else is speculation."

"You attacked me."

"That was the others. Am I going to be punished because I look like someone else?"

I turn away, my hands balling into fists, my jaw clenched hard. I'm engaging again, wasting time. "This ship will crash into a huge pile of rocks, and everyone on-board will die," I say, speaking slowly so as to keep hold of my temper. "Your manoeuvre instructions were found and deleted. Unless you tell me what I want to know, everything you're working towards will be destroyed."

"An obvious bluff."

I glare at him again. "You know me then? Know what I'm capable of?"

"I know what you stand for. The institutions exist because you support them. It is surprising what happens to a person when the option of doing that is taken away."

"Where are you going with this?" I ask. "Is this always all about you?"

"What makes you think I'm just talking about me?" Rocher shakes his head. "Thousands of people are trapped in a system that makes them serve others, makes them slaves in the machine. Mars works like that. You know it does, but you sit outside of it. Your Fleet insignia protects you. A badge that keeps you servile."

I'm about to answer, but then notice my screen flashing in my hand. I glance at the display. The data filter from Mars has completed. I'll need to access all the information in a secure location.

I stand. "People will be coming in to get you set up on an acceleration seat," I say. "I hope when we next speak, you'll be more helpful."

"You'll thank me for what I've done when this is all over."

I smile. "I really won't."

★ ★ ★

The minute I leave the room, I feel better.

Daniel Rocher is different to the other clones I've met. He comes across as less charismatic and more full of shit. I get the feeling he's desperate and fragile, that I've outwitted him, but I'm not taking that as fact. There could be another contingency or two that he's prepared that I haven't noticed.

"Xiua to Johansson?"

I touch the comms bead on my collar. "Receiving. What's up?"

"We're getting close to being out of time, Ensign. Are you on your way up?"

"Yes, I'll meet you there."

I'm looking at my screen. The data filters have picked out a collection of files for me to examine, but there isn't time to go through them now. I slip the device back into a pocket and start moving down the corridor. There's no gravity anymore. The rotation deck has wound down. We're ready to begin the burn.

I touch my comms bead, switching to a private channel. I send a request to Chiu. After a few seconds, she picks up.

"How's it going?" she asks.

"I was going to ask you that. What's the thruster situation like?"

"Fifteen units are back online. We can overload them a little and get sixty-five or seventy percent of capacity. Port side is strongest. Z axis maneuvering is unavailable."

"That's not going to be enough."

"Then you'll need to think of something clever."

I reach the bridge and enter. Xiua is there, with Masson and Wade. I gesture towards them. "Stations please, Xiua comms, Masson pilot, Wade pick a chair."

Wade scowls, but does as she's told. I move to Francalla's old seat and settle in. "Plug into the emergency oxygen and make sure you're strapped down. This may be rough."

"You want me to sound the alert?" Xiua asks.

"Yes, get it done."

The recorded announcement goes out. Francalla's voice, notifying everyone to strap in and prepare for g's. This is the moment that makes it all real. I'm in command. I'm trying to think of how Shann does this, managing the ship and its crew at the same time. Carefully, I guess.

"How did it go with Rocher?" Wade asks. Her tone is casual, maybe a little too casual.

"I didn't get much," I reply. "He spent most of his time railing about how insignificant he is to whoever made him, like he's not entitled to a life."

"The Rocher I killed did that too," Wade says. Xiua and Masson turn around to look at her and she realises she is the centre of attention. "I found him in the communications array on Phobos Station, just before it blew. I got the feeling he wanted to live, but had a task that meant he would die."

"But you survived," I say.

Wade nods and holds my gaze. "Yes, I did," she says.

Whatever, we don't have time for this. I plug my screen into the terminal in front of me and slot it into the holder. My preliminary calculations for our manoeuvre start appearing on the main viewer. Some small updates and we're ready. I'm typing with my prosthetic hand. The fingers are a little clumsier than I'm used to, but the adjustments don't take long. "Masson, time for you to upgrade your wings," I say. "This beast is a little bigger than a shuttle."

"Bigger than nearly anything," Masson replies. "You trusting me with this?"

"I can program the course and execute it, but this equipment is ancient," I say. "We're asking the computer to work with partial thrust capability and fragile systems. I'll post a course plot to your screen. If you can keep your hands on the controls and follow the prompts."

"I'll do my best," Masson says.

"That's all that I ask." The files are uploaded. The course simulation appears on the display in front of me and then on the main display, so everyone can see it. *My little miracle....*

"Johansson," Xiua says. "Am I seeing what I think I'm—"

"Yes, you are," I reply. "Let's get to it."

I've never been a people person. Actions speak louder than words. Two quick commands initiate the burn, a third brings up a screen with Chiu and Diouf in engineering. They are both strapped into their seats. The repair work is done. We ran out of time, now we do what we can to survive.

Deceleration comes first. I'm pushed forwards into my seat straps as the thrusters come online. *Gateway*'s manoeuvring engines were never designed to slow the whole ship and we don't have a full complement of working units. The last time the ship executed a braking manoeuvre, the thrusters were used to flip the ship around, with the main engines fired up to counter the velocity they had generated leaving Earth orbit. That's always been the most efficient way for a ship this size to work. This time, we can't do that before we crash, so instead, we're doing something else.

The pressure shifts; I'm pulled to the right. This is the plan, an adjustment, not a reversal. It won't save us – we're still travelling away from Mars – but it will give us more time.

The trade-off is another problem. Our fuel reserves are being depleted. The main engine tank is fine, but the thruster tanks are being used up. That'll mean we won't have enough to reverse the ship later.

The adjustment is also not going to solve the problem. Our course will be changed, we aren't going to crash into the alien ship, but we are going to end up alongside it at comparable velocities. The trajectories of both vessels will gradually come together. The collision will grind us against the rocky hull of their ship until *Gateway* is destroyed.

    This is a captain's decision. The kind of decision I always wanted to make. I joined Fleet to do this, but now I'm here, I realise what this kind of decision means. People will live or die based on what I choose to do.

    I'm thinking about my time on *Khidr*. Could Shann have done any better with this? Maybe. I don't know what she'd have come up with, but this is my choice, my responsibility. I'm owning it.

    The computer pings. The burn is complete.

CHAPTER THIRTY-FOUR
Shann

What is going on out there?

I'm sitting on the metal floor in the interface room. The panel I pulled out earlier has now been replaced, the screws returned to their slots and tightened.

Around me, activity continues. Le Garre and Sam Chase are around the terminal, talking to Drake. Thylla is with them, watching and listening to everything they do.

Elaine and Marius are closest to me. They are sitting together with their child, Antoni. Occasionally, Marius glances in my direction and frowns.

We need to know what is happening outside of this ship. Beyond us, the world goes on. I want to know about it.

Benjamin Sarandon is in a chair. Savvantine is plugging his immersion headset into the interface terminal. "Okay, ready when you are," he says.

"Begin," Sarandon replies.

I watch Savvantine. She stands and walks over to Thylla and Marius, spending a little time with them both, then to Elaine, who is sitting with Antoni in her arms.

Finally, she looks at me. Smiles and walks over.

"Sam, you can handle things from here, right?"

"Sure, Captain."

I shift across the floor towards the hatch and lever myself through into the laboratory. There is a workstation chair a little way in. I grab hold of it and pull myself up and onto the seat.

Savvantine arrives. Her projected smile has faded. Her lips have settled into a grim line.

"All right, summarise."

"There's a lot," she says. "Fragments from all over the place. It all hangs together though. Your friend, Duggins, he knows.... Well...I can't explain how...."

"By rights he shouldn't be alive," I say. "It's a waste of time trying to figure out how. We're way out of the realm of science that we understand."

"I know about them all," Savvantine says. "I saw their recruitment interviews and heard why they were selected. Marius was a junior lab technician for Hannington and the Odin Corporation. He was part of the team that recruited the Rocher progenitor."

"And Elaine?"

"An award-winning biochemist who lost out on funding for a Mars terraforming project. She was offered more money to come here."

I nod, absorbing it all. "What will they learn that will convince them they are being lied to?"

Savvantine grimaces. "There is a lot. The bits and pieces fit together and verify some of the things I already know. But a bit of it...well... figures in a darkened room, voices disguised as they plot to control humanity. All a bit illuminati." She glances at Thylla, then at Marius. "I'm not sure whether they'll believe it."

"We don't need them to believe everything," I say. "We just need them to realise we're telling the truth."

"Duggins has included what happened to the *Khidr*. Sarandon will see what you had to do, how you were attacked."

"You think that will convince them?"

"If they're reasonable and rational about what they learn, they should be persuaded," Savvantine says. "But we have other concerns to worry about."

"Oh?"

"*Gallowglass* wasn't the only ship being used to bring people here," Savvantine explains. She moves to the terminal at the desk and taps on the screen. A scaled data plot of Mars and Phobos appears. She taps in a few commands and more objects are added. "This is us," she says. "There's at least one other ship on the far side of the planet. That's how they managed to get insurgents onto Phobos Station."

"Do we have up-to-date plots?" I ask.

Savvantine shakes her head. "No, we just know the ships are there."

"We need to get these comms working," I say. "The sooner we're in contact with Johansson and the other ships, the better. We need to warn them."

"Agreed," Savvantine says. "How's it going?"

"Drake should be ready for a walk outside," I say. "But I'm not sure I trust him with all this."

"Then go help him," Savvantine says. "Or send me."

I'm thinking about that. It makes sense. "Will they let one of us go?"

"We'll need to wait until they've been briefed," Savvantine says. "But after, if they accept it, I don't see why they shouldn't."

"Keep on it with them," I say. "I'm going to stay out here." I gesture at the terminal. "Can you hook me up to the interface? Let me talk to Dug?"

"I'm sure it can be done," Savvantine says.

★ ★ ★

Twenty minutes later, I'm staring at a comms request window, watching it flash.

Technically my request is going to the terminal at the interface and then along a cable into an organic node. That node is embedded in the flesh of the alien that inhabits this ship.

I'm waiting. As I wait, I'm wondering about what was happening here before we came along. Sarandon and his people were working with the alien, communicating with it in some way. They haven't told us how.

I'm hoping Duggins will provide more answers.

The window flashes then expands. Duggins is there, in a seat on the *Khidr*'s bridge. A dead man in a room that was destroyed.

I'm blinking hard. The tears stream down my face. I let them. "Hi, Dug," I say.

"Hello, Captain."

He's smiling. It's good to see that smile, even if it's a little sad. "You okay?" I ask.

"I'm good," Duggins replies.

"Are you alone?"

Duggins glances around. Then his attention returns to me. "No, I'm not," he admits. "I don't really know how to explain what that means. Did you get to view all the information I sent you?"

"Not yet," I said. "We need the research team onside, so we're letting them go first, after the colonel."

"Colonel?"

"Yuhanis Savvantine. She's from Fleet Intelligence."

Duggins frowns. "But you're still in charge?"

"For the moment, yes."

"I don't envy you going back," Duggins says. "Fleet are going to want someone to blame."

"Savvantine knows that. I think she might be our best defender, when it happens."

"Yeah." Duggins grimaces. There's something he wants to say. It's a little weird watching the imprint of a man I once knew behaving like a human. The organic computer system that hosts his identity is far more powerful than any human computer, and any human computer would be able to work hundreds of times faster than a human brain. Eventually, he chooses his words. "You may need to accept an outcome that doesn't feel right."

"You predicting the future now, Dug?" I say. My smile keeps the question light, but really, I don't know what my chief engineer is capable of these days.

"Nothing like that," Duggins says. "But keep an open mind. I'm trying to."

"I bet you are." I decide to press my question. "The research team said they were communicating with the alien mind on this ship. How were they doing that?"

"There was a person here, before me," Duggins says. "She's a little...different."

"She there with you now, Dug?" *She telling you what to say?*

"Yes, she is. We're working together."

"Do I need to be worried about that?"

"No, I don't think so," Duggins says. "Ask them about it."

"What?"

"Thylla, Marius and Elaine. Ask them about Irina."

I have a name. Duggins may not see this revelation as meaning very much, but it is confirmation for me. He's said he's not alone, now I know who he is with. "All right, I'll do that," I say. "Thank you."

"Welcome, always," Duggins replies.

"One other thing? We need communications and exterior sensors. We're trying to rig something up, but if there was anything you could do to help."

"This ship has some sort of sensor system," Duggins says. "I don't know how it works. I'll see what I can find out."

"Thank you again," I say.

Duggins smiles. "I may have died, Captain, but I'm still part of your crew."

The image disappears.

CHAPTER THIRTY-FIVE
Wade – Holder – Split

I am....

I am back.

I haven't been myself. I don't know what happened. I remember sitting in my chair on Phobos Station, there was a disturbance and then... this?

I know the station has been destroyed. I know I survived. I know I am on *Gateway*, the old colony ship.

Light flicker, there is a buzzing sound, somewhere here an electrical connection is shorting. I am strapped into a chair on the bridge. I feel sore, injured. The ship has been moving, changing position, but these are old wounds. Blurry images of violence, gunfire, and murder. I am to blame for some of it. I don't know how much.

"Okay, we're done."

A woman's voice. The words are flat, strong, but brittle. She is young and trying to project authority. I don't know her, but I do know her. *Johansson?*

"Thruster reserves down to twenty-eight percent." A man is speaking. I glance around and see him in another chair, the pilot's chair. "Position is as projected, trajectory plot is mapped. We've got six hours until collision."

"Hail *Nandin*," Johansson says. "We need to get them in position for phase two."

"Phase two?"

"Send the comms request and I'll explain."

The pilot turns back to his screen. He taps in some commands. "Okay, I have them," he says.

"On the main display, please."

"Sure."

The data plots disappear. An image of another ship's bridge appears. I guess it's *Nandin*.

"Receiving you, *Gateway*," says the man in the centre of the image. "This is Captain Mattias Elliott of *Nandin*. Who am I speaking with?"

"Captain, this is Ensign Johansson of the *Khidr*. I'm here with Alison Wade of Phobos Station, Lieutenant Xiua and Kras Masson of Mars CorpGov's shuttle corps. Our situation is stable for the moment. The thruster burn has put us on a parallel course with the asteroid ship. The trajectories will intersect in just under six hours. At that point, we're going to need your assistance."

Elliott nods. "Send us your calculations," he says. "We'll verify."

"Confirmed, Captain, sending them over now."

There is a pause as the files are transferred and examined. I'm thinking about the voices around the room and trying to sneak a glance at the people in the chairs. Then I remember I can use the terminal in front of me to look at them.

I log into the system. I shouldn't be able to do this. My work on Phobos Station didn't give me bridge access. I'm not qualified for any of the positions up here. Nevertheless, it works. Windows appear, camera views of everyone in their seats, a duplicate of the main screen and a tactical plot of our position. That doesn't concern me. I'm looking at the faces.

All of these people are familiar to me, but I don't know them. I can't reconcile that. It's a little like meeting someone who you have forgotten the name of, but also, not like that. I should know everyone in this room.

Thankfully, everyone has said their names.

Elliott is talking to one of his officers. Their link is muted so I can't hear the words. Eventually, Elliott nods and the audio returns. "Okay, *Gateway*, we've analysed your data. My team agreed with your preliminary report. Repairs to the thrusters need to continue. The more we can get online the better."

"Agreed, *Nandin*. The team are down, they're doing everything they can."

"In the meantime, *Gateway*, maintain your current efforts to move away. We'll be docking with you in fifteen minutes," Elliott says. "We'll be transferring a command team to the ship. Please prepare a list of your injured to be moved across."

"Understood, *Nandin*," Johansson says. "What about *Gallowglass*? If we can launch her, we may be able to use her to support—"

"The new command team will assess the situation when they arrive," Elliott says, interrupting her. "All options will be considered."

"Sure."

"*Nandin* out."

The window in front of me disappears. I glance at Johansson. She looks irritated. "Get Chiu on comms. We'll need to get a detailed fuel assessment," she says. "I want to go over the numbers again. The *Nandin* team will want to go through it all when they arrive."

They don't need me for this. My hands are on the safety straps, the release button. I press it and push myself out of the chair.

"Wade, where are you going?"

Xiua is talking to me. His words draw the attention of the others.

"You don't need me here," I say. "I thought now the manoeuvre is complete, I should check on the others."

Xiua looks at Johansson, who nods. "Good idea," she says.

They return to their conversation, leaving me to slip quickly out of the room.

★ ★ ★

"Alison?"

Tristan Abernathy is here. I remember he was rescued from Phobos Station. He was one of the middle managers, looking after delivery consignments, managing inventories, that sort of thing. We started on the station at the same time. Rode up on the same shuttle.

Tristan's a little older than me. When we first met, he had thinning grey hair around a bald patch on the top of his head. Now he's shaved all that off.

He is standing in the middle of the corridor. He must have been outside the bridge. He looks concerned. In a moment, his arm is around me. I don't pull away.

"Are you okay, Alison? You haven't been yourself."

I shake my head. "Is there somewhere private we can go?" I ask.

"Sure, they gave me a room. This way."

Tristan leads me down the corridor. We're grabbing for the handrails, pulling ourselves along in zero gravity. They turned off the rotation section before initiating the manoeuvre. I'm glad that he's here. I always found this tricky.

There is a door to the left. Tristan presses the plate, and it slides back. We go inside. It's a small space, one of the single occupancy rooms. "Sit down," he says. "I'll make a drink. Coffee?"

"Yeah. That would be great."

I settle into a chair. There's no *down*, so I'm not really sitting. But this is a nice moment. I don't feel as alone as before.

Tristan is working the machine in the corner. Hot water is injected into a reinforced plastic canister and mixed with a little synthesised milk. Eventually the liquid cools a little and is injected into two pouches, just like every other type of food and drink we get in zero gravity. He passes one of the pouches to me. The contents are reassuringly warm in my hands.

"What happened to you?" Tristan asks.

"I'm not sure," I reply, trying to piece together an explanation in my own mind. "My memories are a blur. I know about the station and that we were rescued, but beyond that...."

"It's been a shock for all of us," Tristan says. "Has there been any contact with the Mars colony?"

"I don't think so," I say. I'm trying to remember. There are words and images all jumbled together.

"People want to get out of here," Tristan says. "They want to go down to the colony. The injured need care and attention up here, but the rest are ready to be transported to Hera. No one has explained why we aren't moving. The shuttles are still there, right?"

I nod. I remember a shuttle. Being sat in one of the seats. "Sure, but the pilots are all telling us we need to stay. The old captain of this ship, he died."

"They'd already cut him out of everything." Tristan scowls. "There's already been one attempt to take over from those people they found in the hold. Do you know anything about that?"

Again, I'm trying to remember. There was gunfire, fighting. Prisoners were taken. I'm about to try and explain that to Tristan, but then decide not to. It's all too much of a jumble. "That's all resolved now."

"But did the right people win?" Tristan asks. "I don't like any of this. Someone needs to get to Mars and find out what's going on."

I'm drinking my coffee. I'm worried about Tristan. He sounds like being here is affecting him. He wants to get away and he's talking himself into doing something. I'm not sure I agree with everything he says, but he's the one person I really know.

I'm worried about staying here too. There's something wrong. I want to leave.

But how?

"The shuttles are fuelled," I say. "The autopilot systems are set up to land on Mars. Once you take off it can all be run by the computer."

"We'd need access," Tristan says. "Could you get us there?"

I think about it. As a Phobos Station administrator, I shouldn't have the access privileges needed for what Tristan wants to do. But I remember a conversation with Xiua. Something about changing my user profile. I shouldn't have been able to log into the bridge control console like I did just now. Maybe I can help?

"I think I can," I say.

"Okay," Tristan says. "Then we need to organise. Give me five minutes."

He moves towards the door. I frown. "Where are you going?" I ask.

"To talk to my friends," Tristan says. "Don't worry, I'll be right back."

Suddenly, I'm alone. That fact helps. The anxiety that has been my constant companion since I found myself in a chair on *Gateway*'s bridge is starting to fade.

I realise I am in pain. Dull aches and soreness that shouldn't be there. Serious enough to warrant investigation.

I unzip my clothes. The overjacket and one-piece suit peel away easily. They are designed to be efficient in terms of temperature regulation, and flexible and removable in case of injuries. Any fashion considerations are quickly dispensed with when you leave Earth.

I discover the extent of the damage. I am appalled. My ribcage is a colourful tapestry of bruises and strapping. I can feel there is more underneath. Broken bones, torn muscles? Sometime in the last few days I've been treated and patched up. I don't remember any of it.

Something is very wrong. I wonder if I've got some sort of head injury as well? I can't remember anything specific, unless something happens, then the knowledge just seems to come to me.

Maybe all this physical trauma is connected?

I glance at the terminal built into the wall of the room. Tristan has left it on standby. The day and time are displayed: *14th of December, 1307 hours.* Hera Standard.

Martian days are just under twenty-four hours. That means time zones work the same as on Earth. Space stations tend to use a synced time with their main transport hub to make things easy for people travelling back and forth, so for Phobos Station and *Gateway*, Hera Spaceport is the correct time.

I was at my desk on the 12th of December.

I'm missing two days.

The revelation doesn't shake me as much as it should. The blur of memories feels like they come from a much longer period of time. I guess, given what's happened, with Phobos Station being destroyed and the evacuation, it might be understandable that it all becomes something I would want to block out.

But why am I working with the CorpGov security people and with a Fleet officer?

I dress carefully, replacing each item as it was, trying to avoid aggravating each injury. As I finish, the door opens. Tristan is back. He has two people with him. I vaguely recognise one of them.

"Alison, this is Samuel and Indira. They're coming with us to the docking bay."

I remember Samuel. Occasionally, he would take the same conveyer as me to work. We never spoke, but I think he was part of the station security team. He's a big man, with that kind of build.

Indira is much shorter and stays at the back in the hall. Her left arm is in a cast of some sort.

Tristan is looking at me expectantly. I raise my plastic pouch to my lips and squeeze out the last of the coffee, swallowing it quickly.

"Okay," I say. "Let's go."

* * *

The corridors of *Gateway* are empty. I recall Xiua's words, mentioning that the people on-board have been asked to stay in their rooms in case they need to initiate an emergency manoeuvre.

We are moving in a line towards the docking bay. I don't know the way but remember it as we go. Tristan is in front, Indira after him, then me, then Samuel. I sense the order is important and intentional. If I change my mind, Samuel is there to ensure I don't slip away. How forceful he'll be is not something I want to test.

There is a door at the end of the passage. Tristan stops there and turns to look at me. "We'll need your thumbprint access here," he says.

I nod and move forwards to the door. I know the security system will register my access into the docking bay. If Johansson is paying attention, she might wonder why I'm doing this.

"They'll know we are here as soon as we open this door," I say.

"That can't be helped," Samuel says. "Cameras will have recorded our movements anyway. Four people moving around during a shelter-in-place order is going to trigger an alert through the system. If someone is on a screen, they'll get an alert."

"None of the people on the bridge are members of the *Gateway*'s crew," Tristan says. "They may not have accessed the security system."

A memory: sitting in a room, wearing an oxygen mask. Opening a door into another room and seeing people unconscious all over the floor. "I think they have used the security functions," I say.

"Either way, we're taking the risk," Tristan says. He nods towards the panel. "Would you, please?"

I reach up and press the authorisation plate. The door slides back. We all move through into the docking bay.

This room is huge. I remember the facility on Phobos Station. It wasn't as large as this. The station was built for shuttle transports, whereas *Gateway* was designed to get massive amounts of cargo down to the planet's surface. Outside the huge glass windows, I can see the shuttles and a larger ship, *Gallowglass*. They are all hanging there, suspended, immobile.

I know this is an illusion, that really, we are all moving, racing through the darkness together.

"This way," Samuel says. "Shuttle *Epsilon* was the last to dock. That means it will be the easiest to launch. We go there."

The open space is more difficult to move across. There are handholds and indentations made to help people move. Painted demarcations indicate where people should be. In the floor and the ceiling, I see tracks and grooves, constructed for cargo. When this place was in active use, it must have been quite an operation.

Again, I have been here. I remember disembarking from one of the shuttles with the other refugees and following a camera drone right up to the door we just came through.

I can see the shuttle Tristan is making for. Beyond it, in the darkness, there is another ship, out there, on approach to the station.

Nandin, the ship Johansson was in communication with.

"Look!" I'm pointing at it, out there. "They'll be down in minutes. Johansson, Xiua and the others will be here to meet them."

"Then we need to get aboard," Indira says. "Right now!"

The shuttle airlock is connected by an umbilical passage. I move to the access plate and touch it. Again, the panel slides back.

I'm turning around as the others pile forwards. I can't turn back even if I wanted to.

* * *

Remember!

Whitewallswhitewallswhitewallswhitewalls....

"She is fading. The identity is starting to break apart."

My vision is blurry, my eyes sore, affected by the light. I can see two figures moving around me. A moment ago, I knew who they were, now I'm not so sure.

"We have established a link to Mars. The arrangement with our new partner means we have access to a relay in orbit around the planet. We should be able to replicate the recovery process she went through and send another operative out there."

These people are talking about me. They have already condemned me, decided I am finished.

"You want to send Vessel?"

"The new partner is keen to ensure they get their desired outcome. The circumstances out there are something of a mess, by all accounts."

A mess? *My mess*. If I had known what awaited me here, I would not have tried to escape the destruction of Phobos Station.

"Okay, compile the asset and tell me when you are ready to transmit."

"Will do."

CHAPTER THIRTY-SIX

Duggins

There is…pain.

The flesh of my body, torn open. Cold metal forced into the wound so that it prevents healing. The humans and their dead machines. Cold components animated with electrical energy. Their languages translated into pulses.

After a time, they recognise the incompatibility of our forms. A new technology is introduced. It is a strange hybrid of their machinery incorporated into organic flesh. The organisms fester in the wound.

The pain worsens.

★ ★ ★

I key commands into the screen and Shann's face disappears. It was good to see her.

"You told her about me," Irina says.

I turn around in my seat and look at her. A woman in her thirties, the memory of her former self projected as her physical self in this space. I am the same. I was similarly projected to Shann and the others through the screen.

"Yes, I did," I say. "I can't lie to the captain, not if we want her trust."

"They will want to know everything," Irina says. "You know they can't cope with it all."

"A flaw of humanity, curiosity, hubris and capacity," I reply. I smile. "I'm guilty of it too. I expect you are as well."

"I suppose so." Irina stares at me. "Will she help us?" she asks.

"Captain Shann is one of the best people I've ever known," I say.

Irina tilts her head to one side and frowns. "When she learns you are withholding key information about the researchers, will she remain onside?"

"I hope so," I say. "She would want me to be honest. I want to be honest, but some of these things need to be discovered and confessed. I hope they'll tell her before it comes to that."

"I heard her request," Irina says. "We can provide them with access to the bio-organic sensors, but their connection to us may not be sufficient to cope with the flow of information."

"Then we'll need to design something," I say. "I may need to learn more about how all of this really works."

Irina smiles. "That is not the first time you have made that request," she says. "Other versions of you have spoken about wanting to understand the machinery of this vessel. It is always an interesting conversation when I try to explain that things do not work the way you think they do."

I hold up a hand. "All right, I'll try to keep an open mind."

"It is important you experience what you are dealing with," Irina says. "Close your eyes."

I sit back and do as instructed. The familiar hum of the ship fades away.

★ ★ ★

I am outside.

The illusion of my previous location and physical form is gone. Instead, I am a presence beyond the confines of the receptacle, beyond the alien vessel entirely. I am in space.

If I were human, and really here, I would be dead. Cold vacuum, solar radiation and all the other fatal dangers of the environment execute life as we know it in seconds. But I am no longer bound by these physical limitations.

I know this, but every time I experience it, I have to reconcile my situation with my previous life.

I am looking at objects in the void. My mind translates the absorption of information into vision. I sense this is the only way it knows how to cope with what I am immersed in. Each of these phenomena is moving. All of their positions are relative to one another in a continual dance.

Below me, I see the alien vessel. A sleek finger of rock, illuminated by the sun, inching through the darkness. An object unlike any meteorite or asteroid I have seen.

Instinctively, I know the ship was brought here. An action in response to the activity of humans living inside its protective shell. An action Irina assisted with. I have not been told the reasons for this.

Beyond this, I see another ship. It is an ancient sprawling hulk, recognisable from media images and literature from my youth. *Gateway*, the colonial barge that brought the first settlers to Mars. For decades it has remained parked in an orbit around the red planet. Now it is moving, coming towards us on an intercept course.

Beyond this, I see the *Khidr*'s sister ships. The *Nandin*, moving towards *Gateway*, then further out, *Seraphiel* and *Asthoreth*. All chunky, utilitarian constructions, with form sacrificed for function. But there is a beauty in these machines. As an engineer, I see them as the apex of human technology.

I remember what happened to these ships. After attacking the *Gallowglass*, there was a mutiny aboard the *Seraphiel*, then a fight between her and her siblings. The people on-board those ships are still fighting. A pathetic struggle in a dangerous environment. They could destroy themselves at any moment.

I focus my attention on Mars. The debris field from Phobos Station is swirling around the edge of the planet's atmosphere. Hot metal and plastic will be raining down on the planet. Beyond that, I see more ships. Two of them on the far side of the planet. Their names are known to me. The *Timore*, and the *Boryenka*. They have come from further out, somewhere around Jupiter.

More ships. Shann and the others are in danger.

* * *

A moment of effort and I am back in the *Khidr* illusion. Irina has turned around in her chair and is staring at me.

"There are other ships," I say.

"Yes," she replies.

"Why didn't you tell me?"

"You were aware that this operation could not have been established and maintained with only one ship." Irina's expression does not change. "Our presence has drawn the attention of the other vessels. Everything gathers here."

"Why here?" I ask. "Why was this ship drawn here in the first place?"

"Marius and Benjamin would tell you they acquired control of the ship's navigation," Irina replies. "The Rocher clones ordered that they move the ship here when Phobos Station blew up."

"But that's not true, is it?"

"No." Irina gets up from her chair. She looks at the other seats. "Where did Mattias go?" she asks.

I frown and stand. I can see he's not here. I didn't notice him leaving, but then this place is an illusion. "I didn't know he was capable of this," I say. "Can you find him?"

"Possibly," Irina says. "But there are hundreds of versions of Mattias, just as there are hundreds of versions of you and me."

"Only one of them is capable of slipping in and out of places like this," I say. "The Mattias I first met wasn't capable of that."

Irina is silent. I look at her. She is standing still, staring into space, as if she isn't really there. A moment later she blinks, returns to herself and looks at me.

"He is still on the ship," she says.

"He can't do any harm," I decide. "Perhaps he decided to explore? I'll go find him in a bit, or maybe he'll come back in his own time."

"You should go and find him now," Irina says.

CHAPTER THIRTY-SEVEN
Savvantine

Benjamin Sarandon opens his eyes.

I'm right next to him. I watch as he blinks, trying to adjust to the room's electric lighting. Then he focuses on me.

This is the moment where I need to determine what he thinks about what he's seen. I have about thirty seconds before he gets up and speaks to anyone else.

There have been several situations in my life where I have seen this happen. Information is obtained and for an instant, the individual who knows has power. They hold something that others do not have; they must make the choice of when to speak and who to speak to.

Leaks, betrayals and secrets. These are the stock-in-trade of the intelligence services. People have been murdered in these moments, executed before their knowledge can be divulged and acted upon.

I stare at Sarandon; he stares at me. Then he leans forwards in the seat. "Would you help me with this?" he says.

"Sure." I help him remove the headset. He says nothing. We work together in silence. Then he stands up and goes over to speak with Marius and Elaine.

I turn to follow, but realise Thylla is standing next to me. I step back and she takes Marius's place in the seat. I hand her the headphones. She adjusts them and slips them on. "Ready when you are," she says.

"Okay." I kneel down, reset the feed and initiate it for another playthrough. Then I step back. Thylla is immersed.

I turn to Le Garre and Sam. The major is looking at me. I gesture her to come over. She does. "Your turn," I say.

Le Garre picks up the headset that I left on my chair. "What will I see?" she asks.

"Fragments," I say. "Bits and pieces of different lives and stories. Some of the events depicted will be familiar to you."

"Fair enough." Le Garre sits down and puts on the headset. "Okay, let's do it."

I reset the feed and set it going for her. Then I glance at Sarandon again.

The conversation between the three scientists has become animated. There is a tense expression on Marius's face and Sarandon looks angry. He looks at me. Then steps away from the couple, gesturing for me to approach.

"You ready to talk?" I ask.

Sarandon nods. "Let's go into the other room," he says.

I follow him through. Shann is there. She sees us both and immediately gets my intention. She slips down from her chair, and makes her way out and into the interface room with the others.

Sarandon takes a seat. I stand a few feet in front of him.

"You are from Fleet Intelligence," Sarandon says. "That's why you defer to Captain Shann. You're not really a leader."

I smile. "I have learned that recent events are best managed by those who are used to working with practical tools. My weapons are less obvious."

"You are a guardian of all this," Sarandon says. "Your organisation was created to maintain the current order. That makes you part of the problem."

I frown. "Is that what you learned from the files?"

Sarandon shakes his head. "That's what I learned from watching you. The files confirmed some of what I suspected."

"You must see that you've been lied to."

"Must I? Are you telling me what to think?"

"No, but even so."

"One of the reasons I came here, why we all came here, was to get away from the slavery of our lives on Earth," Sarandon says. "The research grants we accepted were complete sufficiencies. When the project is complete, we would be taken to a specified location and allowed to live without any financial concerns for the rest of our lives."

I smile. "You would be executed," I say. "Whoever is behind this would not be able to let you live, knowing what you know."

"Just the kind of thing one of your kind would say." Sarandon is angry. The cold truth that his life is based on an empty promise is not what he wants to hear. He points at me, his finger jabbing towards my chest. "You were trained to preserve the status quo, to ensure the corporations and governments stay in charge and keep people down."

"And you think special people should be able to get around all that?" I ask and gesture around the room. "You came a long way to try that, did you?"

"I think we don't move forwards if we don't experiment and try things," Sarandon replies.

"And that justifies breaking human cloning restrictions?" I ask, trying to keep my voice mild, but the criticism is right there. "What other ethical issues will we find when we dig into the science you're doing here?"

"I shouldn't have to justify myself to you!" Sarandon's voice is louder. He is struggling to control himself. "I came here to get away from this bureaucratic shit!"

I open my mouth to reply, but think better of it and turn away. "Tell me what you want to come out of this conversation," I say. "You know what's happened out there. You know what we told you was the truth."

For a moment, Sarandon is silent. I can hear him breathing, trying to get a hold of his temper. Finally, he seems to remember himself. "All right," he says. "We've agreed we need to know what's going on out there. We'll work on repairing the communications."

"And my promise to you stands," I say. "You will be protected when this goes to the authorities. I'll do everything in my power to help."

"But you won't lie to them, will you?" Sarandon says. "If you uncover some deep dark secret, you'll turn it over and let the wheels of the corporation government machine grind it to powder. That's what you people do. Innovations that could help everyone are pulled to bits so all the money people can get their cut before normal people see anything. Hundreds of innovations that would have bettered humanity have been lost to this process. The system is flawed and you're a guardian of it."

I bite my lip, swallowing a harsh reply. I glance at Shann's terminal. She's logged off after talking to Duggins. I never met him in life, but I did see him die. I know he wants to help. Maybe he'll talk to me? Give me something I can use to bring these people into line?

Then again, what if Sarandon is right?

Slowly, I turn towards him again. I'm trying to understand his position. A man surrounded by some of the best minds in the world, left out in deep space to apply his genius to a discovery that is beyond most life experiences of anyone. Now, he's being asked to be accountable again. Sure, the hubris of the man is toxic, but maybe I have to breathe the fumes to understand him at least.

"Some day," I say, "I hope that you and I will have a discussion, where we can be honest with each other. In the meantime, let's try to get along. When everyone has viewed the information from Duggins, then we'll continue this conversation."

For a moment, Sarandon looks like he wants to challenge me further. Then he scowls and turns away.

★ ★ ★

"Okay, you're all set."

Shann is in her EVA suit in the airlock. Sam Chase, Angel Le Garre and I are watching her through the little window in the inner hatch. Thylla is here as well. The others are in the interface room.

Shann's helmet is locked and secure. She touches the comms unit on her wrist and the speaker on the wall activates.

"System check complete. Receiving you. Are you receiving me?"

"Receiving," I say into the transmitter. A little sleight of hand allowed me to establish a spliced link into her biodata. My implant is monitoring her vitals. I'll be able to keep track for some of the journey back across the cavern to the surface facility. "You're ready to go."

The airlock hatch closes, and the depressurisation process begins. There is a tingle in the air as Thylla deactivates the gravity plate, and a moment later, Shann is floating in the chamber.

"Depressurisation complete. Outer door opening," I say and press the button.

In response, Shann waves, then moves backwards out onto the cavern surface. She is confident in this environment. The EVA suits we wear are bulky and awkward, but she makes hers look like a second skin.

The outer hatch closes and she's gone.

The airlock is sealed. I set the repressurisation cycle. Thylla reactivates the gravity plate. Then she leaves.

"Okay, how does this work?" Le Garre asks.

I turn towards her and Sam. "No rank," I say. "Be frank and honest. Live in the moment and do what we need to do. If there is a judgement call to make, I'll make it and explain when I can."

Sam nods. "Works for me," he says. "I guess it's my turn with the viewer?"

"Yes," I say and motion for him to leave us. "The quicker you're done, the quicker we can prepare for the talk with them."

"Understood."

Le Garre and I are left together. I look at her. She has something on her mind.

"You persuaded Shann to leave before she took her turn in the viewer," Le Garre says. "Why?"

I curse inwardly. There wasn't a plan to this, but I guess it looks that way. Le Garre is suspicious. I can understand that. "We need her to help Drake set up communications. The timing is unfortunate."

Le Garre doesn't react. I get the sense that she doesn't believe me. "What do you want me to do?" she asks.

I point at the terminal. "Shann was talking to Duggins here. I want you to raise him and see what additional information we can get before Elaine and Marius have been through the viewer briefing."

"I can do that," Le Garre says.

"We need them onside," I say. "I'll be making an agreement with them. Back that. We'll deal with the repercussions of it later."

Le Garre frowns, but nods. "Do we take other precautions?" she asks.

"You mean personal security?"

"Yes."

I'm thinking about the suggestion, trying to imagine it. "Its four versus three, but I don't think they'll be stupid enough to try something direct. The gravity plates are a problem though. They've already shown they can target the effect on individuals, leaving one of their own immune."

"That'd still be a risk."

"Yes, particularly with the baby."

"Maybe we separate them a little in the meeting?" Le Garre suggests. "Just in where we sit. Two on either side."

"That's good," I say. "But we may need a little more leverage." I'm glancing around the room, looking for something that would help. Tampering with anything obvious might be seen.

I remember what I did with Sarandon. Hacking into his EVA suit's bio-monitors gave us an edge. The researchers will have personal monitors relaying data to the computer system. I might be able to access the feed.

"Wait until Sam is out, then help him with the last of their people," I say.

"What are you going to do?" Le Garre asks.

"I don't know yet," I say. "But I'll think of something."

★ ★ ★

I don't think of something.

I remember training exercises back on Earth. Every few months, teams of analysts would be put in rooms and given scenarios to work through. These were classic 'red team vs blue team' exercises, with each group set objectives in opposition to the other.

Every time, these events would play out the same way. Some tactically minded individuals would explore the parameters, then try to find a weakness, something they could exploit to gain an edge. Others would look for personality traits and 'tells' in their opponents and try to gain an edge. Both of these strategies were entirely situation-dependent and ground against the purpose of the exercise – to try and simulate a real situation.

Now I'm sitting with people I don't know. People who are intelligent and suspicious of me. Gaming them in some way is not going to work.

So, what's left?

Seven people in a room in an awkward silence. I'm tempted to start talking first, to try and shape the conversation, but that's a trap of my own making. These people are far too clever to fall into line so easily.

"I've watched the files," Elaine says. She turns to Sam. "You went through so much. I'm so sorry."

"Thank you," Sam replies.

"I don't know if I would have been able to cope," Elaine says. "But you did."

"We need to be honest with you," Marius announces. His words are a surprise. I'm intrigued. "When we came here, we were promised more than our financial freedom. There is a plan for a new community, outside of Earth's and Fleet's control." He looks around at the others. Thylla shrugs and gestures for him to continue. "We were promised places in that project."

"An illegal colony," Le Garre says. "We found evidence of that on the *Hercules*."

"That might have been connected to it," Marius says.

"Must be the Europa mission," Le Garre says. She glances at me. I motion for her to continue. "We've all seen the conversation between Hannington and his father. They were funded by your employers. The plan must have been to take over and expand the research station."

"Europa would be the obvious choice," Sarandon says. "But none of us were told where we would end up. Only that we'd be taken care of."

"Which is why you didn't believe me when I said you'd be murdered," I say. "Makes sense."

Marius stares at me and his expression sours. He opens his mouth to speak, but thinks better of it, turning to Thylla instead. She nods.

"We are telling you this to be honest and truthful," she says. "That doesn't mean we are giving up on what we have agreed to do."

I frown and look at Le Garre. She shrugs, leaving this to me. Understandable. "The people you're working for. They've committed crimes, broken laws and killed people. Are you saying you support that?"

"You have also murdered people," Sarandon says. "We don't know who started all this. Or who is to blame."

"You saw Phobos Station," I say. "You saw the solar farm on Earth—"

"I did," Sarandon says. "We all saw it."

"You heard the words as well: '*humanity may need a push*'. That tells us who is to blame."

Sarandon sighs. "If only the world were like that. Good and evil, so clearly defined. It must be nice to be able to point at your enemy, see them as a monster, convince yourself you are doing the right thing by killing them. I guess that's how you sleep at night."

"That's not what I meant," I say.

"Isn't it?" Elaine asks. "You're asking us to abandon a lifetime of research because you've decided the people we're working for are to blame for two terrorist atrocities." She shakes her head. "NASA began this mission. Malcolm Palgrave began this mission, one of the greatest scientists in human history. We have good aims, to better our understanding of the universe. We have an incredible opportunity here to do that."

I start to reply, but Le Garre raises her hand. I nod and let her speak.

"I want to know more about what happened to you," she says. "How did you end up here, around Mars?"

"About three months ago, the last supply ship brought in new equipment," Thylla explains. "The interface terminal and a prototype artificial intelligence – *Irina*. Through her, we made contact with the alien and started to understand how to work with it. The gravity devices were our first breakthrough. We managed to get the ship to construct them. The *Timore* left with several prototypes."

"So, you didn't make them yourselves?" I ask. I point towards the fabricators and assemblers in the other room. "They weren't made on those machines?"

Thylla frowns at me. "No. But we did use our facilities to manufacture part of the unit. The objects seem to react to electrical charge. We built a device that provides that when given the correct signal and a data recorder to measure the effect. It was attached to the prototypes made by the ship before they were taken away."

"We also made the resistors," Sarandon adds, tapping a little device on his shoulder. "We were able to isolate an interference signal. That's why when we captured you, I was unaffected."

Sam and Le Garre exchange glances. I know what they are thinking. "When *Gallowglass* arrived here, our communications were disrupted by a distortion field," Le Garre says. She looks at me. "The *Seraphiel* launched torpedoes at us."

I grimace. "The situation was complicated."

"And this one isn't?" Sarandon says.

"For the last few weeks, Irina has been helping us understand the ship's propulsion system," Thylla says, ignoring the cross chatter. "The surface base received a communication for us to come here, so we came."

"How long did it take?" Le Garre asks.

"A few days. No more than a week."

I can see Le Garre doing a calculation in her head, trying to work out the timings against what was happening to the *Khidr*. "Whoever brought you here must have known when *Gallowglass* would be here," she says. "What are they trying to do?"

"That's what we can't figure out," Marius says.

★ ★ ★

[Evidence File #12: Savvantine's Personal Folder. Minutes of board meeting dated 06.07.2104]

Somattawa, Jack: Respectfully, Doctor Palgrave. We aren't here to debate the merits and flaws of matters that have already been determined. We are here to implement a new strategic direction for the collaboration.

Palgrave, Malcolm: Oh? I wasn't aware we were changing things?

Somattawa, Jack: Your project's aims should remain as they are. Outreach and Avensis are important to our organisation, even if they are no longer being funded by the New Space Coalition. Your probes and, eventually, a crewed mission to the Oort Cloud will remain as part of our strategy.

Palgrave, Malcom: Then what's being changed?

Somattawa, Jack: The partners have acquired patents for several new technologies which will become the central focus of the company's efforts. We'd like to explore the potential of a research station to develop these.

Palgrave, Malcolm: Research station? You mean somewhere in deep space?

Somattawa, Jack: Yes, exactly that.

CHAPTER THIRTY-EIGHT

Johansson

I'm annoyed.

Captain Mattias Elliott of *Nandin* is a competent leader. He has assessed what I've told him and made decisions based on all the information available. He trusts his own people and is going to install them here to take over from me.

I can't fault his thinking. If I think about what I would do in his situation, it would probably be the same. There are civilians who need helping. I'm Shann's creature, so is Chiu. I'm an unknown quantity to him, a junior officer who has returned from deep space without their ship. Plenty of questions to answer for all of us from *Khidr* before we are completely trusted again.

That doesn't stop me being annoyed about this.

Chiu is on the screen, talking about fuel reserves and additional repair work. I've told her what's happening. She's calm, competent and focused on the job, ready to brief another engineer sent over from *Nandin*. Xiua is handling the details of all this. I'm listening, but not taking it all in.

This isn't a criticism. Elliott isn't removing me from command because I've done something wrong. But it feels that way. I need to swallow this and move with the tide.

My display flashes. There's an alert from the security system. The ship's camera network will have been activated to detect movement in the corridors. Given the emergency, people shouldn't be moving around, unless they are performing essential work.

I remember Alison Wade leaving the room. Her presence might have triggered the response. I key up the security management console and the video clips load up in separate windows.

I'm watching Alison Wade outside the bridge. I see her meet a man. The database identifies him as Tristan Abernathy, a senior cargo manager from Phobos Station. There are no records of him leaving his room.

The two talk; they seem to know one another. They return to his allocated room. He then leaves her there and returns with two other companions. Other clips show them all making their way to the docking bay.

The computer quickly identifies the others. Indira Attali, Phobos Station executive from Augustus Boipelo's personal office, and Samuel Grimwade, senior security operative.

None of these three have come forwards to help with any of the situations we've been dealing with. They are all from leadership roles on the station.

I bring up the other windows. Xiua and Chiu are still talking. I need to interrupt.

"...handling canisters in the passageways isn't ideal but—"

"We have a problem. Xiua, check your alerts."

I see Xiua look down towards another window on his display. He frowns, then turns to Masson. "You seeing this?"

"Yes, they've initiated a shuttle's auto launch procedure."

"Shit!"

I'm accessing the station's access protocols. "You gave Alison Wade user privileges for the bridge and raised her profile to give her permissions for room access and everywhere else. She's used them to get onto the *Epsilon*."

"We need to get down there," Xiua says. He's getting up from his chair. I get up too and grab him by the shoulder.

"You might be too late," I say. "We also need to notify the *Nandin*. They're manoeuvring to dock."

Xiua grimaces. "Can you lock them out of the shuttle?"

"I can try."

"You do that, we'll head down." He pulls away, moving towards the door. Masson follows. I return to my seat. Chiu is still there on the screen.

"What's going on?" she asks.

"Wade is trying to steal a shuttle," I say. "I need to lock her out."

"Okay, I'll leave you to it."

Chiu's window closes. I pull out my screen and activate the programming tools. Wade's account is easy to access, and I can remove her clearances, but hacking into a shuttle's auto launch procedure could be dangerous.

I'm checking the current status of *Epsilon*. I'm learning as I go. The launch procedure has initiated. The umbilical docking connector has retracted, and the docking arm has deployed. It will grab the shuttle and move it to the launch cradle. The rail pushes the ship out of *Gateway*'s dock, then the thrusters activate and take over. If I disable the engines, they'll be stranded out there.

I need to disable the rail.

This will be more difficult. It requires me either to hack into *Gateway*'s automated docking procedure and foul it up or to find a way to initiate some sort of emergency stop. Maybe there's a manual way of doing that? But I can't see anything in my access panel. I'm not the ship's dockmaster.

Okay, try something else.

How about tricking the system? What worked for Rocher with the transmitter was to broadcast false data, which caused the computers to course correct. He had the advantage of having lived on this station for years. He could record all the data he needed and repackage it for the fake transmission. I don't have any of that.

So, we go with the hack.

The terminal window is on my screen. I'm typing fast with both hands. The prosthetic is still a little awkward; the fingers are slightly shorter than I'm used to. I have some pre-generated code I can use, but because *Gateway* is old, a lot of the stuff I would normally rely on doesn't work.

As I'm assembling the program, I'm thinking about Wade. *What has she done?* I was suspicious before, but this doesn't make sense. If she was going to betray us, she'd try and free Rocher or Aster.

I key up a comms window. "Johansson to Diouf, where are you?"

A camera flicks on. I see a room – one of the personal quarters allocated to the survivors. Diouf's face appears. He looks old, half-asleep. He frowns when he sees it's me.

"What can I do for you, Ensign?" he asks.

"Something's happened. I need you to check on Aster and Rocher," I say.

"Okay, you think they might escape?"

"I don't know. Wade is trying to steal a shuttle. I'm trying to stop her. You trust her, I get that. I want to trust her too, but this—"

Diouf holds up a hand. "Whoa, this is a lot to take in. Wade's trying to—"

"Steal a shuttle! She's with people. I don't have time to explain, just please, go check on Rocher and Aster!"

"All right. I can do that." The connection ends and the window vanishes.

The docking arm places the shuttle on the launch ramp. I check my code. The hack has compiled. It's rough programming, but it might work. I'm targeting an initialisation check that the computer makes before activating any of the launch procedures. There's a motion and visual sweep to ensure there are no unauthorised objects in the arc of the ramp as it deploys. If I can fake a movement, make it think there is something there....

No, too late, the ramp activates and starts to move.

In one of the camera windows I can see Xiua and Masson arriving in the bay. As I feared, they are too late to stop any of this.

I tweak the program and send it again, this time targeting the rail. Movement outside, in the shuttle's launch arc.

No. Rejected.

Damn.

Shuttle *Epsilon* slides out of the dock and into the void beyond.

Diouf's communication window reappears. I pull it up. "You were right, Johansson," he says. "Rocher and Aster are missing. There was a shuttle pilot on guard. I found him unconscious, hit by a taser."

Shit! My fingers move instinctively towards keying up a ship-wide alert, but then I stop. That would only get Xiua and Masson chasing shadows and inform Rocher we know he's escaped.

I think I know where he's going or where he's gone.

"Diouf, get to Engineering. Tell Chiu what happened," I say.

"Will do," Diouf says.

I cut the comms. I need time to think.

★ ★ ★

"Xiua to Johansson."

"Go ahead."

"There's…. There's nothing we can do here. I'm heading back up."

"Understood."

I'm suddenly exhausted. Defeat does this to me. I wasn't fast enough, clever enough or whatever. Someone got around me, got past me. They shouldn't have.

I'm thinking about Wade as she left the room. There was something in the way she looked at me, a confusion that she was trying to hide. I don't know what was on her mind, but we need to—

Another communication window. The *Nandin*. They'll have seen the launch. Elliott will want to talk to me.

All right, let's do that.

"*Gateway*, this is *Nandin*. Explain your shuttle launch please?"

"It was unauthorised," I reply. "We have an issue—"

"*Gateway*, we have targeted the shuttle, we can disable it." Elliott's expression is grim. His words flat, but authoritative. "I need an immediate summary of the situation."

I nod. "Four passengers have commandeered *Epsilon*. They managed to get into the docking bay during a manoeuvring lockdown. At this time, we have no information on their agenda."

"As you know, Ensign, we have a lot of unauthorised actions going on out here."

"Yes, Captain. How long can you maintain target lock on them?"

Elliott glances at the feed on his screen. "If we don't manoeuvre ourselves, about ten minutes or so."

"Understood. I'll try to resolve the situation before that."

"Acknowledged. Five minutes' grace."

"Got it."

The window disappears, revealing the tactical plot behind it. I can see all the objects in our vicinity. *Gateway* has left the Phobos Station debris field. The *Nandin* is close to us, and shuttle *Epsilon* is positioned between us both. The alien ship is a little further away, but getting closer all the time.

Beyond that, I see *Seraphiel* and *Asthoreth*. Two dots grouped together. I zoom out a little further and Mars comes into view.

There are two more dots, emerging from the far side of the planet.

For a moment, I think it's a sensor glitch. *Gateway* has a laser sweep that can verify signals. I activate that, targeting the region. The system confirms the signals. Two objects of significant mass, heading right for us.

I don't have time for this! I key up another comms window. The request isn't picked up, so I try an audio broadcast, directly into their speakers. "*Gateway* to *Epsilon*, are you receiving?"

"*Gateway* to *Epsilon*, please acknowledge."

There is no answer. I switch comms to the *Nandin*. Elliott reappears in another window looking even more irritated. "What is it, Ensign?" he asks.

"We've detected two more ships near Mars. They are on approach. Neither of them has Fleet transponders."

Elliott turns away and speaks to members of his crew, then he comes back to me. "Yes, we see them too. This changes things. We have their estimated time of arrival as thirty-five minutes."

"That matches my calculation," I say.

Elliott grimaces. "Well, that changes everything," he says.

Xiua and Masson arrive. I switch the comms with the *Nandin* to the main display so they can see and hear everything. "I have suggestions, Captain, if you want them?"

"All right, let's have it."

"We abandon the shuttle. Track them but let them go. *Gallowglass* is in dock. We can launch and manoeuvre into position between this ship and the new contacts. Then we raise the *Asthoreth* and get them to join us."

"Three against two?" Elliott says. "Our ships are in no condition for another battle."

"Numbers may discourage them," I say. "For now, that might be all we have."

Elliott nods. The image distorts, then restores. "We'll be docking in ten minutes. My team will board and continue the plan as previously indicated. In the meantime, get your ship ready for launch. Ping us directly as soon as you begin the launch procedure."

"Yes, Captain," I say.

The window disappears. I turn to Xiua. "They'll need you here," I say. "Both of you should stay with the ship and the survivors."

"What are you going to do?" Xiua asks.

"Prepare the *Gallowglass* for launch," I say. I'm already out of my seat and moving towards the door. "Most of the ship is designed to run with a minimal crew. I think I can manage to get her out and in position on my own."

* * *

This is a better solution.

Captain Elliott outranks me. He is in charge and once his people arrive on this ship, he'll be calling the shots through them. He's already relieved me of command, but he can't spare enough of his crew to operate both *Gateway* and *Gallowglass*.

I'm in the docking bay. A few quick instructions given to the automated harbourmaster and *Gallowglass* is ready to depart.

I'm in the umbilical tube when I remember the data transfer. I get aboard the ship and pull out my screen. The file request has completed. There is a store of up-to-date information on what is happening on

Mars available in *Gateway*'s computer system. Quickly, I get through and into airlock control. I log into the *Gallowglass* systems from the terminal. The ship accepts my credentials and the interface I built for myself, Shann and the others appears.

I'm smiling when I see it. The security lockouts that I was fighting before appear to be completely gone. The ship is back under my full control. Immediately, I start copying the files into the *Gallowglass*'s computer.

A comms window appears on the screen. Someone is trying to contact me. I accept the request and Chiu's face appears.

"Hey. What's up?"

"I might ask you the same question," Chiu says. "Where are you going?"

"There are two ships near Mars on approach," I reply. "No transponders, like *Gallowglass*."

"You think it's part of the same faction?"

"It has to be."

"All right. Time to leave, then," Chiu says. "I'm en route."

"What? You can't—"

"I can. Diouf is here too. The *Nandin*'s team will manage without us."

I'm about to protest, but then I realise Chiu is not going to back down on this and I can't order her around. In fact, I don't want to. "I'll wait," I say. "It'll be good to have your help."

"I always enjoy being useful," Chiu says. "We're two minutes away."

"I'll start launch preparations and see you when you get in."

"Aye aye."

The window disappears. I'm pleased. I didn't want to do this on my own.

I initiate the ship's launch procedure. *Gallowglass* runs on a level of automation we didn't have on *Khidr*. Instead of people rushing to their stations and doing all the checks, the ship does nearly everything on its own. Sure, you have to clean and stow away your own mess, but that's about it. Warm-up tests and station-ready confirmations are all under the computer's purview. My hack of the system didn't change any of that.

I'm moving to the bridge. I reach the door and head inside. The captain's chair is right in front of me. I guess I should sit in it.

No. It still doesn't feel right. Not here.

I move to the pilot seat and settle myself in, popping my portable screen into the slot on the side of the chair and activating the terminal display in front of me. The Mars data is there. I access it, pulling up a selection of the filtered records. There are video files, recordings of private communications. I'm reading transcriptions, listening to people, watching them.

I see security footage. Drone cameras outside of Jezero dome tracking a storm of metal and plastic debris. The hot fragments rain down, cracking the shell of the colony. I can see people have already been evacuated, but that doesn't stop the apocalyptic devastation. One breach and suddenly the internal atmosphere becomes a weapon tearing apart buildings and infrastructure.

Hera Spaceport is worse. Explosions wreck the docking cradles and launch silos. Thankfully, the whole place has already been evacuated. Only the machines bear witness to their own destruction.

The audio makes it worse. Fragments and excerpts of different conversations stay with me, haunt me. To start, it's all professional. Registering equipment failures, contact loss, all of that, but then as the storm is detected, the voices start to crack. There is fear and panic, then terror. People died in these moments. No one could help them.

I am a witness, thousands of miles away.

New voices. Communication from shuttle craft. The language is sloppy, less precise than the usual CorpGov transmissions. The system has tagged these files as being from unidentified sources. The shuttles aren't from the colony deployment. These are landing craft launched by the ships on the far side of the planet. The people on-board talking about extraction and achievement. These are vultures being sent to pick over the spoils.

I stop the feed. Give myself a moment. This is hard listening, but at least we know what's happening. I key up a new screen, ready to open a comms request to Xiua. He needs to know not to send anyone down to—

"Hello, Ensign."

The voice is familiar, and not a surprise. I turn around.

CHAPTER THIRTY-NINE

Shann

Zero gravity. Back where I belong.

That's not strictly true. My arms ache. I'm tired from the effort of moving around in the research base. I know that's good for me; the human body wasn't designed to live continually in weightlessness. That's why we have exercise programmes and rotating facilities on our ships. Every member of a spaceship's crew is fighting muscle decay and atrophy.

I'm moving across the rocky interior surface of the cavern. There is a small conveyor transport next to the large dark metal plate we were captured on. That must be how the research team get from the surface site to the base here. I move over to the vehicle and get in. It's like one of the old vehicles they used to use on Mars and the Moon for surface exploration. There are no wheels, but a couple of thrusters on the back and some micro-directional nozzles on the sides. The cabin seats two. For this trip, it'll just be me.

"Shann to Thylla."

"Receiving."

"I'm borrowing your transport, that okay?"

There's a chuckle on the other end of the comms. "I expected that," she says. "Throwing yourself across a mile of empty is pretty crazy. Doing it twice is even worse."

I smile. "Any tips on using this machine?"

"Move onto the metal plate. We'll use the gravity function to push you off. That way you'll save fuel."

"Got it."

The conveyor controls are simple; directional joystick and a thrust slider. The latter shouldn't be needed much. I sit in the seat and deploy the straps, then initialise the computer and gently push on the stick.

The little ship slides to the right. *Great.*

Carefully, I move the machine to the plate, as instructed. The cabin isn't enclosed. Instead, there are a couple of roll bars acting as a frame and that would be the first point of impact if we were to hit something.

"Okay, ready."

"Understood. Prepare for a jolt."

The comms crackles and there is a sharp push, jamming me down hard in my seat. The conveyor is punched away into the darkness.

Quickly, I adjust my orientation, using the joystick to face forwards. I can see two tiny green lights in the darkness. They are markers for the airlock on the other side. I'm moving much faster than before. That's all good now, but when it comes to the other side, I'll need to decelerate.

"Shann to Thylla. Do I need to perform a braking manoeuvre?"

"Engage the pilot, the conveyor will handle it."

I lean forwards and find the button on the console. The moment I press it, I feel the joystick stiffen as the computer takes control. Tiny micro-adjustments are made to my course, lining me up perfectly with the lights.

I'm thinking about my choice. Putting myself out here is an act of trust. If Thylla and the others wanted me dead without repercussions, it would be easy to cut the controls or something. They might be able to do that from a terminal in the base. Right now, without a computer, I'd never recover the controls in time. I'd either smash into the cavern wall, or bounce off and float away, mangled up in a damaged conveyor. Neither option is particularly appealing.

At the moment when I start to think I've been lied to, the thrusters activate and the ship flips around. The main engines kick in and I'm pushed forwards in my seat. The straps bite into my shoulders and around my stomach. Now, we're flying backwards towards the rock wall. I grit my teeth and tense up, but there is no crash; instead, the little ship slows, and I see the arms of a docking cradle gather us in.

Movement stops. Another light appears on the console in front of me. The straps ease and disengage. I'm down.

It takes a few moments to climb out of the conveyor. The cradle is a few metres away from the airlock. There are handholds cut into the rock to help people traverse. I grab the first one and pull myself forwards. This is just like it used to be on the *Khidr*, flying along the corridors....

Shit, I miss all that.

I turn around, peering into the darkness. I can just see the pulsing light of the research base across the vast emptiness of the cavern. As if on cue, the conveyor's thrusters activate and it launches from the cradle, turning and angling itself back towards the lights. A computer-controlled return flight. The little ship quickly disappears into the gloom.

Now for the task at hand. The airlock is right in front of me. I press the plate and watch as the inner door closes, and the atmosphere purge starts. A minute later, the lock releases and I pull the outer door open.

I move inside. Everything is as I remember it. The outer door shuts behind me and the sequence begins. The chamber is filled and once again, I become aware of noises outside of my suit.

I unlock my helmet, twist and remove it. The inner door rolls back, and I see Drake standing in the chamber beyond.

Travers is next to him.

"Hello, Captain," he says.

I glance at Drake. He shrugs. "It is good to see you, Captain Shann," he says. "We have everything set up as you requested."

"Travers...I...." My mouth is dry. I'm emotional. My crew have fought and died. The number of survivors gradually dwindling as all of this has happened to us. Duggins came back. Now Travers....

He looks pale and sick. Words are an effort, but he's smiling. I want to hug him, but I'm afraid he might snap, like a bundle of twigs.

"What are you doing awake, Lieutenant?" I ask.

"He's under medical supervision," Drake says. "I made the call whilst you were in transit. Given how much you were asking me to do around here, I thought having someone on hand who actually knows something about electronics and machinery might be useful."

"But is he—"

"He'll be fine, so long as he doesn't push himself too much."

"God willing, I'll be able to help," Travers says. He gestures into the room. "We've organised everything as instructed. Just a case of running a cable outside to the dish."

"We don't have a dish," I say. "Did you think of—"

"Yes, as a matter of fact, we did," Drake says.

I look past him into the room. The big table from before is gone.

"Took a lot to cut it off the base and drag it up to the airlock," Drake says. "Before you ask, I did it on my own. The lieutenant was still going through his thawing sequence. All you'll need to do is take it out onto the surface with you and wire it up."

I smile at Drake. "That sounds like a pretty good plan. Well done."

I move inside. No point in taking off my EVA suit. Thanks to the conveyor, I have more than enough air supply to manage a second trip out. As I move through each room, I notice Drake has been busy. The dead Rocher bodies are gone, the room organised and ordered.

The upper floor is cleared as well, but there are signs of what happened before. The jagged hole in the hatch is evidence to the struggle that took place.

I can see the round metal tabletop lying on the floor by the airlock hatch. Drake has collected some of the parts and tools I asked him to find. I'm auditing what's here. We should have what we need.

"Right, what's left to do?" I ask.

"I need to dig out a length of data cable," Drake says. "There's a prefabricator that can make what we need. Thylla has sent me the instructions for it." He gestures at the pile. "Otherwise, there's some assembling and jury-rigging to do here."

"If you don't mind, Captain, I'd like to help you," Travers says. "Drake can manage."

I look at Drake. He nods. The time up here on his own appears to have helped him come to terms with his situation. "Thank you, Doctor," I say.

Drake shrugs, but accepts the gesture. "Glad to help," he says.

A moment later, I'm left alone with Travers. "You all caught up?" I ask.

"Just about," he says. "Seems like all this hasn't been easy."

"You're right about that," I say. I'm looking at him, but he's not meeting my eye. There's something on his mind. Best to tackle it head on. "I'm sorry, Bill," I say.

Finally, he looks at me. "What for?" he says. "I should be the one apologising to you for removing you from command."

I shake my head. "No, you did the right thing. Pulling me out and taking over gave me space. I needed that. You and Angel held everything together while I took the time I needed to get my head together. I'm sorry it came to that in the first place."

Travers gives me a tired smile. "You're human," he says. "Who knew?"

I'm laughing at that, sharing a moment with a man who is one of my best friends and closest professional colleagues. "We've been through the wringer," I say. "If we can get communications working, we might be nearing the end of all this."

"I could do with some leave," Travers says. "Back to Earth and two weeks on the West Coast, or someplace like it, would be great."

"Get the tickets booked," I say. "I'm in."

Travers chuckles. Then his attention turns to the broken tabletop and collection of parts Drake has assembled for me. "Looking at all this, I'm guessing you want to bend the circle, so it has focus, then build a pylon out of these panel struts?"

"Pretty much," I say. "We should have some low-noise amplifiers and block converters in the extra EVA suits."

"You mean the ones from the dead clones?"

"Yeah."

Travers grimaces. "Picking over corpses wasn't what I had in mind when Drake woke me up. But you're right, the tech is there, and we should use it."

I nod. "It shouldn't take long to find what we need."

"Then the difficult bit will be bending the table." Travers moves over to the pile of materials. "What's your plan for that?"

"Focused heat and some brute force," I say. "Keeping it even all the way around will be the challenge."

★ ★ ★

Thirty minutes later and I'm in the airlock, waiting for the depressurisation process to complete. The new dish is propped against the wall. On Earth it would be too heavy and awkward for me to carry on my own, even if I were wearing prosthetic legs. But out here, so long as I'm careful, I can handle it.

"Okay, you're clear," Travers says over the comms. "Opening outer door."

The battered hatch peels away and I move out onto the regolith surface of the alien ship. It seems like a lifetime ago that I was here with the others. People have died since then.

The dish is attached to cables. The data lines are carefully rolled up so they don't get damaged. I'm holding a short metal cable in one hand. I grab a handhold near the airlock door and pull on the cable. The dish starts to move, floating towards me. I let go of the cable and manoeuvre around, adjusting the object's trajectory so it will ease out of the entrance, which it does.

Excellent.

I'm holding the cable again, and moving out across the regolith, disturbing the dust as I dig my fingers into the rocks and adjust my momentum. It is easy to get this wrong and add momentum. Slow and steady works. I don't want to get crushed by a dented table.

After a few minutes, I reach an outcrop of rock. As the dish catches up with me, I move around it and pull it down to the ground. This is a good place to set everything up.

"Shann to Travers. You there?"

"Receiving."

"Okay, I'm ready for you."

I'm looking back the way I've come. There is movement around the airlock. The small camera drone Savvantine was using before. Travers is now controlling it, sending it out towards me. When it gets close, I gesture to my right. It moves forwards and positions itself about a metre above the stone hull of the ship.

Attached to the belt of my suit are two metal brackets. I pull them free and use my drill driver to make a hole in the stone. Then I bolt down the bracket and remove the metal cable from the dish. That loops through the bracket and through a handle on the back of the drone, anchoring it in place.

Now for the dish itself. I lever it up and position it above the drone. The second bracket attaches to the top with some chemical seal, then I bolt it on to the back of the dish.

This is a rough fix. We won't be able to do everything we want, but the drone will allow us to rotate our receiver/transmitter to try and make contact with other ships. Travers can control the drone to the right angle and the whole construction should just float where it is, provided the ship doesn't make a course adjustment.

It's only when the job is done that I look up.

I can see a ship. It's heading towards us. It's too far away for me to make out any details, but it's definitely getting closer. I wonder if it's *Gallowglass*? Have Johansson and Chiu managed to fix the computer system?

"Shann to Travers."

"Receiving. How's it going out there?"

"We're all set up. Just have to plug you in. There's a ship on approach. We may need to get comms with them."

"Can you angle the dish in that direction?"

"Doing that now." I take hold of the drone and turn it slightly, so the dish is in line with the growing object. Then I plug the data cable into the improvised 'port' on the back of the device. I'm spooling out cable and move back towards the airlock. I need to go slowly and make sure I don't disturb the alignment.

I'm thinking about Johansson and Chiu. I wonder what they've found out about *Gallowglass*, whether they've managed to regain control of the ship. The other fleet vessels are out there too somewhere. We need to know what's been happening.

I'm at the airlock doors. There's an exterior data port that I can connect the cable to. I sit in the dust and take out my mini driver. Accessing the port from the outside isn't easy, but it can be done. I insert the driver into the recesses and activate it, drawing out four long screws. The panel comes away, exposing the socket. I jam the data plug straight into it.

"All right, we're hooked up. Tell me if it's working."

I check my air. Thirty minutes left before the scrubber kicks in. Plenty of time if I need to—

"Shann, you best get in here, now."

CHAPTER FORTY

Wade – Holder – Split

"We're clear."

I'm strapped into a chair, one of the passenger seats. Indira is sitting just across from me. Up front, Samuel and Tristan have taken the pilot and navigator positions.

I'm leaning forwards, looking over Tristan's shoulder. I can see the darkness of outside through the DuraGlas screen. The initial acceleration has eased. We are leaving *Gateway* behind.

"Can you pilot this?" Tristan asks.

"I think so," Samuel replies. "Just a case of disengaging computer control and aiming for a target on the screen. Once we get there, things might be more difficult."

"Wait a minute," I say. "I thought we were using the computer to take us down to Mars?"

"No, that was what we *told* you," Indira says. "We are going somewhere else."

"Where?"

"There." Samuel points at a large dot on the screen in front of him. "To all intents and purposes, it's an asteroid, but we know it isn't. That's where we're going."

"Why?"

"You ask too many questions," Samuel says. "We have what we need from you. Better to sit still and be quiet now. Let the adults deal with the adult problems."

I open my mouth to reply, but then close it. Realisation of my situation is a hammer blow. I've been used, exploited by these people to get something. I don't know what.

My world shrinks. I'm looking at the chair, at the floor. I remember being in a shuttle like this on the way over. Little flashes of memory, helping the pilot, having my injuries assessed. The faces were there: Xiua, Masson, Diouf.

None of them are here now.

"There's a ship near us," Samuel says. "The computer says it's a Fleet vessel, the *Nandin*."

"They won't fire," Tristan says. "Not unless we give them a reason to."

A window on Samuel's screen starts to flash. I recognise it as a communications request. A moment later, Samuel notices it as well. He checks the tag. "It's *Gateway*. What do you want to do?"

Tristan glances at Indira. She shrugs. "If we don't reply, they have nothing to work with," she says.

As in response, the speaker over my head crackles. Then I hear a voice, twisted by static. "*Gateway* to *Epsilon*, are you receiving?

"*Gateway* to *Epsilon*, please acknowledge."

Samuel stands from his seat and flips a switch over his head. Immediately, the speaker cuts out.

In that moment, I realise, I'm still strapped in. My acceleration restraints haven't retracted, but everyone else is free to move around.

They've made me a prisoner.

I clench my fists. My stomach churns. I have no power in this situation. Whatever decision these people make might lead to us all getting killed. "You need to stop," I say at last. "Respond to that comms request and tell them you surrender."

All eyes turn to me. I meet each gaze in turn, acknowledging the impassive stare from Indira, the implied threat of violence from Samuel and the pitying look from Tristan.

"Alison, I'm sorry things had to turn out like this," he says softly.

"No, you're not," I reply. "If you were sorry you would stop."

"Are you going to be a problem for us?" Indira asks. "Might as well tell me now. It'll make everything much easier."

I glare at her, but that's all I can do. She has her arms free. I do not. "Like I said," I say. "You need to stop."

She moves forwards. There is a syringe in her hand. In one swift motion she grabs my head, exposes my neck, and jabs the needle into my carotid artery.

I—

* * *

Whitewallswhitewallswhitewallswhitewalls....

"The transfer is ready."

"Initiate it. Get Vessel sent. The sooner we have an asset up there, the sooner we will have something to work with."

I recognise that name. *Holder* and *Vessel*. Human test subjects for Project Apertura. I am Holder, she is Vessel. They are sending her somewhere.

Where?

"Link established. Transfer is underway."

* * *

I have been asleep. I am waking up.

I am tired. So very tired. They say exhaustion is a killer in old age. The constant battle to overcome little aches and pains, fighting off sickness. All of it adds up.

I am not old in the grand scheme of things, but I have lived a hundred lifetimes. All in fragments. I have died a hundred times or more.

I feel a connection. I have been woken up by the touch of something. But it is not meant for me and quickly moves on.

Leaving me awake.

Alison Wade is unconscious. She was injected with a sedative. Her heightened heart rate quickly ensured that her body would shut down.

I remember what she has done. Her journey from the bridge, to here. I see it as if it were my own memory. But I know it is not. I know we are different.

I would not have made these choices. But we are where we are.

I twitch my fingers – Alison's fingers. They move. I open my eyes. I am hunched forwards, a dead weight in the seat straps. No one can see my face.

There is an emergency release switch located around the far side of the left armrest. There is always a release in equipment designed for space. It's a holdover from the days when NASA, then Fleet, believed there wouldn't be any wars out here.

They were wrong.

I can reach the switch, but it may draw attention if I move.

People are talking. I can't make out all the words. I'm struggling to process sounds, must be an effect of the sedative.

"… can't just ignore them."

"What do you suggest we say to them, then?"

"Something ignorant and anxious."

"Well, it better be you talking to them, then."

Three people. Two men and a woman. I know who they are. Alison Wade trusted them, and they betrayed her. The men are the ones talking. They aren't paying attention to me.

Old memories come to me. If I can't reach the release, I can escape these restraints, but the effort will cause injury.

The shuttle lurches to the left. I let my body shift and sneak a glance at Indira, who is sitting opposite me. Her face is vacant and slack. Something is happening to her. I think I know what that might be.

I move my hand, straining my fingers around the armrest to the release. I catch the side of the button and immediately, the pressure of the straps eases. I know they are loose. I can free myself at any moment. Then I'll just have three people to subdue.

One step at a time.

Indira inhales sharply. Then moves in her seat. I feel a sharp pain as her booted foot connects with my shin.

"Come on, I know you're awake."

I raise my head and gaze at the person in front of me. Not Indira anymore.

"Hello, Natalie," she says.

Kate Vessel. A woman like me. Somewhere on Earth there is a laboratory with two rooms. In one, there will be a version of Natalie Holder, strapped to a chair. In the other, a version of Kate Vessel.

Vessel, Holder, how many more?

I recognise this woman because we have met before. Emoli's clients have made demands on him that require more than one operative to fulfil. I have woken in the body of a host with her standing over me. I have woken her, helped her, supported her as she has supported me.

Today, we are not friends.

"Indira Attali, personal aide to the Deputy Governor of Mars," Vessel says. She is leaning forwards, her head close to mine so the others cannot hear us. "They wanted Boipelo herself, but she figured out what had been done to her after the surgery. That's why she came out here."

I nod. I sense I have some of the pieces of a larger puzzle. "All this, to get Boipelo?"

"Not all of it," Vessel says. "Indira Attali was a close friend, a lover. She'd also had the procedure and also became suspicious. Both of them out of reach. That couldn't be allowed."

"Why not?"

"You know already. Control. The system works when those with power are shackled to the process. Just like us, shackled to our chairs. They wanted a lever on Boipelo. They tried when she was running for senate on Earth. She escaped and they couldn't have that. So, they went after her. Emoli was paid millions to get it done."

"But she's dead," I say. "Why are you—"

"Here?" Indira chuckles softly in my ear. "I've been sent to clean up. You were supposed to die when that station blew up, Natalie. Surviving like this is unacceptable."

"But that's not the only reason."

"No, you're right, it's not."

The shuttle lurches again. "Okay, we're clear!" Samuel yells. "There's no target lock on the screen!"

"What did you do?" Tristan asks.

"Nothing. I guess something happened."

I look at Vessel. She's smiling at me. *Something to do with her?* She said Mars was out of reach. That doesn't make sense. I got here, she got here, what has changed?

Another hard turn throws me back in my seat. Samuel's piloting skills are rudimentary at best, but now we're heading right for a large grey object right in the middle of the scope.

"Slow down!" Tristan shouts. "We'll crash right into it."

"Not for ten minutes or so," Samuel replies. "It's big. We're still that far away."

I glance at them, then back at Vessel. Her smile broadens, but she shakes her head. I know what that means. If I attack them and go for the ship's controls, she'll intervene.

I can't beat them all.

"The auto-landing system is bullshit," Samuel growls. "There's no option for a free surface touchdown. There's station dock or spaceport."

"The spaceport scenario would be closer to what we need," Vessel says. "Try that."

"All right." Samuel keys in the request. "It's on you if we crash," he says.

"If we crash, we'll be dead," Tristan says. He looks around, noticing I am awake. "How's our passenger?" he asks.

"Compliant," Vessel says. They still think they are talking to Indira; they don't know she's changed. "I think we've come to an understanding."

Wordlessly, I nod. I need to buy time.

★ ★ ★

"The transfer is complete."

I cannot see the people talking. I can only hear their words.

"Time to clean up," says the second voice. "Wipe this one, put it out of its misery."

I remember promises. A bargain made that granted me freedom. I struggle feebly against the restraints. I know I cannot break them, but I was told I would be free.

"You...promised...." The words are an effort, but I get them out.

Hands are on my wrists, then my ankles. The straps are undone. "A moment of freedom," the voice says. I hear laughter in those words. He is laughing at me. "Too bad you're too weak to enjoy it."

I hear a switch flipped. The whirr of electronics, then pain in my head...a flash and—

CHAPTER FORTY-ONE

Duggins

I served on *Khidr* for three years. Firstly, under Captain Bel Ashe, and later Captain Ellisa Shann. In that time, I got to know every twist and turn of the ship's corridors and passageways. I saw crew arrive and leave as their tours on the ship started and finished. Some were sent to other ships, others retired to the colonies or back to Earth.

All the while, the ship remained our constant. The shared missions, the days and nights in space, sheltering inside our benefactor, vehicle, home.

This projected memory of our ship is almost perfect. Behind every panel there will be electronics, cables and stored equipment, but these aren't real, none of it is. I know that instinctively for one specific reason.

There are no people.

I'm floating down the corridor, breathing imaginary air and listening to the hum of imaginary electronics. Every moment brings back other moments from my past. The people I lived with, laughed with, cried with. A part of my mind wants to create them here, just like Irina did, surrounding herself with the components of the life she remembers. A life that wasn't hers but was one that she wanted.

The temptation is palpable, but I don't succumb to it. Therein lies distraction, divergence and soporific rest, a kind of indolent death. My purpose is urgent. I don't have time for any of that.

If this is a near perfect representation of the *Khidr*, then Mattias could be on any deck, in any room.

Or he could be exactly where I want him to be.

Airlock control is on the lower deck, near the ship's hull. I'm through a hatch and down a ladder to the right place. The terminal and chair look like Vasili Arkov has left his post only a moment ago. Through the DuraGlas screen, I can see the airlock chamber.

Mattias is there. Huddled in a corner.

I open the inner door and step inside.

"Doctor Stavinson," I say gently. "Are you all right?"

Mattias raises his head. He doesn't turn around. "If I open this door, I'll die," he says. "All the air will be sucked out of this room, and I'll be drawn out along with it into a vacuum. My blood will freeze or boil, my entire body will fall apart. I'll be alive to experience that."

"Mattias, please come inside," I say.

"An alternative explanation is that I'm already dead," Mattias continues. I can't tell if he's heard me. "Opening the door will just be part of the illusion. I'll be torturing myself, convincing myself that I should be dying and enacting that reality."

I'm at the inner airlock door. I put my hand on the panel, but the door refuses to unlock. "Mattias, I need you to open the door," I say.

Mattias turns around. He blinks, then his eyes focus on me. His face is wet and puffy. He gets up and moves to the door, staring at me through the glass view plate. "Why?" he says. "Why do you care about me?"

For a moment, I wonder about that. Then I realise why. "Because I care about people, and I don't want to see you in pain."

"I can't cope with this," Mattias says. "Knowing it's real, but not real. That I'm dead, but not dead." He's sobbing now as he speaks. Struggling to get the words out. "In the last moments when I was alive, I felt guilty. I saw death as a punishment, but now I'm this, a fragment, an echo of a person. That feels worse than death, knowing I'm broken."

"I get it." I do get it. Mattias has lost a lot more than I have, but I can sense the lack of memories in my own imprinted mind. There is a blurriness around the edges. When I find something that I can't remember, I don't want to focus on it.

"Then you understand why I don't want this anymore," Mattias says.

"Mattias, please...."

"If you do care, you'll know why."

The words are hammers. I know what will happen here. Perhaps I could prevent it. The illusion is one of my memories. I could change it and stop this happening, but that won't change how Mattias feels or what he is thinking about.

"Maybe there's another way," I say.

Mattias frowns. "Another way? What do you mean?"

"If we could find you something, anything that would give you what you need...." I'm thinking, trying to rationalise this. Words are a delay, a delay is good, but I need better than that. "You want penance," I realise aloud. "You want some way to atone."

Mattias nods. Tears stream down his face.

"You're dwelling on those last moments you told me about, the guilt and shame of betraying people. What if we find you another purpose? A positive purpose. A task that lets you give something back."

"I don't know what that is," Mattias says. "I don't know what that could be."

"But you trust me?" I ask. "I promise we'll find what you need. Come out of the airlock and we'll try and find this together."

Mattias stares at me then he nods. "Okay," he says.

★ ★ ★

I return to the bridge with questions.

The door opens. The main display is showing a tactical plot of all the objects around us that I observed when I was 'outside'. Irina is in the same chair, still dressed in the same medical gown she was wearing in the cryopod, the same gown she was wearing in hospital when I first entered her memories. She knew I was here. She was waiting for me.

"Ask," she says.

I shrug and do as requested. "Why is this ship here? I understand the purpose of its presence in our solar system, but why travel here, to Mars, right now?"

"Sarandon would tell you it was their genius that unlocked control of the ship," Irina says. "When they transferred me into the receptacle, I was able to make proper contact with the ship and communicate a better understanding of our purpose here. In turn, I was able to understand the needs of this ship, what it has been waiting for."

"So, you're working for the ship?"

"I am working to align our interests. The ship has been sent here to observe humanity. There are specific conditions that will change its purpose and move matters on to the next phase. My work has expedited that process."

"I'll need you to explain that," I say.

Irina gets up and the tactical display changes, zooming in on the representation of us and *Gateway*, the old colony ship. "You witnessed the meeting of the consortium, the rich and powerful of Earth. They want a new world. They have worked to create that on Europa, to leave their home planet behind."

"They also want to live forever."

"The hubris and arrogance of their agenda are not my concern," Irina says. "But their work to create a new world is something we can take advantage of." The display shifts again, focusing on *Gateway*. "They have spent years acquiring the raw materials they need for their plan. The cargo compartment of this ship contains a selection of cryopods and a library of human DNA. Everything that might be needed for a small colony to survive a long journey on this ship."

"A journey to where?"

"I don't know. The ship does not know, or it is withholding the information from me." The display changes again. Trajectory lines appear. "*Gateway* will reach us very soon. When it does, action will be taken. The ship will be brought inside. Its purpose will be fulfilled, and the next phase will begin."

I'm listening, taking this in, comparing it with information I already have. The last journey this ship undertook was from somewhere far, far away, taking millions of years. "Everyone on-board will be passengers on this journey," I say. "They will never return to Earth."

"They might do. I have no idea."

"But you're willing to allow that? To trap them here?"

"This must happen," Irina says. "You and I have no choice in the matter. The purpose of this ship is greater than any one individual human being. As for anyone else, if there is time and opportunity for them to leave, then they may leave."

"But they don't even know this is going to happen!" I'm angry now, shouting at her, but the emotion has no effect. Her reply is cold and calculating.

"Then perhaps it is time you tell them."

I'm furious and about to complain about Irina withholding this information, but I know there is no point. I have been too trusting, too accepting of her support. I have not considered that there might be an objective, an agenda.

I turn towards Mattias. I should have realised what was happening. There is no compassion for him here. Irina and the alien care only about preserving what is here as a specimen. If he suffers, there will be no support or assistance. If he dies, he will be recreated. So will I. I don't know how many versions of me currently exist, all likely doing different things. All ultimately powerless to prevent the ship's purpose.

"All right, then we open communications," I say. I move to the captain's chair, activate the display in front of me and initiate a communications request to the interface terminal in the research base. I know this is a comfortable illusion, but I'm content to work through the process.

Sam Chase's face appears on the display. "Hey, Chief, what's up?" he asks.

"Where's Shann?" I ask. "I need to talk to her."

"She's outside in EVA at the moment," Sam says. "Major Le Garre is here."

"Get her and stick around," I say. "What I have to say is for you both to hear."

Sam nods and disappears from the screen. A moment later Le Garre appears with him. She looks serious, as if I've dragged her away from something. "Okay, Duggins," she says. "What's so urgent?"

"You need to get off the ship," I say. "It's going to leave and if you stay, you'll never get home."

The two glance at each other. In that moment, I feel pain, a deep soul ache. I am no longer human. They have a choice. I have no choice. I must stay here.

"How long have we got?" Le Garre asks.

The question has a complicated answer or a simple one. I opt for the latter. "I don't know exactly," I say. "But the process is going to start happening very soon. You need to get moving."

"Okay." Le Garre grimaces, then asks the question on her mind. "What about you?"

"I'm here for the ride," I say.

Le Garre nods and the window closes. I take a moment, staring at where it was. This is my old life, my old memories. All of this I will leave behind.

All of this I will take with me.

My attention turns to Irina. She sits just as she was before in the pilot's seat, turned around to face me.

"You heard them say it," she says. "Humanity will need a push. This is the culmination of that effort – a push, but not in the direction they were intending."

"Was it you?" I ask. "Did you blow up the Atacama Solar Array and Phobos Station?"

Irina shakes her head. "Humanity is more than capable of sabotaging its own progress. You have seen the factions in their huddled meetings. The rich want to be powerful, the powerful want to be rich. All of them claim to be acting in the interests of the masses. In reality, they act in self-preservation. All I have done is taken advantage of their conflict."

"But if you do this, you will have acted in a similar way to them," I say. "You will condemn people to a lifetime aboard this ship."

"The real Irina Saranova was deprived of her last years, then exploited to create me," Irina says.

"So, is this revenge?" I ask.

"No. But you cannot ask for special courtesy that humanity does not afford itself." Irina gestures. "The intelligence is curious about its charge. It seeks to understand the culture and societies of our civilisation so it may fulfil its purpose. It does not seek to be some sort of benevolent educator, or benefactor. It is not a tolerant adult schooling children. Such perceptions are a false assumption. They exist in human history as fables. The gods are wise mentors or vengeful enemies. They help the righteous and punish the wicked. Even when pantheons are a collection of diverse voices, polarity is a simple way of organising them. What exists here is neither."

★ ★ ★

[Evidence File #5: Savvantine's Personal Folder. Augustus Boipelo Senatorial Nomination Commencement Speech: 02.03.2113]

[applause]

Thank you very much. Thank you.

Most of you know the reason I am here tonight. The media have been writing stories about what I am going to say for more than a week now. Perhaps on another day we should ask ourselves why? I mean, I get the need for a scoop, but why this scoop? Why so much attention?

So, let's get the headline out of the way. This evening, exclusive to this event, I announce to you, I am running for World Senate.

[more applause]

Thank you. Thank you very much.

To start with, I would like to say, this is not a candidacy and campaign that will be about me. Or, at least it shouldn't be. Those of you who know me and have been on journeys like this with me before are well aware of my views on the popular press....[pause...scattered laughter] Seriously, any platform that I acquire I try to donate and share, shifting the focus away from the person to the people. Whether we're talking about enforced climate migration and enfranchisement, access to free water and power, infrastructure reform, whatever. All of these campaigns should have been about the issue at hand, not the face in the video or on the podium.

Sometimes I'm successful in making the campaign about the issues, sometimes I'm not. Tonight, I know I've already lost the battle, but that doesn't mean I'm not going to fight the good fight.

History has never really been about individuals. I mean, when we read the books, it seems to be all about individuals. The story of humanity is told through the great hands that grabbed hold of the churn of events and solved a crisis. We learn names and dates, as if these are the only important meaningful moments and people.

In turn, that focus on individuals makes us feel we are important and special. Within each of us is the power to be that shaper of destiny, right? The old colonial dream sold to those looking for a better start and a new life. We are raised up as children, given ambitions and aspirations through an arrogant dogma. Out of four billion people, you are special, you are unique and will do great things.

I say maybe, but not above anyone else. We are all capable of great things because of everyone else. We become great by identifying and raising up others.

Humanity is great when it is collective. The will of the community, the global community offers us a chance to change and remake our civilisation.

So, tomorrow, when the headlines are written, they'll focus on me. Character assassination by my enemies, multiple stories, all spin from different directions, but look behind them, see the agenda of the corporations and their vested interests. That's what we should be focusing on.

My campaign will concentrate on exposing those relationships and scrutinising them. Individuals who are acting in the best interests of the people have nothing to hide and should be celebrated. I'm hoping to find them and change the story for us all.

The work begins now.

Thank you very much.

CHAPTER FORTY-TWO

Johansson

Daniel Rocher is standing by the door into the corridor. I reach for the taser on my belt and step forwards. "What are you doing here?" I demand. "How did you get out?"

"You know the answer to the first question," Rocher says. "The second may take a little more explaining, but I'm sure we'll have time for that. After all, we're going to be crewmates now, aren't we?"

"You're going nowhere, other than back to the locked room you managed to get out of," I say.

"I don't think that's the best course of action," Rocher replies. He points upwards. "You need me. I'm the only person who thinks exactly like them."

I smile. We've been down this road before. Rocher on Erebus played the same card and wormed his way out of being a captive, trading his life to escape imprisonment. "What do you want?" I ask.

"Take me there," Rocher says.

"Where?"

"To the alien ship. That's where we want to go."

Another figure emerges in the doorway. Genevieve Aster. She looks brittle and exhausted, but that same passionate fiery independence is still there as ever.

"Both of you?" I ask.

Aster nods.

"Then I'll need more than you're offering," I say.

"What do you want, Ensign?" Rocher asks. "Think about what

matters to you most. Your friends are on that ship, and they are running out of time."

I glare at him. This Rocher is more desperate than the others. This is an all-in play. After coming here, he has no plan B.

"You better explain," I say. "You have sixty seconds before Chiu gets here."

"You already know what my orders were," Rocher says. "I wanted to use this ship to transport the cargo in compartment C. You stopped me from doing that, so I fooled the guidance computers and initiated a burn. I wanted to get there. To the alien ship."

"You were always going to fail," I say. "*Gateway* would have crashed into the ship already if I hadn't intervened. There is no way you could transfer that cargo without a huge amount of manual labour."

"You are assuming the alien ship isn't already aware of our presence," Rocher says. "That ship is *alive*."

I glance at Aster. She isn't looking at me. Her burning gaze roams the walls and floor. She seems unfocused, troubled.

Alive? I'm thinking about Rocher's explanation. Duggins transferred over to the ship. He must have found somewhere to be. A conventional computer system wouldn't hold him. He was falling apart whilst he remained here on *Gallowglass*.

Some sort of wetware computer might work. There have been experiments in creating that sort of technology for decades. The faster processing time available in an organic system has always made it attractive to corporate researchers looking for an edge, but locking down the response states into a coherent language at scale was always the challenge.

"As we get close to the ship, it will react and move," Rocher says. "It has a purpose and a desire to protect itself. We were never in any danger."

"You mentioned we were running out of time," I say. "Why?"

"Because that ship is going to leave," Rocher replies. "It was lured here by humans on-board who have imperfect control of its systems. Sooner or later, it's going to figure that out and return to where it came from. If your friends are still on-board, they'll be going with it."

The hatch alert sounds. Diouf and Chiu are here. I don't think Rocher is going to try anything, but having backup gives me leverage. "How do you know that?" I ask.

"I received a briefing before Phobos Station blew up." Rocher grimaces, his hands are clenching and unclenching. He's frustrated at having to explain. "During the attack, the cargo was supposed to go on this ship and be sent to Europa. But we can seize the moment and do something different! We can escape!"

"By we you mean...?"

"Me and her." Rocher gestures at Aster. "We get to be free."

Aster steps forwards. She's looking at me now, focused, determined. "I want to go there," she says. "There's nothing for me on Earth."

"You think we'll let you?" I say. "Why would I—"

"Ensign, that ship can't be stopped," Rocher says. "Your only hope of rescuing your friends is if you take us there and let us help you." He points towards Mars. "Those ships are crewed by more clones. They are coming for the cargo on *Gateway*. They want to retrieve it and take it to Europa. Those are their orders. They will do everything they can to get in our way."

A flicker of movement. I see Diouf behind Aster. Silently, his arms envelop her, just as Chiu appears behind Rocher and jams a taser into the side of his neck. He cries out, spasms and then goes still.

"Good timing," I say. "I was running out of things to say."

"What do we do with them?" Diouf asks.

"Detach the umbilical and drop Rocher in the airlock for now," I say. "We'll keep Doctor Aster with us on the bridge."

Diouf nods and releases the woman. Chiu approaches her brandishing the taser. "You'll be staying with us, Doctor," she says. It isn't a request.

Aster nods. She and Chiu move towards the comms and engineering seats. I return to the pilot's chair and initiate the final commands for launch. "Tell Diouf to get strapped in. We don't have a lot of time," I say. "*Nandin* is planning to dock at any moment."

"Aye aye," Chiu says. She drops into her seat. The safety straps snake out around her. Aster does the same. I initiate a safety lock on her chair, just in case.

"Moorings retracted," I say. "Directional thruster activated. Ten percent power to withdraw."

"Ten percent," Chiu echoes.

The thrusters kick in and I'm pushed gently against the straps of my seat. There is a temptation to try and do all this faster, to crank up the power and get us away, but that's the kind of thinking that gets you dead really fast in space.

I key up a comms window and ping *Nandin*. The piloting officer will have seen us start to move out of dock and should have taken appropriate action already. The tactical plot is in another window on my screen with scrolling data tracking *Nandin*'s trajectory and thruster burns on approach.

"*Nandin*, this is *Gallowglass*. We are leaving dock."

Elliott appears in the comms window. "We see you, *Gallowglass*. Come about three points relative starboard."

"Acknowledged." I make the adjustment and the pressure on my straps shifts to the left. This is a dance. *Gateway* is travelling in one direction. We have the same momentum, but as we manoeuvre, we will counteract that velocity to drop in behind her. Meanwhile, *Nandin* will approach, decelerate and manoeuvre to dock and take our place.

There is one more thing to deal with. "Captain, I've been informed by the clone, Daniel Rocher, that the alien vessel is going to react. He believes it is sentient and will avoid a collision."

Elliott frowns. "Can we trust that?"

"I don't know, sir. But I am concerned about the presence of Captain Shann and other members of the *Khidr* crew on the vessel."

Elliott bites his lip. He has decisions to make. More than seventy people are on-board *Gateway*. "We'll proceed with docking," he says. "I can't leave those people on a hunch."

"Understood."

Gallowglass is moving away from *Gateway*. In a view from the exterior cameras, I can see the exterior superstructure of the old colony ship, the vast cargo capacity of this grande dame of human engineering, the miracle of her resilience, remaining functional for so many decades after she was retired from active service.

Now I have my own decision to make.

Timore and *Boryenka* will be starting a burn, using Mars orbit as a slingshot, they will accelerate and head straight towards us, following *Gateway*'s path out here to intercept us if they can. At my suggestion, *Nandin*'s tactical plot is to dock and launch, manoeuvring to put herself in the way.

Gallowglass is supposed to do the same, to line up next to the Fleet patrol ship and defend *Gateway*. That was my idea.

I'm changing course, keying in a new pathway, dropping us down in the narrowing gap between *Gateway* and the alien vessel. We need the velocity we had from *Gateway* to keep pace with both ships.

"Johansson, what are you doing?" Chiu asks. Then she realises. "Oh right."

I'm going to get Shann and the others.

I key up another comms window. A camera in the airlock control room. Diouf is strapped into a chair. In the background, I can see a second figure in the airlock. Rocher.

"Diouf, what's your situation?" I ask.

"Locked down and riding it out," Diouf says. He grins into the camera. "Just like tornado season back in New Orleans."

"Tell Rocher we have a deal," I say. "Tell him he better not have lied to me."

Diouf's expression darkens. Then he nods. "I trust you," he says. "Will do."

"Anything I can do?" Chiu asks.

"Get a transmission recorded and sending to that pile of rock down there," I say. "Then get something else looping out to the *Asthoreth* and *Seraphiel*. We need to know what's going on with them."

"Aye aye."

Moving, twisting, turning. A complex series of directional changes that bring the ship into a dangerous position between two larger objects. Our destination is where we left the others. When the trajectory is established, I push the engines a little more. *Gallowglass* accelerates ahead of *Gateway*. We'll pay for that when we need to decelerate, but this ship was built to withstand greater forces than the old colony transporter.

"Destination ETA four minutes," I say. In my window, I can see a priority comms request from *Nandin*. I ignore it. Elliott will think the worst of me. I'm fine with that right now. I remember disobeying Shann's orders and going EVA. I felt a lot worse in that moment than I do now. "Deceleration will be seven point five g's for twenty-five seconds."

"That's a lot," Chiu says.

"Gives us a little more time when we arrive," I say. "Any less is more risk on them."

"*Epsilon* shuttle course is pretty close to ours," Chiu says.

"Where are they going?" I pull up the tactical plot, seeing the little representative dot about five kilometres below us. "I thought they were heading for Mars."

"Doesn't look like it," Chiu says.

Maybe that's a good thing? I remember the images from Jezero. Hera Spaceport is a ruin and none of the people on-board have piloting experience. They might be able to land, but only if the autopilot can compensate and touch down on the surface. "Keep an eye on them," I say. "If our distance gets under three clicks, tell me."

"Will do."

"And get me an inventory of our ordnance. We may need it."

"There won't be much," Chiu says. "Not after we dropped the armoury compartment on the alien ship."

"Anything may help," I say.

The forces fade. *Gallowglass* is on course. I touch the comms. "Diouf, get up here with Rocher," I say. "I want everyone where I can see them. You've got about seventy seconds."

"Got it," Diouf says. "On my way."

"I have Drake on comms," Chiu announces. "He's in the surface structure down there."

"Brief him," I say.

CHAPTER FORTY-THREE

Savvantine

I can't control this.

Le Garre has told me we need to leave this ship. She was told by Duggins that if we don't, we may end up trapped on-board as the intelligence will soon begin preparations for a new journey.

We have told the scientists. We can't withhold this from them. Reactions are mixed. My reaction is one of disappointment. Marius is furious.

"There must be a way we can prevent this!" he says. "We need to talk to Irina—"

"This came from Irina," Le Garre says. She's been at the terminal and been given a detailed briefing by Duggins. "Irina is helping the ship get what it wants – human specimens to take on its journey to who knows where."

"But if we can access the control system, persuade it to—"

"Do what?" Thylla says. "You think you can override millions of years of mission parameters? Who exactly do you think you are?"

"I'm staying," Sarandon says.

We all turn to look at him. I thought someone might make this decision. "The air supply will run out eventually," I say. "Even with scrubbers."

"I'll use the cryopod," Sarandon says. "Wake up every few years. Do experiments, take readings, then go back to sleep."

"We've no way of knowing if the ship's manoeuvre will be something you can survive," Le Garre says.

"Then I'll be taking a chance."

I'm about to reply, talking about the limited power available from the base's power generator, but I realise Sarandon already knows about this. He knows better than I do.

"I want to stay too," Marius says. He glances at Elaine. "But I know I can't. This isn't a life for a child."

"I want what they promised us," Thylla says. "That isn't staying here for the rest of my days."

"You may not get that," Elaine warns.

"Even so, I love my work, but I don't want to stay here."

"We need to move quickly," Sam says. "EVA suits on. Take only what you can travel with. Thylla, Antoni and Elaine in the conveyor. Everyone else goes back the way we came in."

Marius glances at me. I nod. "What he said. Let's get moving."

★ ★ ★

The prize. In our hands, about to be lost.

Alien technology that I have seen perform miracles. Gravity manipulation that should be impossible. Acceleration and deceleration that should kill anything alive. All of it, part of a pandora's box that is being snatched away.

Thylla is packing a box of equipment. I move over to her and touch her shoulder. "We'll need your data," I say.

She looks at me. "We've saved as much as we can in portable storage," she says. "It'll be coming with us."

"When we get out, come to me first," I say. "What you have here will be your bargaining chip. It may also prevent a war."

"My life's work becomes another card in your game?" Thylla snorts. "No thank you."

"You don't understand, you—"

She rounds on me, jabbing a finger into my chest. "No, you're the one who doesn't understand. You and the institution you represent are all about controlling risks, outcomes, activity. You follow the Jefferson quote, don't you? 'The price of freedom is eternal vigilance'? That's your ideology, isn't it? Have you thought about it? What does your vigilance bring?" She waves her arm, gesturing around her. "This ship has stood observing humanity ever since we climbed out of the trees. It outmatches all of us."

"I'm not trying to devalue your work," I say.

"Maybe that's what you think, but you are devaluing it, and everything here. Maybe you think you're doing the work of the angels, but you're not. Your guarding of humanity doesn't bring freedom. It brings a prison, a constraint. We won't ever reach the stars with people like you shackling people like me."

I'm about to reply when Le Garre steps in front of me. "We're wasting time," she says. "Save your arguments for when we're all safe."

She's right. I bury any further arguments. "You're right," I say. "We need to hurry."

★ ★ ★

I'm still trying to control all of this. It's instinctive, part of how I'm conditioned.

I need to face this. No one can control what's going on.

I keep quiet as we organise ourselves and get to the airlock. Thylla and Marius do their best to ignore me and keep their distance. I get it. I'm the authority, the gaoler that they ran away from.

I'm in my EVA suit. My helmet is in my hands. Sam comes over and I stand in front of him with my arms raised, letting him check the seals.

"How are we doing?" I ask.

"Nearly there," Sam replies. "The base suits are older, but they all passed an inspection. They've been well maintained. Adapting this equipment for the baby is going to be tricky to manage, but we're working it out. They have prepared for this. Thankfully, all those printers and prefabricators allowed them to make a lot of stuff as and when they needed."

I lean in towards him. "Do you trust them?" I whisper in his ear.

"Angry words don't mean they'll do something stupid," Sam says. "My advice, Colonel? Let it be for now. We'll work everything out on the other side."

I nod and I put my helmet on. Sam helps with the locks, then touches the transmitter on his suit. I hear the muffled audio pop in my ear and give him a thumbs-up. He moves on and starts helping Elaine and Antoni.

My implant reconnects with the suit's data system. I get an immediate reading on all of my physical information – heart rate, blood oxygen levels, everything. There are some signs of tension, but otherwise, I'm good to go.

"First group ready for the airlock," Sam says. "Le Garre, take them out."

I move into the airlock.

★ ★ ★

I remember Admiral Langlsey's words when I first joined his office. There were six of us brought in from a variety of different organisations. An exciting opportunity that quickly became a cold dose of reality. That cramped little concrete building in the city of Utrecht was a disappointment.

"We're the people thinking long term for the rest of the world. We need to plan for decades ahead, generations ahead. No one else is doing this. That's why we need to be doing it.

"Our approach must be without fear or favour, even to our paymasters. The institutions that exist do so to improve society. The minute that they don't, they become our enemies. We cannot let corruption hide or fester anywhere.

"We must examine ourselves too. Prejudice, morality, assumption, familiarity. These can all blind us from what we're looking for. The best course may not be the righteous one."

The best course...that sentence is the one that stayed with me. Am I trapped and blind in the way I'm thinking about this?

"Opening the airlock," Le Garre says over open comms. "We need to move quickly."

The outer door rolls back, and I stumble out onto the cavern surface, a couple of steps behind Marius and Elaine. We need to get them on the conveyor before the rest of us set off.

"Base to Le Garre?" Sarandon is on the comms. He's staying behind, which means he can operate some of the systems from terminal inside.

"Go ahead."

"Gravity plate is not responding."

"Try again?"

"I've run the initialisation procedure three times. Nothing."

This is a problem. We were relying on the plate to launch us from the cavern surface. Without it, we're back to using spare air and oxygen tanks for propulsion like we were going to do on the way over. Each of us is carrying a fresh cylinder for exactly that purpose, but if we have to rely on that, it will take too much time.

I activate my transmitter. "Sarandon, Savvantine here. Try contacting Duggins and Irina on the interface. See if they can make it happen."

There is a pause. I get the feeling Sarandon doesn't want my help, but if this solves our problem….

"Okay, will try. Hold for an update."

"Will do."

We're moving over to the gravity plate and the conveyor cradle. I can see the little ship sitting inside the safety bars. The conveyor can launch under its own power, so we can get Elaine, Marius and Antoni on their way.

Le Garre reaches the control station for the cradle. She starts up the system and I see the entry panel open. "We have eighty percent charge," she says. "More than enough for what we need."

"Let's hope so," Sam says. "Group two on our way out now."

Elaine leads Marius to the conveyor. She is tethered to Antoni and holding him as well. The two of them get into the seats. Le Garre then helps them secure the baby.

The conveyor wasn't designed for a baby. Nothing humans have constructed in space is designed for a baby. Marius is working the console, changing the acceleration and deceleration maximums to try and avoid high g's. That will mean a slower ride.

But that's the way it has to be.

"Okay, we're ready," Elaine says.

"Acknowledged." Le Garre activates the auto launcher. The cradle safety bars lower, and the little ship is gently pushed away from the plate. Its thrusters kick in and it accelerates away into the darkness.

"Sarandon, any news on the gravity plate?" Sam asks.

"Duggins is working on it," Sarandon says. "The ship is gathering itself for a manoeuvre. That's why the plate isn't working."

The explanation is interesting, revealing more of the real context here. I'm wondering how much the scientists have actually discovered, and how much they have been allowed to access by the ship. "Major, I suggest we all make our way to the gravity plate anyway," I say over comms. "That way we're ready if Sarandon can get us what we need."

"Agreed," Le Garre says.

I'm moving already. The lights from my suit illuminate the rocky tundra beneath my feet but disappear when they hit the absolute black of the gravity plate. It takes a conscious effort of will to step onto it. My mind won't accept there is a solid surface under my feet and thinks I'm about to be sucked into an abyss at any moment.

Thylla joins me on the plate; a moment later, Sam and Le Garre arrive as well. As they step onto the plate, I feel it shift. A microadjustment ensuring we are lined up with the airlock on the other side of the cavern.

"Okay, Sarandon. We're ready for you."

I'm aware what's being done here is pretty dangerous. We're asking for a 'push' to send us off towards the airlock on the other side of the cavern. The velocity we gain from the push will need to be counteracted before we reach our destination, otherwise we'll all slam into an unforgiving rock wall.

The plan is that the conveyor will return and pick us up in two groups. Thylla has already programmed it to lock on to transponders we are wearing on our suits. It will adjust course, grab us and use its thrusters to decelerate to the other side.

Not a plan I'm confident about. But Thylla is trusting her own calculations, so I guess I'll have to trust them as well.

"Sarandon, acknowledge please?"

Clearly, Le Garre doesn't like to wait. Neither do I, not in a situation like this.

"All right we're ready here," Sarandon replies. "Three seconds."

I grit my teeth and clench my fists. My implant flashes a warning about my increased heart rate. *Shut up.*

Three.

Two.

One.

The push is firm, but not violent. A giant hand has thrown us into the darkness.

I'm rotating forwards in a slow roll. An easy mistake. I try to stay calm and go with it. There's nothing I can do to correct. Using my spare cylinder would be overkill and the burn would have to be so precise. Probably impossible.

Motion sickness might be a factor. The 'catch' from the conveyor may also be more difficult if I can't eyeball it. I look around. The research base is falling away, gradually getting smaller. I shut my eyes. The sensation of movement is something I can ignore, at least for now.

"Marius to Le Garre. We've arrived at the cradle. Conveyor is on the way back."

"Great. We're en route. Will join you shortly."

I can't figure out how long we've been moving. The implant has a timer, but when I make a request doesn't give me an accurate reading. I wonder if it's being affected by the rotation.

"Savvantine to Le Garre."

"Yes, Colonel?"

"I'm in a slow spin. Request first seat on the next trip."

There's a pause. "Colonel, I'm going to suggest you take second seat. If we put Sam on-board first, he can help get you on-board."

"Okay, that sounds like a plan."

Le Garre is calling me 'Colonel' – being formal. Am I only just noticing? I don't think she's like that around Shann. Should I read something into it? I don't know.

Another rotation and I can see an object moving towards me. It slips away to my right, then circles behind me. I can see it as I turn. It is approaching me from behind. Lights turn on, spearing into the darkness. I'm blinded by them.

"Colonel, I need you to reach out your hands," Sam says.

I do so, turning myself into a *T* shape. A moment later, fingers grab my right wrist and I'm pulled around backwards. I slam into something solid, and my head is jerked forwards into the padding inside my helmet. Thankfully, the EVA suit's backpack absorbs most of the impact.

"All right, Colonel, I have you."

I twist my body, bringing my arms together and grabbing Sam's wrist. He gets hold of my other arm and pulls me forwards, into the front seat of the conveyor. He lets go and I grip the cabin safety rail, then climb inside.

"Colonel Savvantine is on-board," Sam says. "We're returning to the cradle."

"Acknowledged," Le Garre says. "See you soon."

★ ★ ★

I'm outside the airlock. The conveyor has gone back for Le Garre and Thylla.

The door opens. Sam and I step inside. We'll be sitting here and waiting for the other two. It'll be quicker and safer if we only go through one pressurisation cycle.

I'm thinking about what Langsley said to me again, all those years ago. *We must examine ourselves too* – I must examine myself. Maybe

I'm focusing on the wrong components of this crisis? The two ships heading here. They are coming to prosecute the agenda of those who ordered the destruction of Phobos Station. That single act is the biggest crime in this situation, potentially one of the biggest crimes ever committed by any human being. My part in this may not be to act the guardian of a flawed system, a system that cannot be preserved. Perhaps my part is to bring those who would usurp everything to account for what they have done?

There is another trap here. I can't lose focus, become lazy in assuming all of the enemies of the state are in concert, lined up against us in a convenient binary. For one moment, maybe this action is a collective action, the will of the people in the darkened room. But those agendas will splinter and cut against each other.

I recall what I said to Drake: *'I'm a lighthouse keeper. My job is to keep the lights on, the wheels turning, everything functioning as it should.'* That could mean sacrificing anything, everything for the greater cause.

Perhaps in the aftermath of this, that will be something I can take advantage of.

CHAPTER FORTY-FOUR

Shann

I'm back in the airlock, removing my helmet. I can see Travers waiting behind the inner door. The moment the pressurisation completes he activates the release and starts talking to me.

"We've established contact with *Gallowglass*," Travers says. "She's seventeen minutes out. Johansson says this ship is going to manoeuvre. We need to evacuate as soon as possible."

"Have you told the others?" I ask.

"Drake is doing that now."

I look at him. He's breathing hard, pushed to the limit. "We get you on-board," I say. "No waiting for them."

Travers nods. "You too," he says.

I'm about to object, but then I think about it. Savvantine and Le Garre are with the others. They will organise them, get them here and across the rocky surface to *Gallowglass* when it arrives. "I'll stay until I know they are on their way across the cavern," I say.

I'm moving past him towards the hatch to the lower floor. I pull myself through and down. Drake is here, crouched in front of the terminal. As I approach him, the display goes dark and he turns around, his expression grave.

"We have some confirmation. Le Garre has been told by Duggins that the ship is going to move," he says.

"Are they on their way?" I ask.

"They're leaving shortly," Drake says. "The conveyor will bring over the first group and go back for the others, picking them up as they make their own way across."

I nod. "Do you have tactical information from *Gallowglass*? Where are the other ships?"

"Johansson did send over some tactical data," Drake says. "I'm not sure I'm qualified to make sense of it."

"Let me take a look," I say.

"Be my guest."

Drake moves aside and I take his place in front of the terminal. Johansson has provided a tactical plot, I pull it up on the display in a window, noting all the tagged objects.

"Why is *Gateway* out of Mars orbit? Why is it heading here?"

"No idea," Drake says. "I didn't know it was still able to move."

"Did Johansson say anything about it?"

"No, she just sent the data file."

Shuttle *Epsilon* is also inbound. A quick search reveals it's one of the short-range transports from Hera Spaceport. The last registered flight log was in response to the Phobos Station explosion. *Why are they coming here?*

I note the projections. The shuttle will arrive a couple of minutes before *Gallowglass*. *What's that all about?*

"If I head outside, can you and Travers handle things here?" I ask Drake.

"Provided mother and baby aren't being difficult, sure," Drake says. "I'm aware we need to get them moving quickly, but we'll have a little wait before *Gallowglass* is due."

I look at the projected timings. Marius, Elaine and baby Antoni should be in time, but the others will be cutting it close. We've no accurate calculation of how long their trip across the cavern will take.

I tap on the display. "Have you had any communication from shuttle *Epsilon*?" I ask. "They should be in range of our transmitter."

"Nothing," Drake says. "Until you showed me that image, I had no idea they were coming."

"Send Travers out as soon as the ship arrives," I say. "I'll go and meet the shuttle."

"On your own?"

"Yeah. Best if I handle it." I point to the taser on my belt. "I'll stay on comms."

I push away from the terminal and move to the hatch. As I pull myself upwards, I realise how tired I am. My arms ache from that short stint in a gravity environment and I've been operating non-stop for a long time.

Travers is floating by the airlock. I move over to him. He sees me and turns. "What's the latest?" he asks.

"*Gallowglass* ETA sixteen minutes," I say. "Before that, we have a shuttle coming in."

"A shuttle? Where from?"

"The old colonial ship, *Gateway*. She's also en route. Looks like someone broke her out of Mars orbit."

"Interesting."

I move to the hatch. "I'm going outside to find out who's on the shuttle. Keep the chamber depressurised, just in case I need to make a run for it."

Travers grimaces. "Let's hope it doesn't come to that."

"Yeah."

* * *

The grey stone of an alien landscape. The pitted outer hull of an object that has been a witness to thousands of years of human civilisation.

Right from the beginning to now.

I'm no scholar, no deep thinker beyond tactics and strategy. When the world comes crashing in, I'm the one you go to for decisions, action, motion. A switch flips and I live in the moment from one crisis to the next.

I've been doing that ever since we got the distress call from *Hercules*. Now...I'm here.

This is a moment between moments. I'm alone, waiting for what will happen next. In the waiting time, maybe I'm appreciating what this all is.

One living being, on a rock, hurtling through the void. I guess someone else would be more poetic about it.

I can see the shuttle, a large dot in the blanket of black. A repeating exterior light marks out detail as it gets closer.

Deceleration. Adjustment. Velocities match. The ship turns and descends, touches down.

I wonder if they've seen me. I'm crouched down, near the transmitter dish. I touch my comms. "Shann to Drake."

"Receiving."

"Any update on shuttle *Epsilon*? Have they reached out?"

"No, nothing, Captain."

"Noted. They've arrived. Will update when I know more."

I'm not approaching the shuttle. If there's a small crew on-board it'll take them a few minutes at least to get into EVA suits. If we're dealing with more Rocher clones, then waiting for them is going to be the better plan.

"Drake, what's the *Gallowglass* ETA now?"

"Thirteen minutes."

The timings are going to overlap. These people are going to be a problem if we're going to evacuate. They may get in our way or slow us down.

The shuttle hatch opens. I tense instinctively. Two figures are by the door. They exit the ship. I notice they aren't moving well, as if they aren't experienced with extra-vehicular activity.

I get a little closer, shuffling around, stirring up the regolith, watching them, seeing them stumble and fall in the big suits. Immediately, I'm sure these aren't Rochers. I wonder if they even know how to use the comms.

This is taking up valuable time. I need to make a decision. Either I'm confronting them or I'm boarding their ship. Fleet access codes should open up the hatch and allow me to control the airlock. If there are others on-board, I may have to deal with them, but I'm not overly concerned about that.

"Shann to Travers."

"Receiving."

"People coming to you. No comms so far. I'm going to make contact."

I push off from the rocks. I'm moving at speed, as fast as I can manage. This is dangerous. That's why we use tethers on a spaceship. But the irregular terrain gives me something to grab on to. I just need to make sure I don't do something stupid, like crash into something and bounce off into deep space.

I'm twenty metres away from these people. I take out the hand axe from my belt and dig it into the stony ground. Immediately, I'm slowing down, the blade of the aluminium tool scraping across the regolith, kicking up more dust.

I'm right behind the two. They haven't seen me. I drift right up to them and get in front of them. Suddenly, they see me and I see them. Two men, talking to each other on a private comms channel.

I switch to open broadcast. "This is Captain Shann of the *Khidr*. Please identify yourselves."

There's an audio click as someone changes their comms channel. "Oh...hello." One of the men tries to look at me. He's struggling with the EVA suit, trying to manage the systems and feedback inside the helmet. "My name is Tristan. We came here from *Gateway*."

"You need to get back in your shuttle and head straight back," I say. "There is nothing for you here."

"Actually, there is," Tristan says. "We need to get inside."

"That's not going to happen," I say. The taser is in my left hand, the metal axe in my right. I've angled my body a little, so the taser is concealed. "This is a Fleet operation. Civilians have no business being here."

"This is Mars," Tristan replies. "The Corporation Government has a claim on any unassigned assets in this sector. I am a citizen of Mars, and as such, a representative of the Corporation Government. If you're saying this rock has something to do with the destruction of Phobos Station, then I will back off and leave you to continue your investigation, Captain."

The second man steps forwards, trying to put himself in front of Tristan. I know he is no threat to me. Zero gravity is a specialist environment and moving in an EVA suit takes a lot of practice. He is bigger than me, stronger than me and seems to value those qualities a little too much.

Tristan says he is a citizen of Mars, one of the twelve. That might explain why he is here and why he thinks he has some sort of authority.

The issue is that I don't want to hurt these people.

"This asteroid is about to suffer a collision," I say. "We are evacuating the base that was built here. I can't let you stay here and kill yourself."

"If you have viable evidence of a threat, Captain, then you have authority here. If not, you don't."

I'm thinking about this. My instincts are to resolve this straightaway. Immobilise the second man, threaten Tristan and drag them both back to their shuttle. But those instincts have been established by recent experience. I've had to make binary decisions – yes/no, good/bad, whatever. If this man is telling the truth, he has a point.

"Where did you come from?" I ask.

"What?"

"The shuttle. Where did you launch from?"

"Just now? *Gateway*. We launched and—"

I move, ramming the axe into the ground, pulling myself forwards and jamming the taser into Tristan's ribs. His body twitches violently; vomit spatters the inside of his helmet.

Momentum takes me past him as he falls backwards. His friend is turning, trying to push forwards towards me. I use the axe again, digging it into the rock, pivoting around, facing him.

The taser is out. I'll need a new cartridge or a recharge. My other options are dangerous. "You need to stop and think what you're doing," I say. "This doesn't need to escalate. Just help me get your friend back on the shuttle. I'll set up the autopilot and have you out of here in a couple of minutes."

"What are you hiding here?" the man says. "I was told—"

"Believe whatever bullshit you want. I'm not going to talk about it. This is a Fleet operation. You help or you get put down."

For a moment, he considers it. The old rules of size, strength and power are instinctive to him. Then what he's just seen makes him reassess. "What do you want me to do?" he asks.

"I need to know why you are here," I say. I point to the shuttle. "And I need to know who else is on-board. After that, you sit out here with your friend and wait."

"All right," the man says.

"What do I call you?" I ask.

"Samuel," the man says.

"Great, Samuel. Do what you're told, and we should get along just fine."

★ ★ ★

"Shann to Travers."

"Go ahead."

"Made contact with the shuttle. Two are outside. One incapacitated, the other has agreed to stay out of it. What's the ETA on Le Garre and Sam?"

"Nine minutes or so."

"Get them straight through. Pick up whatever you can find as a weapon for them."

Nine minutes will be too late. Travers is in no condition to be backup. I'm on my own.

I'm at the shuttle steps, climbing them to the hatch. The outer door is shut, but I see movement inside. I touch the panel, locked.

There is a standard Fleet code to override locks on CorpGov vehicles. I open the keypad panel. Tap in the numbers. In that moment, I realise the person who wrote the sequence on the *Gallowglass* plans was Fleet too. He gave us a similar sequence. Not the same number of digits or the same pattern. Too much similarity would make it obvious.

I'm cursing myself for not working it out sooner, but there was no reason I would connect the two situations.

I tap in the code. The door opens.

Violence erupts in my face.

CHAPTER FORTY-FIVE
Holder – Wade

"Why are you here?"

Vessel and I are alone, left in the shuttle. Tristan and Samuel have gone outside, leaving us behind.

Vessel smiles. There is no humour in her expression. "Indira Attali wanted to be here. She believes all of this was an attempt to murder or kidnap her boss, Augustus Boipelo. She thinks they know about her and will finish her off in the chaos. She knew there was a base on this asteroid. She was hoping to get here and hide out, then slip away somewhere. Her plan was pretty desperate and foolish."

"That doesn't account for your transfer," I say.

"I had no choice when or where I arrived," Vessel says. "Indira saw you on Phobos Station, when you were in the lecture theatre. When you started behaving out of character, escaping from there and later, ordering the shuttle pilots around, she decided you were an agent sent to kill her. The breakout from the cargo compartment and death of Captain Francalla were confirmations for her. She thought those were distractions to give you an opportunity to get to her."

I shake my head. "I didn't even know who she was."

"Well, she thought she knew Alison Wade," Vessel says. "You'll be staying here. I fully expect you to try and escape, but it won't do any good."

"You still haven't answered my question."

"Because we're in the lull, the calm before the storm," Vessel says. "Earth is unaware of what's happening here. The first transmissions will be arriving right now, and the authorities will be trying to work out what they can do. They'll realise quite quickly they are powerless in this situation. They'll wait for an update, hoping the crisis will resolve itself."

"So, whatever you tell them will be what they believe."

"Pretty much," Vessel says. "Earth's institutions have enough going on to occupy their time. Atacama has made them look at each other. They would rather everything up here went away. They don't even want to sign the cheques. The aftermath of what's happened needs to be a story they can file away and forget."

"And you're going to take that opportunity to settle a few scores." I shrug. "Makes sense."

"The client mission is one we've been working on for a while," Vessel says. "Mars has become a problem. Some of the subordinates have become too used to being independent. The distance means they are beyond the direct control of their benefactors. The client has wanted us to get here for a while. You made this possible."

I nod. My escape from Emoli and Summers brought me unexpectedly to Mars. They must have figured out how I managed it and sent Vessel after me.

"Indira Attali is a known face, the right hand of Augustus Boipelo. We can use her, after we've taken care of business here," Vessel says.

"But you know what's going on," I say. "You know what you're being forced to do. Why are you obeying their orders?"

"Because I enjoy what I do," Vessel says. "It's a shame you never did."

She stands and starts to unpack another EVA suit. "Tristan and Samuel are on a private comms channel, floundering around outside. In a while, I'll need to go outside after them," she says. "The upload included EVA training and zero-gravity acclimation. It'll take minimal effort to puncture their suits or pull an air hose."

"Why would you do that?" I ask.

"Because Tristan Abernathy is not who you think he is," Vessel says. "Or rather, he is not who Alison Wade thinks he is."

I frown. The memories I have from Alison are limited interactions. They shared a shuttle to Phobos, they socialised a few times. I see Tristan smiling over drinks, Tristan and Jim talking together as Alison joins them for a leisure day. Nothing sinister.

Vessel is ready. She is holding the EVA suit helmet in her hands. "You freed your hands during the trip down," she says. "So far, you've held off making your play. If you want to sort this before I go out there, I'm good with that." She smiles. "Or, if you want to wait, maybe take advantage of an airlock? You need an edge, given the injuries you're carrying."

I shrug. "Makes sense to me. I'm still trying to figure out why you haven't got rid of me already."

"Tristan liked Alison," Vessel says. "I wasn't sure how much I might need Tristan. So long as he's useful, you are useful. When he dies, Alison Wade is of no further use to me."

Noise from the outside. Someone is on the steps. Vessel reacts immediately, putting on her helmet and moving into the airlock. She activates the depressurisation sequence. The inner door slides shut, and I hear the environmental system click and whir as air is drawn out of the transit space.

I'm leaning forwards, undoing the straps around my ankles and waist. Then I race down to the lockers and grab another EVA suit. Alison Wade has no experience of this. I have only what happened on Phobos Station. I had Diouf with me then. There is no one to back me up out here.

Only whoever is trying to get into the shuttle from the outside.

I've never put on an EVA suit by myself, but I just watched Vessel do it and before that, got a few glances at what Tristan and Samuel were doing. I'm repeating the process, copying their movements exactly, step by step. All the seals need to be in place, locked and secured.

But I also need to hurry.

No time for a full air tank. The emergency canister will do. The hoses plug into the same ports. It'll be a little awkward, but I can make it work.

My fingers are fumbling with the connectors. Alison Wade is still dormant, her body/my body still under the effect of Vessel's sedative. Every movement is an extra effort. Nothing feels right.

I'm dressed and at the airlock door just as Vessel exits, charging outside, straight at whoever is out there. I punch the inner door activator and the outer door closes. Nothing will open until there is air between the two doors, but at least the process has started.

I don't know what I'm getting myself into. Whoever is out there could be my ally or another enemy. I know I'm on limited time, but whatever time I have left is not going to be spent serving Emoli's agenda.

I can hear the shuttle's air tanks working. I need to get out there. *Come on!*

The helmet goes on. A twist to the left locks it into the runners and establishes a seal. Immediately, the suit pulls air from the connected canister. It's not designed for EVA, just for a mask attachment, so it won't give me long outside.

The door light changes, the inner airlock opens, I step inside, and the process starts again in reverse. Now I'm close enough to see outside through the DuraGlas window in the outer door.

The shuttle's exterior lights reveal a small area around where we landed. Dust hangs above the ground, stirred up by our landing, the complex forces making it swirl and churn. There is no gravity to help it settle.

Two figures move into view. They are fighting, wrestling on the ground. The contest is a deadly ballet. Every moment of struggle brings them both closer to murdering each other.

The exterior light goes green. The door rolls back, and I push myself from the deck, moving at speed, descending. Momentum can be a weapon; it will be a weapon.

It is the only weapon I have.

I crash into both figures. There are arms and legs and dust. I struggle to get my feet down, to see what I'm dealing with. But the swirling regolith clouds everything, clogs into everything.

My feet are on the ground. Lights flash in my helmet and an alarm sounds. The emergency air tank has been dislodged – ripped away. I take a deep breath and lash out, grabbing an arm, heaving, throwing, pushing away.

A helmet near mine. A cracked visor close to my face. I see a woman inside, her expression grim. She shakes her head, then pushes me away from her.

The dust clears. I'm moving backwards, scraping my hands across rock, trying to slow down. I see another figure flying through the air towards the woman. That must be Vessel.

The woman raises her arm. Light gleams off an object in her hand. It comes down, hard, smashing into the backpack of Vessel's EVA suit.

Vessel goes down on her face. A fresh cloud of dust explodes around her and starts to swirl in crazy patterns. I realise what that means. Her suit's air supply has been damaged; she's bleeding air.

The arm comes up again. Then down, hard and fast.

I turn around. I'm a few metres from the shuttle. The outer airlock is still open. I think I can reach it. I stumble in that direction, making it to the steps, then up the steps to the door. I'm falling inside, my chest starting to hurt with the effort of holding my breath.

I touch the comms control on the wrist of my suit, switching to an open channel. I don't know who the person is who got attacked by Vessel, but she's helped me and the least I can do is try and help in return.

"Hey! Airlock! Quickly!"

The words are a rasped shout. I take another quick breath afterwards, then turn to look out through the open doorway.

A figure erupts from the dust cloud, flying towards the shuttle. A hand snaps out, catches the edge of the gantry rail and the person pivots around, up the steps towards me. There's a burst of static on the comms. I just make out her shouting, "Close it!"

I jam my hand onto the button just as she crashes into me. The door slides shut, and the pressurisation process begins.

* * *

"Who are you?"

The woman is sprawled on the floor of the airlock chamber across from me. Her helmet is off, discarded to one side. Her face is covered in a sheen of sweat. There is blood around her temple.

She works herself up into a sitting position. She's carrying a metal pick of some sort. Its edge is chipped and torn. I notice the legs of her EVA suit are cut off above the knee.

She has no legs.

I'm about to answer, to tell her I'm Alison Wade, but stop before I do. I don't want to lie to this woman. "My name is Natalie Holder," I say. "But if you look me up, you'll find a personnel record on Phobos Station for a woman called Alison Wade."

The woman nods. She shifts her position carefully. "I'm Captain Ellisa Shann of Fleet," she says. Then she fixes me with a hard stare. "Your friend attacked me."

"She's not my friend."

"Figured as much when you jumped in with no more than a can of air on your suit."

"What happened to her?"

"She's dead," Shann says flatly. "Thanks to you, I'm alive."

The words hang between us. I sense Shann has questions, so before she asks them, I start talking.

I tell her my story, right from the beginning. I leave nothing out. There is no point. The adrenaline from throwing myself into a mad fight and nearly killing myself in the process has had another effect. I can feel the sedative wearing off. Alison Wade will wake up soon.

"In a few minutes, I'll be gone," I explain. "The person who I become, the real Alison Wade, she'll be very confused and frightened. Please help her understand, I didn't mean for any of this to happen."

"The woman outside is the same as you?" Shann asks.

I nod. "Her real name is Indira Attali. But the person you fought is Kate Vessel, another one like me."

Shann raises her eyebrows, digesting everything. I'm surprised that she's not surprised, not questioning me and making things difficult.

"Look, I don't know whether you believe me or not," I say. "But I don't have long. I want to do the right thing."

"Then you can start by letting me check your suit," Shann says. "After that, you check mine. Vessel cracked my helmet and shorted out the comms, so we'll need to find a replacement that fits. Once that's done, we invite your friends Tristan and Samuel on-board."

"Are you sure that's wise?"

"Samuel and I have an understanding," Shann says. "We'll use more of that sedative on Tristan. That'll keep him quiet until they're out of harm's way." She hauls herself off the floor and moves into the passenger cabin. "Come on. We don't have a lot of time."

★ ★ ★

I learn more in the next five minutes than I think I've learned in my entire life.

Shann works fast. She finds a rip in the arm of my suit. Some chemical sealant and a patch cover that up. Then she grabs another air tank and straps me in.

As she works, she talks. Explaining what happened to her, her ship and her crew. The *Khidr* responded to a distress call, fought another ship, called *Gallowglass,* and got destroyed. Shann and her crew escaped, boarded *Gallowglass* and took command, killing her original crew.

A crew of Rocher clones.

As soon as clones are mentioned, everything clicks into place. I know why she believes me. All of this is too crazy to be made up.

"*Gallowglass* is on its way," Shann says. "If we want to live, we have to get on-board. This isn't an asteroid. It's an alien ship, and it's about to start moving out of here."

"I met your people, Johansson and Chiu. They came over to *Gateway*."

"They didn't have a lot of choice," Shann says. "*Gallowglass* was programmed to head there after it came here. I guess now we know why. To pick up all those lovely cryopods, embryos and DNA samples."

"I didn't tell Johansson the truth about me," I say. "Maybe I should have."

"You made your choice and had your reasons. I'm not judging you for it." Shann moves into the pilot's seat of the shuttle and activates the display.

"What are you doing?" I ask.

Shann chuckles. "Using the same tricks on your fellow passengers that were used on me. My Fleet ID can override the basic autopilot programming. We're going to pack this crate and send it to Mars. It'll find a safe landing place, turn on its emergency beacon and wait for help."

"You're sending me there too?" I ask.

Shann stops what she's doing and turns around to stare at me. "Not at all," she says. "Right now, you're far too useful." She points towards the door. "I'm sending you back out there to bring those people back in. Once that's done. I'll set the controls and you and I can wave them goodbye as they head to Mars."

CHAPTER FORTY-SIX

Johansson

Five minutes to go. The last possible moment that I can start the deceleration process.

"All right, initiate burn. Run it hot."

"Working," Chiu says. On the *Khidr* she would be communicating with Duggins in the engineering room. On *Gallowglass*, everything is run from the bridge terminals. "Brace yourselves."

The burn hits me like a wave. The ship is running in reverse, so as to maximise our deceleration with the main engines. This is how we wanted to position *Gateway*, but we didn't have enough manoeuvring thrusters to do it. With *Gallowglass*, we're not trying to reverse course, not completely, not yet.

I'm pushed forwards into the straps. Best to relax for some of this, then tense as the force increases. In this position, breathing becomes an effort, but I'm used to this. I've been here a few times.

Six and a half g's. Seven. This is dangerous. We've all had the injections, but Chiu and I have had the training for this. Rocher might have been conditioned, but Aster is older and has been in space for a few years. She can't take this for long.

Ten seconds, then the pressure starts to ease. With an effort, I'm speaking. "Diouf…check on Aster…when we slow."

I get a grunted reply. I think it was an affirmative.

I can breathe without effort now. My hand is working the panel on the arm of the chair, accessing the ship's exterior cameras. New windows appear, an updated tactical plot, a view of the grey stone expanse below. We are one hundred metres from our targeted destination. Below, I can see shuttle *Epsilon*, landed near the building Shann and the others entered before.

"Fifteen seconds until complete," Chiu says.

"We'll need a landing party," I say. "Rocher, you're up. I want all your tactical projections uploaded to our system. We're going up against clones on those ships. I want to know what they'll do when we engage. After that, head down to the surface."

New windows appear on the display. The faces of Diouf, Chiu and Daniel Rocher. "You're trusting me with this?" Rocher says.

"I have to," I say. "Chiu and I are needed to prep the ship. Diouf must help Aster. I could send him with you, but that wouldn't be the right thing to do. We'll tell them you're coming and that you're an ally."

"I'm surprised."

I scowl at him. "Prove yourself. Help them get off this rock and you get what you want. Take a screen, when you meet Shann or any of the others, put me on direct video comms. Then I can talk them around."

"I'll do everything I can to help," Rocher says. "Hopefully, we can get all your people aboard and safe."

I bite back my instinctive reply. . *You were trying to kill me an hour or two ago!* An answer like that will break our fragile alliance. "Get going," I say. "We don't have long before *Gateway* arrives."

When he's gone, Chiu unclips herself from her seat. "You sure you trust him with all that?" she asks.

"I don't have an option," I say. "You and I need to get the ship prepped." I get out of my seat and over to Diouf. "How's she doing?" I ask.

"Not great," he says. "I think the straps cracked a couple of her ribs."

I move forwards, checking his diagnosis. Aster's eyes are closed. Her breathing is shallow and wheezing. A little pressure with my fingers along the lines of her ribs causes her to wince and cry out in pain. "Yeah, I think you're right," I say. "We'll need to strap these, then get her into an EVA suit."

"You're still sending her out?" Diouf asks.

"That's what she wanted," I say. "Doing anything else would make me a liar."

★　★　★

Five minutes.

I can see *Gateway* on the tactical plot. The ship is getting closer. Whatever Elliott's people have done, it hasn't worked.

The *Nandin* separates from the ancient colony ship. I watch as she moves away, getting clear before impact. I wonder how many people they managed to rescue? It can't have been all of them.

Xiua will think of something. He has five shuttles. They can act as lifeboats, provided he can get enough distance between the ship and the place of impact. With a little effort and coordination, there are places for everyone to escape before it smashes into the rocky hull of this place.

"Rocher to Johansson."

"Go ahead."

"Am exiting the airlock now."

I pull up the exterior camera view. I can see him in the doorway, stepping out and down to the surface of the alien ship. His boots hit the surface and kick up rock dust. "Head for the base," I say. "I'll radio them and tell them you're coming."

"On my way."

I pull up a second window. Drake's face appears. "Doctor, this is *Gallowglass*. We're in position. Waiting for passengers."

Drake nods. "I'll send the first group out," he says. "Have you made contact with Shann?"

I frown. "No, I thought she was with you."

"She was, but she went to investigate the shuttle. We've not heard from her since then."

"Understood." I'm weighing up my options. "I'll send Rocher to the shuttle to check on her."

"Rocher? One of the clones?"

"Yes, this one's on our side."

Drake scowls. "He better be."

The window disappears. I switch back to Rocher. "Change of plan. Head for the shuttle. Captain Shann should be there. She may need assistance."

"Hopefully, she'll talk first and act after."

"We'll try to raise the shuttle," I say. "If I can talk to her, or to Alison Wade, we should be able to find out what's going on."

"Keep me updated," Rocher says.

I switch windows again, trying to contact shuttle *Epsilon*. This didn't work before. I try a comms request and an audio transmission patched into their speakers. "*Gallowglass* to *Epsilon*, are you receiving? Please acknowledge."

The comms request flashes twice, then a window opens and Shann's face appears.

I'm smiling. I can't help myself. "Hello, Captain."

"Hello yourself," Shann says. She looks tired and a little worse for wear. "Good to see you, Johansson."

"What's your situation?" I ask.

Shann glances to her left. "I'm here with Alison Wade. Her companions are in the process of being retrieved and secured into the passenger seats before we exit and send them to Mars. After that, we'll come across and join you."

"I'll look forward to that," I say. "A Rocher is on his way to you. He was part of the station crew on *Gateway*. He is helping us."

Shann frowns. "You trust him?"

"I trust he'll act in his own self-interest, like they all do," I say.

"Good enough, Ensign," Shann says. "Be ready to brief me on everything I've missed. Shann out."

★ ★ ★

Everything is moving.

Space is never still. The Big Bang set everything into motion. A huge dense ball of matter exploded. Much was annihilated, and the remaining debris was flung across the emptiness.

That debris became our universe.

When we examine our solar system, we are looking at a region of space that is in constant motion. Each object rotating, turning, orbiting everything else. But also, the whole solar system orbiting a vast entity out there lifetimes away from us. All of this bound together, but gradually flying apart, further and further away.

This motion is relative. We have words like 'stop' and 'halt' that describe our desire to be still, but in reality, we are never still. Human language can't describe the relativity of motion quickly, instinctively. Instead, we need to elaborate, throw more words at our description of activity. That's because this isn't our experience. We live on a planet that has an up and down, and that allows us to stop in relation to everything around us.

In space, it's all different and sometimes the language can't cope.

In this moment, I am looking at specific movements on a tactical plot. *Gallowglass* is moving, our velocity synchronised with the alien ship below us. *Gateway* is on a collision course with the same ship. *Nandin* is moving to intercept *Timore* and *Boryenka*. Shuttle *Epsilon* is preparing to move. Fleet ships *Seraphiel* and *Asthoreth* remain relatively motionless.

Human beings are on-board each of these ships. None of them are inherently evil. They must have rationalised their actions, decided to choose a cause and a side.

There are other movements. Members of the Avensis research team are evacuating from their base, heading for this ship. Shann, Wade and Rocher will be on their way too. Chiu is in the bowels of the ship, running diagnostics and checks, getting us ready to move.

Meanwhile, I'm sitting here, fixed in place, relatively speaking.

I've run the numbers. As soon as everyone is on-board, we'll need to run the engines hard. Another high-g burn to get us clear and catch up with *Nandin*. The projection says it will work, just about.

But these people need to hurry.

I have a moment or two. I pull up the filtered databases of information I downloaded from Mars. The root key database file is the smallest one I can examine quickly. I open it.

Thirteen entries. All of them encrypted with personal codes.

Another comms request flashes. I pull it up and a camera activates in the new window. I see a blurry picture and realise I'm in the airlock of shuttle *Epsilon*. The inner door is open. Wade is standing in front of the camera, her expression grim.

"Hello, Johansson," she says. "Rocher here says you said I'm to trust him."

"Yeah, that's what we're doing," I reply.

"What about the transmission?" Wade says. "Ask him how he can save me."

I frown. "I don't know anything about this."

"Ask him!" Wade shouts then glares at Rocher. "Tell her!" he demands.

The camera moves, then disconnects. I patch in another comms request to the shuttle. Shann picks up. "You need to get Rocher to tell Wade what she wants to know."

"I don't know what—"

"Ensign, this needs to happen. Stand by."

Shann moves out of the seat in front of the camera. There are words being exchanged. I can hear Wade's angry voice in the background.

Eventually, Rocher appears. He settles himself into the chair.

"Johansson, you need to listen carefully. *Gateway* received a transmission from Phobos Station before it was destroyed. The files are covert plans for a device that transfers identities – a subject's brain state and personality. It's proprietary technology, illegal and secretly being used by an organisation on Earth to perform contract assassinations. That's the reason the station was attacked. The people who organised the attack wanted the technology."

"And you were the comms officer on *Gateway*...."

"I received the files, encrypted them using a distribution algorithm. All of the data has been attached to the station's document logs. Tiny parts of every file added to other files. The only way to rebuild everything is to run it through the same program again."

"Or construct a similar assembler," I say.

"That would take more time, though I don't doubt you could do it." Rocher smiles. "Wade needs the program. She's not really Wade. She's someone else in Wade's body. You'll find my assembler in my profile documents folder. It's labelled as a video file. The only one in there."

"Okay, I can get the files," I say. "But even if you have them, there's no way you could manufacture a device without equipment."

"The research base has fabricators and printers," Shann says. "It can be done here."

I'm about to reply, but then realise there's no point. I'm not in control of these people's choices. "I'll get the files and send them over to you," I say. "Johansson out."

I pull the headphones off, disconnect myself from the safety straps and climb out of the chair. I'm breathing hard, my fingers curling into fists. I'm angry. We don't have time for all of this. If they stay here, these people are going to die.

"Johansson?"

I glance around. Chiu is in the doorway. I hear the question and nod. "Yeah, I'm fine, just trying to understand."

"I caught most of it," Chiu says. "We've done all we can. Now they make their own choices."

I'm thinking about Shann. She didn't say she was going to stay. After all this, if she did, I think it would break me.

CHAPTER FORTY-SEVEN

Savvantine

I'm in the operations base, moving through the rooms, up through the torn hatch into the outer airlock. Behind me are Sam, Thylla and Le Garre.

Travers and Drake are waiting for us. The doctor grimaces when he sees me, but that's to be expected.

"Good to see you awake, Travers," Le Garre says. "You up for the last push?"

"I'll make it, Major," Travers says.

I haven't met Shann's XO before. He was badly injured and hasn't really recovered. There's a fragility to his voice over the comms; we may need to keep an eye on him.

"*Gallowglass* is in position," Drake says. "We're moving out now. Two groups in the airlock. Travers, Sam and I are the second group."

I nod and move forwards. Thylla and Le Garre follow. We're in and waiting out the process. Then the outer door opens and we're out on the rocky tundra of the ship's hull once more.

I can see *Gallowglass* ahead, floating almost exactly where it was before. That sight lifts me. I'm smiling. After everything, an old cynic happy to see salvation.

Between us and the ship is a shuttle, parked on the surface. I activate my comms. "Savvantine to *Gallowglass*. What's with the shuttle?"

"Ignore it, Colonel," Johansson replies. "A full explanation will be given when you arrive here."

Figures are moving around the shuttle. I see Shann. She is distinctive amongst them. Instinctively, I make a decision and divert towards what's going on. My curiosity has got the better of me.

"Colonel, what are you doing?" Le Garre asks.

"Pulling rank, Major," I reply and keep moving towards Shann.

I get close and send her a direct private communication request. She accepts. "Something you need, Colonel?"

"Yeah, an explanation. I thought we were leaving this rock?"

"We are, they are not." Shann points to two figures packing away the shuttle steps. "Rocher and Holder. They've elected to stay."

"Rocher? One of the clones?"

"Yes. He's provided an explanation to Johansson. She trusts him and I trust her."

The answer is unsatisfactory and implacable. Shann is taking a stand and making a point. I know what it means. If I want to second-guess this, I'll need to take command.

"They know the risks?" I ask.

"They do," Shann says. "They are also sticking around to help."

I scowl and turn away. I see two more people leaving *Gallowglass*, making for the research base. One of them being assisted by the other. *What the fuck is going on around here?*

"Colonel, we're at the airlock," Le Garre says. "Are you joining us?"

I swallow an irritated reply and start moving to catch up. These people trust each other's judgement. They've been through hell in all this. These are the moments when I'm an obvious outsider to them. "With you, Major. Head inside," I say.

"Acknowledged."

The airlock processing will take a similar amount of time to getting out here from the base. That means if I delay, I'm delaying group two as well. They will already be on their way.

I reach Thylla and Le Garre just as the outer door opens. We go in and wait as the room fills with air.

I'm ignoring the others, sitting with my own thoughts. Why would Johansson trust this Rocher?

I need to know what's going on. Being on-board *Gallowglass* gives me access to the ship's exterior sensors. Immediately, I connect and download the latest tactical plot. All the positions of the ships, all of their trajectories, courses and velocities.

Gateway is going to crash here, about six hundred metres or so from our current position. The projected impact will cause catastrophic damage, throwing up debris that will damage or destroy *Gallowglass* and shuttle *Epsilon*.

I remember what Le Garre told me. Duggins said the alien ship is going to move. *This must be why!*

Gallowglass has a lot of shared activity logs from *Gateway*. I learn that Daniel Rocher was the one who hacked *Gateway*'s controls and initiated a burn to bring the ancient ship out of orbit and into a collision course with the alien ship. Why the fuck did they let this guy out? Why is he being trusted and left behind here?

"Pressurisation complete," Chiu says. "You can come out now."

I turn around. Thylla is by the inner hatch, Le Garre a little behind her. I grasp hold of my helmet, twist and unlock it. Then I start taking off the rest of the EVA suit. Makes sense not to crowd the smaller room beyond. I'll carry everything through when I'm ready.

As I work, the implant is feeding me more information. I see the passenger manifest for shuttle *Epsilon*. Tristan Abernathy is a known alias for Derrin Lomas, one of the twelve citizens of Mars. Indira Attali is the personal aide to Augustus Boipelo, the colony's deputy governor.

I remember Indira Attali. She was with Boipelo when she quit Earth politics in 2114 AD. I know about that incident. An unauthorised piece of brain surgery that we tried to investigate, but before we could get the details, Boipelo and her detail left Earth and went to Mars.

When I learned about her assassination on Phobos Station, I sent marines in to retrieve her head. I wanted to get an autopsy done and find out what had been placed in her brain.

The head is in a case on the *Seraphiel*. Or, it's somewhere else, if Lieutenant Stephen Rivers managed to get hold of it and secrete it somewhere.

I'm moving into the utility room. The EVA suit components need to be stowed. This ship will need to initiate a burn to get clear of the collision. Anything left unattended can become a missile, tearing through the inside of the ship. Le Garre is supervising, taking everything from Thylla and storing it into moulded compartments. She glares at me as I approach them. "Find what you wanted?" she asks.

"Not yet," I say. "I need to get to the bridge."

"You know the way," Le Garre says. "We'll finish up here."

★ ★ ★

"Why did you let him go?"

Johansson is in the pilot's chair. She turns around as I enter. "Good to see you, Colonel," she says. "We're prepping to depart, so I don't have a lot of time."

"Answer my question, Ensign, why did you let Rocher go?"

Johansson sighs and seems to sag in front of me. "Because he wanted to go."

"I've seen what he did. Leaving his post, spoofing the automated orbital controls to get the ship out of orbit and set it on a collision course," I say. "Your reasoning isn't going to cut it in front of a board of enquiry."

Johansson smiles. The expression is almost feral. "You want me to stand down? Want us all to die? I've dealt with Rocher before. Once you find their self-interest, you find a way to deal with them."

"A Rocher you encountered stabbed you," I say.

"Been reading the logs, have we?"

"Every chance I get."

Johansson nods. "All right. Daniel Rocher, communications officer from *Gateway*, offered a trade. He wants to be here and escape from his makers. As a trade, he offered up the tactical procedures those two incoming ships will adopt when they close to weapons range. Currently, given the condition of *Gallowglass*, and *Nandin*, I judged we'd have no chance without that data if it comes to another firefight."

"*Seraphiel* and *Asthoreth* are still out there."

"And we've no communication from either ship. We have no way of knowing whether they are on our side or not. Unless you have something else you want to share?"

I smile. "I like the way you think, Ensign. You're wasted as a communications officer. When all this is over, you should come and work for me."

"What makes you think I'd want that?"

"Just a hunch." I move into the room and take one of the seats. "What about Indira Attali and Tristan Abernathy? How did they end up here?"

"Of their own volition, I think," Johansson replies. "They were evacuated from the station with more than seventy others. The shuttle teams were in charge when I arrived at *Gateway*. Neither Attali nor Abernathy made themselves known to Xiua and Masson, who were running the bridge. Instead, they stole a shuttle and came here."

I nod, absorbing the information. Abernathy is a self-serving idiot who has an inflated sense of his own intelligence. He must have decided there was something worth claiming here. Maybe he thought he could use it as some sort of bargaining chip against whoever destroyed Phobos Station?

Attali is a different deal. She's clever and desperate. After Boipelo's death she'd know they would be sending people after her. Did she think she could hide here and get away?

There are things here I don't know, and I may never know. Sometimes that's what happens, and the mysteries are never solved.

"Tell me about Rocher and *Gateway*," I say. "Why does he want to be here? And why do you believe him?"

Johansson shrugs. "I don't believe everything he told me," she says. "He betrayed the *Gateway* crew and stayed on-board the ship. Then he went down to the cargo compartment, woke up several other clones and hacked the ship computer to break *Gateway* out of orbit. He says the other ships are coming to retrieve the cryopods and genetic vault they've stored here. He says the plan was to build a colony on Europa."

I smile. I know a lot of this already from the records I've been able to access, but it's good to hear from Johansson. "So, his stated reason to try and bring that cargo to the alien ship is, like you said, to try and escape."

"Other Rochers behaved in the same way," Johansson says. "If there was a chance to get away, they were going to take it."

"Makes sense," I say. "But he's complicit in a terrorist operation. Fleet will want him prosecuted."

"I didn't grant him immunity," Johansson says. "Just traded for his tactical acumen to help us get through the next hour or two."

"All right, what about Genevieve Aster?"

"I don't know a lot about her," Johansson says. "Some sort of brain doctor expert that they kidnapped. She went back to them afterwards. I guess she must be important in some way."

Aster's records are available to me from the Fleet archive. A prosecuted researcher who was caught up in a fraud scandal back in the 2080s. After that she fled Earth. There is no record of where she ended up. Maybe these people don't care too much about that, but for me, a product of an organisation dedicated to keeping track of these things, it's a big hole.

Rocher was sent after Aster. I know from what Duggins showed me that the people in the room wanted Aster.

My implant gives me more information about the dMemra trial. Court records and filings. She was set up to be the scapegoat, an academic with enough of a reputation to draw media attention. All of it looks like a power play. The company's assets were bought up during liquidation. She lost everything.

I frown. The alien ship is a huge asset to whoever ends up with it. I'm not convinced that Sarandon, Marius, Elaine and Thylla have made as much progress as they claimed about deciphering the alien technology, but I'm sure there will be many eager scientists keen to get their hands on what's in there. Maybe Aster's expertise is what they need? In any respect, it will be a disruption to the balance we have tried to preserve.

I don't know how to solve that. But I know I will need to act when the time comes.

Le Garre enters the bridge. She glances at us both. "Shann is on-board," she says. "We're just waiting on Diouf, the tech from Phobos Station."

I move around the room towards her. "This isn't going to be easy," I say. "Those ships will stop at nothing—"

Le Garre holds up her hand, interrupting me. "Colonel, don't tell me how to do my job. This might be your first combat experience in space, it isn't mine."

I glance at Johansson. She shrugs, indicating the same.

I smile. "All right, then maybe I'm wrong. I apologise."

Le Garre nods. "First time you've done that," she says. "Least as far as I remember."

CHAPTER FORTY-EIGHT

Holder – Wade

Shuttle *Epsilon* takes off.

The process happens in silence. Thrusters fire and the ship rises. There is little evidence of anything happening. The vacuum of space disperses any burned propellant.

The two men on-board will have to endure a trip from here to the surface of Mars. They will have no control over their fate, no choice but to trust that Shann has programmed the computer correctly and doesn't want them dead.

The shuttle gets smaller and smaller. Tristan and Samuel will have the best chance of being away from here before *Gateway* arrives and crashes into the stone tundra of this place.

I glance at Shann. She looks at me, then at Rocher. "Okay, people," she says. "Last chance to leave."

"Sorry, Captain," I say. "I'd love to come with you, but that would be a death sentence." I turn to Rocher. "This way I have a chance, according to you."

"Then we're out of time," Shann says. "Time I join my people and leave you to it." She raises a hand, touches her fingers to the side of her helmet in that time-honoured military gesture. "Good luck," she says. Then starts moving away.

I'm left with Rocher. Not my preferred choice of companion.

"We need to get to the base," he says. "Come on."

I'm following him across the rocky ground, trying to judge how best to move in zero gravity. I'm awkward and uncoordinated. Alison Wade has no experience of being outside space stations and spaceships.

"I think the reason they organised everything on Phobos Station was to get hold of the technology that made you," Rocher says.

"You're talking about this as if 'they' isn't you," I say.

"My job was to make a life for myself on *Gateway* and wait until I received further orders," Rocher says. "Twenty-four hours ago, I got those orders. I swapped shifts on the comms position and waited. Just before the station blew up, we received a data transfer. I took a look at it and could tell what it was. Then I hid the files in *Gateway*'s file system."

"I was on Phobos Station with another Rocher who sent that transfer," I say.

"A piece of the puzzle," Rocher says. "Powerful people want to transfer their own identities into newly grown clones, wiping out the identities that already existed. To these people, I'm fresh meat and you're a test subject."

I'm seeing the connection and starting to understand why Rocher is here. "You went against their orders," I say. "You weren't supposed to come here."

"The cryopods and DNA library were supposed to be taken to Europa," Rocher says. "That's what the clones on-board the *Timore* and *Aegeas* are coming here for. They'll want the cargo compartment. Everyone else is collateral damage."

"Why bring them here?"

"I'm hoping we can hide them and get out of here," Rocher says.

"*Gateway* is on a collision course with this ship," I say. "I take it that wasn't your plan?"

"I had to work with what I had to hand," Rocher says. "Now I'm hoping the alien is aware of what's happening and that they'll react and move out of the way or something."

We are nearly at the base. There are two figures ahead of us, tethered together. The leader is helping the other.

We are gaining on them.

We reach the airlock door a few steps behind and move inside with them. One of the two turns towards me. I recognise who it is. I activate the open channel on my suit comms.

"Diouf, what are you doing here?"

"Helping," Diouf says. He scowls. "If I ask you the same question, are you going to give me a straight answer?"

I wince. "All right, I deserve that," I say.

"Whatever," Diouf replies. Gently, he helps the person he is with into a corner of the airlock. "You two are here now. You can deal with Doctor Aster."

"You leaving with the others?" Rocher asks.

"I hope so," Diouf says. "I only came here to make sure you were okay."

He hesitates, just for a moment. That hesitation tells me he cares. We shared something escaping Phobos Station.

"I'm sorry," I say. "You deserve an explanation."

"Damn right I do," Diouf says.

I glance at Rocher. He shakes his head. "It'll take too long," he says.

I nod. "You'll get my story," I say to Diouf. "I'll tell you all of it, the whole truth. Nothing varnished."

"I'll listen," Diouf says.

"Get going," I say. "Otherwise, you'll miss your ride."

"Yeah, can't have that." Diouf moves away, then he turns back, waves once, then pushes on.

I watch him go, until Rocher touches my arm.

"Fuck off," I say.

★ ★ ★

We're inside, taking off our EVA suits. Rocher works fast. He's clearly had training and experience. Once he's done, he turns to help Genevieve Aster.

The woman's helmet is off. She looks exhausted and in pain. Rocher told me they had to decelerate hard to get *Gallowglass* in position. She must have known the journey would be arduous, but she still came.

I can't work out why.

"Hello, Holder," Aster says. She smiles at me.

"What did you think you would gain coming here?" I ask.

"Freedom," Aster replies. She glances at Rocher. "He told me about this ship. About what they found here and how they found it."

"I get the feeling he hasn't told me everything," I say.

"We needed to be here," Rocher says. "And, if I'm right, we aren't alone."

Aster is out of her EVA suit. Rocher has stopped helping her and is moving into the room beyond the airlock. He is heading towards a terminal. The display is still active. Shann's people must have been using it before they left.

Rocher climbs into the seat and tries to log in. "Damn! The system has been completely rewritten at this end. I can't access anything."

I pick up my suit helmet and activate the communicator, switching to a private channel. "Holder to Shann, can you hear me?"

The helmet speakers crackle with static, but I make out a couple of words. "This is Shann, go ahead."

"Captain, we need access to the terminal in the base. Can you help?"

"I can help *you*," Shann says. "I asked Travers to modify the system before he left. Log in with your name, your real name. Surname as password."

"Surname as password, got it."

I put the helmet down and move into the room. "Tell me your plan," I say to Rocher. "All of it."

Rocher sighs. "We don't have time for this."

"If you want access to that computer, you'll make time," I say.

Laughter from behind me. Aster is there, moving slowly into the room to join us. "She has you there," she says.

Rocher gives me a pained look. "I've been here before," he says softly.

"What?"

"I've been here before," Rocher says. "*Gallowglass* too. Before I was placed on *Gateway*. I was a member of the crew sent on a resupply mission to the research team when this ship was far out in the solar system. They had people here. Back then, they hadn't got very far.

They were still working on this room, but they knew what they had. I memorised some of the transmission frequencies and encryption codes. Later, when I was on *Gateway*, I used the codes and was able to pick up a few messages. I know they can control this ship. Your friend Shann and her crew might be evacuating, but I think they've been played. There are people here who can make this ship move out of the way."

"We need to tell Shann," I say.

Rocher shakes his head. "No, we don't. We really don't. We need Fleet to get out there and fight the new ships that are coming in. The people who made me will not want to let go of this place. All the possible technologies and innovations, plus the DNA library and cryopods. They'll want all their property back. If my plan goes right, we'll be taking all of that with us too. Ben Sarandon was in charge. We need to contact him. That's why I need access to the computer."

"What happens if I don't help you?" I ask.

Rocher points upwards, he's gesturing towards the ships in space. "To the victor and all that shit. Whoever wins out there will claim us as part of their spoils. You and I become test subjects. Everything about us will be downloaded, dissected and analysed." He points at Aster. "Ask her, she knows what they'll do."

"Holder does not need me to confirm your words," Aster says. "She already knows the truth. She knows you want to use her for your own purposes as well."

"You want what's in my head," I say.

Rocher smiles. "If I do this right, you won't need that container anymore and Alison Wade will have her life back." He steps towards me. "Look, I'm not going to deny that I have an objective, or that I'm self-motivated."

"That would be a lie if you did," I say.

"All three of us have vested interests," Rocher says.

I nod. "Get out of the way," I say. "Let me get to the terminal."

Rocher moves aside and I access the display, typing in the user and password Shann gave me. "All right, do what you need to do," I say.

"Thank you," Rocher says. He climbs back into the seat and initiates a set of instructions. He is working quickly. Command windows appear and vanish in quick succession. "The interface is crude, but given how little time Ensign Johansson had to put it together, I'm very impressed."

"You should be able to establish a communications link easily," I say. "What else are you doing?"

"What needs to be done," Rocher says.

CHAPTER FORTY-NINE
Shann

I'm on-board *Gallowglass*, moving through the corridors, making for the bridge. Diouf is the last person we're waiting for. Once he's inside, we need to move as fast as we can to get clear of the impact zone.

The whole situation is fucked up. With Phobos Station gone, *Gateway* is the only large orbital structure capable of providing logistical support to the Mars colony. Johansson's data brief mentioned they weren't in contact with people at Hera Spaceport or the Jezero dome. Whatever is going on up here has also affected what's going on down there.

A debris storm in the Martian atmosphere could be catastrophic. Maybe it has already been catastrophic down there. Whatever happens after all of this will be about trying to save lives, to repair or begin again on Mars. Without *Gateway*, we might be too late for many people who need help.

Duggins said the alien ship was going to move. We need it to move.

I'm at the bridge. Johansson is here, Savvantine is here, Le Garre is here. The captain's chair is empty. I may have arrived in the middle of a conversation. If I have, I don't care.

"Stations please," I say. "What's our situation?"

Johansson gets out of the pilot's chair, moving towards comms. She is looking at me. For a moment, it's as if she's seen a ghost. Then her usual professional expression returns. "Maintaining current position adjacent to the asteroid, Captain. We're ready for a burn as soon as we get clearance."

"Projection on our safe window?"

"About ninety seconds."

I settle into the chair and deploy the acceleration straps. *Gallowglass* is not my ship, but we've been to war together. I activate the terminal in front of me and open a general channel, audio that will be heard through every speaker on the ship. "*Gallowglass* crew, this is your captain. Prepare for immediate main engine burn. Safety positions and report in."

"What do you want me to do, Captain?" Savvantine says.

"Engineering seat for now, Colonel," I say. "Bridge rules apply. I trust you can keep to that?"

"Noted and yes, I understand."

"Good." I'm pulling up all the tactical trajectory information. Johansson's plot is overlaid onto the current positions. She's been busy, calculating all of the current courses and timings for every ship in the vicinity. "What's our available ordnance?"

"No torpedoes, Captain," Johansson says. "Both lasers are functioning and operating at capacity."

"So, we need to get close," I say. "What about the bafflers?"

"They are repaired and available too."

Great. We have defences, but we have to expect the *Timore* and *Boryenka* have the same defences. "Everybody ready?" I ask.

"All set here, Captain," Le Garre replies. She's back in the pilot's chair. A window appears on my screen, the camera feed from her station showing her in the seat. "Ready to go."

"Ready here, Captain," Johansson says.

"Give me comms with *Nandin*," I say. "Hail *Gateway* too, check if anyone is still on-board."

"All are evacuated, Captain," Johansson says.

"All right, that's one less voice to worry about." I key up a window with Savvantine's camera feed. "Colonel, I want you on weapons, talking to the shuttles and helping Johansson with tactical coordination, once we know who is on our side and who isn't."

"Understood."

Another window appears on the screen. I see Travers in airlock control. With his helmet off, I can see just how tired he is. "Captain, Diouf is on-board. You are clear to manoeuvre," he says.

"Thank you, Lieutenant," I reply. "Le Garre, you get that?"

"I did, Captain, burn initiating in five seconds."

I tense up instinctively. I've been through this a hundred times, but that doesn't stop it being a moment for a few nerves. "What's our projected g?" I ask.

"Eight or nine," Le Garre says. "I'll hold it for as long as we can. Deceleration will be less as we approach *Nandin*."

Dangerous forces and we have a child on-board. "Have you consulted with Doctor Drake?" I ask.

Le Garre nods. "Antoni has been placed in a cryopod. The freezing sequence was slowed owing to the fragility of the child."

I can't imagine Marius and Elaine were happy about that decision, but we have few other options. Our civilian passengers will also need help. They aren't used to high g's. There are drugs we can deploy to lessen the effect on people. We used them when we had to race away from Erebus Station, but they'll make people sluggish afterwards. Given that we may be going straight into combat.... "Shann to Drake?"

"Receiving."

"You're authorised to deploy acceleration medication for our passengers. Leave bridge crew, Chiu and Sam out of it."

"Understood."

The acceleration begins. I'm pushed back in my seat. The tactical display shows us leaving the vicinity of the alien ship on a course towards *Nandin*. *Gateway* is close. Less than five minutes from collision. Projected debris scatter from the impact will get close to us, but we should be able to stay clear.

Six g's, seven g's. Breathing is an effort. I'm suddenly very aware of those two cracked ribs Bogdanovic set for me back on the *Khidr*. The pain is intense. The straps are pushing against the injury. "Le Garre... how...long?"

"Thirty seconds, Captain!"

Instinctively, I'm counting down in my head and trying to hold my breath. I'm trying to tense my stomach and chest against the pressure. I can't relax. If I do, the fractured bones will break.

"Twenty...seconds!"

The display in front of me is a blur. I know everyone on the ship will be suffering just like I'm suffering. There's a risk for all of us. Despite all the precautions, this kind of burn can be fatal.

I remember Jonathan Drake. His brother Emerson is on-board, strapped into a seat. Jonathan died when the straps gave out during our initial burn on *Khidr* to rendezvous with the *Hercules*. I can only imagine what this must be like for Emerson, knowing what happened.

All of that seems like a lifetime ago.

"Ten...seconds...."

Le Garre's voice is thin and desperate. She's suffering too. Somehow, she has to stay focused on the ship's course and intervene if anything goes wrong. How she'd manage to control anything under these g's, I don't know.

"Five!"

I close my eyes. It feels like fingers are pushing on my eyeballs, pressing them so I'm seeing coloured patterns and lines. It hurts, everything hurts.

Then it starts to ease.

I know the numbers. The ranges and calculations have been set by the computer and checked by Johansson and Le Garre. I expect Savvantine has taken a look at them too. We need to go hard and fast, then ease up. The next danger moment is when we slow down.

"*Nandin* is three minutes away," Le Garre says.

"How long until she's engaged?" I ask.

"Ninety seconds after that."

"Can we match speed?"

"Only if we want to lose an advantage," Le Garre says. "I'm planning to reduce speed to twice theirs. That'll save our crew from further trauma. We'll engage first."

I frown. This wasn't discussed, but I trust Le Garre. She's suggesting the best course of action considering the civilians we have on-board. "We go between them," I say. "Johansson, send them our trajectory data. Le Garre, make sure we align our engagement with the enemy, adjust along all axes."

"Aye aye, Captain."

A predictable attack would be some sort of wide pincer, with ourselves and the *Nandin* operating at the same Z-axis position. That's the kind of thing you might see a general do when commanding their infantry and calvary, but this is a battle in space. There are three physical dimensions, we have to use them. Charging in at speed is brave, but it gives them less time to target us.

"Appraisal of the enemy, weapon systems?" I ask.

"Both ships are similar in design to this one," Johansson says. "*Timore* is bigger and potentially less manoeuvrable. *Boryenka* is the same as us, but we have to assume both are carrying a full complement of torpedoes."

"Johansson, direct line to *Nandin* please. Get Elliott on comms, push it to my station."

"Aye aye."

Another window appears on my display. Mattias Elliott's grim face, one that relaxes notably when he sees me. "Captain Shann, good to have you back with us. Remind me to give you my report on your ensign's activity whilst you've been away."

"Mattias, you should have our course plots with you by now."

"Yes, I've seen them. You're going to be taking a lot of heat."

"Least we could do after leaving you out here," I reply. Then turn to my crew. "Savvantine, bring the lasers online," I say. "As soon as we're in range, target both ships."

"Understood."

Le Garre's course plot arrives on my display. Right through the middle, hull rotated to maximise our targeting. Gradual deceleration as we go. Once we're out the other side our speed stops being a weapon. We'll need to cut velocity for a second pass, hoping *Nandin*'s attack will cover us as we come about.

I see the g's marked against the planned manoeuvre. *Fuck, that's going to be rough!* "Approved, Major," I say. "Get this programmed in, in case you black out."

"Aye aye. Tactical viewpoint to main display."

The view in front of us all changes. A black representation of space is punctuated with three-dimensional line drawings of each ship and detected object. Lattice representations of Mars, Phobos, *Gateway* and *Nandin* – everything around us. We are watching the course projection play out in front of us, with the computer anticipating the actions of *Timore* and *Boryenka* as we close.

I flick up the shipwide comms. "All hands prepare for combat. Plug directly into ship tanks and brace for manoeuvres."

"We've entered maximum range," Johansson reports. "Torpedo launches from *Timore*."

"Align baffles to intercept." I'm putting on my emergency mask. On my display, I can see the others doing the same. The advantage *Gallowglass* has is its torpedo countermeasures. We learned about these when we first faced this ship in combat. *Boryenka* and *Timore* will have the same capability, but we aren't carrying ordnance. Drawing their fire will give *Nandin* a chance to get close.

A thought occurs to me. "Johansson, can you do anything about them with your target acquisition program?" I ask.

"Like what, Captain?"

"Reverse it, try to affect their guidance?"

"I'd need to establish a connection," Johansson says. "That would require us to take over their current connection with the launching ship."

"Doable?"

"Not in the time available, Captain." On the screen in front of me, Johansson is chewing her lip. "There might be something else we can do, though."

"You're authorised to proceed. Get on it."

"Aye aye."

We are closing, fast. The ship lurches to the left and rolls over. Le Garre is manoeuvring us into a defensive position, maximising the baffle deployment and giving Savvantine the largest possible targeting profile on the two ships.

"We have a lock on the *Timore*," Savvantine says. "Coming into range in forty-five seconds."

"If we've got a target on them, they will have a target on us," I say. "Get a track on their laser turrets."

This is the imminent, existential crisis. Four lasers to our two. If both *Timore* and *Boryenka* target us, *Gallowglass* will be cut to pieces between them. We have charged straight into this position, placing our head in the jaws of the trap.

But, if they do this, the weapons will not repower in time, and they will leave themselves vulnerable to *Nandin*.

Johansson has decision data from Daniel Rocher. This plan has been discussed, what the crews on *Boryenka* and *Timore* will do has been anticipated. Rocher has indicated they will target us with one laser each, then turn to engage *Nandin*, trying to ignore us as we turn and decelerate. They will hope they can destroy or cripple the ship before we can come about.

"Captain, I think I have something," Johansson says. "Can you initiate a comms request to the enemy ships?"

"Comms?" I frown. "What do we want to talk to them about?"

"Nothing, but it needs to come from you."

"Okay." I activate the panel on the screen and make the attempt. Requesting a ship-to-ship parley at the last moment before either side have wounded the other might be a way to deescalate the situation.

I'm watching the windows on my display. "*Timore* has refused," I say. "*Boryenka* is accepting."

"Got it!" Johansson says. "Shut it down!"

Immediately, I close the window. "What was—"

Explosions. Metal screaming as it twists and tears. DuraGlas shatters and *Gallowglass* lurches, turning over in response to a torpedo impact.

"Direct hit on the port engine!" Le Garre shouts. "I've lost power!"

"Compensate with thrusters," I say. Even as I say the words, I know she is already doing it, acting in the best interests of our survival. "Savvantine, who was down there?"

"Chiu and Sam," Savvantine replies. "Bio-monitors indicate they are both all right."

A ship schematic appears on my display, showing the damage and the salvo plot from *Boryenka*. Two torpedoes were caught by the countermeasures, one got through.

"Lasers in range!" Savvantine shouts.

"Fire!"

The whirr of the system being activated, the build of energy and release. Invisible focused beams projected from our turrets, cutting into the enemy ships, scouring and rending metal and plastic. The pressurised compartments inside punctured, humans dying, dead in seconds as atmosphere vents. The screams and chaotic noise, fading into silence as vacuum takes away all sound.

"Direct hits!" Savvantine says. "*Timore* is returning fire... they missed!"

"Missed? How?"

"The torpedo impact altered our course, Captain," Le Garre says. "They fired as we moved."

"They'll compensate!" I say. "What about *Boryenka*?"

"I fouled their targeting," Johansson says. "When they accepted a comms request, I launched a hack, using the root key and a version of the program Erebus used on us."

"Good work, Ensign, that might have saved us all."

Johansson smiles. "You gave me the idea, Captain, when you said—"

"Brace for burn!" Le Garre shouts.

Gallowglass turns violently and I'm thrown into the side of my seat. The pressure is huge, worse than anything I've experienced. I remember the numbers in the projection – a nine-g turn.

This could kill everyone on-board.

Forces swirl. Le Garre's plot has been adjusted to compensate for the lack of thrust from the port engine. As a result, the manoeuvring thrusters are having to do more work as the ship fights to do what she's asked, to bring us around, give us a second chance to attack.

My vision is cloudy, unfocused. The world seems to darken. I know the signs of a blackout. I squeeze my eyes shut, tense my body and focus on breathing. Every move is pain, agony to survive.

Then abruptly, it eases. The world brightens.

"Report!"

"Manoeuvre successful, Captain." Le Garre's voice is little more than a whisper. "*Timore* will be in range in twelve seconds."

"Savvantine, target and fire!"

No response. I glance down at my screens. The colonel is leaning forwards in her seat, dead or unconscious, I don't know.

My hands are moving across the controls on my seat. Weapons command is transferred to my station. The tactical plot in front of me changes. I can see *Nandin* engaging, *Boryenka* shifting away, with multiple sections of her fuselage damaged. Torpedoes have been launched and at least one has got through.

Timore is in front of us. I target her with both lasers. We have thirty percent charge. Not enough. The weapons will not fire below a certain threshold. "Shann to Chiu, I need more power to the turrets!"

"Working on it, Captain!"

Six seconds, thirty-three percent.

Five.

Four.

Three.

Two.

A small incremental change. Forty-two percent.

I activate both beams, targeting the starboard engine of the *Timore*. The tactical display registers the hit, the computer, detecting and representing fragments of the ship as they are torn away, cut apart by the beams.

"Johansson, update from *Nandin*?"

There is a crackle on the comms channel. I frown. It doesn't appear to be working.

Then all the lights go out and the whole ship goes dead.

CHAPTER FIFTY

Duggins

I'm outside, in the void, looming above *Gallowglass* as she twists and rolls, fighting to survive against her predators. This dance is both fatal and beautiful, but also crude. I'm starting to realise the limitations of humanity, the way we are doomed to repeat the instinctive behaviour of our forefathers. What is happening here is the same as a fight for territory or food between animals, between warlords, between nations.

Can we be better than this? I don't know if we can.

"It is time."

Irina's voice is in my head. She has waited patiently for *Gallowglass* to leave. I sense the alien has been persuaded to allow this. It has no desires and ambitions in the same way humans do, but there are needs, complex requirements that will affect its given purpose.

I blink and I am back on the bridge of the *Khidr*. Irina is sitting where she was before. "What will happen?" I ask.

"Better that you witness this," Irina says. "You have been instrumental in making it happen."

"Are you saying I am to blame?"

"We are all responsible. Decisions like this are impossible without the series of moments that brought us here."

Movement. Awareness. I can feel as the alien reaches out into space. There are others here in the darkness. Children that it crafted before. The anomalies that saved me.

There are more of them here. They were created by the ship at the request of the human scientists. They are different to the others, less self-aware and independent. They were used before to lay down interference when *Gallowglass* first arrived, preventing us from communicating with the Fleet ships.

I know now what was intended. The people here had no idea we were on-board; they acted to cause chaos, so as to give *Gallowglass* the best chance to deliver the anomalies collected from deep space. Then, the ship was to make for *Gateway*, collect the cargo container and escape, making for Europa.

All the chaos on Mars was planned to be a distraction. Fleet and the World Council would spend years fixing the damage whilst a new independent colony would be established on Europa. The people paying for it would then be transported out there.

The technology of cloning and consciousness transfer would be combined. Elderly rich people would have their minds copied and transferred into the bodies of young clones, whose individual identities would be destroyed in the process.

A plan that would take years to be realised, but it would give a privileged few the chance of immortality. What they always wanted.

I'm pleased that what we're doing right now will wreck that plan.

The anomalies begin working at the direction of the alien. Forces affect the ship. It begins to move, turn and change position.

Gateway is close. The forces affect the ship. There is damage. It is fragile and not made for what will be done.

Both ships are moved apart, their trajectories corrected, made parallel. Now for the change.

Stone grinds against itself. More forces are brought to bear, shaped by the intention of the alien. My engineering experience makes me curious about how this works, how it is possible, but I know instinctively my humanity is a limitation. I can't comprehend what is being done. I may never be capable of understanding the process.

But I know the intention and the outcome.

The stone hull of our vessel changes shape. The huge cavern inside is exposed. A way in from the outside appears and grows.

When the entrance is large enough to accommodate *Gateway*, the anomalies alter their work. Slowly, the ancient colony ship starts to move into the space.

I'm focusing on *Gateway*. I know instinctively that there are no humans on-board the ship. The survivors from Phobos Station have been evacuated on the shuttles. Even the cryopods from the cargo bay have been dragged out and taken away.

But the DNA library is there. That's what Irina and the alien want.

Mars colony has been crippled. The destruction of its orbital platform and the removal of this old colony ship leaves the surface settlements isolated. People on the planet are on borrowed time. *Gateway* might have been a focus for those sent to resupply and rebuild what has been destroyed, but we are stealing it. That will set them back years.

"This is necessary," Irina says. "The crisis you worried about will be resolved in a fraction of the time it has taken to bring us here."

"People will die."

"Yes, that is unfortunate."

"But it won't stop you."

"No."

Gateway is inside the cavern. Now the anomalies are moving, gathering, slipping inside as well. When they are done, the stone shifts again, like a growth, boiling across the hole, sealing the ship within.

These are the fingerprints of makers who live far beyond humanity's reach. Their ancient purpose is here, in the workings of the alien vessel, in the anomalies. They are like gods to me. I am part of their work now, contained as I am, watching all of this from the receptacle.

"Everything we need is here."

Another shift. This time a gathering of energy. This is a new purpose, an old imperative unknown to the alien intelligence. Prerequisites have been fulfilled. There is a new mandate.

Acceleration. Velocity. We are gone.

There are fragile things on-board this ship. Benjamin Sarandon remains in his laboratory undisturbed. He is protected; the created anomalies ensure his survival.

There are other humans too, new arrivals. I sense them near the surface. Again, they are protected.

The aftermath we leave behind. I can sense the wider effect of what has been done. The forces used to shift objects in space are not gentle. Humans are trapped aboard disrupted and damaged ships. Their electronics, thrown into disarray by changes their operators cannot understand.

I feel for them. My friends, colleagues and enemies. Even the latter are not really what I name them. Their agendas are small and self-centred, contradictory to ours.

But that doesn't stop the pity.

"What's going on?" Mattias says.

I had forgotten about him. I blink and am drawn back into the bridge. He is standing by the door, almost as if he wants to leave again. "Something amazing," I say. "We are ready for you now."

Irina moves out of her chair. She walks towards Mattias. "We are going on a journey," she says. "We are taking people with us. There are humans on-board who chose to be here, and there is a ship, with a genetic library of human life. It will need a caretaker. A purpose for which you are ideally suited."

"You're going to put me on that ship?"

"This version of you, yes," Irina says.

Mattias glances at me. I smile to reassure him. "I have been transferred like this before. In fact, I think we were both transferred together. This time it will just be you. There will be some discomfort as you get used to the restrictions of a digital environment, but the fragment of 'Mattias Stavinson' that is you should be able to fit in *Gateway*'s computer system."

"Do I have a choice?" Mattias asks.

"You always have a choice," I say. "But you wanted a purpose. This is it."

*   *   *

Mattias is gone.

Irina and I are alone on the bridge. She senses my questions but is courteous enough not to answer them before I ask.

I allow the silence between us. Every moment makes me feel a little more comfortable about what is being done. Rationalisation and processing of actions and events. These things are necessary.

The display behind Irina flashes. A face appears, one that I know.

Rocher.

"Hello, can you hear me?"

Irina frowns. Then turns towards the image. "We can," she says. "I know who you are."

Rocher smiles. "My name is Daniel," he says. "I'm here with two others. We came here on a shuttle, just before you left."

"Then you made your choice," Irina says. "We cannot go back."

"I know that, we all do," Daniel replies. "But there is someone here who would like to talk to you."

Rocher moves away from the screen. Another face appears – a woman, older than him and somehow, fragile. "Hello, Irina," she says.

For a moment, Irina does not speak. She just stares. Then, finally she replies.

"Hello, Doctor Aster."

EPILOGUE

Johansson

The emergency lighting kicks in, low-powered electrical strips installed in the floor and ceiling.

Most of *Gallowglass* is based on a Fleet ship. The system runs on an analogue dead switch. When electrical power cuts out a clockwork timer starts running a countdown. After a prearranged amount of time, a new circuit is connected to a backup battery.

All the systems that activate now are redundant. They are only meant to be used when a ship encounters an electromagnetic pulse, or an equivalent catastrophic incident.

"Is everyone all right?"

The bridge is a darkened place. The illumination, intentionally dim, to save power. Every movement casts huge shadows around the room. Captain Ellisa Shann discards her mask, unbuckles herself from her chair and pushes herself up and out towards me. "You okay, Ensign?"

I nod. But in reality, I'm not okay. My prosthetic right arm is a dead weight. I don't need to examine it to know that the circuitry inside is fried. I use my left hand to remove my own emergency mask.

"We need to check on everyone else," Shann says. She moves towards Savvantine's chair. I hear her murmuring words, assessing the colonel. "She's alive," Shann adds eventually. "Just out of it."

"Any injuries?" I ask.

"Blood around her nose," Shann says. "Nothing else I can see."

"The doors may not be functional," Le Garre says. "The atmosphere cycling and scrubbing will also be running at minimal capacity to conserve power. There is no way of determining if we have atmosphere in each room, so as soon as we manually open any exit, we could kill ourselves. We may do better staying where we are."

"The cryopods should be okay," I say. "They have an isolated independent backup system which is designed for solar phenomena."

"We were winning," Shann says. She looks at me with a grim smile. "That trick with the code you pulled…amazing. By rights, those ships should have cut us apart."

I flinch at the compliment, but find myself smiling. "The *Timore* and the *Boryenka* are probably in the same position as us. A little better or worse, depending on damage."

Le Garre moves out of her seat to one of the storage compartments. With some effort, she opens it, pulling out a Faraday bag. She opens it. Inside, is another portable screen. She presses the power button. "These are working," she says and hands the device to me.

I take it and examine the display. Fleet user IDs won't work on this. I try logging in using the root key, but that doesn't work either. "Not sure how helpful that'll be," I say. "The backup devices on this ship purposely have no connection to the computer and network. Looks like they used fingerprint identification on this. Could be everything is like that."

"Then we're screwed," Le Garre says. "*Merde!*"

"If backup power on this ship is a Fleet system, it'll activate an emergency beacon," I say. "Someone will hear that."

"Who?" Le Garre asks.

"I don't know."

"Keep it together," Shann says. "What happened to us? What did you see?"

I shut my eyes, trying to picture all the data on my display before everything went out. I remember seeing the tactical display, seeing *Gateway* disappear, inside.… *No, did it? Are you sure?*

"The alien ship started moving," I say. "Some of the readings were impossible. I was ignoring them because our current situation was more urgent."

"You think whatever did this came from that ship?"

"Yeah. I do."

"If it was an electromagnetic pulse, it probably hit everything around us," Le Garre says. "That means there's not much left that could receive an emergency beacon transmission."

"Could be that *Asthoreth* was far enough out?" I suggest.

"If so, what can they do?" Le Garre asks.

"All right, that's enough," Shann says. "Let's try the exit. Get yourselves plugged into the emergency oxygen just in case. I'll grab a tank and a mask from the compartment."

I pull on my mask as instructed and turn around in my chair. Shann moves to the bridge door and hooks up to the small canister in the panel beside it. Then she opens another section, revealing the manual crank handle.

Shann grabs the edge of the panel with one hand and the grip of the crank with the other. She takes a deep breath and starts turning the handle.

It moves. The door opens into the corridor.

"All right, that's a start," Shann says. "Let's get to it and work the problem."

★ ★ ★

Fleet Command in Alberta, Canada, has confirmed reports that an update on the Mars situation has been received. Details have not been released as yet, but a press conference has been scheduled for 10:00am MTZ (GMT -7).

It is believed that one or more orbital facilities around Mars has suffered catastrophic damage. The cause of this is unknown.

A request for immediate assistance in the region is being met with a strong response. Corporate ships from the asteroid belt are being sent directly. The Chinese government has also pledged support, although what they can offer in practice remains to be determined as the Luna orbital dock is several months away from Mars.

The incident demonstrates just how fragile humanity's continued presence on the red planet is. With the next resupply freighter not due to arrive for three to four months, the colony will need to find solutions to its problems on its own.

Fleet experts have been working to re-establish contact with the colony and its orbital facilities ever since contact was lost three days ago. If any colonists or Fleet personnel are stranded, then it is unlikely help will reach them for several weeks.

Meanwhile civilian protests over the resources allocated to the global space programme are growing with the latest demonstration occurring in....

ABOUT THE AUTHOR

Allen Stroud is a lecturer and researcher at Coventry University. Stroud completed a Ph.D. at the University of Winchester entitled 'An Investigation and Application of Writing Structures and World Development Techniques in Science Fiction and Fantasy'. He has worked in computer games, roleplaying games, novels, short stories and scripts. He currently runs the Creative Futures research project with the Defence Science Technology Laboratory (DSTL).

Stroud was a founding host of Lave Radio, an *Elite: Dangerous* fan podcast that started in February 2013 and ran the annual convention Lavecon. His novel set in the *Elite: Dangerous* game world, called *Elite: Lave Revolution* was successfully funded on Kickstarter and published in late 2014, with a second edition published in 2015. Stroud then supported Spidermind Games in developing the *Elite Dangerous Roleplaying Game*. Stroud worked on *Chaos Reborn* (2016) with Snapshot Games, as well as *Phoenix Point* (2019) and *Baldur's Gate 3* (2023).

Stroud was the 2017, 2018, 2021 and 2023 chair of FantasyCon, the annual convention of the British Fantasy Society, which hosts the British Fantasy Awards. In June 2019, he became Chair of the British Science Fiction Association, taking over from Donna Bond. Stroud continues to write academic papers, reviews, articles and fiction in science fiction, fantasy and horror.

Stroud's previous Flame Tree Press novels in the *Fractal* series are *Fearless* (2020), *Resilient* (2022), and a set of six ebook episodes: *Europa* (2023), *Ceres* (2023), *Lagrange Point* (2023), *Terra* (2023), *Luna* (2024) and *Jezero* (2024). He has also composed music as part of the series.

FLAME TREE PRESS
FICTION WITHOUT FRONTIERS
Award-Winning Authors & Original Voices

Flame Tree Press is the trade fiction imprint of Flame Tree Publishing, focusing on excellent writing in horror and the supernatural, crime and mystery, science fiction and fantasy. Our aim is to explore beyond the boundaries of the everyday, with tales from both award-winning authors and original voices.

•

Other titles in the *Fractal* series by Allen Stroud:
Fearless, Resilient

Fractal series ebook episodes:
Europa, Ceres, Lagrange Point, Terra, Luna and *Jezero*

You may also enjoy:
The Sentient by Nadia Afifi
The Emergent by Nadia Afifi
The Transcendent by Nadia Afifi
Second Lives by P.D. Cacek
Second Chances by P.D. Cacek
The Widening Gyre by Michael R. Johnston
The Blood-Dimmed Tide by Michael R. Johnston
What Rough Beast by Michael R. Johnston
The Sky Woman by J.D. Moyer
The Guardian by J.D. Moyer
The Last Crucible by J.D. Moyer
One Eye Opened in That Other Place by Christi Nogle
The Goblets Immortal by Beth Overmyer
Holes in the Veil by Beth Overmyer
Death's Key by Beth Overmyer
A Killing Fire by Faye Snowden
A Killing Rain by Faye Snowden
A Sword of Bronze and Ashes by Anna Smith Spark
Idolatry by Aditya Sudarshan
Screams from the Void by Anne Tibbets
The Roamers by Francesco Verso

•

Join our mailing list for free short stories, new release details, news about our authors and special promotions:

flametreepress.com